THE JOYS OF BEING SINFUL

As Vivienne attempted to break away from Aidan's grasp, the sound of voices entering the other end of the long gallery caused them both to freeze.

In horrified alarm, they stared at each other, aware of their scandalous position. Before she could protest, Aidan placed his hand over her mouth and dragged her through the nearest doorway. It was dark inside. This was the last place she should be.

Alone in the dark with Aidan Kavanaugh.

The length of his strong, muscled body leaned against hers and the intense heat between them radiated through the many layers of their clothing. His warm breath on the back of her neck sent a shiver to the core of her body.

His thumb actually caressed her cheek, tracing a gentle path back and forth along her cheekbone, while the hand at her waist was stroking the curve of her hip, oh so faintly. He barely touched her, yet she felt his contact throughout her entire being. And shivered.

Suddenly, he used both hands to spin her around to face him, although she could barely distinguish his features in the darkness. She gasped as his mouth came down on hers. Fiercely. But she welcomed him with an eagerness that matched his own. They kissed with a desperate hunger, as if all that time had never passed. As if this were their last chance to ever kiss again. It was reckless, crazy. It was heaven.

It was Aidan kissing her.

And that was all that mattered . . .

Books By Kaitlin O'Riley

SECRETS OF A DUCHESS

ONE SINFUL NIGHT

Published by Kensington Publishing Corporation

ONE SINFUL NIGHT

KAITLIN O'RILEY

ZEBRA BOOKS
Kensington Publishing Corp.
www.kensingtonbooks.com

ZEBRA BOOKS are published by

Kensington Publishing Corp.
850 Third Avenue
New York, NY 10022

All Kensington titles, imprints, and distributed lines are available at special quantity discounts for bulk purchases for sales promotion, premiums, fund-raising, educational, or institutional use.

Special book excerpts or customized printings can also be created to fit specific needs. For details, write or phone the office of the Kensington Special Sales Manager: Attn. Special Sales Department. Kensington Publishing Corp., 850 Third Avenue, New York, NY 10022. Phone: 1-800-221-2647.

Zebra and the Z logo Reg. U.S. Pat. & TM Off.

ISBN-13: 978-0-8217-8093-0
ISBN-10: 0-8217-8093-X

First Printing: March 2008
10 9 8 7 6 5 4 3 2 1

Printed in the United States of America

For Grandma Aggie

~

And for my mother, as always

Acknowledgments

I want to thank my wonderful agents, Jane and Miriam, for taking a chance on me and for their unerring advice, and my editor, John, for loving what I write.

I happen to be blessed with the most incredible family and amazing friends who have helped me immeasurably in one way or another along my writing journey. From inspiration and encouragement to technical support and business advice to simply making me laugh, I could not have accomplished anything without all of you. I give much love and deepest gratitude to Jennifer, Greg, Janet, Scott, Maureen, Richard, Bob, Adrienne, Billy, and my father, John. The same thank you applies to Danny, Lynn, Mark, John, Jeff, Brian, Cela, Albert, Kim, and Eric. I also thank Yvonne, my best friend for over thirty years and the bravest woman I know, for her unfailing faith in me. (And for wanting to read every rough draft.)

Above all, I thank my sister Jane, my partner in romance novel crime, for her invaluable critiques, insight, and support, and for not letting me forget that good things are possible.

Note to Riley: You are the best little boy in the world.

Chapter 1

The House Party

England
Spring, 1870

"Come and meet my cousin now," Gregory Cardwell said eagerly.

"You mean the pretty one?" Aidan Kavanaugh, the Earl of Whitlock, asked with slight skepticism, fresh drink in hand.

For the last few minutes Gregory had been extolling the heavenly attributes of his newfound cousin. Truth be told, Aidan had only been half-listening to his garrulous friend, although the point that Gregory was describing an unusually attractive person had penetrated his preoccupied mind.

"All my cousins are pretty, my fine friend," Gregory explained with an unabashed grin, his merry eyes twinkling. "We're a handsome family."

It was a true enough statement, for Gregory was an attractive man despite his ruddy complexion and many freckles. Since their days at Cambridge years ago, he and Aidan had been good friends.

"You know I was speaking of your meeting my most beautiful cousin. But I must warn you, Aidan. She may just tempt you away from the fair Helene." Gregory raised and lowered his eyebrows in a devilish manner.

Aidan gave him a doubtful look as they made their way through Bingham Hall's massive ballroom, where sophisticated and fashionably dressed people swarmed about. A full orchestra played at one end of the elaborately decorated ballroom and couples danced in the center. The Duchess of Bingham's invitations were always extremely popular and highly coveted, for she was renowned for her lavish and extravagant entertaining. Her informal style and manner were often imitated but never matched, for no one could host a party quite like the Duchess of Bingham and her house parties, like this one, were particular favorites. Tonight was the Welcome Ball to commence the weeklong round of lively and engaging activities for the fortunate guests who were extended an invitation.

As he and Gregory pressed through the crowd, Aidan ignored the heads that turned in his direction, the majority of which were of the female persuasion. As one of the most eligible bachelors in England, he was used to women flirting with him and fawning over him. In fact, he would be surprised if women did not look his way, but he paid no attention to them. He idly wondered where Helene was and knew he would have to seek her out sooner rather than later.

A decision about Helene Winston was one that Aidan needed to make in the near future. He probably should just propose to her and be done with it. She expected it by now, and perhaps even deserved it, but she was too much of a lady to ever pressure him about it. Somehow he could not bring himself to take that final step and ask her to marry him. Oh, Helene was desirable enough for a wife. He did not know why he held off on this, much to his mother's dismay and, he presumed, Helene's.

He truly did not even wish to be at this house party in the first place.

More than a little worried about his shipping business, Aidan recalled the dreadful week that passed. After one of his largest shipments ever of cotton from America was mysteriously lost, there had been a disastrous fire at his shipping warehouse two nights ago. The double financial blow of missing an entire cotton shipment in addition to losing a large warehouse filled to the brim with merchandise was almost ruinous, but fortunately not one of his employees had been injured in the terrible, late-night blaze. For that Aidan was most thankful. He had spent years building his shipping company up from nothing, devoting himself to making it a success. He was not about to let it go up in smoke.

Yet he had his suspicions that the fire was not accidental. There had been too many "accidents" lately, and the events of the past week were clearly deliberate.

And he had a fairly good idea of who was responsible for it. Proving it would be a most challenging enterprise, however. He would rather have stayed in London to manage these matters personally, but he had made a promise to his mother, as well as Helene, that he would attend the Binghams' party, and he could not break it. He had finally arrived at the estate, although rather later than expected. His mother had not been pleased by his delayed appearance but, then again, she rarely was pleased by anything.

His mother's wishes were not easily thwarted; she had wrangled this particular promise out of him when he had been overly distracted with work and afterward he had seen no decent way out of it. If it had not been for the mysterious fire the night before last, he actually might have enjoyed a week of relaxation in the country: going for long walks, riding and hunting. Lord knew he needed to clear his head. However, he was too anxious about the cause of the fire to relax now.

Clearly not in the mood for the evening's unavoidable social obligations, he took another sip of the excellent whiskey in his glass and followed his friend around the crowded and noisy perimeter of the dance floor, nodding briefly in greeting to the many faces who recognized him.

Then Gregory stepped aside, nudging Aidan lightly with his elbow and whispering to him in a low tone, "There she is."

As Aidan glanced ahead, he stopped short, almost spilling his drink down the front of his expensive, finely cut evening jacket.

There, on the arm of Gregory Cardwell's identical twin brother George, was a woman of incredible beauty.

He stared as she gracefully turned her head and laughed at something George said to her, the sound of her laughter rich and warm. Her luminous smile lit up her exquisite face, which would melt the heart of any man looking at her, including—obviously—George Cardwell's. But then, how could a heart not melt?

Silky black hair framed a face flawless and delicate in its bone structure. Her deep blue eyes were fringed by long, dark lashes with graceful brows arching lightly above them. She had a small, straight nose with high cheekbones in a slightly heart-shaped face with a creamy complexion. Full, sensual lips smiled charmingly to reveal pearly white teeth. As he watched her, the breath in his chest constricted and his heart pounded forcefully.

He could not move.

Suddenly Aidan was hundreds of miles away. Rolling green hills spread before him, covered in a soft gray mist. The waves of a wild surf crashed on the shore below high, windswept cliffs. The fresh scent of the sea saturated him. Heated kisses and sweet words; hands clasped and promises made. He could feel his heart pounding and his gut clenched.

He knew this woman.

No one else could have that face. That hauntingly beautiful face.

It couldn't be anyone other than Vivienne Montgomery.

He could tell by the elegant curve of her neck. The graceful way she held herself. The ivory white skin that beckoned to be touched. The sultry sapphire eyes that sparkled and teased. The black hair that would fall in long, silky waves to her waist. He knew, for he had seen her wear it that way. God, he had run his fingers through it! Now those glossy tresses were piled fashionably around her head in sophisticated ringlets. The pale blue gown she wore covered perfectly rounded breasts that gave way to the slender waist of a petite body.

Desire coursed through his blood at the sight of her, although he fought against it. Anger surged through him next. White-hot anger.

What in hell is Vivienne Montgomery doing in England?

Gregory pulled Aidan closer and said in a low, satisfied voice, "As you can see for yourself, I did not exaggerate her beauty. You can close your mouth now."

At his friend's words, Aidan mentally shook himself and closed his mouth, unaware that he had been gaping like a callow school boy.

Good Lord! The enormity of the situation hit him. *Vivienne Montgomery is Gregory Cardwell's cousin!*

"Vivvy, dearest, this is my good friend, Aidan Kavanaugh, the Earl of Whitlock," Gregory introduced them easily. "Aidan, may I present my beautiful cousin, Miss Vivienne Montgomery."

He stepped forward woodenly to greet the only woman who had ever turned his world upside down. She stood there composed and serene, looking for all the world like she had never laid eyes on him before. There was no air of recognition about her. Did she not remember him? Was she going to ignore him? How could she possibly have forgotten what had happened between them? So many years had passed, but not a day went by that he did not think of her, however unwillingly.

Vivienne's sapphire-blue eyes were looking up at him from beneath her long sooty lashes. Aidan's heart almost stopped beating completely. She had become more breathtakingly beautiful than he remembered. Even in his dreams. Perhaps dreams were not an accurate description. Tortured nightmares was the more precise term for the images that endlessly haunted him in his sleep.

He simply stared at her, not oblivious to the watershed of emotions that were crashing through him at the sight of her before him. He had never thought to see her again. Yet here she was, in the flesh and more beautiful than ever.

"Vivienne has just come to live with us," Gregory had gone on to say in his usual blithe manner, unaware of the stilted silence between Aidan and his cousin.

Aidan cleared his throat. "Miss Montgomery and I have already met."

The surprised expressions of the others were not lost on Aidan as he waited for Vivienne's response to him. Had she wanted to pretend they did not know each other? That they had never met? Well, he was not going to let that happen.

"Has it been ten years already, Aidan?" she asked softly.

The subtle brogue in her voice was one that Aidan recognized instantly and again it pulled him back to another time and place. He felt himself immersed in emotions he had long since buried of a time he most definitely did not wish to recall. Their eyes locked and, for a moment, it was as if they were the only two people in the room.

"Time has done nothing to change you, I see," he answered.

"I've changed more than you know," she responded gently, although there was a wealth of meaning in that comment just for him.

"I doubt that." Aidan's words were like ice.

"How in the world do you two know each other?" Gregory asked, a curious expression on his boyish face.

"Galway." Aidan and Vivienne stated in unison, surprising each other.

"I knew you spent time in Ireland when you were a boy, Aidan, but I had no idea you were in the same town as my cousin!" Gregory exclaimed in amusement.

"What a remarkable coincidence that you two should meet again!" George Cardwell chimed in. "You knew each other as children?"

"You could say that," Vivienne retorted calmly, although her little barb was lost on the others. It was meant for Aidan alone.

It puzzled him that she could remain unruffled by his presence. How could she be so composed when he was overwhelmed with emotion at seeing her again? His jaw clenched as he stared at her. Now that he really looked he noticed a family resemblance between Vivienne and the Cardwell twins in their eyes. But while the twins' eyes were light blue, Vivienne's were a tumultuous sea-blue, constantly changing to match her moods.

"Tell us, Aidan, what was our cousin like as a little girl? We've only just met her for the first time," Gregory said, always wanting to know more than he should.

Aidan watched as Vivienne glanced up at him, meeting his eyes directly. For the briefest instant he pictured Vivienne the day he first met her. Lord, but she was pretty even back then, all dark hair and impish smiles, with the constant hint of laughter in her fascinating eyes. A vivid image of the last time he saw her immediately took its place and his stomach tightened in reflex. "I'm sure she has not changed at all."

Vivienne's expression hardened at that remark. "People rarely change their characters, although they may try to change their outward appearances to make it seem as though they have changed."

"Surely you must have a lot to catch up on," George offered with a grin that matched his brother's.

Aidan watched the briefest shadow flash across her

face. "I don't believe there is anything we need to catch up on. Is there, Miss Montgomery?"

"Nothing at all that I can think of, Lord Whitlock." She glanced coolly at him, as if he did not matter a whit to her.

Gregory Cardwell, carelessly unaware of the tension between them, said, "Can you believe a girl this beautiful has been hidden away in Ireland all this time? My parents are set on finding her a husband. Don't you think she'll be the hit of the Season in London?"

Aidan could barely get his mouth to form intelligible words. "Quite."

"Lord Whitlock, there you are!" Lady Helene Winston declared in her typical breathless rush, as she came to Aidan's side. "I've been looking for you everywhere!"

For once Aidan was oddly grateful for Helene's presence. Smiling warmly, he extended his hand to her. Her flaxen hair was fashioned in an intricate knot of curls upon her head, which emphasized the angular lines of her rather aristocratic-looking face. She was delicately boned, willowy, and taller than average. The pale seagreen color of her gown accentuated her hazel eyes. Aidan had always believed Helene to be pretty, but now he was startled by how she paled completely in comparison to Vivienne's vivid coloring and radiant presence.

George Cardwell made the introductions between the women. "This is Lady Helene Winston. My cousin, Miss Vivienne Montgomery."

Unconsciously sizing Vivienne up and down with a cool glance, Helene uttered politely, "It's a pleasure to make your acquaintance, Miss Montgomery."

"I am pleased to meet you as well, Lady Helene," Vivienne responded.

"If you'll excuse us, I believe I promised Helene this

dance." Aidan knew he seemed curt, but he could not endure standing there any longer. Good God! If he had known he would be trapped at Bingham Hall with Vivienne Montgomery all week, he certainly would have made up some excuse, any excuse, not to come.

He drained the rest of his whiskey, handed the empty glass to a passing footman, and escorted Helene to the dance floor. As the orchestra played a waltz, he maneuvered her with expert skill through the elegantly attired couples and began to dance.

"You are very late. I was afraid you wouldn't arrive in time for the dancing," Helene scolded him in a mild tone, looking up at him sweetly. She had many admirers but her mind was set on Aidan Kavanaugh, the Earl of Whitlock. "Your mother said she expected you this afternoon."

"I had some business to attend to in London that took much longer than I anticipated," he muttered distractedly. He tried to forget that Vivienne Montgomery was in this ballroom. In this house. With him. For the next week. "I apologize if I kept you waiting."

"I'm just grateful that you are here at all," Helene said prettily.

He forced a smile at her, thinking he would rather be anywhere else on earth than at Bingham Hall. As much as he was grateful for the temporary escape Helene presented, he could not ignore the fact that his senses were reeling.

He was completely unprepared for the desirable woman that Vivienne had become. Ten years had barely left a mark of age or time on her. He had always imagined her married and fat, with a passel of babies by now. Obviously that was not the case. What had she been doing all this time? Why had she suddenly appeared in his life now?

As he and Helene moved in time to the music, the knot in his stomach only tightened at the thought of enduring a week of Vivienne's company. Dinners, card parties, picnics, games, musicales. He would be in contact with her constantly. Even a house as massive as Bingham Hall was too small, too confining, too intimate for both of them to survive the week unscathed. There would be no polite way to avoid interacting with her.

"May I cut in on this dance, Aidan?" Gregory Cardwell asked in his casual, easy manner. "I've grown very weary of dancing with my little Irish cousin all night."

Aidan could hardly refuse Gregory's simple request without appearing boorish. And, judging from the look of surprised dismay on Vivienne's beautiful face, she was not at all inclined to dance with him either. His gentlemanly manners were too ingrained in him. He had no choice but to dance with her, although Gregory was oblivious to how much Aidan wanted to throttle him.

"Of course," he mumbled, releasing Helene.

Before Aidan quite realized it, Gregory had waltzed away with Helene and he stood alone with Vivienne. She waited, her eyes downcast, the long dark lashes contrasting against her smooth, ivory skin. Was she that nervous to be with him? Or that disdainful?

Suddenly an exuberant young couple unwittingly bumped Vivienne from behind, causing her to stumble against him. Acting on instinct he grabbed her upper arms to steady her. Her head fell against his chest and then she gazed up at him in surprise.

He swirled in the deep blue of her eyes, unable to

speak. His heart raced at the unexpected feel of her so close to him. He had forgotten how petite she was, how easy to hold. The light floral fragrance of her washed over him, recalling the scent of the ocean along a rocky coast, drenching him in an achingly sweet memory: the first time he ever kissed her. It had been heaven to kiss Vivienne by the sea.

She struggled to right herself, pushing away from him. Instantly he released her as if scalded. His hands trembled slightly and his heart raced. He squared his shoulders and mentally shook himself, taking a deep breath to steady his raw nerves.

"We might as well dance, Vivienne. We shall be trod upon if we stand here any longer." His voice sounded harsh, even to him.

"Can you bear dancing with me, Aidan?" she questioned cryptically.

"If you can bear dancing with me." He held out his hands to her.

She merely nodded her head and accepted his hands, which trembled still. Her contact undermined his steady nerves. They moved together awkwardly at first, then fell in rhythm with the strains of the music. The distinct uneasiness between them was to be expected, yet it irritated him that she kept her eyes downcast and refused to meet his gaze, while he could not help but stare at her.

"You did not seem as surprised to see me as I was to see you," he stated when he could endure the awkward silence no longer.

She shrugged lightly, the delicate movement of her bare shoulders almost knocking the wind out of him. "I knew when I came to England that it was bound to happen sooner or later."

Her coolness left him unnerved, but he could not stop himself from asking, "You did not marry after all?" The impulse to know her answer was too strong to resist.

"No." She answered simply, with no explanation, although an unspoken name hung in the air between them. She looked directly at him, as if daring him to say it aloud.

His gut clenched yet again at the sight of her dazzling blue eyes fringed by long black lashes. Had she always been this beautiful? He'd never seen her dressed so elegantly, but that was not quite it. Vivienne had grown more . . . womanly. More lushly feminine. She held herself gracefully, with a surprising air of confidence. He fought an increasing desire to lean close and drown himself in kissing her soft, sensual lips. He could barely breathe at the thought of it.

She suddenly asked him, "I gather you have not married either?"

He did not wish to discuss his marital status with Vivienne, of all people. Instead he asked, perhaps rather edgily, "What are you doing in England?"

"What does it matter to you what I do or where I go?" she stated, surprising him again with her coolness.

He responded, "It matters that we have to spend the week here in each other's company."

"If it distresses you so, Lord Whitlock, you may certainly leave if you wish."

His annoyance rose at her airy dismissal of him. He was definitely not running off as if he were afraid of her. He had considered leaving Bingham Hall as soon as he could make a respectable getaway, but now he was forced to finish out the week, just to spite her. "Unfortunately I must stay, for reasons I need not go into with you. So we will just have to tolerate each other's company as best we can."

"Does it upset you that much to see me again?" She questioned him in a curious tone, her eyes flashing.

Once again he was lost in her liquid sapphire eyes. He had to remind himself to breathe. "Not in the least, Miss Montgomery. I'm simply surprised that you had to come all the way to England to find a husband. I gather no one in Galway would marry you?"

Vivienne stopped short, pulling away from him, and stood completely still, a devastated look on her face. He didn't feel the slightest bit of remorse. Suddenly her eyes flashed in anger and she made a motion to slap his face, but as if he could read her mind, he caught her hand before she could strike him. Deliberately he lowered it to her side. They stared at each other in heated silence.

Fortunately the dance ended before their motionlessness caused a scene. Without another word, he escorted her to the seating area, bowed politely, and left her standing with a group of giggling young ladies in pastel dresses.

Aidan walked directly to the Duke of Bingham's lavishly stocked bar. It was going to take a hell of a lot of liquor for him to survive a week with Vivienne.

Chapter 2

The Last Letter

Vivienne Montgomery cautiously opened the door to her bedroom, which was tastefully decorated by the Duchess of Bingham in shades of pale yellow and rose and, seeing it was empty, she breathed a grateful sigh of relief. She did not want to squabble with Glenda tonight. If she managed to undress hurriedly, she could pretend to be asleep before her cousin returned.

As she stepped into the room, the door to the small adjoining dressing room opened and a slender young woman, wearing a neat gray uniform and a white mobcap, came to assist Vivienne out of her intricate, blue silk gown.

"Thank you, Lizzie. If you could just help me undo these back hooks, I can do the rest myself," Vivienne said as she turned her back to allow Lizzie to reach the endless row of clasps that enclosed her body in the latest fashion.

She was truly helpless to remove the gown herself. It still amazed her that she had lived her whole life wearing clothes that she was perfectly able to get herself in and out of without any assistance, but since moving to England she had been obligated to wear the elaborate garments that required her to have another person dress her. In spite of this, she adored her gorgeous new wardrobe and all the lovely accessories that went with it; silks, satins, velvets, ribbons, fancy slippers, fans, bonnets. Those little luxuries were unheard of in her former life in Ireland.

"Oh, I don't mind helping you none, miss," Lizzie volunteered, eager to please her new mistress. "'Tis no trouble at all."

Lizzie efficiently unhooked the small clasps along the back of the soft blue silk. Vivienne breathed deeply as the tight fitting gown was loosened and Lizzie deftly unlaced her corset as well.

"Please sit, Miss Vivienne, and let me take the pins out of your hair."

Vivienne sat upon the small chair in front of the mirrored dressing table, and allowed Lizzie to unravel the mass of pins and curls that she had painstakingly weaved together only hours earlier. Luxuriating in the feel of her hair falling free of the tight coiffure, Vivienne unconsciously tilted her head back and let Lizzie's nimble fingers massage her aching scalp. She sighed heavily and closed her eyes.

The evening had been more than exhausting. Her body felt tense and edgy, and she wanted only to bury her head under her pillow and cry. This had been her first foray into society to prepare for her arrival in London next week, and she had been enjoying herself immensely until Aidan Kavanaugh walked in the ballroom. Seeing him again had shaken her to the core.

Aidan.

For the first time in ten years she had spoken with Aidan. And he still loathed her.

She had sensed his hatred spilling over and slapping her like an icy hand. Well, the feeling was mutual. She despised him just as much as he despised her. It was impossible to forgive him for what he had done to her. Yet she prayed that his gentlemanly breeding would prevent him from ruining her. That nasty comment he made about having to come to England to find a husband because no one in Galway would marry her hurt deeply and hit painfully close to the truth. How she wished she had been able to slap that detached and superior look off his face!

"Miss Vivienne, let me fetch you a cup of chamomile tea," Lizzie offered kindly. "You look a bit peaked."

"I'm fine, really. I just need some sleep. You go on to bed now."

"Oh, but I have to wait up for Miss Glenda anyhow. And you look like you could use a cup," Lizzie said as she helped Vivienne into her long white nightgown. "I won't be more than a minute." The obliging maid hurried off before Vivienne could utter another protest.

Vivienne stared at her reflection in the cheval glass mirror. What had Aidan seen when he saw her tonight? Did he think her very changed? No longer a girl of seventeen with eyes full of love and adoration? Most likely not. She no longer loved nor adored him. And she had definitely changed over the years since he left. She had matured. She had learned from her mistakes. She was now a woman who knew better.

Aidan had certainly changed too. There was a dark,

remote quality about him that she didn't recall being there, although his looks still managed to take her breath away. Tall and muscular with broad shoulders, he had a classically sculpted masculine face; strong jaw, straight aquiline nose, intelligent forehead. He had gorgeous thick black hair and penetrating green eyes with impossibly long jet lashes. Yes, Aidan Kavanaugh was still one handsome son of a bitch.

She laughed ruefully to herself for using the vulgar expression the twins had recently taught her. The description fit Aidan perfectly, though, for she had the great misfortune of knowing his mother.

"Good, you're awake," a shrill voice caught her off guard. "I won't have to tiptoe around and be quiet."

"Hello, Glenda," Vivienne nodded, amused at the thought of Glenda ever tiptoeing around anyone. "Did you enjoy the ball?"

She watched as her cousin gracelessly crossed the room, leaving a trail of her possessions upon the floor: her silk fan, her beaded reticule, her kid gloves. It was the one drawback to living with Aunt Gwen and Uncle Gilbert.

Glenda Cardwell was a nightmare.

"Where is Lizzie?" Glenda whined petulantly, as she pulled the servant's cord with an air of beleaguered impatience. "How am I supposed to get this gown off me?"

Vivienne idly wondered how they got the gown on her in the first place, but she walked over to her cousin and began to undo the buttons that were fairly bursting with the weight they contained. It was truly unfortunate that Glenda had inherited none of the Cardwell family good looks or charm. She was heavy and short, whereas her brothers were tall and lean. The other Cardwells all had unmistakable ginger hair and sparkling sky blue eyes, but Glenda's hair was a dull brown and her eyes an indeterminate shade of gray. Her looks might not have seemed half as bad if her disposition were not so unbearable.

"No, Vivienne, I did not enjoy the ball tonight. And I wish I did not have to spend an entire week in this dismal house."

Glenda's strident voice echoed through the room as she continued to enlighten Vivienne regarding all that had gone wrong with her evening, although Vivienne would hardly describe the stately, elegant, and quite enormous Bingham Hall, as a "dismal house." Her cousin had a flair for the dramatic, if nothing else.

"I'm sorry you did not have a good time," Vivienne murmured when she was able to get a word in between complaints.

"And Lord Browning was terribly rude to me, when all I said was perhaps he needed more dance lessons. Honestly, the ridiculous man stepped on my feet the entire dance." Glenda continued her saga of her evening's miseries.

Vivienne felt sorry for her cousin. During the weeks she had been with the Cardwells, it was obvious that Glenda was a disappointment to her parents. Her twin brothers, George and Gregory, were good-looking men, outgoing, fun and well-liked in society, whereas Glenda was abrasive and bad-tempered. Aunt Gwen and Uncle Gilbert despaired of finding a husband for her, for after six seasons no one even once made an offer.

Lizzie returned to the room with a cup of tea for Vivienne.

"Where have you been? Off getting something for Vivienne, as usual," Glenda snapped crossly, her plain, round face pinched in consternation. "My cousin was required to help me in your stead. No. No, don't bother me now, Lizzie. I've finished changing, no thanks to you. You might have thought to bring some tea for me, though," Glenda sniffed, as she wrapped the ties of her dressing gown around her thick waist. "But no one in this family ever thinks of me. I'm always the forgotten one."

When Vivienne first came to live with the Cardwells, she immediately felt accepted into their home. She tried to befriend Glenda, who was close to her in age, thinking it would be nice to have a sister-like companion in her life. However, Glenda made it clear from the outset that she wanted nothing to do with Vivienne.

Not unaware of the growing animosity between her and Glenda, Vivienne continually endeavored to make peace with her cousin. But Glenda only distanced herself from Vivienne's attempts at friendship. It did not alleviate matters that they were forced to share a bedroom while visiting at Bingham Hall, due to the large number of guests.

Lizzie, her kind eyes worried, hurriedly apologized. "I'm sorry miss. I didn't know you were back already. I'll fetch you some tea straightaway."

"Glenda, you can have mine. I'm really too tired to drink it." Vivienne intervened.

Glenda peevishly took the cup from Lizzie. "It's tepid now," she whined. "It's no wonder Vivienne doesn't want it. Bring me some hot tea immediately."

"Yes, Miss Glenda." Lizzie hurried from the room.

Vivienne sighed in futility and padded to her four-poster bed. As was her nightly ritual, she kissed the palm of her hand and placed it lovingly on the intricately carved wooden box inlaid with ivory on her nightstand.

It was the last gift her father had sent to her from his travels before he disappeared, and she cherished it.

Two years had passed since she had last seen him and she missed him desperately. When she had been a little girl she could not wait for her tall, handsome father to come sailing into port bringing exotic gifts for her from around the world. He would lift her high in his arms and swing her around while she shrieked in delight. She was so proud of him! He always promised that one day when she was old enough that he would take her sailing across the blue sea on his beautiful ship. But he never did think she was old enough to go with him, so she stayed behind and waited for him to come home.

Opening the beautiful box, her last link to her father, she removed the yellowed note inside. It had arrived one day early last summer, while she was still living with her grandmother in Galway. The note simply said:

My Dearest Vivienne,
I'm sending this wooden box to you because it is a beautiful work of art from South Africa, and indeed, whatever is mine, daughter, is yours. I know you will care for it well and keep it safe until I return, for it is worth more than you know. Keep it close to you. I will explain its importance to you as soon as I return home. I love you very much.

~Papa

Only a few weeks after she received the box she was notified that her father and his newest ship, the *Sea Star*, were missing after a storm off the coast of Africa and Captain John Montgomery and his entire crew were presumed dead. Although heartbroken at the loss of her father, Vivienne harbored suspicions that he was still alive. The strange note that came with his pretty box meant something more. She just knew it.

"I know you will care for it well and keep it safe until I return, for it is worth more than you know. Keep it close to you."

She had puzzled over the meaning of those words for hours and she had studied the box over and over, wondering what could make it so valuable. To her it seemed an ordinary box, although it was unusually beautiful and delicately carved and inlaid with ivory in diamond-shaped patterns.

Maybe it was instinct or a sixth sense, but even the words "presumed dead" haunted her. Of course she had no way to prove her feelings at the time, stranded as she was in Galway. But prove them she would! One way or another.

The main reason she agreed to come to England was to do her own investigation of her father's disappearance. She confided her suspicions to Aunt Gwen with the hope that her father's sister would help her in her quest, but Aunt Gwen firmly believed her brother was dead and implored Vivienne to accept that painful fact once and for all. Vivienne would not. She could not. So far she had spent all of her time in England at her aunt and uncle's country estate, but after this week at the Binghams', they were finally going to London. Once they were there, Vivienne was determined to find a way to visit the office of Harlow Shipping International to ask some questions.

Placing the faded note back in the box, she glanced inside. The dark blue velvet lining held the few precious objects that meant the world to her: the simple gold band that had been her mother's wedding ring, a tiny Celtic cross that had belonged to Aggie, and a silver locket in the shape of a heart that Aidan had given to her when she was seventeen.

Taking the locket in her hand, Vivienne popped it open to reveal a miniature painting of Aidan. Her heart ached at the sight, for she had not looked at it in years. The artist had captured his handsome features remarkably, down to the slight smile on his lips and the intent look in his green eyes. She used to wear the locket close to her heart every day. Even after he left her. Once, in a fit of tearful anger, she almost tossed it into the waters of Galway Bay, but she could not bring herself to discard the last tangible memory she had of him. Instead, she kept it as a bittersweet memento of what could have been.

Carefully returning the locket to the beautiful box, Vivienne closed the lid with the ivory diamonds and climbed into bed. As she slipped between the soft sheets and settled back into the down pillows, Lizzie returned with the tea.

"Never mind, Lizzie. I've decided I'm too tired to drink tea after all," Glenda's nasal voice intoned, her gray eyes glittering in triumph. "Now put away my things before you go." She waved a plump hand at the mess she had left in the room.

Too overwhelmed by emotions to wrangle with Glenda about tormenting poor Lizzie, Vivienne sighed. Glenda played a continuous game of criticizing their lady's maid for every little thing. Nothing Lizzie did ever satisfied Glenda and no interference on Vivienne's part could persuade her to think otherwise. Glenda insisted that Lizzie favored Vivienne and neglected her. It was often better for Lizzie if Vivienne remained quiet.

Attempting to ignore Glenda's ridiculous instructions

to Lizzie, Vivienne closed her eyes and buried her head
in the pillow.

Aidan Kavanaugh.

She had always known in her heart that she would see
Aidan again someday. Aggie had told her they would
meet again, and her grandmother was usually right
about those things, but Vivienne hadn't expected to see
him so soon. She certainly never suspected that she
would be trapped under the same roof with him for an
entire week! Upon her arrival in England, the thought
crossed her mind that there was a possibility, however
remote, that she might encounter him at social events.
But she had been completely unprepared for the fact
that he was acquainted with Gregory and George. Her
two endearing, rambunctious cousins were friends with
Aidan Kavanaugh. And apparently had been for years.

Or must she now refer to him by his lofty title, the Earl
of Whitlock? He seemed so self-important and remote
tonight. Powerful, reserved, cool. Quite different from
the earnest, caring boy she once loved with all her heart.

He had devastated her. Shattered her heart into
tiny pieces and swept them away with his carelessness.
He had left her hollow and alone, hurting beyond
belief by his lack of faith in her love.

But she had learned her lesson from Aidan Kavanaugh quite well. The weeks and months of tears and
recriminations, as well as the shame and humiliation
that followed in his wake, had hardened her resolve
and her character. No longer a naïve and trusting girl,
Vivienne had grown wiser and stronger from her lone-
liness and pain. Ten years ago she vowed to herself
never to allow anyone to hurt her that way again.

It was even more important to protect her heart
now that Aidan had entered her world once more.

Chapter 3

The Morning After

The next afternoon Aidan woke up with his stomach queasy, his throat parched, and his head throbbing. Still wearing his evening clothes, he noticed wearily that the room reeked of stale whiskey and, judging from the crushing, nauseating pain in his head, he had consumed more than quite a lot of it.

Finley, his steadfast valet, stood over him with a wicked grin, for it wasn't often his master was in such dire straits. From the look on his face, Finley took great delight in the consequences of Aidan's overindulgence the night before.

"What happened to you last night? It's not like you to get foxed."

Aidan groaned and made the monumental effort to sit up in bed.

"Shall I open the curtains?" Finley tormented him. "It's a lovely day and the sun is shining brightly."

Aidan shook his head, only to place both hands to his temples, wanting to strangle his irreverent valet.

"Water," he mumbled thickly. His tongue felt wrapped in cotton gauze.

Finley poured a cool glass of water from a china pitcher on the sideboard and handed it to Aidan, who gulped it down greedily.

"Where the hell am I?" Aidan asked when he had drained the last of the water, looking at the unfamiliar but very elegant room in which he found himself.

"The Duke and Duchess of Bingham's. Remember the little house party you are attending this week? We arrived here last night. I've got some coffee and toast for you and have ordered a bath. I think you could use one, by the smell of you. I thought I'd let you sleep it off for a while longer, but Mr. Grayson is here to see you. And you might want to hurry. He's waiting in the duke's private library."

"Tell him I've died," Aidan moaned and lay gently back into the pillows, although the smell of coffee was mildly tempting. His head throbbed relentlessly. What in bloody hell had he done last night? He clearly remembered arriving at Bingham Hall and talking to Richard and Jane Havilland, the Duke and Duchess of Bingham. He had greeted his mother, who was angry with him for being late. Then Gregory Cardwell grabbed him and . . . *Good God!*

It all came rushing back to him in a sickening wave. Now he remembered why he drank like the very devil.

Vivienne Montgomery.

That beautiful Irish witch would drive any man to drink.

"What brought all this on?" Finley inquired calmly while laying out clean clothes for Aidan.

"You don't want to know," Aidan muttered crossly.

"I daresay I know already." He raised a brow and looked in Aidan's direction. "A certain Irish lady?"

Finley knew the entire Vivienne Montgomery saga, having lived through it with him years ago. Aidan was not surprised that Finley already knew Vivienne Montgomery was here, since Finley somehow managed to know everything about everyone. He prided himself on it.

"I don't want to discuss her," Aidan mumbled.

"Fine. Have it your way for now. I'll hear it all from you eventually." Finley smiled with satisfaction. "Anyway, I believe Mr. Grayson has some concrete information about the warehouse fire."

"Why didn't you say that in the first place?" Aidan grumbled in annoyance.

Finley knew very well that such news would rouse Aidan; he had simply been irritating him for sport. He had been with Aidan's family for years. When Aidan inherited the title Earl of Whitlock from his great uncle, Finley came with Aidan from Galway and officially became his valet. He and Aidan had developed a good friendship over the years.

"Oh, and your mother has demanded to see you right away," Finley said gleefully.

An anguished groan erupted from the depths of the feather pillows.

Three quarters of an hour later, Aidan was freshly shaved, dressed, and nursing a terrible hangover as he sat in the luxuriously appointed library of the Duke of Bingham, who had kindly lent the room to Aidan for this meeting. The Duke's library, outfitted with mahogany shelves from floor to ceiling and stocked with books of every type and description, had a massive oak table in the center of the room surrounded by comfort-able leather armchairs and framed by a picture window commanding a stunning view of the glistening lake in the distance.

Aidan's assistant, Daniel Grayson, sat across the table from him. The thin, wiry man delivered his words with quiet efficiency. "It was as you suspected, my lord. Arson. The fire was deliberately set. They found a tin of kerosene in the front office, where it started. No one had been in the office that afternoon and there was no possible reason for a fire to ignite that room. Unless it was set on purpose."

"That's because it *was* set on purpose. And I have my suspicions of who set it."

His assistant questioned astutely, "The same person who caused you to lose the cotton shipment?"

Grayson had been Aidan's right-hand man since he began his shipping company five years earlier. Aidan had trusted his advice on many matters in the early stages of the business and Grayson's keen knowledge of the industry paid off profitably for both of them, for Kavanaugh Enterprises had grown steadily from his wise counsel. Aidan trusted the man implicitly. Today, how-ever, Grayson only had bad news to share, which did not improve Aidan's wretched condition or dismal mood.

"Yes, I believe so. Can you look into the matter qui-etly, Grayson? I don't want to show our hand until we have absolute proof." Aidan rubbed his throbbing temples with the pads of his fingers. It was foolish of him to drink to excess last night, but seeing Vivienne brought back so many painful memories he needed to drown them to block them out of his head.

"Of course, my lord."

"I'm stuck here in the country until this hellish

week is over. Then I'll be back in London. It's actually fortunate that I'm out of town. He won't believe that I suspect him if I'm here."

"He's here as well, my lord." Grayson offered the news calmly.

Aidan frowned in surprise. "Jackson Harlow is here at Bingham Hall?"

"He arrived just before I did this morning. Another guest of the Duchess of Bingham."

"I thought Jane Havilland had more discriminating taste than that." Aidan closed his eyes briefly in silence and opened them again. "Actually it may just be a fortunate bit of luck that Harlow is here. Now I can keep an eye on him myself, and perhaps attain some information from him. Meanwhile you can continue the investigation of his affairs in London and keep watch over those hired thugs of his."

"Yes, my lord." Grayson paused, then questioned hesitantly, "If you don't mind my asking, are you quite well? You don't look very good."

"Just a little too much to drink last night, and I'm paying for it dearly today," Aidan admitted wearily.

Grayson smiled sympathetically, but raised his eyebrows. "That's not like you, my lord. I trust all is well?"

"Yes. It's fine," he answered dismissively. "I shall return to London on Monday. Hopefully you will have discovered some evidence before then. Please send a messenger the minute you learn anything new."

"Be careful of Harlow. He's a rough character," Grayson warned.

"So are those thugs of his in London. Watch your back as well, Grayson." Aidan rose to his feet and escorted him from the library.

Once his assistant was in a carriage on his way back

to London, Aidan still had another task to accomplish. He would have preferred to go back to bed and recover in peace from last night's debacle, but a meeting with his mother was unavoidable. As much as he did not want to, especially in his present condition, he had to see her. Aidan walked through the grand house, one of the largest estates in the country, in search of Susana Kavanaugh, and he had a fair idea of where he could locate her.

As expected, he found her playing cards in the ladies' drawing room. It was a light and airy room, bearing the distinctive flair of the Duchess of Bingham's decorative touch. And there sat Lady Susana Kavanaugh, the Countess of Whitlock, in her usual regal pose, her head held high, her back ramrod straight, playing cards with Lady Downey.

His mother looked up as he entered, her keen eyes missing nothing. He could tell by the look on her face that she was not in the least bit happy with him.

Aidan greeted the two women. "Good afternoon, Mother. Lady Downey. How are you ladies this fine day?"

Lady Downey smiled warmly at him. "It's always nice to see you, Aidan, dear. It seems your mother has beaten me yet again. But if you will excuse me, I think I shall take a little nap before supper. And I expect you to sit beside me this evening, Aidan." The sweet elderly woman had the audacity to wink at him. "It's not every day that I get to spend time with the most eligible and handsomest bachelor in London!"

"Oh, really, Margaret!" Lady Whitlock rolled her eyes at her friend.

"It would be my honor to escort you to supper, Lady Downey." Aidan gallantly kissed her hand while she batted her lashes at him. Might as well give the old bird a little thrill.

As Lady Downey shuffled with dainty steps from the room, Aidan sat on the opposite side of the mahogany card table from Susana. He grinned at her as he idly picked up the deck of cards. "You always win, don't you, Mother?"

"Yes," she said definitively in her clipped voice. "You look terrible." Her lips formed a tight line of disapproval and eyes flashed with hardness and accusation. "I expected to see you at breakfast, Aidan."

Most people were slightly in awe of his mother's imperious manner and haughty disposition and thought her cold and unfeeling. Aidan had to admit that his mother possessed a prickly and irritable side, but in her own fashion she loved Aidan dearly. He was probably the only person she had ever loved in her life, for she certainly had not loved his father. It seemed to him that she devoted her life to making things perfect for her only son, even if that sometimes conflicted with Aidan's own wishes.

"I had certain business to attend to first."

She gave him a contemptuous look that left no doubt what she thought of his business matters. "You should have been out riding with Helene this morning."

"I was not aware of such an arrangement with her." He continued to shuffle the cards with skilled ease.

Susana retorted sharply, "Well, you would have been had you come to breakfast instead of laying abed all morning while she went out riding with Lord Gardner."

Aidan could say nothing to refute that. He *had* been in bed until after noon, and he continued to pay the painful price for his heavy drinking last night. His head still throbbed, although less so than it had been. He was angry at his loss of self-control, for he rarely overindulged. "Harry Gardner is a fine gentleman."

His mother raised an eyebrow and continued, "You had better propose to her soon. The Winston family is one of the finest in England and her father is the Earl of Hartshorne! Helene is perfect for you. You could speak to her father this evening. In fact, he's expecting it. If you don't make your move soon, you'll lose her to another. A girl like Helene won't wait around for you forever, Aidan."

He responded with quiet determination. "We have been through this before, Mother. I'll ask for her hand, or the hand of someone equally suitable, when I'm ready, but not before."

There was a moment of silence, but her eyes flashed with obvious displeasure. Though Susana was a domineering woman, she had met her match in her only son. He loved her, to be sure, but he did not let her control him as she did everyone else around her. However much Aidan respected his mother, and at times gave in to her inexplicable demands or whims, he stood his ground with her when it was important to him.

He could be stubborn if the circumstances warranted it. He had been determined to begin his shipping business when his mother had been completely against the idea of him being in trade. And he was being quite obstinate about not proposing. Yet, to be fair, Aidan did not know why he felt so apathetic about Helene. As much as he hated to admit it, his mother's assessment was correct. Helene would make a perfect countess for him. Well-bred, accomplished, and refined, she possessed an agreeable disposition, he found her attractive, and he enjoyed her company.

By far, she was the most preferable candidate to be his wife. Yet somehow he could not bring himself to ask for her hand in marriage.

Susana suddenly leaned in closer to him across the card table and spoke in a furious whisper. "I saw you dancing with that dreadful girl last night."

Aidan stopped shuffling the cards. He knew exactly to whom she referred. His mother had no love lost for Vivienne Montgomery and Vivienne had always been a bitter source of contention between them. Interestingly enough, his mother had won that battle in the end, although through no skill of her own.

He asked with a careless look, "Yes, what of it?"

"What of it?" she echoed him in stunned disbelief. "I must say you're taking this rather lightly. I for one was astonished to see her here, of all places, in the home of such a distinguished family. One would think that such a renowned man as the Duke of Bingham would know better than to invite some Irish peasant into his home. But then I learned that she is actually the niece of Lord and Lady Cardwell, and therefore related to the Duke and Duchess! Were you aware of that?" Her icy gray eyes, the same shade as her tightly coiled hair, peered intensely at him.

"I only learned of it myself last night." He had been as surprised as his mother by the fact that Vivienne was related to the Cardwells. Once he thought he knew everything there was to know about Vivienne but, as he learned once before, he actually knew very little about her.

"What on earth is she doing here in England?" The blue veins on his mother's forehead throbbed as she spoke. "And what were you thinking, dancing with her? Everyone saw you!"

"Her cousin Gregory cut in while I was dancing with Helene. I could hardly be rude."

"Well, you should have been." She gave him a fierce look. "Don't you become involved with her again."

He let out a breath of exasperation. "I have absolutely no intention of doing that."

"Well, you had better not. She's a witch, that one. Mark my words. She hurt you once, Aidan. She could do it again if you let down your guard." Susana pointed a long finger at him.

"Believe me, Vivienne Montgomery is the last woman I would want to become involved with again."

Susana seemed to relax slightly at that, but she was not about to end her little tirade. "What terrible luck to run into her. Why didn't she stay in Galway where she belongs? She'll probably tell everyone that she knew us in Ireland too. As if we needed reminders of that dreadful time in our lives." Susana turned up her haughty nose in complete disgust, as if smelling something offensive. "Do you think she means to cause trouble for you?" Her keen eyes glanced suspiciously around the room, as if Vivienne Montgomery could be there plotting their humiliation at that very moment.

Confused by her question, Aidan found himself defending Vivienne. "What would she possibly have to gain by making trouble for me, even if she could?" He neatly stacked the deck of cards, lining the edges up precisely, and set them down on the table.

"The girl is a common trollop. She was nothing but trouble then and I've no doubt she's even more trouble now. She could easily ruin your engagement to Lady Helene. The only probable reason she's here in the first place is to ruin you."

Surprised by that comment, Aidan asked, "Why would you say that?"

"Really, Aidan!" Susana uttered in complete frustration. "Don't be a simpleton. Of course the girl harbors ill will toward you! You broke off your engagement to her."

It was difficult to imagine that he had ever wanted to marry Vivienne at all, knowing what he knew about her now. Somehow that still stung. Yet, unable to bear his mother's contentious complaints about Vivienne, Aidan abruptly stood.

"You've got it wrong, Mother. She broke off the engagement with me, remember?" He turned and strode from the room, leaving his mother with a stunned look on her face.

Chapter 4

The Coincidence

Vivienne laughed impetuously at the bawdy limerick Gregory Cardwell had just whispered to her. "You boys really shouldn't tell me such things," she said, still giggling about the young man from Kew and what he could do. It did have quite a ring to it.

"You love it when we tell you such things. And you have to admit, it was a good one!" Gregory grinned mischievously.

Vivienne, smiling, nodded her head in agreement. She sat in the massive drawing room of Bingham Hall in an overstuffed leather chair with a twin bordered on each arm. It was late afternoon and most of the houseguests were out walking or resting before supper. The three of them had been whispering so the elderly baron dozing in the corner would not hear them.

"You have a remarkably good sense of humor, Vivvy, that's why we like you so much," George declared gallantly, his reddish hair rakishly flopping over one eye. "That and you are a pleasure on the eyes."

The pair of them were quite handsome in a healthy, outdoorsy way; reddish hair, ruddy complexions with freckles sprinkled across strong, manly features, and the Montgomery blue eyes. They were virtually identical and most people had difficulty distinguishing between the two, but Vivienne could tell them apart. Aside from the fact that George had slightly more freckles than Gregory, Vivienne could hear the difference in the timbre of their voices.

"You are much more fun than our sister," George said. "Glenda never likes our jokes."

Gregory promised wickedly, "If you are a very good girl, I'll tell you another one later."

Vivienne laughed helplessly. The Cardwell twins had taken her on as sort of a mascot. They regarded her somewhere between a little sister and a comrade. By turns they were teasing and admiring, treating her like a child and then as the grandest lady, protecting her vehemently from any sort of trouble. They entertained her with bawdy jokes, taught her to drink champagne, said irreverent things to make her laugh, and instructed her in the proper use of expletives. One day they laughed themselves senseless when Vivienne turned the tables on them and taught them the only Irish swear word she knew. Gregory and George adored her and she adored them in return. They were like a pair of lovable dogs, innocently getting into mischief, but so loving, loyal, and endearing, one had to forgive them any transgressions.

Vivienne was quite unused to such innocent and brotherly male attention and enjoyed every minute with them. The twins had made her feel like family the instant she arrived on their doorstep. After so many years alone in Ireland with only her elderly grandmother for company, she delighted in being part of the boisterous Cardwell clan.

"Now that's enough for today, you two," Vivienne scolded them with a smile. "I can't bear to listen to any more of your limericks."

"Hullo, children!" the Duchess of Bingham called as she approached the trio on the arm of a well-dressed gentleman.

Vivienne had liked Jane Havilland immediately, for the Duchess of Bingham had warmly welcomed her into her home and into her extended family with a cordial and generous manner that immediately made Vivienne feel accepted. A vivacious and witty blonde, Lady Bingham was an impeccable hostess with a flair for entertaining whose social invitations were always in demand, and anyone who was anyone coveted invitations to her parties.

"Aunt Jane, you look as beautiful as always," Gregory said with a wink, as both he and his brother jumped to attention.

"Don't put on airs with me, Gregory Cardwell, I've known you since you were in swaddling clothes. But tell me I'm beautiful anyway!" She laughed, and her eyes danced in merriment. "Now behave yourself, boys. I'd like you to meet the very nicest gentleman, who is a friend of my dear friend, Lady Swansea. This is Mister Jackson Harlow, of London. Mister Harlow, these two redheads are my brother's twin sons, Gregory and George Cardwell. And this lovely creature is their cousin, Vivienne Montgomery, so therefore she is related to me somehow but I don't know the technical terms. I just have her call me Aunt along with the rest of them. My sister-in-law Gwendolyn is Vivienne's father's sister. Can you follow that little family tree?" The Duchess of Bingham's laughter was light and airy as she spoke.

"Without any trouble at all," said Jackson Harlow smoothly. He shook hands politely with Gregory and George, but his demeanor changed completely when he smiled winningly at Vivienne. He bowed with an elegant gesture and declared, "It is an absolute honor to meet you, Miss Montgomery."

"Thank you, Mister Harlow." Vivienne studied him closely, for his name intrigued her. He was a handsome young man, of that there was no doubt. With his tawny blond hair and light brown eyes he had the looks of a golden god come to life. Taller than the twins, he possessed a sense of muscular strength beneath his finely cut and fashionable suit. His eyes were intelligent and his smile quite charming.

The Duchess of Bingham placed her petite hand on Gregory's sleeve. "Now you three, I need you to play host for me, since Richard is out riding with Gwen and Gilbert. I'd like you to introduce Mister Harlow around." She turned gracefully to her guest. "I'm not abandoning you, dear Jackson, it is just that there is some commotion in the kitchen about tonight's supper menu that I must deal with straightaway."

Jackson Harlow responded, "I'm certain I can manage well enough in such good company."

"Are you sure you trust us with him, Aunt Jane?" George asked with a wink.

"Not entirely," she called over her shoulder as she walked away, "but I do trust Vivienne."

The boys laughed raucously.

"Is this your first visit to Bingham Hall, Mister

Harlow?" Vivienne inquired as the twins' laughter subsided.

"Yes, this is the first time I have had the honor of an invitation, although I have known the Duke of Bingham for many years," Jackson stated.

George said, "We practically grew up here, didn't we, Greg?"

"Yes, and we always had fun hiding on Aunt Jane. There are so many secret staircases in this house, she could never catch us." Gregory laughed at the memory.

"Did you visit here often as well, Miss Montgomery?" Jackson Harlow asked, his gaze lingering on her.

"No. I've only just come to England recently. Although my father was English, my mother was Irish, so I was raised in Ireland."

"You hardly have an accent. One would never guess." He smiled at her, showing even, white teeth.

"We've been training her," George explained easily. "It's a good thing she's an excellent mimic. But we would have forgiven the Irish accent anyway, because she's so pretty."

"I must agree with you, Cardwell. Miss Montgomery is the most stunningly beautiful lady I have ever seen."

Vivienne felt self-conscious under the scrutiny of such an attractive man. "Now, now gentlemen, you must not talk about me as if I were not present."

"Were we doing that?" Gregory teased, an innocent look on his face.

As she smiled at the three charming gentlemen standing in front of her, her senses suddenly tingled and the hair on the back of her neck stood on end. She knew without a doubt that Aidan Kavanaugh had entered the room.

She turned her head slightly, to see past Gregory,

and there he stood. Lord, but he was devastatingly handsome. His powerful, firmly muscled body strode into the room with a confident grace. His jet-black hair was combed back, accentuating his aquiline nose and the inherent strength in the masculine lines of his face. His emerald green eyes were hooded, searching the room, and his sensuous mouth was fixed in a tight line, as if he were displeased about something.

Feeling her heart race, she rose from her chair. After last night's disastrous encounter she had no desire to see or speak to Aidan again anytime soon.

"Shall we go for a walk in the gardens now?" she suggested brightly to the others.

"I would be honored to walk with you, Miss Montgomery," Jackson offered with a gallant smile, extending his arm to Vivienne, which she accepted gratefully.

"George and I shall let you two go on ahead," Gregory said with a broad wink. "We'll meet you in the rose garden."

Vivienne would have laughed at Gregory's obvious attempt at matchmaking if she were not so anxious to escape Aidan Kavanaugh's presence. But it was too late, for Aidan had walked directly toward them.

"Aidan, you look like the very devil!" George blurted out with a laugh. "What happened to you?"

"Nothing," Aidan said through gritted teeth, apparently annoyed by the question. "I'm fine."

"If you say so," Gregory conceded with a knowing grin. "Have you met Mister Jackson Harlow?"

"The Earl of Whitlock and I have met on many occasions," Jackson said smoothly. "In fact, we have done some business together. It is good to see you again, Whitlock."

"Oh, Aidan's going to talk business now," George yawned mockingly.

Vivienne watched as Aidan took in the scene before him. His face registered surprise. Whether at seeing Jackson Harlow or seeing Vivienne on his arm, she was not sure which. On closer inspection he did look terrible, as the twins had so gleefully pointed out to everyone. His eyes were heavy, and he seemed a little bit green around the gills.

Vivienne looked from one handsome man to the other. Although both were quite taller than average, muscular, and fit, side by side they were a striking study in contrasts. Even in his current state of health, Aidan's tall, dark, and handsomely seductive looks left her a bit breathless. Then there was the golden-blond beauty of Jackson Harlow, which had a sensual allure of its own. A girl would be hard-pressed to choose which was the more attractive of the two. Fortunately, it was not a decision she was required to make.

"Good afternoon, Miss Montgomery," Aidan said coldly, sparing her the briefest of glances with his amazing green eyes. "I didn't expect to see you here, Harlow."

Jackson Harlow explained affably, "I just arrived here this morning. Before I left London I was sorry to hear about the fire at your shipping warehouse, Whitlock. That was a tremendous loss for you. A terrible misfortune."

Vivienne was surprised to discover that Aidan had acquired some sort of shipping business, although she knew it had always been a dream of his to own one. He used to spend hours talking to her father whenever he was in port, questioning him about all aspects of the shipping industry. It was one of the reasons she had loved Aidan. He had wanted to work, to contribute something and to be productive in the world, when he certainly didn't need to earn his living. Most young men of his age and class, like her cousins, were content with idle pursuits and thought working in trade beneath them. Aidan had always been different that way.

Well, it seemed that Aidan's childhood dreams had finally come true.

"Yes, the fire was a great calamity." Aidan's brow furrowed in response.

Harlow asked casually, "Do you know what caused it?"

"They are still searching for the cause."

"You mean to say that it is being investigated?" Jackson's eyes widened slightly.

"Of course. Wouldn't you conduct an investigation if it had been your warehouse that burned to the ground in the middle of the night?" Aidan asked, looking intently at Harlow.

Jackson nodded heartily in agreement. "Certainly I would."

"It is the only logical course of action."

"What do you expect they will find?"

"That remains to be seen, doesn't it?" Aidan answered. "It was most fortunate that no one was injured or killed."

"Yes, good thing," Harlow said. "Although a loss of that magnitude must have set you back quite a bit financially. If my company can do anything to help you, please let me know."

Aidan's tone hardened. "I don't think we'll be needing your help, Harlow."

"We were just going to walk in the gardens to give Harlow a tour about the place. Care to join us, Aidan?" George offered, breaking the sudden tension.

Aidan cast a disapproving glance over the two of

them. Vivienne noticed his eyes lingering on Jackson Harlow's hand on her arm. "No, thank you."

"You two go on ahead. We'll catch up with you shortly," Gregory said.

"Best of luck with your investigation, Whitlock. Well then, we shall see you later," Jackson responded with a casual attitude. "If you will excuse us . . ."

Vivienne left the room escorted by the handsome Mister Harlow, sensing a palpable tension between him and Aidan. Immensely relieved to remove herself from that curious state of affairs, it occurred to her that she had not uttered a single word to Aidan. So, it was to be cold civility while speaking to each other as little as possible, was it? At least now she knew what the rules were for surviving the week with him. Feeling oddly out of sorts with the entire exchange, she resolved to put Aidan out of her mind.

Aidan watched Vivienne leave with narrowed eyes. It was quite apparent that Vivienne could not be bothered to acknowledge his presence. He still felt like hell and so far the afternoon's events had not eased the pounding in his head. After his meeting with Daniel Grayson about the warehouse fire and Jackson Harlow's involvement and listening to his mother's irrational fears about Vivienne Montgomery, discovering the two causes of his current agitated state of mind going for a walk together was a bit of a shock.

"What is Jackson Harlow doing here?" he asked, not able to mask the irritation in his voice. As much as he distrusted Vivienne, he could not ignore the uneasiness he felt at the idea of her in Harlow's company.

"He's a friend of Uncle Richard's apparently. Just

met him. He seems a decent fellow though," Gregory answered smoothly, a bit surprised by Aidan's attitude.

"You just met the man, yet you let him escort your cousin about unchaperoned?" Aidan questioned impatiently.

"Calm down, Aidan. You know how relaxed Aunt Jane is with the rules here. That's why her parties are such fun. Besides, we're going to join them in a minute or two," George explained. "He's hardly going to make advances on her in broad daylight!"

"You sound jealous," Gregory added, looking at him curiously. "Are you?"

"I am not remotely jealous of Jackson Harlow." He could hardly start casting aspersions on Harlow's character at this point. He had no proof yet, but he would soon. Aidan did not trust the unscrupulous man at all.

And it did not surprise him that Harlow was taken with Vivienne. He could tell by the smitten look on the man's face that he was. What man wouldn't be infatuated with as beautiful and desirable a woman as Vivienne? She looked particularly enticing this afternoon, wearing a pretty green muslin gown that accentuated her slender yet shapely figure. The sight of her delicate beauty and sensual mouth had sent a powerful jolt of pure desire through him, leaving him shaken. That after all these years he could still feel such intense attraction for her, even knowing what she was, astounded him.

Steeling himself to ignore those feelings of desire, as well as the creeping sense of alarm he had at seeing her walk off with Harlow's arm in hers, he focused instead on the fact that Vivienne and Harlow shared the same character.

They were both treacherous, deceitful manipulators,

skilled at appearing to be what they were not and only interested in getting what they wanted: gaining material possessions by any means at their disposal. When he really thought about it, they were actually perfect for each other, but it did not make him feel any better. For some reason he could not quite place Vivienne in the same low category as Harlow.

Gregory continued to stare at him. "And just what *do* you think of our little cousin?"

Aidan shrugged. "She seems pleasant enough."

"Aidan, surely it cannot have escaped your notice that Vivienne is a rare and stunning beauty." George prompted him, "Admit it."

Reluctant to acknowledge that fact aloud, Aidan merely nodded his head. Yes, Vivienne was incredibly beautiful. But he also knew that beauty was only skin deep, for she had taught him the hard way to beware of what lay beneath.

"She'll be a sensation this Season. George and I will have our hands full watching over her."

Again Aidan silently agreed. Every man worth his salt would be after her. No doubt Vivienne would land herself a wealthy nobleman and be married before the Season was out.

"It will be good for her to have a little fun, poor girl," Gregory said his tone full of concern. "It seems as though things were a bit rough for her back home."

"What do you mean?" Aidan's brow furrowed in confusion at that news. "How was it rough for her?"

"You should know, Aidan. You were there in Galway, weren't you?" George asked looking at him intently.

"Well, it was ten years ago and I hardly knew her," he stated warily. He realized with a touch of irony that

that statement was closer to the truth than he first thought. As it turned out, he did not know Vivienne Montgomery at all.

Gregory continued the story, "Vivienne won't say a word about any of it, but mother has gathered that her life in Ireland was not the easiest. Vivienne's father didn't take the best care of her. While she was raised by her maternal grandmother, he was away at sea most of the time and not great about sending funds, if you know what I mean, especially the last year or two. Mother feels terrible that she was unaware of how dire Vivienne's circumstances actually were. After Uncle John died at sea—"

"Vivienne's father died?" Aidan interrupted in disbelief. He had not been aware of that fact. Knowing how much Vivienne adored her father, he knew she must have been utterly devastated by that loss.

George picked up where Gregory left off. "Yes, last year. And her situation went from bad to worse after he died, leaving her no money or anything, and all the while she cared for her invalid grandmother by herself. My parents finally went to Ireland to collect Vivienne after the grandmother died. They found her living in a run-down little place, with barely anything to eat. Mother was appalled, but Vivvy had been too proud to ask for help all that time."

Aidan was stunned. He had never given a thought to what life was like for Vivienne after he left Ireland. He had always assumed she had married that brawny farmer, Nicky Foster. And was shocked to discover that she hadn't. What had happened to her after he left? Why had no one taken care of her?

Gregory let out a low whistle. "Can you imagine a

rare beauty like her simply wasting away in the wilds of Ireland? It's criminal."

"The city of Galway is hardly the wilds," Aidan said softly. Thinking about what Vivienne had endured made him distinctly uncomfortable. "Why didn't she marry? She must have had offers . . ." Perhaps that caustic remark he tossed at her last night was closer to the truth than he realized.

"I don't know, but I suppose she refused them." George went on to explain, "So the whole family has spent the last few months polishing her up a bit, not that she needed much, truth be told."

"Yes, we fattened her up, got her some new clothes, worked on her accent, taught her to dance, and instructed her in proper manners and all that," Gregory said. "But she's so bright that she learned everything in record time."

"You'd think she was born to be in society," George exclaimed with pride. "She's a great girl."

"Speaking of which, we should catch up with her and Harlow," Gregory stated. "Are you coming with us, Aidan?"

Aidan declined their offer and watched the twins leave, pondering the new information he had learned about Vivienne. Surely her situation at home in Ireland was not as dire as they depicted it? It certainly had not been that bad when he last saw her. Perhaps the twins had overly dramatized Vivienne's plight in their compassionate devotion to her. Gregory and George were obviously besotted with their lovely cousin and only saw her finer qualities. In their eyes, the girl could do no wrong, and it was not Aidan's place to destroy their pretty illusions.

They would discover Vivienne's true character in due time.

"And here is the rose garden where we are to meet my cousins," Vivienne pointed out after they had walked the lengths of the expansive wildflower garden and the herb garden. "They can tell you more about these gardens than I can. I only arrived at Bingham Hall the day before yesterday myself, so I have not seen much more than you have. I'm a very poor guide, I'm afraid."

Vivienne smiled at Jackson Harlow as they walked arm in arm through the lush and fragrant grounds of Bingham Hall. The late afternoon sun hung low in the sky, bathing everything in its soft golden rays, and the air was fresh with the early scent of spring.

"I think you have been a most enchanting guide, Miss Montgomery, and I can honestly say that I haven't much of an interest in gardens myself. I don't care for them, except as a lovely setting for walking with a beautiful lady."

"I wonder what could be keeping Gregory and George?" she asked helplessly.

Vivienne found Jackson Harlow to be quite charming and exceedingly handsome. His blond hair glistened gold in the sunlight and he had the most intriguing dimples on either side of his mouth when he smiled, as he was doing now. Vivienne noticed her heart beating a little faster than usual. It had been quite some time since she had been alone with someone who made her pulse quicken.

Ten years in fact.

"Shall we rest on that bench and wait for them there?" he asked and, without waiting for an answer, escorted her to a white marble bench flanked by tall, green-leafed topiaries in white marble pots. Once they were seated, he said, "Ah, yes, this is better. I suspect that your cousins will be along soon enough. So tell me, Miss Montgomery, what brings you to England?"

"My Aunt Gwen invited me to live with them," she explained.

"And what of your family?"

"My mother died when I was an infant. And my father is . . . missing." Vivienne fiddled nervously with the lace edging of her bell-shaped sleeve. Now was her chance. She had nothing to lose by asking him.

"Missing?" he asked in confusion. "What do you mean?"

"He was lost at sea."

"How terrible for you." His brows furrowed in concern and he touched her lightly on the arm in comfort.

"Yes, it is. Yet, I was wondering . . . When I heard that your last name was Harlow, I wondered if you were at all connected with Harlow Shipping International? In London?" She turned to look up at him, for he was very tall, even sitting beside her. She also noticed that he smelled very nice. Of something clean and spicy.

His handsome face broke into a wide grin. "How funny you should ask. That is my family's company."

The skin on the back of Vivienne's neck tingled. "Then you are related to Miles Harlow?"

"He is my brother. Harlow Shipping was our father's company. Now my older brother Miles and I manage the business, and our brother Davis is a sea captain. What prompted you to ask about us?" Jackson asked.

"My father was a captain on one of your family's ships."

Again, Jackson's face clouded. "Oh, I see. It was from one of our ships that he disappeared, wasn't it?"

Vivienne could hardly breathe. Her main purpose in coming to England in the first place was to go to London to learn more about her father's disappearance, and here the information just fell into her lap! Her good fortune astounded her. This man was quite possibly the only link to learning the truth about her father. She took a deep breath to steady herself.

"Yes. My father is Captain John Montgomery. His ship was the *Sea Star*."

"Ah, the *Sea Star*. Yes, I recall that ship being lost in a fierce storm off the coast of Africa. They never did find a trace of it. I confess I do not remember all the details for it was many months ago. I am terribly sorry. I had no idea your father was Captain Montgomery for I did not connect your name, as you did with mine. This is quite a coincidence. But you have my deepest condolences."

"Then you think there is no hope either? That he is not alive, perhaps stranded on an uncharted island somewhere?" Her Irish brogue became more pronounced in her urgency to make him believe her. "Since the ship has not been found, then could it not be safe *somewhere*?"

Jackson took her hand in his. It felt warm and strong, and his touch comforted her instantly. "My dear Miss Montgomery, it would be my fondest wish that your father is still alive. I would hate to raise false hopes, but stranger things have come to pass."

"Thank you," she whispered, looking into his light brown eyes.

He was so goldenly handsome it unsettled her. He possessed a classically sculpted face with a broad brow and a strong jawline. His aquiline nose was straight and his lips full and sensual. His skin had a tanned glow, as if he spent a great deal of time outdoors. There was something wild and untamed about him, as if he could barely contain himself, that left her a little breathless.

"You are very kind, Mister Harlow. It's just that no one in my family shares my belief that my father could be lost and still alive somewhere. No one will even discuss the possibility with me. They think I'm foolish to keep believing that he might return someday." She paused for a moment. "Do you think you could—"

"I could contact my brothers to find out what they might know about your father and his ship?" He finished her question for her.

She breathed a sigh of relief and smiled gratefully. "It is terribly presumptuous of me to ask, but could you please? I would be forever in your debt."

"Next week I will enquire into the matter of the *Sea Star*. I shall talk to Miles and look over the records we have in my office in London and I shall write to Davis to see if he knows anything. Let's not talk of debts, Miss Montgomery. I would never take advantage of you in that way. This is the very least I could do for you after the tragic misfortune you have suffered while your father was employed by my family." The genuine look of sincerity on his face warmed her and filled her with a glimmer of hope.

"Thank you, Mister Harlow." Vivienne felt almost dizzy with her success. He really wanted to help her find out what happened to her father!

"You are most welcome, but . . . I shall ask a small

favor from you in return." He smiled at her, a smile that made her stomach flip-flop in a way she had not felt since she was seventeen.

"That only seems fair," she consented with a helpless grin. "What is your favor?" Was she was actually flirting? It had been so long since she had flirted with anyone, she felt giddy.

His golden eyes warmed her. "May I have the honor of a dance with you at the ball Saturday night?"

"Yes, of course."

"I am so pleased to have met you, Miss Montgomery. I think this week at Bingham Hall will prove to be a most enjoyable visit after all."

"I can only agree with you, Mister Harlow."

"Shall we go in search of your cousins?"

"There is no need. Here they are now." Vivienne waved happily as Gregory and George approached them. She had not felt so lighthearted in years.

Chapter 5

The Countess

Lady Susana Kavanaugh, the Countess of Whitlock, frowned in displeasure as she watched Vivienne Montgomery. She chatted and laughed with Helene Winston, the Cardwell twins, the Atwood sisters, and others of the younger set in the grand parlor after supper that evening. Where Aidan had gone off to, Susana did not know, but it irritated her that he was not there paying court to Helene as he should be.

After last night's revelry at the ball, everyone was enjoying a quiet, leisurely evening at Bingham Hall. All the guests wanted to be well rested for the outdoor activities planned for the next morning. While the younger people flirted with each other, the others immersed themselves in quiet pursuits; discussing politics, reading, playing chess, doing puzzles, or playing cards.

Stealing glances at Vivienne between the cards she held in her hand, Susana Kavanaugh grew angrier. It took all her strength not to leave the room in utter disgust, but she would not dare risk social ruin by offending the powerful Duchess of Bingham. Jane Havilland was a force to be reckoned with in Society and it would not do to get on her bad side. So Susana continued to play cards with Lady Gwendolyn Cardwell, Lady Downey, and Glenda Cardwell, while the Duchess of Bingham, and Lady Helene's mother, the Countess of Hartshorne, chatted and watched.

"How lovely of your niece to pay you a visit, Gwendolyn," Susana said with false sweetness.

"Yes, Vivienne is a credit to the family," Gwen agreed pleasantly.

"She's the daughter of my brother's wife's brother," Lady Bingham chimed in merrily. "I simply adore saying that."

"Vivienne's not just visiting. She's living with us now. Until we can marry her off. Which according to my brothers, won't be long," Glenda uttered in a doleful voice, obviously unhappy with the current state of affairs in her household. The plain and plump creature made her discard with a sulky toss of her dull, brown hair.

Susana watched Glenda Cardwell with a keen eye, intrigued by why she did not associate with girls her own age. Especially her cousin Vivienne.

What terrible luck that Vivienne Montgomery turned out to be related, however loosely, to the Duchess of Bingham! After another furtive glance at Vivienne, Susana grudgingly admitted to herself that the girl cleaned up nicely. One would not recognize her as the dirty, untamed little girl from Galway. Vivienne was beautiful and Susana could understand to a certain extent why Aidan found her attractive, if in a somewhat common, earthy way. But she was completely unsuitable for her son. Aidan needed a proper English lady, not some awful peasant from Ireland.

Her hatred of all things Irish began even before she was forced to marry Aidan's father all those years ago. Lord Joseph Kavanaugh. She had detested him on sight, but her parents sold her into that marriage without any regard for her feelings on the matter and shipped her off to Ireland. Ireland, that Godforsaken, blight-ridden nightmare of a country!

At sixteen Susana was ripped from her family, friends, and all that she loved. Yes, Joseph Kavanaugh was titled and owned property and a manor house, if one could call a drafty, damp, rambling, run-down limestone mess with nothing comfortable or stylish to recommend it a proper manor house. Susana did her best to repair the place and make it more respectable, but Joseph was tightfisted with funds and happy with the place just as it was. An unpretentious man who liked his life uncomplicated, Joseph enjoyed his liquor too much and was more than content with his thoroughbred racehorses. His simple mind could not comprehend how his wife could want for anything more in life and her constant misery irritated him.

And miserable she certainly was.

Susana submitted to his husbandly demands until she produced a son and heir, at which point she considered herself finished with Joseph and focused all her attention on her adorable baby boy. She hired the best English tutors for her son, determined to raise a proper English gentleman even if they were only in Galway. And what an exceptional child Aidan was! Handsome and bright, ambitious and charming. Traits he obviously inherited from her side of the family and not the Kavanaughs, heaven knew!

Good fortune finally smiled on her when her husband broke his neck and died from a fall from one of his racehorses when Aidan was eighteen. Dropping dead was the one and only favor he ever granted her in all their marriage. Then all the money was hers, to do with as she wished. Regrettably, she could not sell the Irish property since it was entailed to Aidan, but she immediately made plans to return to England and buy a fine, new house of her own.

However, the greatest stroke of luck of all occurred at the end of the summer that Joseph obligingly broke his neck. They received word that Joseph's uncle, the Earl of Whitlock, died along with his wife and only son in a tragic fire at an inn outside London. That sudden and strange twist of fate made Aidan the new Earl of Whitlock. It was a most unexpected but fantastic change of events. Aidan inherited the title, the lands, and the considerable fortune of the earldom. Finally, Susana could leave Ireland and return to London in high style. And as the mother of an earl, no less!

That miracle couldn't have happened at a more opportune time either. For she needed to get Aidan as far away from the enticing Vivienne Montgomery as quickly as she could. It proved to be a difficult situation because Aidan was determined to marry the girl, in spite of the fact that Vivienne Montgomery would, undoubtedly, ruin his life. But Susana managed to turn the tables and finally allow Aidan to see Vivienne's true character revealed in the light of day.

Everything had worked out to her advantage and she and Aidan made a splendid new life for themselves in England, taking up residence in their grand country estate, Whitlock Hall, and their elegant new townhouse in London.

If only she had managed to secure his marriage to Helene Winston before they came to Bingham Hall, everything would be perfectly settled. Instead Vivienne Montgomery's presence threatened her plans for Aidan once again. The looks her son cast in that girl's direction during supper worried her. No, it did not bode well for anyone that the Irish witch had returned. Something had to be done.

As the card game drew to a close, Susana laid down her winning hand with a triumphant look.

"You win again! That's twice today you've beaten me, Susana!" Lady Downey cried in exasperation.

Susana glanced up to see Vivienne Montgomery, the very object of her thoughts, standing next to their card table. Lady Helene had joined them as well.

"Excuse me, Aunt Jane, but George and Gregory would like to know if it would be all right for them to teach us a new parlor game," Vivienne asked politely. Susana noted that the girl had lost her Irish accent. Clever baggage.

Lady Bingham responded with a knowing look, glancing in the direction of the twins, who were attempting to appear innocent and failing utterly. "And those rapscallions sent you two lovelies over to me, because they know I can't refuse your sweet faces. I'm sure whatever they want to teach you is both highly improper and decidedly wicked, but I will probably let them do it anyway. And I'll more than likely join you!" She laughed in spite of trying to appear stern. "But let's make them stew a bit, shall we? Oh. Vivienne, dear, I don't believe you have formally met Lady Whitlock yet? Susana, this is my 'niece' I was telling you about, Vivienne Montgomery."

For the first time in ten years Susana had to speak to Vivienne. She gave her the most withering glance. Might as well be out with it.

"She was not the Countess of Whitlock when I knew her, but Lady Kavanaugh. However, we are already acquainted with each other, are we not, Lady

Whitlock?" Vivienne said with what Susana suspected was a contemptuous tone. Ah, the little witch.

"Why, of course, Miss Montgomery," Susana murmured with false sweetness, "I remember you. We met in Galway when you were a child. My, but you have grown since then. You used to come and visit us at the manor. You were one of Aidan's many little friends."

Vivienne's color paled and Susana knew she had hit her mark.

"You and Lord Whitlock knew each other as children in Ireland? How wonderful!" Lady Helene declared, her elegant features marked in surprise.

"Yes, we'd see each other from time to time in the village, wouldn't we, dear?" Susana glanced at Vivienne sharply. "Galway is so provincial, but then you know that now that you've come to England. I haven't been there in years. My word, Vivienne, I thought you would have been married by now. Especially at your age, dear. One of the local boys . . ." Susana tapped her finger to her chin as if she could not recall the facts. "Oh, what was his name? The one you used to go around with? That farm boy? Foster, was it?" She arched an eyebrow at Vivienne.

"No, I did not marry him, Lady Whitlock," Vivienne responded tightly, and Susana was satisfied by the devastated look on the girl's face.

"And I for one am thrilled that she did not marry over there," Lady Bingham added with a kind smile, patting Vivienne's arm. "For we shall have such a grand time with the stir Vivienne will cause this Season. She will be married by fall, mark my words."

"Oh, Aunt Jane, please," Vivienne protested.

As the others murmured their assent at Lady Bingham's prediction, Susana watched the look of pure hatred that Glenda Cardwell turned upon Vivienne. Well, well, well. So that was it. The ugly duckling was jealous of her beautiful swan cousin. But of course she was! The two girls were close in age and no one was saying that Glenda would find a husband. Miserable creature, who would want her really? Season after Season had passed over the unfortunate and ill-tempered Glenda with not a bit of interest. Her parents, God bless them, did their best to doll her up and parade her about each year, but to no avail.

"Let me go talk to those two hellions and see what they have up their sleeves." Lady Bingham stood, brushing the skirts of her gown. "Excuse me, ladies."

Vivienne turned to her cousin and offered kindly, "Come join us, Glenda. They say it is an amusing game."

"You may be amused by my brothers, Vivienne, but I am not," Glenda declared with a frown. "They are quite boorish."

"Oh, Miss Cardwell cannot leave us just yet!" Susana objected on her behalf. "I need her as my partner for the next game. Isn't that right, dear?" She gave the dismal girl a bright smile and was rewarded with an eager nod.

Glenda, her fat face pinched in a frown, stated dismissively, "I'm sorry, Vivienne. I cannot join your little games now. I'm busy."

While Susana dealt the next hand, Vivienne returned to the Cardwell twins with Helene at her side. Lady Bingham joined them to give her approval. A few moments later, Susana's eyes narrowed and a frown crossed her features as she watched Aidan enter the drawing room and immediately walk toward Vivienne.

Chapter 6

The Parlor Game

While Vivienne listened to Gregory sweet-talk his aunt, she still shook from her unpleasant encounter with Lady Whitlock. She had never liked Aidan's mother and obviously time had done nothing to soften the woman's malevolent disposition. No longer in the mood for fun and games with her high-spirited cousins, Vivienne trembled with hurt and resentment. Refusing to give the bitter old dragon the satisfaction of thinking that she had succeeded in upsetting her, she remained in the drawing room to play although she no longer had any desire to stay.

One of Aidan's many little friends, indeed!

Lady Whitlock knew very well what she and Aidan had meant to each other, but she had acted as if Vivienne had been nothing to him. And that remark about Nicky Foster almost knocked the wind out of her! She wished she had thought of a cunning remark to answer her, but she had not her wits about her. And after all, what could she say? She was fortunate the old harridan had not made aspersions on Vivienne's character. How that woman ever raised a son as wonderful and caring as Aidan had always been a mystery to her.

Vivienne took a deep breath to calm herself and plastered if not an enthusiastic smile on her face, then at least one that appeared to be interested. After Aunt Jane gave her consent for them to play and left them to themselves, Gregory explained the rules of the new parlor game.

"It's a harmless little game called, 'Facts and Forfeits,'" he stated with a gleam in his eyes. "It is possible to learn quite a lot about a person from this game."

"Oh, you're not playing this again, are you, Greg?" Aidan's deep voice resonated behind her, causing Vivienne to startle as she turned to face him.

She had thought he had retired for the evening and his unexpected presence stunned her. Still dressed in a black dinner jacket with an immaculate white cravat, Aidan looked dashingly handsome. The sharp contrast of black and white set off his masculine features to perfection and his jet-black hair gleamed in the warm light of the room. The color had returned to his face and his dark eyebrows arched in mild amusement as he glanced at them.

"Lord Whitlock, you're here!" Helene squealed, clapping her hands together in delight. "You'll play with us, won't you?"

"This game got Whitlock into a bit of trouble back at Cambridge once, didn't it?" Gregory taunted him. "I think he might have some secrets to hide."

"The truth is something I value highly and I, for

one, have nothing to hide," Aidan answered smoothly, his intense eyes lingering for the briefest moment on Vivienne. "In fact, I'm most eager to play. Please continue."

Vivienne had not expected Aidan to join them. Suddenly very nervous, she wished she could gracefully make an exit, but it had been her idea that they try the new game, and Gregory and George would never let her leave now.

Gregory continued the explanation of the rules with renewed enthusiasm, his eyes lively. "The way it works is that a person is asked a question from one of the group. After hearing the question he or she gets to decide if they want to answer that question. If they answer, it has to be honestly, as a fact. If they choose not to answer the question truthfully, they have to pay a forfeit."

Their small group consisted of some of the younger, and still unmarried, houseguests: the Cardwell twins, Lady Helene Winston, Lord Harry Gardner, Miss Sarah Atwood and her younger sister Victoria, and Mister Wesley Lawrence, as well as Aidan and herself. Vivienne idly wondered where Jackson Harlow was, since she had not seen him since supper ended. She had so enjoyed his company that afternoon and would have appreciated his charming presence with her now.

"What are the forfeits?" asked Sarah Atwood, a pretty brunette with a matching set of dimples framing her wide mouth.

"Whatever the Questioner decides," George said. "For example, if someone refuses my question, I can make up a forfeit for them to pay for not telling the truth, such as doing something as ridiculous as having to recite one of Shakespeare's sonnets."

"Or you can demand a kiss as a forfeit . . ." Gregory whispered with a devilish gleam in his eyes.

"What my charming cousin won't do for a kiss." The others laughed at Vivienne's dry remark.

"How do we decide who begins the first question?" asked Helene, smiling with excitement.

"We'll draw straws. The shortest becomes the first Questioner and asks a question of the person of his choice. When that person has answered the question honestly or paid the forfeit, then he or she may ask the next question," Gregory said as they began to arrange the chairs in a close circle. "And if we know you are lying or if you do not perform your forfeit satisfactorily, you are out of the game. The winner is the last one in."

It seemed an amusing game to Vivienne, and if Aidan were not there she would have actually enjoyed playing. As they settled into their seats, Vivienne found herself sitting between Harry Gardner, a tall, lanky fellow with brown hair and eyes the color of coffee, and Wesley Lawrence, a fair-haired man with a broad nose. She was positioned directly across from Aidan, who sat between Victoria Atwood and Gregory.

Since the shortest straw went to Lord Harry Gardner, he asked the first question.

"Miss Victoria, which Cardwell twin do you think is more handsome, Gregory or George? Fact or forfeit?"

Amid much laughter, Victoria answered confidently. "I can honestly answer that one. It's a fact that the boys are identical. They are equally handsome."

They applauded her answer. Victoria said excitedly, "Now, my question is for Lord Whitlock."

They all turned to look at Aidan. With a self-satisfied smile Victoria asked, "Why have you yet to marry, Lord Whitlock? Fact or forfeit?"

A chorus of oohs went round the circle. "You could have asked that same question of any of them," Sarah Atwood called laughingly to her sister.

Managing a bland smile, Vivienne felt uncomfortable with that question to Aidan. The answers would be too painful. Yet she could not resist a quick peek at Lady Helene Winston, who blushed prettily at the mention of the Earl of Whitlock and marriage. Her cool, refined features were beautiful and her wheat-colored hair was elegantly coiled in a knot at the base of her neck. From what Vivienne had gathered from her cousins, it was generally believed that there was an understanding of sorts between Aidan and Helene that they would eventually marry. Vivienne had to admit that Helene seemed a perfect match for Aidan. She already appeared every inch a countess.

Aidan rose to the challenge and answered Victoria's question without hesitation. "The fact is I have chosen not to marry because I do not believe I am ready to settle down." He gave a droll look around the circle and winked at Helene. "Not yet anyway."

"Nicely evaded, old chap," Lord Harry commented with a chuckle. "Your question."

A moment of silence ensued as they waited expectantly for Aidan to ask one of them a question. With a sudden, sickening sense of dread, Vivienne knew, just knew, he was going to question her.

"Miss Montgomery," Aidan said clearly, his narrowed emerald eyes pinned on Vivienne, as he crossed his arms across his chest.

Her heart beat a little faster and her mouth went dry

at the endless possibilities of his questions. *Not here. Not in front of everyone. He wouldn't dare. Would he?*

His rich voice rang out clearly, "Have you ever done something of which you are ashamed?"

His odd words left them all silent, and the air was charged with the palpable tension between the two of them.

"Fact or forfeit?" Aidan added, urging her to make some response.

Feeling her cheeks flush scarlet at the obvious implication of his question, she realized how much Aidan despised her. Even after all this time, he thought so little of her that he would attempt to dishonor her in front of her family and newfound friends. He seemed so utterly spiteful, so self-satisfied with the embarrassment he was unmistakably causing her, that she flinched at his stare. *Oh, Aidan.*

"That's not a proper question to ask a lady, Whitlock," George declared with a frown, his dissatisfaction with Aidan's manner quite apparent.

Lord Harry offered gallantly, "You are not obligated to answer that, Miss Montgomery."

"Then pay the forfeit," Aidan stated with a cold look, challenging her.

Vivienne's pride would not allow that. She met his eyes defiantly. They were hard and unfeeling, judging her. Her chin went up unconsciously and she did not hesitate to answer. "The fact is I have never done anything the least bit shameful in my life."

"Of course you haven't, darling. You couldn't possibly have," Gregory said in her defense, frowning with disapproval in Aidan's direction. "Your question, Vivvy."

She cleared her throat, but did not miss the dark look of complete skepticism Aidan gave her answer.

How she detested him in that moment! She fashioned a wide smile on her face and asked brightly, "My darling cousin Gregory. What was the worst trick you ever played on your brother?"

Grateful for the change in tone, they all expressed amusement as Gregory opted to forfeit rather than confess his sins in front of his twin. In return, Vivienne demanded he ask old Lord Worthington for a puff of his expensive cigar. As they all watched Gregory gallantly saunter across the expanse of the grand parlor to the elderly man snoozing by the fire, Vivienne dared a glance at Aidan.

He was still staring at her. His emerald eyes had been fixed on her since the game began and it utterly unnerved her. Struck senseless by his masculine presence and steady gaze, she attempted to appear nonchalant by brushing the dark curls from her face.

His task complete, and triumphant from his return, a teasing Gregory then asked a question of Helene Winston. Amidst much playful speculation, Helene refused to name who, if anyone, gave her her first kiss. Gregory demanded that she sing the nursery rhyme "Mistress Mary" with a French accent. After their laughter subsided at her atrocious pronunciation, it was Helene's turn to ask a question.

"Miss Montgomery, I have a question only you can answer for us." Her pale hazel eyes peered at Vivienne expectantly, her refined, fair features still flushed from the laughter of her earlier consequence. "What was Lord Whitlock like when you knew him years ago as a little boy in Ireland? Fact or forfeit?"

Vivienne froze for a moment, although not so much from surprise at the question, but more from the uncertainty of how to answer it. Since Lady Whitlock's comment earlier, she had been half expecting this question from Helene Winston. Due to her complicated history with Aidan, Vivienne couldn't help but feel uneasy with the girl, although Helene seemed a very congenial person. She was just the sort of woman that a distinguished earl such as Aidan should marry, and naturally she would want to know what Aidan was like as a child. Any lady would be curious about her future husband's childhood.

"That's the question to which we'd all love to know the answer, Lady Helene! Was he a stick in the mud then as well?" George asked inquisitively. "Because we certainly know he can be now!"

Again Vivienne felt the heat of Aidan's intense stare on her. She flashed him the briefest of glances, but now his handsome face held an unfathomable expression. Should she avoid answering and pay the penalty? But after Aidan's pointed question to her, they would surely guess that something had happened between them back in Ireland if she did not answer.

Vivienne had never been a coward . . .

"Come on Vivvy, we're waiting!" Gregory urged.

"The fact is . . ." she whispered, her throat tightening at the words.

The truth it would be then, however much she would like to viciously flay his character. It confused her that they referred to him as being dull or boring. Aidan must have changed greatly over the years. Her voice was soft as she spoke. "Well . . . He wasn't the Earl of Whitlock back then. Just Aidan Kavanaugh. And he wasn't a stick in the mud at all . . . He was wonderful. He was great fun and always full of adventure and laughter. We played together often. He was . . . he was the sweetest boy. Smart, sensitive, and kind—"

"That's enough," Aidan interrupted in a low, harsh voice. The expression on his handsome face darkened menacingly and a muscle tightened along his jawline.

"Aw, come now, Whitlock!" Wesley Lawrence called out tauntingly, his grin beaming. "It was just getting interesting!"

Gregory, astutely taking in the tense look between Aidan and Vivienne, came to the rescue. "Yes, that's all we need to hear Vivienne. It's your turn to ask a question now."

Grateful for Gregory's intervention, Vivienne rallied quickly, not meeting Aidan's eyes. She laughed brightly and said, "I shall ask a question of Lord Harry. Is there a particular lady in this room you are sweet on?"

That question caused a chorus of exclamations and nervous giggles from Sarah Atwood. Harry chose to pay the forfeit rather than name one of them, so Vivienne declared he had to kneel at the feet of each lady present and profess his undying love for her. As Harry met the demands of the penalty in the midst of titters and teasing laughter, Vivienne let out a deep breath, unaware that she had been holding it for so long. Her hands were shaking in her lap. Like a magnet to steel, she could not help herself from looking up and meeting Aidan's intense glare head-on.

His green eyes were still fixed on her but his expression was unreadable. Her stomach flip-flopped. As they stared at each other and the moment stretched into minutes, she suddenly felt that they were alone. Just the two of them. Something in his eyes changed and became familiar. They seemed to soften, to warm to her. He looked at her as if he cared. It was the briefest glimmer of Aidan. The real Aidan that she had once loved. Not the haughty, cold, Earl of Whitlock who barely acknowledged her presence, but the Aidan who loved her. Without speaking a word, he asked something of her, questioned her with his eyes.

Helpless to answer, she just gazed back at him, filled with an incredible sense of longing that made her want to cry. Seeing him again left her feeling open, vulnerable.

"Hey, Whitlock!" Gregory called loudly, finally breaking their little reverie, waving his hand. "Gardner just asked you a question."

Blinking, Vivienne disengaged from their powerful stare to see Gregory looking at them with a curious expression. They were all observing her and Aidan. Surely they were as confused by their behavior as she was herself.

"Sorry," Aidan said in a rather clipped voice. "Could you please repeat the question?"

"I asked you to describe what Miss Montgomery was like when you knew her. It's only fair." Lord Harry smiled engagingly at Vivienne. "Fact or forfeit?"

Again Vivienne looked toward Aidan. But whatever they had shared in that brief, fleeting moment of intimacy completely vanished. Aidan, her Aidan, had disappeared and the haughty Earl of Whitlock took his place. That hardened, distant look returned to his green eyes and his dark brows furrowed in consternation. Everyone's attention was fixed on him, waiting expectantly to see what would happen.

"What was Miss Montgomery like when I knew her?" he echoed the question blankly as if he did not understand the meaning.

Oh, this game was interminable! Would it never

end? She felt the avid stares of the others, watching her reaction. How could they not sense the animosity between them? Could they not feel it?

"The fact is . . ." Aidan stated softly, but there was an edge to his voice that did not bode well.

Vivienne held her breath. If he chose to, Aidan could ruin her completely with a few simple words. She looked toward him once more, but he avoided her eyes.

"Tell, tell," Lord Harry prompted excitedly.

When Aidan spoke his voice was calm and low, his posture tense. "Miss Montgomery was much the same as she is now. She is a woman, just like any other, who knows how to manipulate situations to get exactly what she wants."

Vivienne held her head high, appalled by his remark. There were many negative connotations in what he said, none of which reflected nicely upon her.

"Well," Helene whispered after an awkward silence, her injured expression betraying her surprise at Aidan's harsh words, which in essence insulted all the women present.

Vivienne uttered not a word.

"Aidan, my friend, your manners are sorely lacking this evening," George said, obviously confused by Aidan's antagonism of Vivienne. "This game is supposed to be fun. Remember?"

"I told you this game gets Whitlock in trouble," Gregory mumbled under his breath.

"Maybe we should play something else," suggested Sarah Atwood with an uncertain smile.

"The game is not over. It's my turn to ask a question now," Aidan continued casually as if nothing at all were amiss. Before anyone had a chance to make an objection, he asked pointedly, "Miss Montgomery, have you ever been in love? Fact or forfeit?"

All eyes, once again, turned to Vivienne. It was ridiculous, really. What was Aidan thinking to confront her this way? And honestly, how did he expect her to answer such a barbed question? To say yes? No? To say that she was once desperately in love with him? Would he dispute her if she gave a "wrong" answer?

Her anger rose at his manipulative measures to back her into some sort of a corner. Her presence at Bingham Hall obviously disturbed him, causing him to make a spectacle of himself, in front of his future fiancée no less. He acted as though she had come there to deliberately ruin his visit. As if Vivienne had any choice in the matter! To be technical about it, this was her family's home and *he* was ruining *her* visit. If he didn't like it, he could very well leave! Was it a battle the Earl of Whitlock wanted? Then she would certainly give it to him.

She glanced around the circle at everyone, seeing the unsmiling expressions and confused looks. She managed a light laugh. "Apparently Lord Whitlock is taking this little game far more seriously than the rest of us." Then she turned her gaze pointedly at Aidan. "I choose not to answer that. I shall pay the forfeit, please." Her heart pounded and she knew from the stunned look on his face that he had expected her to answer.

Gregory stared between the two of them and whistled low, sitting back and folding his arms across his chest.

Aidan wanted to kiss Vivienne. Wanted to demand it as her forfeit. He wanted to pull her against him and place his mouth over hers in a searing, possessive, mind-numbing kiss. He could think of nothing else.

And he did not know what had gotten into him, why he had even bothered to play this absurd game in the first place. He should have just stayed in his room and gone to sleep early as he originally intended. Lord knew he needed the rest. But after catching half-glimpses of Vivienne through the flickering candles across the formal dining table all through supper, he was intrigued. She looked as if she belonged in this manor house and seemed different from the young girl he remembered. Chatting vivaciously with the guests near her, she looked beautiful and elegant, making him wish he were the one sitting beside her.

Her beauty fascinated him. With her dark hair fashioned atop her head providing a view of the graceful curve of her neck, her silky skin glowed like warm ivory. Her blue eyes glittered with animation. The low décolletage of her rose silk evening gown showed her perfectly proportioned breasts to their best advantage. He could not take his eyes off her. Not once did she look in his direction, and again that irritated him. Especially after what the twins had divulged to him about her life after he left Galway.

He thought he had recovered from what happened. It had been ten years. He should have no feelings left for Vivienne Montgomery at this point. She had betrayed him, wounded him so deeply he didn't think he would ever survive the pain. He had worked hard to forget her, devoting his every waking moment to building his shipping company and taking up with beautiful women with black hair and blue eyes. None of them made him forget her. He simply became accustomed to his new life without Vivienne. Over the years he had moved forward, managing his growing business and creating some semblance of a social life in his position as the Earl of Whitlock. But nothing had prepared him for the shock of seeing Vivienne again and having to deal with the onslaught of turbulent and powerful emotions that she conjured within him.

And here he was, making an ass out of himself over her.

After supper, his head still throbbing, he had slipped away to his rooms to take a draught to ease his headache. But he could not resist the temptation of seeing her again, knowing she was just downstairs, and he had been compelled to join his group of friends in the grand parlor.

And ended up playing this preposterous game.

He was in the wrong, asking her those questions. He had behaved boorishly in reaction to her coldness, but some angry part of him wanted to get a rise out of her. Get her to admit something, *anything*. He wanted to trap her with her own lies.

Then she answered Helene's question about what he was like years ago, her candid and earnest response taking him by surprise, and they had shared something, looking into each other's eyes. For the briefest instant he saw Vivienne as he had always loved her. His sweet, sincere, adoring girl, with her laughing smile and flashing eyes.

It was almost his undoing, because he could feel himself falling under her spell again. It terrified him, for he could not allow that to happen. She had irrevocably destroyed his love for her ten years ago and there was no going back. He knew her true nature. Deceptively cruel and treacherous, he could never trust her again.

Although he admired her sense of spirit, for she did not shy away from anything, even when he quite callously attempted to embarrass her. In trying to wound

Vivienne, he knew he appeared rude and surly, and he had clearly upset Helene. All he succeeded in doing was making a fool of himself.

Now he forced himself into a position where he had to give her a forfeit for refusing to answer his more than inappropriate question. Although he truly wished to demand that she kiss him, he opted to do the decent thing.

"The forfeit is that you must accept my sincerest apology for my ill-mannered questions to you this evening," Aidan said in a low voice.

Vivienne's blue eyes widened in surprise and he realized he had startled the others as well. He watched her carefully, holding his breath, awaiting her answer. According to the rules of the game she had to pay the forfeit or be disqualified, but she could in all honesty, refuse his apology. Sitting there in her rose silk, a few dark curls framing her exquisite heart-shaped face, she nodded her head gently.

"Yes, Lord Whitlock. I accept your apology."

Gregory called out, "Let's play something else, shall we?"

"Actually, I think I shall retire for the evening," Lady Helene stood abruptly, bringing the gentlemen to their feet. Aidan knew she was irritated with him, and rightfully so.

That signaled the end of the evening, for the jovial lightheartedness that had set their little game in motion had been darkened. The ladies bade them a stilted good night and left the parlor. Ignoring the stern looks from the Cardwell twins, obviously unhappy with his treatment of their beloved cousin, Aidan ventured outside for a solitary walk in the cool night air to clear his head.

* * *

"That's it, my pet," Jackson Harlow whispered with increasing urgency as Lady Annabelle Worthington took his large cock into her mouth, licking and sucking it with skillful, practiced movements. He ran his hand over her curly blond head, but Annabelle slapped at his arm, abruptly stopping her decadent ministrations. His eyes flew open in startled surprise.

"Don't muss my hair, Jackson." She looked up at him with pert annoyance. "You know I hate that."

From her position on the floor kneeling between his legs and wearing only her lacy garters and stockings, he laughed at Annabelle's outrage over her elaborate coiffure's disarray. She practiced a whore's tricks but worried about her hair. He grinned at her in helpless apology as she stood and came to him.

Jackson wondered idly what Annabelle's husband would say if he could see his wife at this moment. She straddled his hips, her creamy white thighs spreading for him, as he reclined in an armchair in his guest room at Bingham Hall. Lord Worthington, who was down in the drawing room playing chess, was an old buffoon who did not deserve his gem of a wife. Jackson grunted in satisfaction as Annabelle slid over him, taking the large girth of him within herself, and he reached for her luscious breasts.

As she rode him expertly, he gripped her wide hips to move the momentum along. Groaning with pleasure, he strained against her, both of them panting with exertion. A few frantic moments later, he exploded within her and then she cried out his name and collapsed against his bare chest, which was still heaving. He sighed deeply, replete and relaxed.

All in all it had not been a bad day.

Coming to the Duchess of Bingham's house party had turned into an incredible bit of luck. He rekindled the little affair he had had going with Annabelle Worthington *and* managed to taunt the pompous Earl of Whitlock.

But the best part of all was finally finding Vivienne Montgomery!

"I have to go now, darling," Annabelle whispered in a seductive voice, as she delicately removed herself from his embrace. "Same time tomorrow night?"

"Absolutely," he promised her. He slapped her shapely bottom to send her on her way.

"Oww!" she squealed, staring at him crossly.

He flashed her a beaming and devilish grin, meant to apologize for his rough teasing of her.

Annabelle sighed in exasperation, gathering up her clothes and dressing hurriedly. "Honestly, Jackson, you know I cannot resist that smile of yours. Those dimples just melt me and I can't stay angry with you."

"Go back to your husband," he whispered wickedly, as he helped button up the back of her burgundy dinner gown. "I'm sure the old fool is missing you."

"You make me crazy, you know that." She planted a wet kiss on his mouth.

"And that's what you love about me, Lady Worthington." He grinned. "I'll see you tomorrow night."

She gave him a flirtatious wink and flounced from the room.

Jackson lit a cheroot and laid back on the bed, his powerful, muscular body still naked, and inhaled deeply.

Yes, it had been a splendid day. Lord, how he loved big house parties! He could live in the lap of luxury for a week and enjoy himself to the utmost. They certainly made conducting affairs an easier task. He idly wondered how many husbands would be spending the night in beds other than those of their wives . . . Or vice versa. Relaxing, he took a long breath on the cigar and exhaled slowly, watching the pungent smoke drift lazily around him.

Vivienne Montgomery. He had finally found Vivienne Montgomery!

He had been seeking John Montgomery's daughter for weeks now, traveling all the way to the Godforsaken country of Ireland and the city of Galway, only to discover that she had already gone to live with her English relative, Lord Cardwell. After that fruitless journey, he returned to London empty-handed, much to his older brother's dissatisfaction. Pompous, ailing old Miles, looking at him over his spectacles in disappointment. Shortly afterward, Jackson learned the Cardwells were visiting the Duchess of Bingham, and he manipulated an invitation to their house party. And there, to his immense surprise, he discovered the elusive Miss Montgomery.

And she was a stark, raving beauty.

He could not believe his good fortune. She could have been an ugly cow like her wretched cousin Glenda. He got stuck sitting next to the awful Cardwell chit at dinner. Miserable creature that one! Fat and mean.

But Miss Montgomery . . . Ah, she was going to make the business of stealing from her all the more pleasurable! Not that it mattered to him one way or another to steal from an ugly girl or a pretty girl. It just suited him better to spend time with a beauty rather than a homely creature. Hell, what man wouldn't?

Flirting with Miss Montgomery would be fine sport, for she was quick-witted and charming to boot.

And, even more perfect, *she* was attracted to *him*.

He was far too experienced with the fairer sex not to see the signs that Vivienne was quite taken with him. She practically fawned over him in the rose garden that afternoon, flirting like a schoolgirl. The incredible part was that she had come to him first, asking about her father. The fact that she wanted his help finding her father made it ridiculously simple. He would have a lovely time with her, for she trusted him already. And he would be more than able to finagle the right information out of her and obtain the papers he wanted.

It was a remarkable coincidence that he ended up with the Earl of Whitlock, his prime business nemesis, and Vivienne Montgomery, his intended quarry, both in the same house. He laughed aloud and then drew another long breath on the cigar.

The Earl of Whitlock, he scoffed to himself in derision. Ever since his brother Miles had suffered from an attack of apoplexy last summer, Jackson had taken over most of the responsibilities of his family's shipping business and the sainted Earl of Whitlock had become a thorn in his side. That spoiled, entitled, do-gooder, thinking he was so much better than everyone else. He was so blasted wealthy, the man didn't even have to work! Yet he usurped the long-standing trade routes that had belonged to Harlow Shipping for decades, causing them to lose a fortune in revenue.

Jackson hated Whitlock for everything he was and everything Jackson wasn't. Jackson hadn't been raised with a silver spoon in his mouth and had been required to work in his family's business—even though he hated shipping and everything to do with it—or be thrown out on the streets without a shilling by his father. And there was the pampered Earl of Whitlock, coming along on a whim and taking hard-earned business away from people who had no choice but to toil for a living.

But he had finally managed to put Aidan Kavanaugh, the mighty Earl of Whitlock, and his infernal shipping company in their proper place after all. And just as soon as he got his hands on enough money, he would leave London and his brothers for good.

Which was where Miss Montgomery came into the picture. Jackson's life was finally heading in the right direction. Today had been so successful, he couldn't wait for tomorrow.

Chapter 7

The Picnic

"Miss Montgomery, over here!" Jackson Harlow called across the lawn. With a toss of his head, he motioned to a blanket spread under the shade of an elm tree while his hands were filled with two crystal glasses.

Vivienne snapped her frilly white parasol shut and raced to the impossibly handsome blond man who beckoned to her with a winning smile. They had just finished a spirited game of croquet, which her team won, and she felt giddy with pleasure. Jackson Harlow had gone to fetch her a glass of fresh lemonade from the elaborately arranged picnic area on the north lawn of Bingham Hall.

It was a lovely day, warm and sunny with a light breeze, and the Duchess of Bingham had declared it Picnic Day. Everyone had been roused from the house early and made to bask in the glorious spring sunshine. Groups of people milled about, picnicking, playing games, chatting, and there was some talk of taking the boats out on the lake.

In high spirits and thoroughly enjoying herself, Vivienne reached the blanket and collapsed inelegantly upon the soft coverlet. Laughing, Jackson Harlow joined her, handing her a glass.

"Thank you, kind sir." Vivienne accepted it gratefully, her white gloved hand absorbing the small beads of moisture on the surface of the glass.

He grinned at her as she sipped her lemonade. "You are most welcome, my lady. Although I would rather be drinking champagne with you under this tree."

"Why, Mister Harlow!" She batted her eyelashes at him in an exaggerated manner. "I do believe you are flirting outrageously with me."

Vivienne felt very pretty and utterly feminine in a pale pink and white striped dress. Silk ribbons in a darker shade of pink trailed daintily at the end of her short elbow sleeves and she wore an adorable white straw hat trimmed with more pink ribbons. It was one of her favorite gowns from the collection she had acquired after an extravagant shopping spree with Aunt Gwen when she first arrived in England. It was a flirtatious dress and she acted the part with surprising ease. Something she had never done before with such abandon.

"Because I am flirting with you," he whispered decadently, his voice dropping low. "I have a decided weakness for flirting with beautiful ladies. And you, Miss Montgomery, are the loveliest one here by far. So you see, it's all your fault, my lady. You are preying upon my most dreaded weakness."

She glanced at him playfully above the rim of her glass. "Am I really?" It was very satisfying to be in the company of a man such as Jackson Harlow and to have his complete and undivided attention.

"Most definitely."

"How shall I end your misery then?"

"I'm afraid you cannot," he said with a sly laugh, "and still remain a lady."

Vivienne felt her cheeks turn scarlet at the implied meaning of his words. She had to remind herself that he was not flirting and teasing her in the same innocent manner that she was used to with the twins. This charming man belonged in another league of men all together and she needed to remember that.

"Judging from the look on your pretty face, I'm afraid I have offended you, Miss Montgomery. Please forgive my blundering foolishness." A solemn and serious expression appeared on his handsome face. "I assure you that was not my intention."

Wanting to return to the easy bantering they had enjoyed all morning while playing croquet, she nodded her head and smiled. She did not want to put him off, especially after he had agreed to look into the matter of her father's disappearance next week in London. He was quite possibly the last link she had to her father. Besides, she really did think him charming. "Mister Harlow, I am positive you had no intention of saying anything in the least to offend me."

He simply said, "Thank you."

Vivienne gazed up at the bright green leaves on the tree above her. The light breeze rustled them gently. It was quite beautiful outside, and she was having a lovely time at Bingham Hall. With the exception of interacting with Aidan. She briefly scanned the lawn for a glimpse of him, but did not see him any longer. He had not joined in their game of croquet, but watched them from the sidelines. She caught him looking at her a few times, but he had kept his distance from her, and after their awkward exchange the night before, she was grateful.

After the disastrous parlor game, Gregory had cornered her on her way upstairs to ask what had happened between her and Aidan in Galway. She explained very little and rushed off to bed. But her cousins and new friends were not oblivious, and they surely suspected there was more to her and Aidan's acquaintance than appeared on the surface.

"You play a determined game of croquet, Miss Montgomery," Jackson interrupted her thoughts.

Vivienne glanced back at him with a sly smile. "Is that a compliment?"

"Of course. It was a pleasure being on your team. I admire a competitive spirit and you are a girl who plays to win."

"Hmm. I suppose I do sometimes. It depends on the game. Do you like winning, Mister Harlow?"

"That is something you should know about me, Miss Montgomery." He leaned in close to her and whispered, "I always play to win."

"And do you always win?" she asked with the strangest feeling that he was referring to something quite specific, and not just a picnic game.

"Always." He moved back from her and she exhaled, realizing she had been holding her breath.

Intrigued by his words she questioned him, "What about playing for the fun of it? For simply enjoying oneself?"

"I am not talking about a mere game of croquet. I am referring to winning life in general."

"What is it that you hope to win?" She stared at him, puzzled by the predatory gleam in his eyes.

"Everything I want."

"Be careful what you wish for, you might just get it."

"What made you say that?" he asked, his expression curious and intent on her.

"I don't know," she laughed lightly. "It's something my grandmother always said to me growing up and I was never sure what it was supposed to mean. Isn't that the only reason we wish for things? To get them? But as I grew older, I eventually began to appreciate the meaning of wishing wisely."

"And what do you wish for now, Miss Montgomery?"

She stated clearly, with no hesitation, "I wish to find out what really happened to my father."

He tilted his head to one side and looked at her carefully. "Then I have the power to grant that wish for you. But again, remember your grandmother's words. Your wish may come true, but you may not like what you learn."

"I am well aware of that, Mister Harlow. It is the very fact of *not knowing* that is unbearable to live with. I have already been told that my father is dead. There is nothing I could learn about how he died that would be worse than knowing I will never see him again."

"I understand that feeling, which is why I am more than willing to help you. As long as you understand what the possible outcomes are. Tell me, what do you know of your father's last voyage? Was there anything unusual about it that you can recall?"

She shook her head. "It seemed just like all his others."

"Did you hear from him during the voyage?" Jackson

paused for a moment, then asked, "Did he send you anything before he disappeared?"

"Yes, he did. With the last letter I ever received from him, he sent me a beautiful jewelry box of carved wood and ivory. He always sent me things from his travels that he thought I might like."

"Did he mention anything in the letter that something out of the ordinary or unusual was happening?"

Vivienne hesitated. She wanted this man's help, but something held her back, preventing her from telling him what her father had written her in his last letter. Unsure what kept her from divulging the contents of that letter, she trusted her instincts. At least for now, she would wait. She would reveal that information if she thought it necessary, until then she would bide her time.

"No, he wrote nothing unusual, just that he missed me."

"I'm sure that was the truth," he said staring at her with intense brown eyes.

Vivienne smiled gratefully at Jackson's thoughtful remark.

"Well, we shall see what, if anything, I can discover when I return to my offices in London. In the meantime, you must try to recall every fact he mentioned to you from his last voyage. Even the smallest detail might be of importance."

Vivienne agreed to try but felt a little pang of regret at not telling him about her father's strange words regarding the box.

"Hullo!" Gregory called out to them, as he came sauntering over the grass with George, Helene Winston, and Sarah Atwood.

Their conversation thus interrupted, she and Jackson Harlow greeted the others.

"Are you ready to go out on the lake?" George asked enthusiastically. "Aunt Jane is having the boats prepared now for those who wish to row out and have a picnic on the other side of the lake."

"Oh, that sounds like fun!" Vivienne exclaimed. "Let's all go, shall we?"

"Anything for you, Miss Montgomery," Jackson declared. He stood and helped Vivienne to her feet, while she brushed the bits of grass from her dress.

As they made their way down to the dock, they joined Lord Harry Gardner, Wesley Lawrence, and Victoria Atwood. Vivienne was disheartened to see Aidan already waiting there for them. Well, at least she had successfully avoided him for most of the day. Looking darkly handsome in his buff-colored breeches, crisp white shirt, and bottle-green coat, he stood taller and broader than any of the other gentlemen. The unusual brooding look on his face had finally disappeared, and he seemed relaxed, his green eyes cool. She did not relish having a picnic with him.

They learned that in all there were four small rowboats: two boats that held three passengers each and two that held only two passengers. If more than ten people wanted to journey to the other side of the lake, it would have to be done in shifts. With the addition of Jackson Harlow to the group that played games together the night before, their total reached ten.

After much discussion, it was determined that Lord Harry and Wesley, and George and Aidan would take the two smaller boats with the picnic supplies out first, while Gregory and Jackson would row out the four ladies, and then come back for any others who wished to join them. As they settled into the wooden boats, which were painted in crisp colors of royal blue, cherry red, bright yellow, and leafy green, bursts of laughter and girlish squeals punctuated the spring air.

Aunt Jane admonished them to behave, but to have a good time, and waved at them from the dock.

Vivienne rode in the bright blue boat with Lady Helene and Jackson Harlow, who moved them across the calm waters with long, easy strokes. It was a rather large, kidney-shaped lake. Once they made the turn they were out of view of the Bingham Hall dock and the sandy beached shore of their destination was almost visible.

Peering under the brim of her lace parasol, Vivienne observed Aidan rowing his little boat ahead of them, almost across the lake already. His tall, muscular figure impressed her as he rowed with a fluid, effortless grace. Once again they had not spoken to each other at all while on the dock, and she had been relieved she had not been placed in a boat with Aidan.

In fact, she had maneuvered herself to sit with Jackson Harlow and she did not think she imagined that Jackson was quite pleased with her choice. He had given her a winning smile when he assisted her into his boat. However, she would have preferred to be with either of the Atwood sisters, rather than Helene Winston. She felt uncomfortable in her presence, although she really could say nothing against the girl.

"Isn't this picnic a lovely idea?" Helene asked Vivienne with a shy smile.

She answered, "Yes. And it is a perfect day for it."

"How did I get so lucky as to have the two most beautiful ladies in my boat?" Jackson said gallantly.

Surprised to see Helene roll her eyes at Jackson's remark, Vivienne grinned at her conspiratorially.

"Mister Harlow, do you think you could reach the other side before Mister Cardwell does?" Helene asked with an arch look as delicate wisps of her wheat-blonde hair wafted in the breeze.

"With one hand tied behind my back, Lady Helene." Jackson grinned with a mischievous twinkle in his eyes. "Would you care to race, ladies?"

"Oh, yes!" Helene exclaimed excitedly. "But only if you win!"

"Oh, I'll win," he declared, with a knowing look at Vivienne. "I always win." He turned his head toward Gregory and called out, "The lovely ladies in my boat wish to race you to the other side, Cardwell."

With his face breaking into a defiant grin, Gregory heartily agreed to the challenge. Instinctively, Vivienne snapped her parasol shut and instructed a perplexed Helene to do the same. She wasn't a sea captain's daughter for nothing.

"But why?" Helene asked, as she closed her yellow parasol.

"If they are open, they will create a drag on the boat," she explained.

"Good thinking, Miss Montgomery!" Jackson praised as he exerted all his effort into rowing. His movements strong and powerful, their boat flew across the water.

A little thrill raced through Vivienne as their speed accelerated and she gripped the sides of the boat tightly. She faced backward, looking at Lady Helene and Jackson Harlow and had to turn her head to see where they were going. Now the two boats moved neck and neck, since Gregory quickly caught up with them. The girls were shrieking in delight and shouts of encouragement were heard across the water. Vivienne, filled with a growing sense of excitement, glanced ahead and could see the opposite shore. Lord Harry, Wesley Lawrence, and George and Aidan had already beached their boats, and having gathered that a race was under way, cheered them on loudly. Both men rowed fiercely; their speed increasing. Jackson's oars glided swiftly through the water as they pulled ahead of Gregory's boat.

Suddenly a panicked shout erupted from Gregory. "Watch out!"

An odd scraping noise grated from beneath their boat and it suddenly lifted out of the water, tilting sharply to the left and throwing all three off balance. Startled cries, one must have been her own, pierced the air and the little blue rowboat tipped over completely. Vivienne caught a brief glimpse of Helene's terrified face and Jackson's stunned expression before she was tossed out of the boat and plunged into the cold, dark waters of the lake.

Watching the race from the shore, Aidan had seen Gregory's boat overtake Harlow's and immediately felt better. It rankled him that both Vivienne *and* Helene had elected to ride with the likes of Harlow. They were both more than likely still vexed with him for his churlish conduct last night. And justifiably so.

Suddenly Jackson's boat overturned, throwing them all into the lake. With his heart in his mouth, he watched Vivienne, who was seated near the bow, thrown clear of the boat, while Helene and Harlow were trapped beneath the upturned rowboat.

Amidst shrill screams from the Atwood sisters, Gregory had already jumped into the lake and was swimming to the scene. Aidan and George jumped back into their two-seater boat and raced across the lake with Harry and Wesley following close behind them. Aidan rowed as fast as his arms would go. As he intended, his boat neared Vivienne first.

"Go help the others. I'll get her!" Aidan called to George as he tossed aside his jacket and dove into the lake.

Immersed in the bone-chilling water, Aidan saw Vivienne surrounded by the pink and white fabric of her dress, looking like a wilted spring flower floating on the surface. Aidan knew from experience Vivienne was a strong swimmer but now, stunned and cold, she struggled to stay afloat with her cumbersome dress weighing her down.

"Are you all right?" he asked as he reached for her.

"Aidan?" she gasped, looking up at him with wide blue eyes.

"Hold on to me," he commanded, wrapping one arm around her waist and pulling her close to his chest. "Are you all right, Vivienne?" he repeated more softly, close to her ear, his lips brushing lightly across her wet cheek.

She nodded numbly, not saying a word. Although thankful she was not hurt, he knew he needed to get her out of the very deep and cold water. He guided her to the side of his boat. Lifting her up by her waist, he managed to get her and himself into the small craft without tipping it over, which was no easy task.

When they were both safely out of the water, he saw that George and Gregory had already returned the hysterically wailing Helene back into their righted boat. On the other side, Wesley and Harry wrestled

Harlow's limp form into the smaller boat. Blood dripped from his forehead and he lay motionless.

"What in blazes happened?" Aidan called out incredulously. He had been so intent on Vivienne's safety that he had nearly forgotten about Helene and Harlow.

"I think their boat hit that large boulder," Gregory explained, pointing to a shadowy outline in the water. "Do you see it there? The waterline barely conceals it below the surface. I saw it just a second before they hit it, but it was too late. They were going too fast. Looks like Harlow hit his head on the rock, judging from the gash on his forehead."

Fortunately, the boat was not badly damaged and was deemed seaworthy enough to ferry them back. Harlow lay sprawled in a boat with George, while Wesley climbed in the boat with the distraught Atwood sisters, who were the only ones still dry by that point. Aidan observed Gregory comforting the sobbing Helene, who, aside from being wet, seemed perfectly fine, while Harry rowed them slowly toward the dock. He could not help but admire Vivienne's calm manner, especially in comparison with Helene's hysteria. They both had been unceremoniously dumped into the lake, but Vivienne bore the upset with a surprising calm.

As each boat made its way back across the lake, he and Vivienne were left alone. Aidan looked toward her. Her little straw hat now floated in the lake and her black hair hung in long, wet strands around her delicate face, which was dotted with crystal droplets of water. Her pretty pink and white dress clung seductively to her lush curves, the front of which had torn apart, revealing a more than tantalizing amount of her creamy breasts.

She looked like an exquisite water nymph come to

life. To Aidan, the most amazing part of it was that she was completely unaware of how desirable she looked and the effect she had upon him. Suddenly the urge to hold her in his arms again raced through his veins. He wanted to kiss each tiny droplet of water off her soft cheeks, her pink lips, her graceful neck, her full breasts . . . Good Lord, he had wanted to kiss her last night as well. Vivienne had always had that power over him and the cold dunk in the lake had done nothing to cool his ardor.

"Aren't you going to row us back?" she asked with a puzzled expression. She wrapped her arms around herself for warmth, unaware that she only amplified her bosom's exposure.

"Of course," Aidan answered shortly, surprised he could find the breath to speak. Wishing he'd had the foresight to toss his jacket into the boat instead of the lake, he removed his wet shirt, leaving himself bare-chested. Better him than her. Casting another hungry glance at her open dress front, he handed her his shirt and muttered, "You might want to cover yourself."

An aghast "Oh!" sprung from her lips when she glanced down and saw where he had been staring. She accepted his sodden shirt and struggled to slip it on, clutching the front together with her hand. Because it was wet, the white cotton shirt was almost sheer and virtually useless, but at least it gave her the appearance of a covering.

"Thank you, Aidan," she murmured with a shiver.

He nodded. "You're welcome." He picked up the oars, not taking his eyes off her. "Are you sure you're not hurt?"

"I'm fine. Just cold."

He slowly began to row, realizing how drained he

felt. The wind had picked up a bit and the lake began to get a slight chop to it. The oars cut through the water, making little splashing sounds amidst the awkward silence. He could not find the words to say what played over and over in his mind since yesterday. He knew he should say something. Simple good manners dictated he say something, anything, to her. He had known Vivienne longer than he'd known anyone else in his lfe. She deserved at least an expression of sympathy from him. Now might not be the best time, but at least they were alone.

"Vivienne?"

"Yes?" Her dark blue eyes turned to him.

If he kept looking into them he would be lost. Or do something entirely stupid.

He swallowed and tried to look away. "I'm sorry about your father. And Aggie."

An expression of utter sorrow shadowed her beautiful face; the grief was still raw for her. For a brief instant he wished he had not mentioned her loss, for her anguish was painfully obvious.

"Thank you," she whispered in a tight voice.

"Gregory and George just told me yesterday."

She did not respond, nor encourage him to continue the matter. Yet he did so anyway. "I always admired your father. And I loved Aggie, you know. She was more of a grandmother to me than my own."

Almost everyone in Galway believed Agnes Joyce to be a witch, but Aidan knew her only as a wise old woman, with a wry sense of humor. As a child he had spent many hours in Aggie's warm and cozy kitchen, listening to her recount Celtic fairy tales and legends. She was a riveting storyteller, Aggie was. Spry, witty, and with a zest for life, Aggie offered sage advice and had touched something, given something, to Aidan that he was unaware was lacking in his own family until he met Vivienne.

And Aggie *knew* things. Aidan couldn't explain it, and it was the reason half of Galway believed her to be a witch, but Aggie knew certain things were going to happen before they happened. Her ability both frightened and fascinated him. At the time she had been the only person in Galway who had recognized Aidan and Vivienne's love for each other as something real. Although she had been utterly wrong about him and Vivienne, Aggie had once told him that he would be living in London years before he actually did. Some said Vivienne possessed the same otherworldly talents, but Aidan had yet to see evidence of that.

Aggie had been so full of energy, so full of life, he could hardly imagine her gone. He could still picture her in her neat black dress, her hands always busy, sewing, cooking, making, creating something. She wore her dark hair, without a single strand of gray, pulled into a tight knot on the back of her head and her wrinkled but elegant face had merry eyes. He had always pictured Vivienne looking like her grandmother in fifty years.

Now Vivienne's blue eyes brimmed with tears at his words and she murmured, "She loved you, too, Aidan. Even after everything . . ."

"You were with her at the end?" he asked, although he knew the answer. Vivienne would not have been anywhere else but at her grandmother's side.

She nodded her head. "She had not been well for years, and Aggie knew it was her time to go. She passed peacefully in her sleep one night."

"What happened to your father?" he asked after some time.

"His ship was lost at sea."

"I'm sorry, Vivienne. I always admired your father."

"I know," she choked out.

"So that is why you came to live with your aunt and uncle?"

"Only because before she died, Aggie told me to go live in England. She said that I would find happiness here."

"And are you happy?" he asked before he could stop himself.

"The Cardwells have made me feel quite at home."

"They are set on finding a husband for you?"

"What else would you expect them to do, Aidan?" she said matter-of-factly.

Again he thought of Jackson Harlow. He and Vivienne had looked very cozy together earlier that afternoon. Aidan had watched while they sat on a blanket beneath a shady tree, talking quite earnestly to each other. Obviously Harlow was interested in pursuing her. But Vivienne could not possibly entertain the idea of marrying the likes of Jackson Harlow. Just the thought of it made his blood run cold.

Then again, what business was it of his who Vivienne married at this point? It was not his place to give his advice or opinion. If she wanted to ruin her life by becoming the wife of Jackson Harlow there was not anything he could do to prevent it. There seemed to be nothing more to say after that and they rowed the rest of the way back to shore in awkward silence.

Glenda Cardwell watched with stormy eyes as the boating party returned to the dock. The entire day was ruined now. Oh, the fuss that ensued over her foolish brothers and their ridiculous friends! It infuriated her. Truly. They were not even capable of simply rowing to the other side of the lake and back. One would think they had been shot at rather than simply fallen into the water. The idiots.

That haughty Helene Winston acted as if she'd been dragged by wild horses, the way she carried on. The sobbing and the tears. It was really too much, how everyone was fretting over her, coddling her. And there was Gregory, preening about as a great hero for rescuing the little blond twit. Sarah and Victoria Atwood were wailing and describing the events dramatically, and nothing even happened to them! They all made her sick.

At least that handsome Jackson Harlow had the good grace to actually get hurt, judging from the nasty gash on his head. He deserved it, too.

Glenda was familiar with his kind. He never gave plain girls like her the time of day, but would fawn all over the pretty girls. Even the silliest ones. Glenda had tried her best to be nice to him at supper last night, for she had thought him most attractive, fascinated by his golden coloring and thick, tawny hair.

At supper she attempted to discuss the fine spring weather, and how delicious the food tasted. But he only murmured a decidedly dismissive, "That's nice," and practically turned his back to her. As if she were not good enough! She hoped he had scarred his face terribly in the accident. That would teach him, for he was too handsome to be tolerated.

Aunt Jane had already rushed inside with Uncle Richard to send for the doctor to care for Mister Harlow. Glenda, however, raised her eyebrows as she watched Lord Whitlock and her cousin Vivienne arrive alone together in the last boat, he bare-chested and she wearing his shirt. Well, well, well. This was most interesting. What had the saintly Vivienne been up to with the Earl of Whitlock?

Now Lord Whitlock, there was a true gentleman! Even though he was a friend of Gregory and George's, she could forgive him that flaw, because at all times he treated her as if she were the greatest beauty. He always made a point of asking, "How are you today, Miss Glenda?" as though he truly cared if she were fine or not. What a pity he was practically engaged to that feather-headed Helene Winston! Glenda would have liked being *his* wife, if she had to be someone's. Not that anybody was offering, mind you. There was no fear on that account.

By now Glenda had quite grown resigned to the idea of spinsterhood. She could not abide fools, and all the men of her acquaintance were nothing if not foolish. Most men she knew were not worth much as far as she could see.

But the Earl of Whitlock, now he was different, a genuinely good man. He was industrious and hard-working, when he certainly didn't have to be. He had even built a shipping company on his own. Being devastatingly handsome did not deter from his appeal either.

No, she would not mind being married to someone like Aidan Kavanaugh, but he was destined to marry someone typically conventional like Helene Winston.

As she watched Vivienne being escorted from the boat, she could not help but think that something was not quite right between Aidan Kavanaugh and her cousin. It was patently obvious to everyone that the pair disliked each other intensely and from what she had gathered, they had known each other as children in Ireland. There was more to that story, she was quite sure.

Ever since Vivienne Montgomery had come to live with them, Glenda's quiet life had been upended. She was now constantly compared to her lovely cousin and found lacking in every way. Her parents thought Vivienne could do no wrong and treated her as if she were a crowned princess. Her idiot twin brothers were besotted with the girl, singing her praises till Glenda thought she would scream. Even her older brother Gerald, who was married and lived in the country, had been won over by Vivienne when Glenda had always credited Gerald as having more sense than Gregory and George combined.

"Glenda, lend Vivienne your shawl," her mother commanded, startling Glenda and forcing her to focus on the present. "Can't you see she's shivering?"

Indeed Vivienne's teeth were chattering and her wet dress clung to her. She looked a mess.

"Oh, by all means," she answered sarcastically. *Shall I remove my dress for Vivienne also?*

Glenda sullenly whipped off the light gray knit shawl that she had draped over hers shoulders and tossed it to her mother. She wrapped it around Vivienne's petite shoulders and they ushered her off the dock and back to the house. As everyone made their way inside, it was obvious the picnic day had ended. Ruined. By her feeble-minded brothers and their dim-witted friends.

"Aren't you fortunate you didn't join the boating party, Miss Cardwell?"

She turned to see Lady Whitlock standing beside her. Tall for an older woman, Susana Kavanaugh perpetually wore a serious expression. She carried herself like a queen, and unconsciously Glenda stood straighter.

"I have more sense than that, Lady Whitlock. If I had gone, believe me, I would not have ended up in the water."

"I have no doubt of that," Lady Whitlock murmured approvingly. "You, unlike some others, are a sensible girl."

"And even if I had ended up in the lake, I wouldn't be carrying on the way those silly girls are," Glenda declared as they walked slowly across the lawns toward the house together.

"You have a point there. They were very dramatic. Except for Miss Montgomery, that is." There was an edge to Lady Whitlock's brittle voice.

"But she got all the attention anyway," Glenda could not help pouting. "Everyone loves Vivienne and I don't know why. There's nothing particularly special about her."

"I happen to agree with you."

"You're the only one who does."

"Have you forgotten that I have known her for years? The real Vivienne. Not this sweet façade she displays for all the world to see." Lady Whitlock's voice became a sharp whisper.

Glenda glanced at her quizzically. A determined look gleamed in the woman's cunning gray eyes. She was quite intimidating, but Glenda did not fear for herself.

Glenda had known Aidan Kavanaugh socially for years, due to his being close friends with her brothers, but she had only recently met his mother. She liked Lady Whitlock immediately because she could see through Vivienne's sweet but false exterior to her true heartless character. Lady Whitlock had not divulged much, but she credited Glenda's good judgment in not being taken in by Vivienne and that made Glenda feel worthy.

"How would you like to help me reveal Vivienne's true character to everyone here, expose her for what she really is, before this week is over?" Lady Whitlock asked her.

Making Vivienne look the fool in front of everyone? Now that was an intriguing thought. Someone finally understood what it was like to be Glenda. Suddenly seeing the advantages of an association with Aidan's mother, Glenda gave a most eager smile. "Why, I would be happy to help in any way I could."

Lady Whitlock smiled knowingly. "I thought you might, Miss Cardwell, being the clever girl that you are. Why don't you come for a nice long walk with me now and we can have a little chat?"

Chapter 8

The Portrait Gallery

The next day dawned with dark gray skies and a steady dripping rain. Vivienne groaned inwardly at the thought of being inside all day. After a hot bath last night she had completely recovered from the boating accident and, with her very legitimate excuse, she kept to her room. This morning she had breakfast in her room also, grateful that Glenda had already gone downstairs without her.

Dressed in a simple day gown of dark blue with pale yellow trim, she was now restless. She knew the twins would be more than willing to entertain her, but she was not in the mood for their sort of fun this gray day. And she *felt* gray today. Maybe there had been too many social activities over the past few weeks for her.

Living with the Cardwells had provided her with constant companionship, a concept that was new to her. For the first time in years, there was always someone with her: her aunt, her uncle, one of her cousins, or a servant. She enjoyed this novel life tremendously, especially after she had spent so many years living with just her and Aggie. Now she realized that she was never alone at all anymore and she needed some of that solitude again to sort through her thoughts and clear her head. Of Aidan.

Aidan.

She wondered why he dove in the lake to rescue her instead of Helene Winston yesterday. Given that the two were practically engaged, it made no sense for Aidan to come to her first. Yet he held her so tenderly in the water, and she could have sworn that he kissed her cheek. His concern for her welfare confused her. When they talked, he seemed genuinely hurt by the deaths of her father and grandmother. She did not know what to make of Aidan's behavior. His compassion toward her had been so unexpected, especially after the obvious hostility he displayed during the parlor game the night before last.

Longing to take a solitary walk along the shore of Galway Bay and to feel the brisk sea air on her face, she succumbed to a restlessness inside Bingham Hall. She missed Ireland; she missed home. Everyone in England looked down on the smaller island nation, but Vivienne loved her country even more because of the hardships the country endured. Admittedly there were problems, for great sorrow and tragedy reigned in her home country. The famine years had been devastating, although her family, fortunately, had been spared much of that anguish.

But now, she yearned for misty days and green fields. The sound of the sea. The scent of burning peat fires. The lilt of a gentle brogue. In spite of the luxury that was lavished upon her now in England, pangs of homesickness washed over her.

A stroll by the sea was out of the question today, however. She toyed with the idea of walking in the gardens, but the torrential downpour outside deterred even her love of walking in the rain. Instead she opted to explore the seemingly endless maze of corridors that comprised Bingham Hall. Although she had been in the house for days, there were wings of the massive estate in which she still had not set foot. With everyone trapped inside for the day, most of the houseguests engaged themselves in solitary pursuits, while the servants were kept busy preparing for the grand masked ball the following evening. But the section of the house that Vivienne intended to explore was still and quiet.

However, after more than an hour of wandering aimlessly through the dim hallways, her troubled spirit was not soothed. Although she peeked in the many drawing rooms and gazed out tall windows washed with raindrops, the restlessness she felt was unappeased. As she made her way down to the corridor to return to her room, she noticed an oddly shaped wooden panel just outside her bedroom.

Intrigued, she ran her hands over the smooth, polished oak. She pressed one corner and the panel sprung open, revealing itself to be a little door. Peering in, she saw stone steps leading down in a spiral and she laughed. She had actually found one of the secret staircases the twins had mentioned! Nothing if not adventurous, Vivienne went through the opening, closing the door carefully behind her.

Her eyes took a moment to adjust to the lack of light. Keeping one hand on the wall, she descended the steps cautiously in the darkness, feeling her way. When she reached the bottom she could see the outline of another door, for a faint light shone through from the other side. Pressing her hand against the door, it sprung open, and she stepped out to find herself in the portrait gallery!

Pleased with the prospect of telling Gregory and George what she had discovered, she closed the door, purposely noting that it was next to the painting of some elderly Bingham relative in a violet frock coat.

Vivienne walked aimlessly along the white marbled floor of the silent portrait gallery, hung with formal pictures of generations of the venerable Bingham family. The imposing array of paintings left her feeling very small. What would it be like to have the history of such an illustrious family supporting you? It was certainly unlike anything she had known in Galway, although her mother's side of the family boasted a long and colorful past.

Vivienne was half English, but she felt more Irish, because that was how she was raised. Aggie had always taught her to proud of her heritage, unlike Aidan and Susana Kavanaugh, who hated Ireland and everything about it. Even though she believed Aidan didn't truly feel that way in his heart. That was just his mother's influence over him.

Aidan.

His feelings for her were a mystery. He acted cold and standoffish with her and had been unbelievably rude and nasty to her during the parlor game. Yet, yesterday on the lake he treated her with such caring and tenderness. It seemed he was cruelest to her in front of others . . . Why?

And how did she feel about him after all this time?

She had to admit that she cared for him. He was more handsome than ever, and in spite of everything he made her heart race. She still felt a strong attraction to him, wanted to be near him, wanted to talk to him. When he entered a room, she could not help but look at Aidan. His presence demanded all her attention, no matter how desperately she attempted to ignore him. As it had always been with him.

Suddenly she became aware of heavy footsteps echoing in a familiar rhythm through the marble corridor. And she knew, just *knew*, without turning around that Aidan stood behind her. She did not even need to look to confirm her feelings.

"Looking for me, Aidan?" Her tone was sardonic.

"Believe it or not, I had no idea you would be here." His deep voice resonated slightly through the empty portrait gallery and his footsteps continued as he walked closer to her. "Or I would not have come."

She turned to face him, her breath catching in her throat, for he was nearer than she had realized. His mere presence always made her a bit light-headed. She was cursed by it. Aidan was too handsome. His sensual mouth was drawn into a grim line, giving him a menacing appearance. Which, surprisingly, only enhanced his looks. "Please leave," she stated calmly, although his closeness had unnerved her more than she wanted to admit, even to herself.

He folded his arms across his chest in defiance. Obviously he had no intention of leaving her.

"Forgive me, Miss Montgomery. Am I interrupting a secret little tryst with Jackson Harlow? Or were you waiting for one of your many other admirers, perhaps?" Aidan asked caustically, his contempt for her apparent.

Before she realized what she was doing, she slapped him. A slap that made an impression on his cheek and left her hand stinging.

"I despise you," she breathed heavily. "You always think the worst of me."

He glowered, his green eyes like dark fire, as he

stepped toward her. For a panicked moment she was not sure if he meant to slap her back or—wild thought—kiss her. She did not know which would hurt more.

"Vivienne, I just—" Aidan broke off and reached for her arms, drawing her roughly against his broad chest. He was shaking and his breath was rapid, as he placed his forehead against hers, beseeching her in some way, wanting something from her.

His stare penetrated her and she looked down. The familiar scent of him—clean, spicy, and distinctly Aidan—saturated her. As she attempted to break away from his grasp, the sound of voices entering the other end of the long gallery caused them both to freeze.

In horrified alarm they stared at each other, aware of their scandalous position. Before she could protest, Aidan placed his hand over her mouth and dragged her through the nearest doorway. It was dark inside. The thin sliver of light that glimmered from beneath the door hardly gave enough to see by, but she gathered they were in a storage closet of sorts. She struggled at Aidan's handling of her, but he gripped her tighter, not allowing her to move. What was he thinking to force her into a closet with him?

"Shh," he breathed in her ear as the voices grew nearer.

She stilled.

Just outside the door Glenda's sharp voice declared, "I know I saw someone come this way and I'm sure I heard voices."

"Perhaps you were mistaken," Gregory offered lazily. Their footsteps echoed in the corridor just beyond the door to the closet.

"Where could Vivienne be? I've looked everywhere for her," Glenda whined.

If they found her with Aidan now . . .

Vivienne's back pressed against Aidan's broad chest while he held her in place with one arm tight around her waist and one hand over her mouth to keep her quiet. Her breathing was heavy and panicked as she wondered how long they would have to stay hidden. This was the last place she should be.

Alone in the dark with Aidan Kavanaugh.

The length of his strong, muscled body leaned against hers and the intense heat between them radiated steadily through the many layers of their clothing. His warm breath on the back of her neck sent a shiver to the core of her body, which she desperately tried to ignore. They stood motionless for a few silent minutes, but it felt like ages. Their heartbeats echoed in the darkness as they waited. And waited. Neither Glenda's nasal tone nor Gregory's deep laughter could be heard in the gallery any longer. Clearly, it was safe to leave the storage closet now.

Still they did not move.

Aidan's warm hand continued to cover her mouth. He certainly was not holding her to keep her quiet any longer, for she had not uttered a sound nor moved a muscle.

But he moved. His thumb actually caressed her cheek, tracing a gentle path, back and forth along her cheekbone, while the hand at her waist was stroking the curve of her hip, oh so faintly. He barely touched her, yet she felt his contact throughout her entire being. And shivered.

His lower hand then slowly slid up her waist to the swell of her breast. He breathed in deeply, pulling her tighter against his chest.

It had been so long since Aidan had held her. Years and years. It was so familiar and yet so new. Recalling images of the last time Aidan kissed her, she gently tilted her head back until she relaxed against his chest. On an impulse she could not control, Vivienne flicked her tongue lightly along the inside of the palm of his hand.

His body tensed. His breathing stilled, as if he feared she would stop if he moved. She continued licking his hand, delicately twirling her tongue in intricate patterns against his palm, until he carefully inserted his index finger into her mouth. She took it easily, sucked it softly, nibbling with her teeth, slowly running her tongue down the length of it, circling the tip in lazy swirls. His skin tasted warm and salty. One by one, she did the same to each of the fingers on his hand as he offered them to her.

She felt his heated breath on the nape of her neck and the tender brush of his kisses on her hair, sending shivers down her spine. She pushed her body against the length of him, his thumb still in her mouth.

Suddenly he used both hands to spin her around to face him, although she could barely distinguish his features in the darkness. She gasped as his mouth came down on hers. Fiercely. But she welcomed him with an eagerness that matched his own. They kissed with a desperate hunger, as if all that time had never passed. As if this were their last chance to ever kiss again. It was reckless, crazy. It was heaven.

It was Aidan kissing her. And that was all that mattered. "Aidan."

The sound of her voice startled her as she realized she had whispered his name aloud. He murmured something she could not understand, but she did not care as his mouth claimed hers again.

Her heart slammed into her chest as a thrill went through her. Aidan still wanted her after all this time. Aidan was kissing her as if she still belonged to him.

She arched against him as one hand encircled her breast, fully cupping her, squeezing her. Desire coursed through her veins like a living thing. Instinctively she knew where this was leading and she let herself be swept completely into the tide of passion that washed through her. This was going to happen.

She felt a forceful tugging on the bodice of her gown and before she realized it, she was exposed to him. His head lowered to her chest and he had his mouth on her bare breast. The exquisite sensations of his heated tongue sucking on her taut nipple coaxed a soft moan from her lips. His mouth was hot on her skin, burning her. Her hands weaved into his thick black hair and she buried her face in it, inhaling the familiar scent of him.

She was with Aidan again.

It seemed as if he had a hundred hands, for now one hand was sliding up her inner thigh, pulling her skirt up with it, and moving between her legs. He touched her through her undergarments with intent, persistent strokes. She sucked in her breath with a hiss as he slipped his fingers beneath the thin fabric and caressed her intimately. He placed his hand against her throbbing flesh and eased a finger inside of her.

"You're so ready for me," he whispered in her ear.

She breathed his name. Yes, she was ready . . . Her hands clung to the lapels of his jacket for support and she gasped for air. There was more rustling of clothing and her petticoat and crinoline were no longer under her skirt. He was undressing her and she was doing absolutely nothing to stop him. Because she didn't want him to stop. She didn't care what they were doing, fool that she was. This was Aidan, and despite her anger, she'd always loved him. This is what she was made for. For him. She wanted this to continue through to the end and savor every minute of it. Oh, Lord, but it had been so long.

Vivienne was all but naked, in nothing but her gartered stockings and heeled shoes. How had he done it? Were there classes a man took to learn how to undress a women with such ease? Still he kissed her and she was grateful for the dark.

His shirt and jacket were still on, but his breeches were missing. Again she wondered how Aidan did it so effortlessly. All the while he was still kissing her, devouring her. Her body thrummed in response to the naked feel of him pressed close to her bare skin. That elemental, primal part knew this made her feel like a woman. She knew what was coming and longed for it. Ached for it. Would go mad if she didn't get it. She wanted him inside of her desperately.

His voice, thick with lust, whispered seductively in her ear, "Tell me what you want, Vivienne."

Was he mad? How could he not know what she wanted? Had she protested in some way? She was obviously agreeable to the situation, albeit he had dragged her into the closet unwillingly. He had to know how she felt, for she had not resisted him in the slightest.

"Ah . . . I . . . ah . . . I want you," she managed to murmur.

"And just what do you want me to do?" His voice was wickedly decadent. She gasped as he pressed his hardness against her.

"Th-that . . ." she panted in short, gasping breaths.

"You mean this?" he asked with false innocence as he thrust himself inside her.

"Yes," she cried, but before she could even get the word out of her mouth he had withdrawn from her and she almost wept with the loss of it. She arched toward him trying to get him close to her again, but he backed away.

"Tell me first . . ." He kissed her mouth again, cupping her breast harder.

Her cheeks were burning. "Aidan . . ."

"Tell me why . . ." He plunged into her again and pulled out skillfully, leaving her whimpering. "Tell me," he demanded in silky tones.

"I want you inside of me because you belong there," she blurted out breathlessly, shamelessly.

He drove into her as a reward, remaining longer this time before he withdrew. "Tell me . . ."

"I'll tell you anything, Aidan, just please don't stop," she begged. She must have given him a satisfactory answer because he was inside of her again. This time she wrapped her leg around him to hold him to her.

"Oh no," he laughed low in his throat, "Oh, no, you don't." He thrusted deeply once, twice, and then a third time before he withdrew. He was impeccably controlled in his movements, whereas Vivienne was weak and quivering. She would die if he didn't continue.

"Tell me who else has had you." His voice was edgy, demanding.

"Aidan!" she cried, her eyes open wide in the darkness. She could feel his gaze piercing her.

"Tell me." He lunged into her and withdrew once more.

She pressed against him, begging him, "Aidan, please, please." She was sobbing now. She had to have him. She was going mad.

"Who else?" He was pounding her hard now, thrusts deep and long, in rapid succession. It was what she had wanted. Her body rocked against the wall.

Her words came in sobs on short breaths in rhythm

with his thrusts. "No one else, Aidan! There has . . .
never been anyone else. Just you, Aidan. Only you."

"Ah, Vivienne." He kissed her face, her hair. "Why,
why . . . ?" He leaned his head against hers.

She whispered to him, "It's always been . . . you for
me. It will only . . . ever be you. Only you can make me
feel this way. It's you I love."

He kissed her to silence her sobs, kissed the hot tears
on her cheeks, but he kept giving her what she needed
and wanted from him, "Yes, love. It's only me now."

He was losing that control he had earlier, lost in the
feel of her body, and his movements became more
forceful, more demanding of her. Their passion intensified. It was about possession and need. Vivienne
belonged to him. She always had.

Then she whispered, "Now tell me, Aidan. Why me?"

"Because, *muirnin* . . . you're mine—" Carried away
in the emotion, his body's response grew more frantic.

She was lost then, clinging to him, crying. Tears
spilled down her cheeks. But the intense feelings between them only increased in fervor. With one hand
braced on the wall behind her, he lifted her and she
wrapped her stocking-clad legs around his waist. He
drove into her then, giving way completely to their passionate need. She felt herself explode in waves of pleasure and Aidan called out her name. They climaxed
together, drowning in a sea of emotional and physical
bliss that was unlike anything they had felt in years.

After a few moments, Aidan gathered her in his
arms and sank to the floor, resting his back against the
wall and cradling her on his lap. He could barely catch
his breath, but he tenderly kissed the top of her head.
She cried softly, burying her face against his chest.

"Ah, my beautiful Vivienne . . . What have we done now?" he whispered into her silky hair, stroking her with long, soothing motions.

How had he managed to lose control of himself? He certainly had not planned on seducing her this afternoon, although the thought was in his mind that if he had her once, then he would get her out of his system. Now he had just taken her standing in a closet, while her cousins searched for her outside in the hallway. It had been the most incredible encounter of his life. But, good God, what was he thinking? Why did he come completely undone when he was with her? What power did she hold over him?

Vivienne, his lying, deceitful, lovely Irish witch. She now wept against his chest. She seemed so fragile and lost, not at all the fiery woman who slapped his face or sucked on his fingers or set his blood to boiling only a short while ago. His heart ached at her tears. How was he going to get her dressed and out of there without getting caught together?

"Vivienne, Vivienne . . . Stop, love. It's all right."

"You left me, Aidan. You asked me to marry you and then you left me." Her tears soaked his shirt. "You didn't believe in me. In us."

He froze then, choking out the words, "I saw you with Nicky Foster."

"No, Aidan." She shook her head against his chest. "You didn't see what was really happening. And you never asked me about it. You never spoke to *me*. You made assumptions and you just left." Her voice was low and husky from crying.

"What was there to say? I know what I saw, Vivienne," he whispered tightly, feeling the familiar anger rise within him. "You—half-naked and kissing Nicky Foster."

He knew why he didn't believe in her. He'd seen it

with his own eyes. Still etched clearly in his memory was the image of Vivienne, her long hair tousled and loose hanging to her waist, and Nicky Foster, a simple farm boy, locked in a passionate embrace. With her dress unbuttoned and her bare breasts showing, they kissed each other passionately. It was quite clear what had been going on between them. His stomach clenched at the mere recollection of the day he caught them together.

"Are you sure about that?" she asked, her voice shaking.

"Yes."

"Did you believe that I ever loved you, Aidan?"

"I thought so at one time."

She sighed heavily. "You asked me to be your wife. We were going to be married and go to England together, weren't we?"

He nodded at her descriptions of the events. He remembered that time most clearly. He loved her with a fervor that left him weak. When he found out he had unexpectedly inherited the earldom of Whitlock and had to return to England, he was desperate to marry Vivienne and bring her with him, in spite of his mother's opposition to her as his wife. Determined to marry her, Aidan scheduled an earlier date for the wedding. It would not be the grand wedding that he had envisioned for her, but time was not on their side. He needed to claim his earldom, and he wanted to do that with Vivienne at his side, as his countess.

But then . . . Then she ruined everything. As his mother predicted, Vivienne did not really love him. He'd been completely wrong about her. She only desired him for his money and title. All his dreams with her were destroyed. Completely and utterly destroyed. By her.

"I loved you, Aidan. We were in love with each other. I wanted to be your wife. What earthly reason would I have had to be with Nicky Foster, of all people, when I had you?"

He was silent for a long moment considering her words. His hands continued to stroke her hair. "What are you saying, Vivienne? That I was wrong? That I didn't see you with your arms around him with my own eyes?"

"My arms were not around Nicky. They were trying to push him off of me. And I was not kissing him. He was kissing me. Against my will," she sobbed.

He stiffened at her words. "Am I supposed to believe that?"

"Why wouldn't you believe me, Aidan? At the time, what did I have to gain by deceiving you?"

"And you had everything to lose by telling me the truth," he countered quickly.

At her silence he wondered, what *did* she have to gain by being with Foster? Nothing. Not a bloody thing. That's why it wounded him so deeply. She threw everything they had away for nothing. Nicky Foster, that brawny, beef-headed, potato farmer. Foster had escorted her to a few dances before Aidan returned from school that summer. And now she wanted him to believe that she wasn't willingly in Foster's arms? Dared he believe her words? Could what she said be true? No. He saw it with his own eyes. He saw her kissing Nicky . . . saw her undressed . . . smiling, laughing, even . . .

"You certainly didn't look as if you needed to be rescued from him, Vivienne."

"I was explaining to him that I loved you, not him."

"And he just happened to know you were at our cottage and he picked that exact moment to declare his love for you? And with your dress open to your waist?"

"I was waiting for you. I honestly don't know why he was there or how he knew I would be at the cottage. I guess he just followed me."

Good God! Did she think him an idiot? He didn't want to hear anymore. He had put all of this behind him years ago and felt no need to revisit it now. He buried that part of his life, yet it seemed she had just unearthed it all again. Just how had he ended up in this dark, little closet in the portrait gallery with Vivienne this afternoon mystified him. If she was found there with him, she would be ruined. Hell, *he* would be ruined.

"We have to get out of here," he said, taking his arms from around her warm body.

Her voice was very soft, "You still won't believe me?"

Aidan stood up and began to fix his clothing.

"After everything we meant to each other, after everything we did together, after what we just did—" her breath caught in her throat.

Aidan stilled and stared at her in the dim light, wanting her to stop talking. He pulled her to her feet roughly. "Get dressed."

"Ten years ago I gave you everything, Aidan. I gave you my heart, my soul. I even gave you my virginity," she continued ruefully, wiping the tears from her eyes. "Do you think I gave all that away for nothing? I loved you. I believed in you and trusted you."

"And I trusted you. I asked you to be my wife and you betrayed me. You gave yourself to another man." He handed her the gown he had removed from her body with such passionate need only moments earlier. "Get dressed, Vivienne."

She grabbed the gown from his hand and angrily

turned her back to him, while she fumblingly donned her clothes. Although it was a small comfort, at least she had stopped crying. He reached to help her fasten the back of her gown and she slapped at his hands.

"Don't touch me."

She didn't want his assistance, but she had no choice. She couldn't very well go around with her dress undone. He tried not to let himself dwell on the thought that he had dressed Vivienne this way many times before and she had always welcomed the feel of his hands on her back. That was before she had betrayed him. Standing stiffly with her back to him, almost flinching at his touch, she allowed him to refasten her dress.

"I'm sorry for what happened in here just now," he whispered contritely.

She turned and faced him in the dark, but he sensed her coldness. "Not nearly as sorry as I am."

Pushing past him she angrily swung open the closet door. Light poured in and his eyes adjusted to the glare. He tried to grab her arm but she flinched from his grasp.

"I said don't touch me," she ordered with undisguised bitterness.

"Vivienne, be careful. You can't just prance through the house looking like that. Someone might see you and—"

"And what?" she interrupted scornfully, giving him a hard look. She continued in a pronounced Irish brogue, "I'd be compromised and you'd be forced to marry me? A common Irish whore?"

"You said it. Not me."

"But you were thinking it," she accused him.

In response to his guilty silence, Vivienne continued

with an icy calm, "Don't worry, Aidan. I wouldn't have you."

Turning from him, she stepped heedlessly into the portrait gallery, taking purposeful strides down the hall. With the house full of guests anyone could see her. He followed carefully behind her, watching as she stopped and pressed her hand against the wall. To his surprise, a small door sprung open.

"Where are you going?" he demanded in an angry whisper.

"Again, don't worry yourself, Lord Whitlock." She gave him a scathing look. "No one will see me."

He watched her slip inside and close the door behind her. And he felt like the worst kind of heel. For taking advantage of her just now. For what his words implied. Why did everything with Vivienne end badly?

He waited a few moments and then followed her through the secret door. The stone staircase led him to an upstairs corridor. Quietly he opened the panel at the top of the steps and peered down the hallway just in time to see Vivienne enter her bedroom.

What a mess his neat, orderly life had suddenly become. In a matter of days, Vivienne Montgomery managed to turn his life upside down yet again.

Chapter 9

The Musicale

No house party would be complete without an evening musicale and the party at Bingham Hall was no exception. That rainy night all the guests assembled in the grand parlor to listen to the varied musical talents of those present. Chairs had been arranged for viewing and a large dais had been set up for the performers. While their mother accompanied them on the piano, the Atwood sisters sang a charming duet, their voices ringing clearly through the salon.

As she sat in one of the elegant chairs arranged for the audience, Vivienne inwardly cringed in embarrassment and shame, still in shock over what she and Aidan had done in the portrait gallery that afternoon.

They had been completely reckless and impulsive. What were they thinking to start acting that way again? Even worse, how could she let herself be used by him that way? And he had so obviously used her! He could barely stand to be in her presence, yet he would gladly fuck her in a closet if no one would know about it.

There she went again, using those foul words Gregory and George taught her.

But what other word better described what they had done together?

Next Lady Annabelle Worthington, a pretty blonde with a wide mouth, began to play a rather sad tune on the harp. The strings moved magically under her fingers.

Again Vivienne shrank at the shameful memory of being naked in Aidan's arms. But even more embarrassing than the things she had *done* with him, were the things she had *said* to him. She had admitted her love for him, left all her feelings exposed, and he hard-heartedly trampled all over them. She acted like a lovesick schoolgirl, not a mature woman of twenty-seven.

And he was the worst sort of scoundrel to take advantage of her in such a way!

Instantly anger replaced her humiliation. Anger at herself for letting it happen. Anger with Aidan for the way he had treated her afterward. In her hands she twisted a Belgian lace handkerchief into a tight knot.

Then she watched as Lord Abernathy, a short balding gentleman with a pronounced paunch, situated himself on the dais and began to play a Vivaldi piece on his violin. "Spring." Very fitting.

The music continued and Vivienne glanced furtively at Aidan, who sat across the room from her with Helene Winston by his side. Just a few hours ago she was naked in a dark closet with him and had reveled in every minute of the feel of his powerful body rocking hers against the wall. Of his hot mouth kissing her skin. Of his skilled hands touching her intimately. Of his strong arms around her again. It had been heavenly.

Now, Aidan appeared as handsome and elegant as ever, although his green eyes reflected calm reserve and distance, showing none of the fire and passion she had felt that afternoon. Nonetheless, a jolt of pure desire washed through her body in response to his physical presence. She wanted him again.

She cringed in mortification. How could she still want to be with him after the way he had treated her? This incredible desire for him mystified her.

She and Aidan had not uttered one word to each other since she left him in the portrait gallery earlier that day. She toyed with the idea of feigning a headache and not attending the musicale, but she did not want to give Aidan the satisfaction of thinking she cared that much.

Her eyes casually searched the room to see if Jackson Harlow had arrived yet. Not seeing him, she assumed that he was still in his room, recovering from yesterday's accident. Apparently, he had suffered quite a blow to the head. His gentlemanly presence would have comforted her tonight. Especially now, seeing Aidan seated beside the lovely Lady Helene Winston.

The musicale dragged on interminably. Her Uncle Gilbert sang an old English love ballad, his deep bass echoing through the room, the lyrics prompting Vivienne to doubt her interpretation of the word love, or at least romantic love. What did love really mean?

She thought of her parents, her father a dashing English sea captain and her mother a beautiful Irish girl. They had loved each other once. According to her father's stories, he fell in love at his first sight of the captivating Ellen Joyce during his first trip to Galway. They were married after a whirlwind courtship, before John Montgomery sailed away again. Their story was tragically cut short when Ellen died giving birth to a daughter, Vivienne. Her brokenhearted father never remarried. Was their love all for nothing? Did all love end in tragedy and heartbreak?

So what was love? To desire someone? To feel affection for someone? Could it be merely a special attachment or connection between two people? Was it something destined by fate or just a whim? Was there a biological chemistry that attracted certain people to each other? Did it need to be fortified with commitment, devotion, faith, and trust? A blend of all of these things?

She had once believed that she and Aidan were deeply in love with each other and that they were fated to be together. Now she was not sure what they had felt for each other at all. Had it been simply youthful adoration? A passing physical attraction? Once Aggie had foretold that their love was true, but it obviously had not stood the test of time.

Apparently the physical attraction between them had not waned over the years, judging from their actions that afternoon.

Vivienne idly wondered if Aidan loved Helene Winston. Helene, whom Aidan respected, trusted, and treated like a lady. Her heart unexpectedly ached at the thought of Aidan whispering words of love to Helene, when Vivienne had once been the one he whispered to. What would Helene say if she knew what went on in the portrait gallery that very afternoon between her and Aidan? A pang of guilt pierced her at the thought of Helene. She seemed a decent girl who deserved better than a hard-hearted man who took advantage of his childhood sweetheart in a darkened closet.

Come to think of it, they both deserved better than Aidan Kavanaugh.

"Vivienne, darling, please sing for us," the Duchess

of Bingham called to her. "I have been told your voice is quite lovely."

Shaken from her reverie, Vivienne looked up at her aunt in startled surprise.

"Oh, Vivienne must sing for everyone!" Aunt Gwen echoed her sister-in-law's sentiment and smiled proudly. "My niece takes after her mother's side of the family for no one in the Montgomery clan can carry a tune!" Turning to Vivienne, she urged gently, "Please do, Vivienne."

"Thank you, but—" Vivienne had no chance to refuse her aunt's request as Gregory and George, with much laughter and fanfare, hurriedly ushered her up the step to the dais and clamored for her to sing for them.

"Come on and sing something pretty, Vivvy!"

Vivienne had sung her whole life with her grandmother, but never in front of an assembled audience. Yet she could find no way out of this predicament except to acquiesce to their demands. "What shall I sing then?" she asked with a little laugh, glancing nervously around the room.

A few people called out the names of familiar tunes. She heard one distinctly rich, masculine voice more clearly than the others.

"Sing, 'Give Me Your Hand.'"

The voice belonged unmistakably to Aidan, and Vivienne's heart slammed into her chest. She stared wordlessly at him. His green-eyed gaze pinned her in place. She could not breathe when he looked at her like that, let alone be expected to sing. And after what happened that afternoon, she did not have the strength to sing that song of all songs.

Much to the surprise of everyone in the room, Aidan stood up. Heads turned to watch, wondering what he was going to do, as he purposefully made his way toward the gleaming grand piano. To Vivienne he stated simply, "I shall play for you."

Vivienne's mouth went dry. He was stark, raving mad!

He wished to accompany her on the piano while she sang, just as they had done together years ago in her grandmother's tiny parlor. Stunned, she dared a glance at the many faces watching them. Most were merely curious, but Gregory watched with open amusement, his smile enigmatic. Helene Winston's expression held a mixed look of bewilderment and interest, her eyes searching. Susana Kavanaugh's brittle face was drawn into a most definite frown of displeasure. Never one to back down from a challenge, and once again Aidan was challenging her by daring her to sing with him in front of everyone, Vivienne took a deep breath to calm her racing heart. They were actually going to do this.

"Are you ready?" he asked in a low whisper. He barely looked at her as he sat at the piano, yet she felt the warmth from his body as she stood beside him.

Vivienne answered with a soft "Yes," and cleared her throat, as Aidan began to play, his long fingers moving expertly across the keys. The familiar chords pulled at her heartstrings and flooded her with warm memories of evenings in Ireland with her beloved grandmother. And Aidan by her side.

Just give me your hand.
Tabhair dom do lamh.
Just give me your hand
And I'll walk with you . . .
Through the streets of our land,
Through the mountains so grand
If you just give me your hand,
Just give me your hand,
And come along with me . . .

> *. . . If you just give me your hand,*
> *Just give me your hand,*
> *In a gesture of peace.*
> *Will you give me your hand*
> *And all troubles will cease,*
> *For the strong and the weak,*
> *For the rich and the poor?*

It was an old Irish song that played with meanings on a number of levels. It could be a love song to one's country, a song of forgiveness and reconciliation, or it could even be interpreted as a proposal of marriage. That Aidan had chosen that song for her to sing left her mind spinning. As her lilting voice carried around the room, she wondered if he were asking her forgiveness for what happened that afternoon or for what happened ten years ago. Tears welled in her eyes as she sang the chorus.

> *By day and night*
> *Through all struggle and strife*
> *And beside you, to guide you,*
> *Forever, my love*
> *For love's not for one,*
> *But for both of us to share*
> *For our country so fair*
> *For our world and what's there.*

As she sang the last lyrics, she felt her voice falter, but Aidan's strong baritone joined her mezzo soprano in perfect harmony to finish the song together. She wiped the tears from her eyes and realized that everyone in the room was silent, staring at the two of them. She could not bring herself to look at Aidan.

"Oh, that was lovely!" the Duchess of Bingham

finally said, breaking the silence. "Just lovely!" At her words, everyone applauded enthusiastically and called their congratulations.

"Did you two practice together?" Gregory asked, an amused expression on his face.

She could not speak. Yes, they had practiced together, but the thought of Aggie was too much to bear. Vivienne gratefully accepted the handkerchief Gregory silently handed to her.

Aidan said only, "Vivienne's grandmother taught us that song years ago when we lived in Ireland."

"Well, that was simply beautiful. Do you know any others?" the Duchess of Bingham asked with enthusiasm.

"I'm afraid not tonight," Vivienne apologized with a small sniffle. "I'm sorry, but that song always makes me cry. It reminds me of my grandmother."

"I'm sorry, dear," the Duchess murmured softly before turning from her. "Well then, that concludes the musical portion of our evening," she announced to the room in general. "Let's have some cake, shall we?" Heartily agreeing to that proposal, the guests began filing out of the rows of chairs to follow the duke and duchess into the dining room.

Vivienne stood still, wishing to say something to Aidan, but not sure what.

He merely nodded his head briefly in her direction, and followed the others from the room, leaving her standing there feeling awkwardly bereft. Singing that song had filled her with a heartsick yearning for him, how had it left him so untouched? Especially after they were so intimate together in the portrait gallery only a few hours ago.

Gregory still stood by her side, saying in a low voice, "What was that all about?"

"It was just a song," she murmured noncommittally. "And I'm overly sentimental."

"It was more than that, Vivvy." Gregory gave her a meaningful look, his bright blue eyes intent on her. "What really happened between the two of you?"

"We've known each other since we were children, that's all. He spent some time with my grandmother and me. She taught us both to sing and play the piano."

Gregory eyed her skeptically, as if he didn't believe her for a minute. Vivienne knew Gregory was no fool, but at that particular moment she had no desire to discuss her history with Aidan. Breathing deeply, she took Gregory's arm and followed him into the dining room.

Waiting his turn near the dessert table, Aidan ignored the furious looks from his mother. Susana would not dare berate him here in front of everyone, but he would get an earful from her at some point. Aware that she was doubly angered, not only by his singing with Vivienne but also by publicly flaunting his Irish heritage, he felt a pang of remorse for upsetting her. Singing with Vivienne had been a mistake, but he could do nothing about it now. It was done.

He managed to retrieve a slice of lemon cake for Helene and brought it to her.

"Thank you, Aidan," she said sweetly, taking the plate from him and resting it awkwardly on her lap.

"You're welcome."

"I had no idea you had such a wonderful voice. You and Miss Montgomery sounded lovely together. And that song was quite touching." Helene praised his singing, but her eyes betrayed her confused feelings. "You must have been very close at one time."

"We were just children then. Her grandmother was kind to me."

She nodded her head, but he knew she suspected he was not being entirely truthful. Guilt over his treatment of her gnawed at him; Helene deserved better from him.

Feeling like an idiot, he wondered what had possessed him to sing with Vivienne in the first place. When he saw her standing alone at the piano, the words came out of his mouth before he could reconsider them. He had to play for her. She stood so proudly, beautifully, and he suddenly ached to hear her sweet voice again. The scene so vividly recalled the familiar memories of their time together that he had reacted with an automatic reflex.

Just as having her in the portrait gallery that afternoon had been.

That would be a memory that would haunt him forever. Vivienne in the portrait gallery. She had been astonishingly sensual. His body throbbed with desire at the mere thought of Vivienne sucking his fingers. Vivienne kissing him in the darkness. Vivienne declaring she had only ever been with him. If only he could believe her . . .

He lost all control of himself with Vivienne. For whatever reason, she had that effect on him. She always had. He had never been with another woman who had that type of influence over him, and there had been plenty over the years since he left Ireland. Like a witch, Vivienne caused him to act irrationally and recklessly, going against his better judgment and defying all logic. All the more reason to stay away from her.

For Vivienne Montgomery had been a force that turned his world upside down from the moment he met her.

Chapter 10

The Beginning

Galway, Ireland, 1852
Eighteen years earlier . . .

"Nothing's ever good enough for you, is it, Susana?" Joseph Kavanaugh's deep voice slurred and he slammed his glass on the mahogany table, some of the whiskey sloshing over the sides.

"What a surprise," Susana stated in utter disgust. "You're drunk again."

Listening outside the door, Aidan wished his mother would be quiet. Couldn't she see how angry his father was? Why did she continue to taunt him like that?

"Not so drunk that I don't know what you are trying to do," Joseph asserted nastily, scowling at her. "I know what you're after. And you're not taking Aidan anywhere."

"Oh, for pity's sake, Joseph, let me take my son!" she cried in exasperation.

"Your son!" He mocked her, his laughter laced with bitterness. Joseph's once handsomely rugged face had become red and bloated, filled with too many years of unresolved resentment and too much alcohol. "Oh, yes, your son. He is your son, isn't he?"

Ignoring his intonation, Susana continued, "He needs to go to England with me, Joseph. Unlike you, Aidan shall learn to be a proper English gentleman."

"For what? To come back here and inherit Cashelwood? He'll stay in Galway, *just like I did.* Why does he need to go off to England only to come back with lofty manners? What good will it do him, I ask you?"

She cried out in frustration, "You don't understand anything important!"

"I understand more than you think. The boy is ten years old and needs to toughen up a little. If I left him to you, you'd keep him protected under glass, like some fragile hothouse plant. You pamper and spoil him too much as it is. Aidan must learn how to manage this estate, and he needs to know about the country he lives in. *Ireland,* not England."

"He *is* English!" she exclaimed hotly, her cheeks reddened in anger. "The Howard family, *my* family, is one of the best families in England!"

"So you've told me a thousand and one times." He sneered at her. "But what does it matter, woman? You're married to me. Joseph Kavanaugh, Lord of Cashelwood. Nothing's going to change that. You may think Aidan only belongs to you, Susana, but he's mine, too. And it is *my* name he carries, not the name of your high and mighty English family."

"Aidan is all I have," she declared crossly.

"Aidan is all I have, too." He gulped more whiskey from the crystal tumbler he had slammed on the table just moments before. Wiping his mouth with his sleeve, he continued his tirade. "Since I've long given up any notion of getting another child from you."

Outside the room, Aidan's heart pounded in his chest. He hated when his parents fought with each other. The same argument always ensued and they always argued over him.

Joseph stated calmly, with a cold determination, "Aidan stays here with me."

Susana tried a pleading tactic. "Please let me take him to visit my parents. They've never even met him. My mother is not well and I need to see her."

"No. If you want to visit your family in England, then go alone. If your family even wants to see the likes of you. They were well rid of you when they foisted you upon me. But you're not taking Aidan to England, for I don't trust you to bring him back home to me!"

Aidan tiptoed away from the library where his parents were now screaming at each other. He felt his stomach tighten and the threat of tears pricked behind his eyes. They hadn't known he was listening outside the door, but that wouldn't have stopped them anyway. His mother and father always fought over him, and it made Aidan sick inside.

Blinking back the tears and brushing his thick black hair from his eyes, he hurried along the corridor until he found himself by the servant's staircase. An idea occurred to him then. He'd show his father that he was tough. That he wasn't a spoiled baby.

Aidan never left the house without permission or without being accompanied by one of his parents or a guardian but, weary of his father's constant derision and his mother's overprotectiveness, he crept as quietly as he could down the back staircase. Surprisingly, he found the large kitchen empty. Feeling his stomach rumble, he grabbed a loaf of freshly baked bread, wrapped it in a checkered cloth along with a big hunk of cheese, and managed to slip out the servants' entrance into the gardens without being seen. Amazed at how easily he escaped, he smiled to himself in satisfaction.

As he followed the path along the garden, he wondered nervously what his parents would do when they found him not in his bedroom. His father would give him a beating for sure, but Aidan didn't care. For once a beating seemed worth the risk.

Aidan raced across the green grass and toward the stone fence that encircled the perimeter of the estate. Carefully manicured lawns and gardens surrounded Cashelwood, an elegant and stately gray stone house that resembled an ancient castle. The estate had belonged to the Kavanaugh family for a century. Although the area had seen hard times from the famine, when the potatoes turned black, most of the Kavanaugh's farmers had survived, for Joseph Kavanaugh, being partly Irish himself, was not an absentee British landlord as most others were. He lived on his land, raising sheep and Connemara ponies, working with his tenants and helping them when in need, which made Cashelwood a prosperous estate. Lord Joseph Kavanaugh was well-liked by everyone and popular with the locals, unlike Lady Kavanaugh. Because of his father, Aidan had grown to love the land and the estate that would one day belong to him.

A thrill of exhilaration surged through Aidan at the prospect of venturing out on his own for the first time. After he climbed the stone fence and landed

with an emphatic thud on the other side, he sat down
and ate the bread and cheese while he figured out
where to go.

He didn't understand why his mother was so angry
all the time or why she hated everything Irish and only
talked of England. He loved her, of course, but sometimes he wished she were not so critical of his father.
Maybe then his father wouldn't be so critical of him.

His father's moods were mercurial and Aidan never
knew if his father would be happy or displeased to see
him. Sometimes Joseph would take Aidan riding or
into town and he seemed proud to show his son to his
friends. Then, for no apparent reason that Aidan
could discern, his father would beat him for the slightest infraction. Aidan tried his best to be a good son.
He studied hard and did very well in his lessons. Polite
and obedient, he used his manners and never caused
any trouble. Aidan was as good as he knew how to be.
While his mother continuously heaped praises upon
him, his father's kind words were few and far between.

But today was different. Today Aidan was defiant.
He needed to get away from his parents. But where?
There was only so far a person could go in Ireland
before he reached the shore.

The sea! That's where he would go. He would go
down to the bay and watch the ships. How he loved
the water! Someday he would sail off on his own and
battle pirates and find buried treasure. After reading
Daniel Defoe's *The Life and Strange Surprising Adven-
tures of Robinson Crusoe* last year he couldn't think of
anything more exciting than sailing across the ocean
and having to survive on a deserted island. Maybe he
would stow away on a ship and leave home for good!

He finished off his makeshift meal, licking his fin-

gers, thinking it the best he'd ever had. Tucking the
checkered cloth in his back pocket, Aidan then ran
with strong, steady strides through the green fields
dotted with sheep and lined with stone walls, his mind
spinning with this newfound freedom.

Determinedly, he followed the road into town and
made his way across the Salmon Weir Bridge into the
city. He loved watching the waters of the River Corrib
rushing by, knowing that in the spring salmon would
make their way up to Lough Corrib. An important ancient city, Galway boasted a distinguished past and
Aidan had learned all about it from his tutor. It had
once been a walled city and wealthy trade center, ex-
porting fish, wool, and leather, and self-governed by
the fourteen families who built grand townhouses.
The Irish called it Gaillimh, but its population shrank
dramatically during the last decade as people fled Ireland and the famine, flocking to Galway port to sail to
the United States. But things were getting better.

Aidan followed the road into Eyre Square and marveled again at the Great Southern Hotel, which had
been built only a few years earlier. The tall stone building dominated the square and made him feel hopeful.
Exciting things were happening in Galway. Queens
College recently opened and the railroad to Dublin
had been built the year before. His parents planned to
take him on the train to Dublin during the summer.

He walked along the streets until he caught a
glimpse of the River Corrib again. Aidan could hear
the shrill calls of the fishmongers who were selling their
day's catch near the Spanish Arch, a stone fortress
which was built to keep out the Spanish Armada hundreds of years ago. Carts and drays pulled goods for
sale in the market and people milled about, deciding

what to buy. He could see pucans, the little fishing boats from the Claddagh village, out on the water. He loved it there in the fish market, where the salty smell of the sea was strongest. He'd been there before, of course, on the trips with his father and he always enjoyed visiting the city. He could not imagine how big Dublin or even London was compared to Galway, although his mother assured him they were much finer cities.

Aidan wandered over the Claddagh Bridge and followed the road around until he came to a path that veered off to the shoreline. He looked across the bay at the horizon and dreamed of sailing to the edge and beyond that thin line that touched the sky. The Aran Islands were visible and he wished he could at least sail out to Inishmore, the largest island, and visit Dun Aengus, the ancient fort. Some day he would, he promised himself.

A light breeze ruffled his dark hair. It was a clear day, rare and beautiful, and the sunlight glinted brightly on the water, causing his eyes to water at the brightness. He walked for some time, making his way closer to the shore, until he noticed a group of children up ahead playing some sort of game.

Children!

He rarely had an opportunity to play with children his own age and he smiled to himself at the prospect. How fun it would be to play with them! Being a cautious boy, he moved toward the group with care and realized as he approached that they were not playing at all, but were in some sort of argument. He managed to position himself behind an overturned rowboat and observed them for a time without being noticed.

What he saw intrigued him.

Standing with her hands on her hips, her black hair whipping in the wind, and her blue eyes flashing, a little spitfire who seemed about nine years old gave orders to a ragtag group of boys who were decidedly bigger than she was. They stood in awe of her.

"And don't you be thinking that I won't know what you're up to," she scolded them indignantly. She wagged her tiny finger at them for emphasis. "If you bother her again, you'll have me to deal with."

"Ahh, go on with ya," a tall boy of about thirteen yelled back at her.

"No, Nicky." A shorter boy tugged on his sleeve. "She's telling the truth. Her grandmother's a witch. She'll put an outlandish spell on us, she will."

"She don't scare me," the boy called Nicky blustered, but his wary eyes narrowed in suspicion.

Looking at these children on the beach, Aidan knew his mother would not approve of his associating with them in any way. He smiled to himself at the prospect.

The little girl countered fearlessly to the bigger boy, "Your little brother's right, Nicky Foster, and you should take heed. My grandmother is a witch. A most talented witch. Besides that, we're descended from one of the original tribes of Galway, and that gives us special powers as well. She'll put a spell on you so bad, you'll be wishing you had it as good as poor Annie here." The little girl seemed to become taller as she spoke, her words falling upon them with a frightening surety.

Apparently that last threat worked, for one by one the children wandered away, even the big one called Nicky, not willing to take a chance against the fiery little girl who claimed to have witches on her side. When they were gone, Aidan watched her turn to help another girl of maybe sixteen hobble up the beach. The older girl, wearing a tattered dress, had a sort of deformed leg and leaned awkwardly on the younger girl while holding a crude wooden crutch in her other hand.

He had never seen anything like it. Fascinated, Aidan hurried over to them, not wanting to lose sight of the strong-willed little witch.

"Can I help you?" he asked in a rush, for the little black-haired girl struggled to keep the older one from falling as they made their way over the rocky ground. Aidan, tall for his age, took the deformed girl's arm, and, being bigger and stronger, assisted her over the rocks and back onto the flat road with ease.

Both girls stared at him in surprise.

"Now, who would you be?" the little witch asked skeptically.

Startled by the deep blue of her eyes as they narrowed in on him, he answered, "I'm Aidan Kavanaugh."

"I haven't seen you around here before." Her sharp eyes looked him over, as if trying to discover if he were worthy enough to be in their presence. She must have found him acceptable because after a moment she introduced herself, saying, "I'm Vivienne Montgomery and this is my friend, Annie Sheehan."

Aidan immediately turned to Annie. "What happened to your leg?"

Annie blushed, hiding behind her long brown hair, and shrugged self-consciously. "Born this way."

"Yes, and those eejits don't use the sense God gave them, and they tease her, as if Annie could help how she was born," Vivienne uttered scornfully, rolling her eyes heavenward. "It could just as easily be one of them to have a twisted leg, or arm, or head, for that matter."

Aidan saw the look of utter contempt on Vivienne's

pretty features, for even at ten he recognized her childish beauty, but he admired her for her fearless protection of her unfortunate friend.

"I'm right as rain now, Vivienne. Thanks for taking up for me. I've got to get home or my mother will be worrying." As Annie turned to make her way to the little cottage a few yards away, she gave a shy smile in his direction and said, "Thank you for helping me, Aidan Kavanaugh."

He nodded his head and answered, "You're welcome."

Vivienne turned and walked back toward the rocky beach. Aidan saw her go and hurried after her.

"Are you really a witch?" he asked her, half hoping in his ten-year-old heart that she was. He'd never known a real witch before.

Vivienne laughed. "Sure I'm not a witch, you daft boy!" She smiled again as she continued to clamber back down the rocks they just climbed up. Slight and pixie-like, her movements conveyed quickness and agility. "I just say that to scare off the idiots who don't know any better."

Aidan followed alongside of her, hopping from one large rock to the next with careless ease. "I watched what you did. They were teasing her and you stopped them. Good for you."

"You're smart for a boy, Aidan Kavanaugh," she pronounced with some surprise, as she jumped from the rocks to the beach and looked up at him, her blue eyes questioning. "I've never seen you around here before. Where do you come from?"

"Cashelwood," he answered as he landed in the wet sand beside her.

Vivienne let out a long, low whistle, which was most impressive for a little girl. "Fancy place, that."

Aidan shrugged. "It's just my home."

"You don't seem to be very happy about it."

He picked up a small stone and threw it into the bay. "You wouldn't be either if you lived there."

"Now why wouldn't you be happy there? Everyone knows that Cashelwood is a lovely place." She still continued to stare at him in wonder, as he picked up another stone.

"No one is happy living in a prison." It surprised him that he shared this feeling with a little girl he just met. He flung the stone as hard as he could, satisfied with the splash it made when it landed in the water.

"So you escaped your grand prison today, did you?" she asked.

Aidan smiled ruefully. "I did. And one day I'm going to have a ship of my own and sail far away from here. I'll go to some island and become a pirate. I might just stow away on a ship tonight."

"Have you ever even been on a ship before?" she challenged him, folding her skinny arms across her chest.

He shook his head and admitted, "Well, no."

Vivienne sighed wearily, as if talking to a simpleton. "Don't you know what they do to stowaways on a ship?"

"Oh, and you do?" he questioned contemptuously. Honestly, did this little girl think she knew everything about everything?

"As a matter of fact I do. They throw you overboard and feed you to the sharks." At his stunned expression, she added, "After they beat you senseless, of course."

"And how would you know such a thing?" he challenged her. "Don't tell me, you've been a stowaway?"

"Don't be daft," she said with derision. "But I certainly know more about ships than you do."

"Prove it."

"All right then." She grabbed his hand firmly in her small one. "Come with me, Aidan Kavanaugh of Cashelwood."

Vivienne began to run and Aidan had no choice but to run with her. She was as fast as a cat, and he raced to keep up with her, but found himself grinning. He'd never met anyone like this girl. She was fearless and self-confident, and obviously free to do as she pleased. Following the path along the bay, they ran back over the Claddagh Bridge, past the Spanish Arch, up Shop Street and back into town. They ran between the alleyways and side streets of the city until they came to a stone building with a shiny red door. Without knocking, she swung the door open and charged inside. Instinct warned him that his mother would be horrified at the idea of her son in such a modest dwelling, but Aidan ignored the thought and followed the girl into the little house with perverse determination.

Surprisingly, it was neat and clean inside, for he expected worse from the dire warnings that his mother gave him about the Irish being filthy, dirty peasants. Somewhat disappointed to not find pigs rooting about the floor, he looked around the small parlor with interest. This house had lots of lacey things covering the tables, shelves lined with books, curtains in the windows, and rugs on the floor. A small piano stood in the corner. It was obviously not the mud-covered and filth-laden hovel he had been led to believe would constitute an Irish home. Why would his mother tell him such things? Perhaps she had never taken an opportunity to visit an Irish house. He would set her straight one day.

"Aggie!" Vivienne called out as she walked into the parlor.

"Do you live here?" he asked the little witch. Even though she denied being a witch, he couldn't help but think of her that way. He wanted her to be a witch. For some reason, he also wanted her to be on his side, like she had been on Annie's.

"Of course, I do. Do you think I'd just be walking into someone else's home without a by-your-leave?"

"Of course not." He smiled ruefully at her and nodded his head, agreeing that he had asked a silly question. He glanced around once more, noting the delicious smells coming from the kitchen.

"This is my home," she stated proudly. "I live here with my grandmother."

Nervously he watched as Vivienne climbed upon an overstuffed armchair, teetering on the side arm while balancing on the tips of her toes to reach up to the shelf on the wall above it. He feared that she would fall, but she managed to take something from the many strange and curious objects that lined the shelf. She jumped from the arm of the chair to the floor in a graceful swoop. Thoroughly impressed by her actions, for he wouldn't dream of doing something like that in his mother's house, he thought it must be heavenly to jump from furniture without a care.

"Where are your mother and father?" he asked her in wonderment for surely a mother would scold her for climbing heedlessly on the chair.

"My mother died when I was born," Vivienne

said matter-of-factly, looking at him in her straightforward manner.

Aidan had nothing to say to that.

She then gave him a most glorious smile. "But my father stays here when he's not at sea."

Aidan was suddenly riveted to the spot and knew exactly why the little witch had brought him here. "Your father has a ship."

"Oh, and a grand ship it is," she declared proudly nodding her head. She handed him the small object she had taken from the shelf. "My father found this on one of the islands near Florida when I was a little girl and brought it home for me. It's a conch shell. Now I want you to have it."

He reached out to take the shell from her and held it gingerly, reverently, in the palm of his hand. Delicate and fragile, its colors were of the softest, palest pink, with concentric spirals swirling within each other. He had found lots of shells on the beach, of course, but nothing that evoked images of hot sun, blue waters, and tropical palm trees that he had seen in his picture books. "I've never seen anything like this. Why are you giving it to me?"

"So it can remind you of all the places you want to go someday and you won't have to be a stowaway. If you hold it up to your ear and listen very carefully, you can hear the ocean."

He placed the conch shell to his ear, and indeed, heard what sounded like waves crashing. "It's amazing! It really came from across the Atlantic Ocean?"

"Yes. My father brings me things from all over the world." Before Aidan realized what she was doing, again she scampered up the armchair, grabbed something from the shelf above, and swooped down to the floor. With a grand flourish she presented him with a long whitish object of some sort.

"Touch it," she urged excitedly as he took it from her. "It's an alligator tooth! From a real live alligator in Florida. My father brought me that, too."

This bit of news left Aidan speechless. He had many, many fine store-bought toys in his lavish playroom at Cashelwood: tin soldiers, beautifully illustrated picture books, wooden puzzles, stuffed animals, paint sets, and all sorts of musical instruments. But this little girl, who lived in a house so tiny that it could easily fit into his bedroom, seemed to have more than it first appeared.

"Did your father kill the alligator?" he asked in utter fascination.

"No, but one of his crew did. Now my father's somewhere in South America. If you promise not to stowaway on a ship tonight or ever, the next time he comes to port, I'll take you on my father's ship, the *Great Wave*."

His eyes widened in astonishment. "You will?"

She nodded, an excited smile lighting her pixie-like face.

"Why?" he asked incredulously, amazed that she would be so generous with him. He, the young lord of the manor who lived on the grand estate of Cashelwood and supposedly had everything, while she was merely a little Irish girl with no mother. Somehow he felt that she had more in her life than he ever would. He was more than a bit in awe of her.

"That's what friends do, Aidan Kavanaugh. You helped Annie. So you are my friend now."

Aidan felt his cheeks turn scarlet and was not sure whether he would burst from pure joy or utter embarrassment. He had made his first friend. He'd never had a real friend before, being kept under his mother's watchful eyes his whole life. She had never deemed anyone good enough to be his friend. Now Vivienne Montgomery was just a little girl, and perhaps she really was a witch, but he wanted to be her friend more than anything he had ever wanted in his life. He smiled shyly at her.

Just then an older woman entered the room, wiping her hands on the white apron around her waist. Smallish, with dark hair like Vivienne, she wore a kind expression on her wrinkled face. This had to be the witchy grandmother!

"I was out back in the garden and didn't hear you come in, Vivienne," she began, until she saw Aidan. "Now, who have we here?" she asked with a warm smile, looking at him as if she knew him.

Vivienne said, "Aggie, this is Aidan Kavanaugh. I met him on the beach. Aidan, this is my grandmother, Agnes Joyce."

"From one of the original tribes of Galway," Aidan blurted out, wondering if the woman had the power to cast spells. He politely shook hands with her, keeping the precious shell carefully in his left hand.

Aggie chuckled lightly, "Well, now, aren't you the knowledgeable one? I can see Vivienne's been bragging again." She gave her granddaughter an exasperated look and turned back to Aidan. "You are just in time to join us for some tea, Master Kavanaugh of Cashelwood. Vivvy, get the cups."

As Vivienne scrambled to set the table, Aidan followed them into the little kitchen and apparently found the source of the delicious smells. The clean and inviting room had a large and sturdy wooden table surrounded by an assortment of mismatched chairs in various shapes and sizes. The room had obviously hosted many guests and was the heart of this house.

Aidan quietly seated himself in a bright red chair with a ladder back and watched with wide eyes as the two of them maneuvered around the cluttered kitchen. Aggie placed a plate of freshly baked brown bread with creamy butter and a cup of piping hot tea with sugar in front of him. Vivienne climbed onto a faded yellow chair beside him and began eating without ceremony. Aggie sat across the table from them.

He had never eaten in a kitchen in his life! In fact, he was always chased out of the kitchen by the cook at Cashelwood. As a rule, he took his meals upstairs in the nursery. Although at his mother's insistence, he was frequently expected to dine with both his parents in the formal and imposing dining hall where not a pleasant word was spoken. Either way, mealtimes were somber experiences for him.

But this . . . This little house was heaven! Aggie and Vivienne talked excitedly, and actually laughed, while they had their tea and bread. Their simple meal became a joyful affair. For the first time in his life, Aidan felt warm and peaceful inside, as if he had suddenly come home, as if he belonged there.

Vivienne retold how they met earlier on the beach and how they helped Annie Sheehan, the poor crippled girl. In no uncertain terms, she let her feelings for the local boys on the beach be known.

"Oh, Aggie, they were horrid, just horrid, to Annie," Vivienne continued, her blue eyes flashing. "They called her the most vile names and had taken her walking stick from her. They poked at her and tried to make her fall down. The poor girl was in tears. Those Foster boys make me so angry!"

"Well then, it's good you put a stop to them, love. It's up to us to help those less fortunate." Aggie placed more bread on Aidan's plate.

Aidan spoke up, "Vivienne said she'd put a curse on them if they didn't stop tormenting Annie."

"Did she now?" Aggie winked at him.

"No, I didn't. I just let them think that *Aggie* would curse them," Vivienne corrected him with a satisfied grin. "I can't help it if they believed me!"

Aggie laughed and turned her gaze upon him. "Well, Master Kavanaugh, tell us a little about yourself." She smiled warmly at him, encouraging him to talk.

As briefly as he could, Aidan recounted his rather dull life at Cashelwood. "I live with my mother and father. I have lots of lessons every day with my tutor, but one day I'll go away to school in Dublin."

"That sounds grand for a boy of ten years," Aggie stated, with an approving look.

Aidan worried that Vivienne would tell her grandmother that he had referred to his home as a prison. He didn't want to explain that. He glanced nervously in her direction, but she did not say a word.

"Thank you for the tea and bread, Mrs. Joyce."

"Oh, you must call me Aggie. Everyone does. Even Vivienne calls me Aggie. It's only fair that you should, too."

Aidan nodded his head, pleased with being accepted so warmly into this amazing little world.

"Oh, play a song for us, Aggie!" Vivienne exclaimed, clapping her hands in excitement. "Aidan would like that, wouldn't you, Aidan?" She scampered to the little piano in the parlor and readied the stool for her grandmother.

"All right," Aggie agreed with a smile, "but Vivienne must sing with me."

Mesmerized, Aidan sat in the flower print armchair Vivienne had climbed upon earlier and listened as she sang a jaunty tune while her grandmother played the piano. They enjoyed being together and obviously spent a great deal of time together. He watched the old woman and the little girl with an unexplained longing in his heart. He suddenly wondered if other families were like Vivienne and her grandmother—close, and warm, and joyful of each other's company. And was his cold family the peculiar one?

Then they insisted that he learn a song and sing with them. Gamely Aidan joined in, laughing more than actually singing. They encouraged him cheerily, pleased with his strong voice, and he sang even louder until they all collapsed with laughter.

"Well, Master Kavanaugh, did you enjoy your visit?" Aggie asked after their musical interlude had ended.

"More than anything I've ever done," he said earnestly. In truth, it had been the nicest afternoon he had ever spent in his life. Being with them satisfied a need for companionship he had not realized he was missing. They had made him feel he was a part of their family.

"Well, isn't that a lovely thing to say!" Aggie proclaimed proudly, her warm smile beaming at him. "You will have to come visit us again."

"I will?" he asked in amazement. Even though he wanted to return to this little house, with the witchy, but not witchy, grandmother and granddaughter, his mother would never permit him come back here. He was sure of it.

"Of course you will, sweet child!" Aggie smiled at

him in such a way that Aidan knew she meant what she said and he desperately wanted to believe her.

Vivienne added, "He can come anytime he wants, can't he, Aggie?"

Although he was mortified, he felt he had to tell them the truth. He looked up at Aggie, pleading with his eyes for her to understand. "My mother will not allow me to come here again. She does not even know I'm here now."

Vivienne gasped in wonderment, her expression perplexed. "Whyever not?"

But Aggie knew why and Aidan silently blessed her. She took his hand in her soft and gently wrinkled one and squeezed it reassuringly.

"My dear boy, you must respect your mother's wishes, but you will always be welcome in our home whenever you can manage to stop by and visit us."

Humbled by her kind words, he whispered in relief, "Thank you."

"Aidan, you're my friend now, so you must come see me," Vivienne declared, and Aidan knew he had no choice but to find some way to visit them again.

However, Aidan did not return soon to Vivienne's house, for when he arrived home later that evening, his father stewed in a drunken rage and his mother was in hysterics, convinced that Aidan had been abducted. After searching the house from top to bottom, they had scoured the nearby farms to find him. By the time he returned home, his parents did not want to hear about Aidan's wonderful adventure, nor about the amazing little girl he met on the beach and her magical grandmother, nor that he made his first friend.

Instead they lectured him on obedience and

responsibility, traits that he was surely lacking, and gave him a reminder he would not soon forget. To impress the lesson upon him, his father dragged him out to the stables and whipped him with a belt so severely, Aidan could not sit down without pain for two whole days. He bore the agony by remembering the time he spent with Vivienne, which made that day worth the price of the beating. Anytime he wanted to escape his home, he placed the beautiful Floridian conch shell from Vivienne against his ear and imagined himself on a grand ship at sea.

From time to time, he managed to escape from Cashelwood and visit Vivienne, and that, oddly enough, was due in large part to his father. Horrified at the thought of Aidan associating with common Irish peasants from the town, Susana forbade her son to go out alone again. And that was when Joseph Kavanaugh stepped in, declaring that it would be good for Aidan to learn the local ways and that being outdoors would toughen him up a bit. Joseph also delighted in infuriating his wife.

So, in a manner of speaking, Aidan was set free.

Whenever Aidan knocked on their little door, Vivienne clapped her hands in delight and Aggie warmly welcomed him into their home. An unspoken bond of friendship developed between Aidan and Vivienne. They understood each other. Vivienne never questioned his situation at home, but accepted Aidan as he was. She sensed he needed comfort and she gave it freely.

One special summer Aidan spent almost every day with Vivienne, because his mother went to England for her mother's funeral and stayed there for two whole months. Aidan and Vivienne ran wild along the shores of Galway Bay. They competed with each other in foot races on the sand and swimming contests in the sea, and sometimes Vivienne actually beat him. They played together, hiked the green fields together, and fished together. They spent hours in Aggie's bright kitchen, concocting all sorts of delicious goodies to eat, for food always tasted better at Vivienne's house. He listened avidly as Vivienne read aloud the letters she received from her father, describing his trips to far off lands. Aggie taught Aidan to play the songs that she and Vivienne sang. Before he knew it, Aidan had become a part of their intimate family scene and he loved them for it.

When he was thirteen and she was twelve, Aidan finally met Vivienne's father for the first time. Captain Montgomery arrived in port from America and Aidan managed to escape from Cashelwood for the day because his mother and father had taken a trip to Dublin. Vivienne and Aidan spent a magical afternoon exploring the ship, the *Great Wave,* together.

Aidan thought Vivienne was the luckiest child in the world to have a father like the dashing and exciting John Montgomery. It amazed him that a father could be so loving to his child. Captain Montgomery's whole face lit up when he saw his daughter. And he let Vivienne, who was just a girl, climb the rigging and give orders to the crew. It was a beautiful ship and Aidan was in heaven.

Vivienne became an essential part of his life somehow. As the years passed, they became confidantes as well as playmates, sharing their secrets and dreams of the future with each other. Aidan was going to sail ships around the world and Vivienne was going to travel to far off lands and become a princess.

One time Aidan even dared to bring Vivienne to the manor house to meet his parents. His mother, not surprisingly, was most displeased with Aidan's Irish peasant friend. However, Joseph Kavanaugh thought Vivienne an intelligent and charming girl and encouraged the friendship, and for that reason alone Aidan blessed his father.

At his father's insistence and amidst grudging approval from his mother, Aidan was finally sent to school in Dublin, which, in any case, provided him with a convenient means of escape from both his parents. He didn't mind school. In fact, he enjoyed his studies, received the highest marks, and ranked in the top of his class. The best part of school turned out to be meeting boys his own age. Aidan made many good friends and was popular with the students and the teachers at school. For Aidan the only drawback to being away at school, was being apart from his best friend. He missed Vivienne terribly, but they stayed in touch by writing endless letters to each other.

When Aidan turned eighteen, he completed his last term at school and returned home to Galway after almost a solid year of being away. Instead of witnessing yet another ugly argument between his mother and father over how Aidan should spend his summer, Aidan snuck away that first afternoon home. Naturally he went straight to Vivienne's house and knocked on her door, anxious to see her after so much time had passed. Disappointed when no one answered, he made his way lazily down to the shore.

As he always did, he sat on the rocks along an empty stretch of coastline, just watching the low waves roll in and looking across to the Aran Islands. The sky was covered with a dark blanket of low clouds and the ocean was a steely gray. He loved when the water looked like that, as if it couldn't contain itself. Enveloped in the briny scent of the ocean and the salty sea spray, he breathed deeply, still longing for the day when he could escape both his parents and go off to sea on a ship of his own. Shaking his head ruefully, he knew his childish daydream was just that. He was a man now and would soon manage Cashelwood.

He glanced south and noticed the figure of a woman walking unhurriedly along the beach. Her self-assured and fluid movements caught his attention first. Possessing the graceful bearing of a queen, she paused and gazed out to sea, as if searching for something. She appeared deep in thought. Her build was slender and petite, and her thick, dark hair was swept up in a knot behind her head, exposing the tender curve of her neck. Something familiar called to him and his heart raced. And then he knew exactly who the woman was. She couldn't be anyone but Vivienne Montgomery.

Continuing her stroll across the sand, she came closer to where he was sitting on the rocks. She didn't notice him yet, nor was she even expecting him to be there. As far as he knew, she was unaware that he had returned from Dublin earlier than planned. So he took this opportunity to observe her at his leisure. It had been a year since he had last seen her, and he was astonished to realize that she was no longer a little girl.

Vivienne Montgomery had grown up while he was away at school! His daring little witch and his best friend had, quite simply, changed.

Not only had she grown a little taller, but the cut of her plain navy gown revealed a very shapely seventeen-year-old figure with the well-rounded breasts of a woman. Her dress billowed around her, exposing glimpses of lovely, stocking-clad legs. And then there was her face. He'd always thought her a pretty, spirited little thing, but now . . . now her beauty left him speechless.

Vivienne had always been the one person he could turn to when things at home were terrible. He never needed to explain to her, she just knew. Her presence comforted him, filled him with contentment. She made him laugh, with her flashing eyes and witty tongue. Vivienne was the first friend he ever had.

Seeing her now, he felt overwhelmed by a new emotion he had never associated with Vivienne before. Desire.

Perhaps sensing his presence, Vivienne glanced up and saw him looking at her, and her beautiful face lit up in delight. She smiled wholeheartedly and waved her hand, as she picked up her skirt and ran across the sand toward him.

"Aidan!" she called excitedly. "Aidan, you're home!"

For Aidan, the earth turned upside down watching Vivienne run to him, so obviously happy to see him. This beautiful, warm, smart, and caring girl was running to him. He could barely breathe. Feelings he never realized he possessed crashed over him in a tumultuous wave. Desire, longing, tenderness, protectiveness, possessiveness, need. Love.

Vivienne belonged to him. She always had. She always would. He felt it in his heart, his soul, his blood. They just belonged together.

He rose to his feet as she reached him, and she was out of breath from her dash across the shore. Still smiling at him, she marveled, "It's been so long since I've seen you, Aidan! When did you get back?"

Seeing her sapphire blue eyes alight with happiness at the sight of him, he stepped toward her, cupped her exquisite face with both of his hands and kissed her full, tender lips. Almost as if she had expected him to do that very thing, she did not resist, but returned his kiss with an openness that touched his soul. He parted her lips and his tongue met hers and their kiss deepened. Aidan lost himself in her, thoroughly consumed by the warm feel of her skin, the sweet sea-misted scent of her. He breathed her in, wanting her in a manner that shook him to the core of his being. His world now centered on one person, one woman. One incredibly beautiful woman.

Completely unprepared for the intensity of kissing Vivienne, he could have willingly drowned in her sweetness, warmth, and passion. He should have guessed it would be that way with her. His heart flipped over and a potent desire for her spread unchecked through his throbbing body. He wanted her.

Slowly Vivienne pulled back from him, her beautiful face serious, and looked directly into his eyes. "So that's the way of it, then?"

"Yes," he whispered hoarsely, overcome with emotion. "That's the way of it."

He kissed her again to emphasize his point. There was no need for words or explanations. It was as if they had just come home. To each other. They were connected as one being in that moment, locked in a breathtaking, soul-searching kiss that left them both reeling with the knowledge that their friendship had irrevocably changed.

Still shaking with desire, his arms moved around her shoulders and he pulled her closer against him. She rested her head against his chest and a soft sigh escaped her. He pressed a kiss to the top of her silky hair, breathing in the floral scent of her perfume that mingled with the fragrance of the sea. She smelled heavenly. He wanted to hold her close to his heart that way forever.

"Aidan," she whispered against his chest, when she was able to catch her breath.

"Yes?"

"There is something you should know."

"What is it?" His heart began to pound. She was going to tell him something he didn't want to hear. That she was in love with another boy. That she didn't want him. He could not bear it. He looked into her sapphire blue eyes and became lost, for she gazed up at him with such honesty and tenderness, he was thunderstruck.

"I love you, Aidan." Her lilting voice caught a little, but she continued. "I think I always have."

Aidan held her to him again, flooded in relief and happiness, relishing the feel of her small body next to his. Leave it to Vivienne to be brave enough to state what she felt in her heart first. Her sweet confession completely undid him. "Ah, my beautiful Irish witch, I think I loved you from the moment I met you."

His mouth sought hers and they kissed each other again, his arms holding her tightly to him.

Rain began to fall. Big fat drops plopped onto their faces as the gray sky turned stormy. Vivienne giggled but kissed him harder while his hands ran the length of her back. Her kisses tasted of the rain and salty air, and their tongues intertwined in heated eagerness in spite of the cold dampness that enveloped them. The rain fell and within minutes they were both drenched. He gazed reverently at her, as her long, black hair clung to her face, her soft cheeks glistening with raindrops.

Smiling lazily, Vivienne disengaged from his embrace. "Hurry!" she called out, reaching for him as the shower intensified. Hand in hand, they ran through the downpour back to her house.

Once safely inside and out of the storm, they found the house unusually cold and dark, and they were completely soaked to the skin.

"We need to get ourselves out of these wet clothes," Vivienne stated in a soft voice as they both stood dripping on the wooden floor.

"Where is Aggie?" he asked hoarsely, glancing around the room.

Vivienne looked into his eyes and again he felt his heart race. "She went up to Tuam to visit her brother. She won't be back until sometime tomorrow."

The clock ticked loudly on the mantel, echoing in the empty little house. He knew immediately what that meant. So did Vivienne. The implication hung unspoken in the air as their wet clothes dripped on the floor and the clocked ticked by the minutes.

His brave girl was suddenly shy, eyes downcast. "I'll get some towels," she murmured. She turned and fled the darkened room.

Aidan threw some peat turf into the fire to warm up the place. As the familiar smoky scent filled the room, his heart beat triple-time and his mind raced with possibilities. He also wrestled with his conscience. He and Vivienne were alone together in this house for the night . . . A million thoughts sped through his head.

As Aidan knelt before the fire trying to warm up, he heard Vivienne return. First he noticed her bare feet against the polished wood floor. He blinked at the pretty pink toes in front of him. She must have taken off her shoes and stockings. He was still low to the ground, but his eyes moved upward from the sight of her slender ankles to her shapely calves. The bare expanse of legs became covered as her thighs were draped with an embroidered quilt. He looked up at her face. Her gaze was steady, but vulnerable, and her sapphire eyes spoke volumes. The soft blanket draped around her body tantalizingly exposed the flawless skin of her shoulders, arms, and legs. His heart slammed into his chest with such force he couldn't breathe for a moment. Nor could he move a muscle.

Vivienne was naked beneath that blanket.

With her long, dark wet hair, and wearing nothing but a blanket, she was stunning.

"You can wrap this around you while your clothes dry." She held up another blanket for him, suggesting he do the same.

He slowly rose to his feet. He stood before the fire and, while Vivienne watched him, he unhurriedly removed his shoes, soaking shirt, trousers, and underclothes. Her eyes were riveted at the sight of his naked body, and wordlessly she handed him the blanket to cover himself. Instead of taking it, he dropped the blanket to the floor. He extended his hand to her.

Vivienne gazed at him, knowing what he asked of her. He saw the brief look of hesitation in her eyes, and the sudden lift in her chin. Slowly, slowly she let her blanket slip to the floor revealing herself to him as he had. She stepped toward him and took his hand. Tightly Aidan held her small hand in his, never wanting to let her go. He could not breathe at the sight of her.

They both knew where this path led, and Vivienne nodded her head in silent assent. Overwhelmed by her gift, her beauty, her sheer perfection, his heart pounded and his blood rushed in his head. He loved her.

"You are a fine figure of a man, Aidan Kavanaugh." Her voice was the barest whisper.

"You, Vivienne," he murmured, "are more than beautiful."

In the firelight her skin shone like fine alabaster. Perfectly proportioned, her petite body curved lushly in all the right places. He pulled her to him, their damp naked bodies pressing against each other, instantly creating a smoldering heat between them. He kissed the hollow of her throat and her head tilted backward. He moved lower to the swell of her breasts.

"Oh, Aidan, is this really happening?" she breathed, her voice low and filled with passion. Her hands slid over his upper arms, across his chest and his cool skin warmed beneath her tender caress.

He kissed her rosy lips softly as an answer, for he was too overcome with passion to speak. Her body felt exquisite, warm, incredible in his arms.

"Make me yours, Aidan."

"You were always mine," he murmured possessively, his body throbbing with an intense need and desire for her.

He lowered her to the floor onto the two soft blankets that they had dropped in front of the fire instead of wrapping around themselves. Astonished that he was not more terrified, for he had no idea what he was doing, he covered her delicate body with his. He brought his lips to hers once more, devouring her. His tongue swirled with hers and she gave of herself with utter abandon. Her small hands pressed into his back, her fingers caressing his skin, inflaming his already heightened desire. He wanted her more than he ever wanted anything in his life.

They melted into one another, their intense love for each other overcoming their complete lack of experience. In their little cocoon of firelight and soft blankets, they explored each other's bodies and hearts, amidst whispered words of love and fervent kisses. Hesitant touches gave way to passionate caresses, shyness gave way to boldness as they learned how to please one another.

His lips kissed a path to her fully rounded breasts and he licked and suckled her nipples until she writhed beneath him. Aidan caressed across the flat plain of her stomach, while his hand moved lower, stroking her shapely hips and creamy thighs. Gently his fingers glided between her legs, pressing into her soft flesh. Vivienne held her breath while he touched her, and she arched against his hand, wanting more.

Slowly Aidan adjusted his weight over her, rising up on his arms. Instinctively he eased himself inside her, feeling her virgin body stretch to accommodate his size. She gasped with her eyes closed tight. He stilled and her eyes fluttered open, glistening with teardrops, but she smiled reassuringly, kissing his mouth. He began to move within her gently, engulfed by the exquisite sensations she provided. His motions became more urgent, more demanding, more fervent. He could not get enough of her, did not know if he ever would. He loved Vivienne and she loved him. She was a part of him; she was his life. Unaware of where he ended and she began, he heard her cry out his name in pleasure. Suddenly complete bliss flooded his entire being and he collapsed next to her.

He held her lovingly in his arms, their legs inter-

twined. They were so interconnected he did not think
he could live without her. He wanted to keep her with
him that way forever. He knew it was time for him to
put away his childish dreams of going off to sea. They
were silly dreams, really. One day he would inherit
Cashelwood and become Lord Kavanaugh. He would
manage the estate and lands as his father had. And he
wanted nothing more than to have Vivienne share
that life with him.

"Marry me, Vivienne," he whispered fervently to her.

"You really want to marry me?" she asked in wonderment.

"More than anything I've ever wanted in my life."

"Oh, Aidan, who would I be, if not your wife?" she
asked with a smile that lit up her beautiful face.

Chapter 11

The Masked Ball

England
Spring 1870

"Come with me, Vivvy. Here comes Lord Hunting-ton and he looks about ready to devour you," Gregory Cardwell said as he took Vivienne's hand and led her from the crowded and noisy ballroom. "Let's get some fresh air."

Grateful for the respite he had offered, for she had been dancing non-stop for the past hour, Vivienne followed her cousin outside. The Duchess of Bingham's masked ball was reaching its peak and the night had been a veritable whirlwind of activity. Wearing a daringly low-cut and stylish gown of sapphire blue shot through with silver thread and a peacock feather mask over her face, Vivienne had barely had a moment to herself all evening.

Out on the portico, the cool night air carried a light breeze.

"So, explain why you don't want me to dance with Lord Huntington," Vivienne said, wondering at Gregory's reasons for finding a potential suitor lacking. "He's seems a perfectly nice gentleman."

"Oh, he is. It's just that I've heard he has certain . . . uh, predilections, shall we say?" he answered with a sly wink through his black mask. His reddish hair lent a look of boyish charm to his already handsome face, while his sky blue eyes seemed to be always alight with laughter.

"Such as . . ." she encouraged.

"Gambling and wearing women's undergarments."

"Greg, honestly!" she protested, but couldn't help laughing at his falsely innocent expression. "That's a terrible thing to say about a man. Besides, how could you possibly know such an intimate detail? About the undergarments, I mean."

He turned and leaned lazily against the balustrade, folding his arms across his chest. "I heard it from a most reliable source at my club."

"Well, I don't believe you!" Vivienne grinned in spite of herself, but she found herself observing Lord Huntington a little more closely. "Enough about him already. I don't wish to hear anymore. Let's look at ladies for you, shall we?"

"I'm not ready to settle down yet. You know that."

"Nonsense! At twenty-eight years old, of course you are! Look over there. How about that one?" Vivienne suggested gamely, tilting her head toward a sweet, dimple-cheeked brunette in a blue gown walking by the open French doors. "Now, she's very pretty."

"But as dumb as a post. I couldn't abide a stupid wife, Vivienne." He smiled charmingly at her.

"No, I don't suppose you could."

"And no offense to you, of course, but I prefer blondes."

Vivienne arched an eyebrow in his direction. "Someone more along the lines of Helene Winston perhaps?"

Gregory responded with a pained look below his mask, his teasing smile gone, his voice low. "Is it so obvious then?"

"No," Vivienne said kindly. "I think not. Maybe I'm just very observant. But Helene is in love with Aidan Kavanaugh, you know."

"She just believes she ought to be in love with him," Gregory stated with a sense of forcefulness. "Their parents wish for them to marry eventually, but nothing is definite."

"Aidan is your best friend," she cautioned.

"Yes, but he is all wrong for Helene. I'd be doing Helene a favor by taking her away from Aidan. He doesn't love her or even want to marry her, truth be told. I know for a fact that he's in love with someone else."

Surprised by his admission, Vivienne felt her pulse quicken. "You do?"

"Yes, and I think you know who I'm talking about, Vivvy."

She shook her head with a rueful little laugh. "Oh, you're quite wrong on that score, Gregory. Aidan is not in love with me. He may have been once, but not anymore."

"So there was something between you all those years ago, wasn't there?"

"Yes," she admitted reluctantly. Thank goodness he had no idea what happened yesterday afternoon! Grateful for the cover of her exotic peacock mask, she felt what she and Aidan did in the portrait gallery was written all over her face and Gregory could see it.

"Do you mind if I ask what happened when you were in Ireland?"

"It's a rather complicated story." Vivienne let out a resigned sigh. "We were friends since we were little children and fell in love as we got older, but in the end, I suppose Aidan simply didn't have enough faith in me."

"Yet he still has feelings for you. Anyone with eyes can see that. When you and Aidan sang that pretty Irish song together, there wasn't a doubt in my mind that the two of you are in love with each other."

Shaking her head, she murmured anxiously, "Don't say that, Gregory."

"Why, not? It's true."

"Even if you believe that, I promise you that nothing good will come of it. Aidan despises me." She needed to put Aidan Kavanaugh out of her thoughts and she certainly did not need her cousin filling her head with fantasies that could never come to pass.

"And you . . . ?"

"And I . . . I know better now." Vivienne stepped forward to return to the ballroom.

Gregory put his hand on her arm in a gesture of comfort, stopping her. "I think you are wrong about that, Vivienne. Things have a way of working out the way they were meant to be, and they just might work out for the both of us."

She gave Gregory a look of thankfulness and was about to add that she thought his situation would work out more easily than her own, when they were suddenly interrupted by Aunt Gwen and Uncle Gilbert.

"Hullo there, you two!" Aunt Gwen called, waving her hand gaily as they joined them on the portico. She and her husband looked charming in their coordinated black-and-white harlequin ensembles and matching masques. Lord and Lady Cardwell were a married couple who clearly still adored each other.

With his florid face and reddish beard, Uncle Gilbert boomed in his usual raucous way, "Vivienne, my dear, you are the belle of the ball! I've had more compliments about you this evening than I know what to do with."

"Thank you, Uncle Gilbert," murmured Vivienne, now used to his effusive blustering. The affection she felt for her aunt and uncle had grown quickly in the weeks she had been with them. They could never take the place of her father or Aggie, but she loved them and was grateful to be a part of their warm and loving family.

Aunt Gwen, a thoughtful and gentle woman, nodded her head enthusiastically. "It's true. And the Season doesn't officially begin until next week. I declare, Vivienne, your uncle has had quite a few inquiries about you from some very eligible gentlemen."

They were thrilled at her popularity, which they believed guaranteed a successful debut in London next week, but tonight Vivienne could not have cared less. Her family simply wanted to see her safely married to an English lord before the year was out. Yet marriage seemed so unlikely to her at this point. There had only been one man she had ever wanted to marry. And he wanted absolutely nothing to do with her now.

"Has anyone caught your eye?" Aunt Gwen asked with a mischievous smile. There were moments when Aunt Gwen smiled that way that Vivienne thought she looked so much like her father. A painful ache at missing her father tugged at her heart. She wondered what it would be like to have him there at the ball, watching over her and proudly accepting offers from gentlemen to court her.

Vivienne shook herself and stated blandly, "No, no one has caught my eye yet."

"She's very discriminating in her tastes," Gregory pointed out. "Give her more time, Mother. She's hardly met anyone yet. Wait until she gets to London at least and has had a good look around."

As Aunt Gwen and Uncle Gilbert chattered away about Vivienne's likely prospects in town, Jackson Harlow stepped out onto the portico and was greeted heartily by the Cardwells.

"I've been looking for you everywhere, Miss Montgomery. I do believe you owe me this dance," Jackson Harlow said, his masked eyes on Vivienne.

"Go on and dance, Vivienne," Uncle Gilbert said with a benevolent grin.

After they excused themselves, she followed Jackson back into the noisy and crowded ballroom. The orchestra played a familiar tune.

"You are looking particularly lovely tonight," he said gallantly taking her arm in his. "Your gown is stunning. But then, you would shine in anything."

She blushed at his flamboyant accolade and murmured, "Thank you."

It was the first time she had seen Jackson since the boating accident on the lake, and he seemed none the worse for wear. In fact, he appeared in good spirits and looked dashingly handsome in his black suit and mask, the dark color contrasting sharply with his blond brilliance. The golden brown of his eyes gleamed behind the elegant mask, making him appear somewhat roguish and he moved with a panther-like grace.

She said to him, "I trust you are completely mended from our ill-fated boat trip."

"Yes, I'm fine now, nothing but a nasty gash on the head and my injured pride. But I thank God it was only I who was hurt. I sincerely apologize for acting so irresponsibly with both Lady Helene's and your safety in my hands. I would never have forgiven myself if either of you ladies were harmed, especially due to my own recklessness."

"Your apology is not necessary, and you must not fault yourself, Mister Harlow. Helene and I both were excited at the prospect of racing and eager to win. No one had any idea we would overturn in such a manner."

"Thank you," he said. "I appreciate your graciousness."

"Your mask hides your injury perfectly, Mister Harlow. One would never notice."

"And you are the loveliest lady in attendance this evening, Miss Montgomery," he said with a charming smile.

"You are making me blush with your extravagant compliments!" she exclaimed laughingly.

"That was not my intention, although I must say the color becomes you."

Vivienne laughed and shook her head at his flirtatiousness as the music for the next dance began. Jackson took her in his arms and she felt her pulse race slightly at the contact. He was a good dancer and they marked the steps to the quadrille quite well together.

Afterward he escorted her to the refreshment area and handed her a glass of champagne in a crystal glass.

"We shall all return to London shortly. Are you looking forward to it, Miss Montgomery?"

"Yes, if only to have you find out about my father. You haven't forgotten, have you?" Vivienne asked and sipped some of the sparkling wine. Champagne had a distinct taste and she was becoming more accustomed to it. Gregory and George would be so proud of her.

"How could I forget a request of yours? Looking into the disappearance of the *Sea Star* is my first priority Monday morning. It is my honor to assist you in any way possible."

"You have no idea how much that means to me."

"I can only imagine how much it means to you and all I can hope is to bring you a measure of peace. This morning I dispatched a letter to our office, requesting that the files on the *Sea Star* be readied for me. I shall leave no stone unturned in finding evidence of what really happened to your father, Miss Montgomery. You have my word on that."

She thanked him profusely.

"And I hope I'm not too presumptuous in believing that you will allow me to call upon you when we return to London. I've already asked and been given permission by your uncle to court you, but I would prefer your consent."

Glancing up, her heart skipped a beat as she caught sight of Aidan across the room. He stood out from everyone and in spite of the black mask he wore, she would have known him just by the way he carried himself. Helene Winston, who looked lovely in a pale yellow gown that matched the color of her hair, stood beside him. They truly were an elegant-looking couple. Vivienne suddenly fought an overwhelming urge to cry.

Then Aidan's dark green eyes met hers, and even through his black mask the blatant look of disapproval he shot in her direction left her feeling sick inside, yet angered her at the same time. She didn't need him in her life and she deserved to be with a man who truly wanted her and treated her like a lady. She would show him.

She forced her gaze back to Jackson Harlow. He was about as different looking from Aidan as one could find. He grinned encouragingly at her. Jackson would be a good husband, she supposed. At least she liked him and felt comfortable with him and, unlike Aidan, Jackson Harlow regarded her as a respectable and trustworthy woman.

"I would be honored to have you call upon me, Mister Harlow."

"Nothing would make me happier, Miss Montgomery."

The gleam in his eyes sent shivers down her spine. She recognized that look of desire, but she did not know if she desired *him* in return. There was not a doubt that she desired Aidan and the thought of being intimate with Jackson Harlow left her feeling hollow, especially after yesterday. In an effort to block Aidan Kavanaugh from her mind she smiled brightly at Jackson and sipped her champagne.

Although the Earl of Whitlock made concerted efforts to ignore Vivienne Montgomery, he found himself helplessly looking for her in the crush of masked guests in the ballroom, hoping to catch a glimpse of her. When he did finally see her, he was overwhelmed with feelings of desire for her. She wore a peacock feather mask that framed her face exquisitely and lent a bit of drama to her features and was clothed in a deep sapphire blue gown shot with silver that matched her eyes perfectly. A gown cut daringly low, showing too much décolletage. She was a walking temptation.

Unable to shake off the memories of what happened between them in the portrait gallery and acutely aware of her presence in the ballroom, Aidan's eyes followed her all evening attracted by her graceful movements. He watched as she laughed raucously with the Cardwell twins, conversed with her aunt and uncle, and waltzed with the likes of Harry Gardner, Wesley Lawrence, and Peter Templeton. Oh, they were nice men, all of them. He could not fault her on that account, as much as it tried his patience to see them fawn over her. It was typical of Vivienne to have all the men after her.

After all, it was what she excelled at.

Wasn't it?

However, when he saw her dancing with Jackson Harlow, he could stand no more. The sight of Harlow's scheming hands on Vivienne's body, that beautiful body Aidan had made love to only yesterday, made him insane. To see Vivienne's pretty smiles and laughter in response to Harlow's blatant overtures only increased his torment. He wanted to punch someone, namely Harlow.

Vivienne could not become involved with Jackson Harlow. She simply could not. He wouldn't allow it. He shouldn't care what happened to her, but unfortunately he did. He felt responsible for her welfare, especially after yesterday. The girl had no idea the type of man she was flirting with. Harlow certainly did not entertain honorable intentions toward her. He would ruin her and destroy her spirit.

Only this morning he had received a dispatch from Daniel Grayson that he had finally found a witness that linked Harlow to his warehouse fire. And that witness was willing to talk to them. Aidan planned to attend to that first thing Monday morning when he returned from London.

There had been bad blood between Aidan and Harlow since Kavanaugh Enterprises won a substantial contract over Harlow Shipping International. Aidan definitely had not imagined the mysterious string of "bad luck" that plagued his company since that incident. He and Grayson suspected that Harlow and his double-crossing brothers were the responsible parties, for their company had a reputation for dirty dealing, but they had a difficult time coming up with some solid proof against the Harlow family. But at last it seemed they finally had it.

Any man who would have a warehouse burned to the ground, risking the lives of the people inside just to promote his own financial and business success, had no scruples. Besides he had heard unsavory tales about Harlow's many affairs with married women. Aidan ought to at least warn Vivienne away from Harlow. She deserved that much from him, especially after he behaved so badly with her. He could not allow Vivienne to fall into the hands of a man like that.

Vivienne.

He had been shocked by the undeniable passion that ignited between them. Crazy and reckless. Completely irresponsible. Aidan knew better than to behave that way. Vivienne at the very least deserved an apology from him for accosting her in a closet. He had treated her like a wharfside doxy. But wasn't that what she was? Oh, she denied it of course, but he didn't believe her . . . With his own eyes he had seen her with another man when she was promised to him.

She was not to be trusted.

Ever again.

Yet he could not take his eyes off her. He could not help thinking about her. He wanted to talk to her, confide in her again. He could not help wanting to be near her, to touch her, to kiss her. To make love to her again.

Instead Aidan had danced his obligatory dance with Helene Winston, afterward escorting her to the dining room, and he suddenly knew what was wrong. Everything he did with Helene seemed *obligatory*. Where with Vivienne he felt wild and reckless. He felt free. And at the same time he felt at home when he was with Vivienne. But this time he could not trust her again.

Could he?

His stomach knotted and his jaw clenched thinking about Vivienne. The Duke of Bingham's bar beckoned to him as a way to drown his feelings for her, to obliterate them with alcohol, but he did not want to go down that hell-bound path as his father had.

"Are you feeling well, Aidan?" Helene asked, obviously concerned about him, her pretty face drawn and worried. "You don't seem to be yourself this evening."

"I'm just preoccupied with some business matters," he responded noncommittally and gave her a false smile.

As she stood looking up at him with questioning eyes, Aidan felt remorse over his behavior. Helene did not deserve this careless treatment from him. She was a lovely woman and should be with a man who had true feelings for her. He'd seen her dancing with Gregory Cardwell earlier and she seemed to enjoy herself. There was a dreamy expression on her face that he had never seen before.

Perhaps there was a chance she felt the same obligatory feelings toward Aidan and would actually prefer to be with someone like Cardwell.

The more he thought about it, he realized it was quite possible that Gregory had feelings for Helene. Recalling the way Gregory rescued Helene in the lake the other day, Aidan was amazed he had not recognized it sooner. Yes, Gregory would make Helene happy in a way that Aidan never could.

Whereas Aidan needed to find a woman who could make him forget about Vivienne Montgomery. There had to be someone who could make him stop thinking about her, and unfortunately he knew it was not Helene. But as a gentleman, he also knew he had to set her free.

"Helene, may I speak with you privately?" he asked her.

"Of course, Aidan," she responded, her delicate brows raising slightly at his unusual request.

She followed him from the crowded ballroom and they stepped inconspicuously into an empty drawing room. He left the door partially open for propriety's sake, and faced her, removing his black mask. A few flickering lamps burned in the quiet room. Helene removed her mask as well, looking pretty in her pale yellow ensemble, but he could not help but notice how she lacked Vivienne's vivid coloring.

"I'm sorry, Helene . . ." Aidan began somewhat awkwardly. "I know there has been an 'understanding' between our families for some time that you and I would eventually marry. I would just like to apologize to you, for I have not been the most caring or considerate suitor to you."

Helene merely nodded her head in acceptance of his words.

"In fact, I have been a terrible suitor—"

"Oh, no, Aidan, don't say that," she protested politely.

"Let's be honest, shall we? I respect you too much and consider you too lovely and too special a woman to waste your time on me . . . You deserve much better than I can give you, Helene, and I don't wish for you to feel obligated to me by our families' wishes."

She was silent, her hands pressed together tightly.

"What I'm saying is—"

"I understand perfectly what you are saying, Aidan," she interrupted him with a soft voice. "That I am free to choose another." Her clear hazel eyes met his. He saw the strength and determination within her and that surprised him. "And so are you . . ."

He responded gently, nodding his head. "Eventually, perhaps."

She asked, "Does this have anything to do with Miss Montgomery?"

"In some respects, yes."

A small sigh escaped her. "Thank you for being honest with me. And to be perfectly honest with you as well, I must say that I feel relieved that we have ended this arrangement."

"Thank you, Helene." He sighed in relief at her calm acceptance of the situation. He had half feared hysterics from her. "I shall speak to your parents now and inform them that we have both decided that we do not suit. I am not deserving of your kindness, but, for what it's worth, you shall always have a very indebted friend in me."

She smiled ruefully and extended her hand to him. "And you in me."

He took her hand and kissed it tenderly.

Giving him one last bittersweet glance, Helene retied the ribbons of her mask. "Good night, Aidan." She turned gracefully and left the room, and Aidan felt as if a huge weight had been lifted from his shoulders.

Now he would take care of Vivienne. He would make his apologies to her for his reprehensible behavior in the portrait gallery yesterday and warn her of the dangers Jackson Harlow. He owed her that much at least. Then with his conscience cleared, first thing in the morning he would leave Bingham Hall and his past, and begin his life anew. Without Vivienne Montgomery.

Chapter 12

The Sinful Night

Susana Kavanaugh worded the note purposefully, choosing each word with consummate care, her eyes glittering in anticipation. The servant was given precise instructions on exactly when to deliver it to Mister Jackson Harlow. Timing would be critical on this. Once again, her entire plan hinged on perfect timing.

Tonight would be the night she ruined Vivienne Montgomery permanently and the miserable witch would be gone from her son's life once and for all.

Susana was no fool. She noticed the look in Aidan's eyes when he saw Vivienne. She knew what it meant because she had seen that same look before. Ten years ago. Aidan was still in love with the Irish harlot, as much as it pained her to admit it. And just how he could be in love with the likes of Vivienne Montgomery when Helene Winston was clearly his for the asking, frustrated and angered her. If only her son had better sense!

Last night during the musicale had been the final
straw. Seeing Aidan's face while Vivienne sang that
maudlin love song, made her ill, physically sick to her
stomach. Having their Irish background flaunted
before everyone, when Susana had worked years to
downplay that very aspect, left her shaking with rage.
It was too much to endure. Aidan simply could not
get involved with that woman again!

Vivienne Montgomery had been a thorn in her
side for too long. From the moment Susana met the
little baggage, she did not like her. Even as a child,
with her long black hair and fair skin, Vivienne had
an uncanny witchiness about her, as if she could see
right through Susana's exterior. Vivienne's change-
able blue eyes unsettled her and her very manner
felt disrespectful. That little Irish girl, in her thread-
bare clothes, had always comported herself as she if
she were Susana's equal! The impudence! Susana
didn't care for the old grandmother either and
blamed her as the reason Vivienne ran wild. Imagine
allowing a little girl to play and run around with a
boy as if she were a boy! But Aidan had been fascinated by the two of them, wanting to spend every
minute in their dilapidated little house. And her im-
becile of a husband allowed and even encouraged
their outlandish friendship!

Then, that pivotal summer, Vivienne blossomed
into a temptress, artfully and cleverly casting a spell
over Aidan until the poor boy lost all the reason and
good judgment Susana had fostered in him over
the years and proposed to her. Anyone could see
that Vivienne did not really love Aidan and only
wanted to better her station in life with Aidan's title
and wealth.

And here they were again.

Drastic times called for drastic measures. She could not sit idly by while her precious son ruined his life by asking that woman to marry him again. She had to take action. She had to save him from himself. As she had ten years earlier. What mother wouldn't protect her son from the clutches of the wrong woman? And Susana prided herself on being a good mother. In fact, she was an excellent mother. Aidan would thank her someday for saving him.

Now Susana needed only to wait and time her appearance perfectly. Through her own cleverness and Glenda Cardwell's assistance, Vivienne's true nature would be her undoing. By this time tomorrow, Vivienne Montgomery would be out of Aidan's life forever.

As the masked ball drew to a close and guests were either leaving Bingham Hall or retiring to their rooms upstairs, Glenda Cardwell acted according to Lady Whitlock's specific instructions. She went to her mother to complain of an illness.

"Oh dear, Glenda, what is it now?" Gwen Cardwell murmured, looking at her daughter in distracted despair.

"I said I'm not feeling very well." Glenda placed her hand over her stomach and groaned as if in terrible pain. "I think I may be sick."

"Did you eat something spoiled? I'd wager it was that salmon," Gilbert Cardwell declared loudly. "I thought it tasted funny."

"Perhaps that's what it is, Father. I did have some salmon at supper. And now my stomach . . ." She grimaced to show her anguish. "Mother, I don't wish to be alone tonight. Might I stay with you and father?"

"Aren't you a little old for that?" Gwen asked uncertainly as she touched Glenda's forehead to test for a fever. "You don't feel warm, but you do look a bit sallow."

"Mother, please. I want to be with you for a little while," Glenda pleaded with a whimper. She just had to be in her parents' room tonight. "It would comfort me."

"Well, I suppose you could come to our room and rest for a spell."

"Thank you, Mother. I truly don't feel well . . ." Glenda moaned with a bit more drama than before.

"Come then. Let's go upstairs to bed. I'll have Lizzie fetch your nightclothes from your room and we'll get you some chamomile tea."

Lord and Lady Cardwell did not see the sly smile on their daughter's face as she turned to follow them up the grand staircase of Bingham Hall.

As he was on his way to meet Annabelle Worthington for their nightly tryst, a little mobcapped maid hurriedly handed Jackson Harlow a note. She bobbed a quick curtsy to him and ran off without waiting for a reply from him. Feeling slightly annoyed as he broke the wax seal and unfolded the thick paper, he assumed it was from Annabelle canceling their encounter. Surprised to find that Annabelle had not penned the note, he read the elegantly scripted words with mounting curiosity.

Mister Harlow,

I need to speak to you on a private matter of the utmost urgency. Could you please meet me in my bed-chamber when everyone has retired? I implore you as a gentleman to be discreet. I will explain everything to you when you arrive. Please, please don't fail me.

Vivienne Montgomery

Jackson stood in stunned amazement. The note was unfathomable! The silly chit just invited him to her bedroom! What could she possibly be thinking? The note surprised him because he hadn't picked up that signal from her. Vivienne was an innocent as far as he could tell, not the type that invited men to her bed-chamber for an illicit romp in the sheets.

The note could only mean that she was in some sort of dire predicament. Although what could have happened in the few hours since he last danced with her at the ball to warrant such a drastic message, he could not imagine. The note did bode well in that she trusted him enough to ask him to help her with something that obviously worried her. And that was a good indication of her feelings. For lately he'd been doing a great deal of thinking about the lovely Miss Montgomery.

She would make a perfect wife for him.

She came from a good family and had a substantial dowry settled on her by her uncle. Aside from her undeniable beauty, it had been her smart, witty nature and complete lack of guile that attracted him to her in the first place. Not only did he find her incredibly desirable physically—and his unfailing male instinct told him Vivienne would be an unrestrained lover in bed with the right man—but he actually enjoyed the time he had spent with her. And if he married her he would have unlimited access to that luscious body of hers anytime he wanted. A little icing on the cake there. Best of all, marrying her would make stealing from her completely unnecessary, for all that she owned would become his.

She must have the deeds somewhere in her possession and it was only a matter of time before he found them. He'd do just as well to marry her and then the papers would belong to him legally.

Making Vivienne his wife would just kill his brother, too. Jackson would own the mines outright, and Miles wouldn't be able to touch them. Then Jackson could leave the infernal shipping business that he had hated his whole life. Davis and Miles could fight it out for control of their father's failing company. He'd have the money and a beautiful wife, and his brothers would be saddled with a bankrupt business. He was done with being their disrespected, undervalued little minion. He deserved more out of life than that and he aimed to get it.

He would visit Vivienne tonight and move the relationship along.

Jackson smiled with satisfaction as he continued down the corridor and made his way to his room. Annabelle would join him shortly, which would work out perfectly. He could have Annabelle first to take the edge off his growing desire for Vivienne before he went to Vivienne's room. Decidedly, he would have to play the gentleman with Vivienne, even if she were hot for him.

Intrigued by the mysterious note, he wondered what could possibly be so urgent that Vivienne would summon him to her bedchamber. That she would risk having him there only demonstrated her desire for him. The girl wanted him, but it was a hugely dangerous thing for her to do for if he were caught in her bedroom, he would undoubtedly be made to marry her. Which, of course, would only speed up the process and further his cause anyway. It would not be the way he would choose to marry her, under the shadow of a scandal, but it would serve his ultimate goal and he would attain her, regardless of the circumstances. And in a lot less time. It seemed to be a win-win situation.

And winning Vivienne Montgomery was all that mattered to him now.

He whistled gleefully as he entered his bedroom.

"What are you doing here?" Vivienne demanded in surprise later that night when Aidan knocked on her door. She had not been able to fall asleep and the late night visit from Aidan startled her. She stood with her hand still on the doorknob. "Won't your spotless reputation be tainted in my presence?"

Ignoring her barbed comment, he glanced past her inside the bedroom. "Is Glenda with you?"

"No. She's not feeling well and is spending the night with her parents in their room."

"It's good that she's not here," Aidan said. "I wish to discuss something important with you."

His eyes flickered over her and she realized she was clad only in a nightgown, her bare toes peeking from beneath the delicate pink material. Suddenly feeling self-conscious, her chin went up. "Well, I don't wish to speak with you. Now please leave my room." She motioned to close the door on him, but he braced his arm between the door and the wall, pushing it wide open and shoving her out of the way.

"I'm not leaving until I speak my peace. This is important, Vivienne, and you need to listen to me very carefully," he said, ignoring her outraged glare and striding past her into the pale yellow and rose bedchamber as if he owned it.

"I don't have to listen to you at all." Who did he think he was, storming into her bedroom of all places, in the middle of the night? But she swung the door closed behind her and turned to face him, her face alight with anger. "Especially after yesterday."

"It is exactly because of yesterday that I am here, Vivienne. I have two things I need to tell you."

She stared expectantly at him, waiting, her hands on her hips. He was still wearing his evening clothes, although his shirt collar was unbuttoned, giving him a roguish appearance that was immensely attractive. His black hair, usually so neatly combed, was slightly tousled, forcing her to curb a ridiculous desire to run her fingers through its thickness. Dark emerald eyes glittered at her behind a purposeful expression, his sensual mouth drawn in a stern line. He seemed taller and more imposing than he usually did, perhaps because she felt undressed and vulnerable in just her bare feet and simple cotton nightgown.

Aidan's voice was low but his words were rushed, "First, I want to apologize. I behaved abominably yesterday, and I'm sorry for losing control in the portrait gallery and for hurting your feelings."

"That's very noble of you, Lord Whitlock," she muttered sarcastically, crossing her arms over her chest. "What's the second thing?"

He gave her a hard look, obviously annoyed by her

airy dismissal of his apology. "What are your intentions with Jackson Harlow?" he demanded heatedly.

"What business is that of yours?" she snapped back, stunned by his question. So Aidan had noticed her dancing with Jackson Harlow earlier that evening. She felt oddly satisfied by that thought.

"You know exactly why."

"Jealous, are you?" She arched an eyebrow at his remark.

A brittle laugh escaped him. "Hardly."

If he wasn't jealous then what could it possibly be? Irritated with his possessive attitude, she asked, "What do you want from me, Aidan?"

"I want you to listen to me," he said with a deliberateness that unnerved her. He spoke his next words slowly and clearly, "Stay away from Harlow."

Vivienne shook her head in disbelief. He really had nerve to come to her bedroom in the middle of the night and think he could order her about. "You cannot tell me what to do. I don't belong to you anymore, Aidan. Remember?"

"And you belong to Jackson Harlow now, is that it?"

"What if I do?" she challenged him, her hands on her hips. His fists clenched and she knew he was angry with her. *Are you angry or jealous, Aidan?*

"I am telling you not to become involved with him. He's not the man you think he is."

"And you are?" she scoffed at him. "I don't suspect Jackson Harlow is the type who would seduce me in a closet and then humiliate me afterwards."

Aidan actually flinched at her words. "That was different . . . And this isn't about me—"

"This is all about you, Aidan. That's the only reason you are here right now. You obviously don't want me, but apparently you don't wish for anyone else to have me either."

There was a moment of silence in which they regarded each other warily. She could not help but think that he wanted her yesterday. And she had wanted him. They both knew it.

"This has nothing to do with us," Aidan began grimly. "I see the way Harlow looks at you. I saw the two of you dancing together tonight. He wants you, but I forbid you see him anymore."

"You forbid me?" she echoed him with incredulity. She would have laughed at the absurdity of such a statement if she weren't so incensed by his meaning. "You forbid me? How dare you forbid me to do anything?"

"I'm just trying to tell you—"

She interrupted him. "You have no right to tell me what to do, and you gave up any rights to me when you broke our engagement and left Galway ten years ago."

"I think I have some claim over you after all the years we've known each other and grew up together," Aidan persisted indignantly. "You have to listen to me on this, Vivienne. It's for your own good. You don't know what he's like. He is a ruthless, heartless man."

"Then he's just like you," she seethed. The stunned expression on his handsome face told her that her words hit home. He rallied quickly though.

"I see you had many admirers this evening," he taunted wickedly, his green eyes narrowing on her. "But then again you always did have more than your fair share of ardent admirers, did you not, Vivienne?"

Her eyes flew open at his insinuation that she had taken countless lovers. He thought her a loose, immoral woman. But after yesterday, what else could he think? She stared up at him angrily. "Your jealousy is quite apparent."

"Jealousy implies that one covets something," Aidan said smoothly, the lines of his face filled with disgust. "I was merely stating the obvious."

"Get out of my room. I'm not interested in anything you have to say." She glared at him. "Nor am I interested in a repeat of yesterday."

He took a step toward her and said wickedly, "Liar."

Her heart pounded in her chest at the predatory look on his face. "Get out of my room before I scream to high heaven."

His smile was seductive as he advanced on her. "You won't scream," he dared her.

"Don't try me, Aidan." The air fairly cracked with the impassioned tension between them so intensely were they aware of each other's physical presence.

"Are you going to cast a spell on me, little witch?" he taunted her, his face coming closer and closer to hers.

"I already have, don't you know?" she said fiercely as her brogue became more pronounced. "And I'll haunt you forever," she threatened him.

Her pulse quickened and there was a tingling in the pit of her stomach. He was so close she could smell the light cologne he wore, but the scent was distinctly Aidan. She was suddenly fearful of what could happen between them. Half hoping for it, half dreading it.

"Oh, I know you have haunted me, Vivienne. You've haunted me for ten years. Tortured me. That's the only reason I can explain why I care enough about what happens to you to warn you from Harlow. It's the only reason I can explain why I'm here in this room alone with you," he said low, his expression dark and forbidding. "To try to get you out of my head once and for all."

"Get out!" she cried. With both hands, Vivienne shoved as hard as she could against his broad chest.

Catching him off guard, Aidan stumbled briefly, but then steadied himself and lunged for her in an instant. She stepped away from his grasp in an agile movement and continued scurrying backward as he advanced on her. The determined look on his face caused a rush of panic to rise within her. Suddenly she felt herself falling backward as she tripped over a small footstool that was on the floor behind her. Aidan's arms grabbed her before she fell, steadying her.

"Don't touch me," she cried, although she did not resist when he pulled her closer to him, against his chest. A sense of strength and warmth radiated from his chest and the sound of his heartbeat echoed wildly in her ears. She could not breathe when she was so close to him. His muscled arms held her tightly. It should not feel so good to be embraced by him. But it did.

"If I recall, that's not what you said to me yesterday afternoon." His voice sounded huskier than usual. She could feel his warm breath on her cheek and she shivered in response.

"That was before I knew just how much you still despise and distrust me. Now, let go of me, Aidan," she demanded forcefully, unable to break his grasp on her.

"First look me in the eyes, Vivienne, and tell me that you don't want me to kiss you right now," he whispered seductively, brushing his lips across her cheek.

His mouth moved closer to her lips, and she murmured a weak protest, "Don't . . ."

"Say it, Vivienne," he whispered provocatively into

her mouth, his lips hot against hers. "Tell me not to do . . . this."

One hand held her to him, while the other moved down the length of her back. She felt his heated touch on her skin as if the sheer cotton of her nightgown were not there at all. She arched involuntarily toward him. His hand cupped her buttocks and squeezed, pressing her against the hard bulge between his legs.

She had every intention of saying no. In fact, her mind screamed it quite forcefully. But her body betrayed her. She could not resist him. She could not withstand the desire that flooded her senses. It was Aidan, after all.

Her hands clasped eagerly around his neck and her mouth sought his. He had expected resistance from her, and when she responded by placing her arms around him and pressing herself against him, he murmured an oath and kissed her deeply, his tongue entering the warmth of her mouth. She was lost then. There was something about this man that weakened all her resolve. All her restraint. As it did with him in the portrait gallery just yesterday. As it did when she was seventeen.

As it did now. So she surrendered to him.

"Vivienne, Vivienne," he murmured as he backed her slowly toward the bed.

"Aidan," she breathed his name in response, her voice tremulous and soft. She returned his kiss passionately, her tongue swirling into his mouth.

His heated kiss, his warm tongue, his gentle hands guided her where she wanted to go. Step by step they moved slowly toward the bed. Toward the inevitable. The back of her legs hit the edge of the bed and they stopped and gazed at each other. She almost could not breathe in anticipation.

Aidan unfastened the clasp on the back of her nightgown and tugged it below her shoulders. The sheer pink material slid from her body, and she stepped out of it, leaving her naked before him. He growled low in his throat and gently pushed her backward. Vivienne's pulse raced and her hands shook in response to his need.

It was happening again and she could not stop it. Would not stop it. She wanted it too desperately. She wanted him to kiss her senseless. She wanted to feel him inside of her. As they fell onto the soft mattress together, he positioned himself over her. His mouth came down over hers and they kissed hungrily, as if yesterday hadn't happened. As if this was their last chance together. And it more than likely was. But she could not let herself think where this would lead. There was no thinking now. Only feeling.

Only Aidan.

Naked beneath him, she lost herself in the feel of him on top of her. More, more, more. She wanted more from him. Yesterday was not nearly enough. In her heart she knew she could never have enough of Aidan.

Her hands found the front of his shirt and her fingers hurriedly worked the buttons free. He groaned in pleasure as her hands touched his bare skin. She splayed her fingers across his broad chest, his skin hot to the touch. His upper body was smooth and muscled with only the finest curls of dark hair covering him. Her hands stroked lower and lower, pressing against the swelling hardness in his trousers. Impatiently she tugged him free, greedy for him. Within seconds he was as naked as she was.

At one time they had known each other's bodies so intimately that now it was like coming home again. The familiarity, the possession, the knowing. It was all theirs.

He rolled over, placing her above him so she straddled his hips. Vivienne began placing hot kisses along his chiseled chest, her hands caressing him, her dark hair falling like a curtain around her. She kissed his taut stomach, inching lower and lower, below his waist until she eventually took the length of him in her mouth. Aidan groaned her name in a long hiss as she stroked his hardness with her tongue. He was heated silk and smooth firmness in her mouth.

After yesterday's frantic session in the portrait gallery, she wanted to savor this unexpected time together. Aidan must have wanted the same thing, too, for he slowed them down by urging her to release him, pulling her back up toward him. Her mouth sought his and they rolled over each other again, the heat between them making their skin hot to the touch.

With Vivienne beneath him once more, he took both her small hands in his and held them above her head, languidly lavishing kisses upon her cheeks, her neck, her breasts. Her eyes fluttered closed and she shivered in expectation. His hand moved down the length of her, cupping her, his fingers playing her expertly. Her breath mingled with his, their bodies fused together. In essence, they were home again. He released her hands and she reached around and caressed his back, running her hands up and down his firmly muscled arms and shoulders, the back of his neck, and stroking his thick hair. He kissed her breasts, licking her nipples. His mouth moved lower, along the firm plane of her smooth stomach, across the sensual curves of her hips, to rest intimately between her legs. Spreading her a little wider, his tongue delved deep within her until she squirmed restlessly. It was heaven. Deliciously wicked to have Aidan touch her so thoroughly. Until she could not breathe from the pleasure he created within her.

Suddenly Aidan's mouth and fingers ceased their decadent ministrations upon her body, and she gasped in protest. He raised himself up on both arms, positioning himself between her legs. He plunged into her, sinking deeply into her warmth, inch by delectable inch. This is what she wanted, what she had craved. What she had missed for ten years. The feel of Aidan inside of her. The pleasure was almost unbearable. She opened her eyes to find him staring at her, his eyes impassioned and questioning.

"Oh, Aidan," she murmured low, feeling as though she might cry from the swell of tangled emotions that bubbled within her.

He kissed her tenderly in bittersweet understanding. He touched her face, her hair, almost reverently. He breathed her name in the softest sigh. This wasn't like the frantic, mad coupling in the portrait gallery. This was something entirely different. This was deliberate. Soulful. Cherishing. Aidan began to move within her unhurriedly, and the sensations were so exquisite she lost herself. There was nothing except the two of them, locked in this intimate dance and nothing else in the world mattered. They gave of each other freely, savoring each touch, each kiss.

They made love dreamily, intensely, as if they had never been apart. As if they were still together. From his indolent caresses, his movements became more sensuously frantic, more urgent and a fine sheen of sweat covered his skin. Vivienne panted with exertion to keep up with him. She didn't want it to end, but heavens, she was so close . . .

A shrill scream of outrage suddenly split the silence in their room.

Frozen in place, a sick sense of dread in the pit of her stomach and the feeling of ice water in her veins, Vivienne peeked over Aidan's shoulder, as Aidan turned his head toward the source of the scream.

Lord and Lady Cardwell stood in the doorway wearing their nightclothes, their expressions horrified. Glenda Cardwell's wide mouth hung open in awe.

Chapter 13

The Second Engagement

Beneath Aidan, a mortified Vivienne released a shrill exclamation of sheer panic. Rolling off her, Aidan hurriedly concealed both his and Vivienne's nakedness with the bedspread, a feeble attempt at dignifying an extremely embarrassing situation.

Aghast, Lady Cardwell covered Glenda's curious eyes and ushered her daughter frantically from the room, while Lord Cardwell's voice thundered in outrage.

"Good God, boy, what gives you the right to take such liberties with my niece?"

"What is going on? I heard a scream as I was walking by—" Lady Whitlock called lightly, then she saw her son. "*Aidan?!*" she shrieked. Horror-struck by the sight in the large four-poster bed, her hand flew to her heart.

Aidan's low voice rang out, "If you would allow us a moment of privacy, we can discuss this later."

"There's nothing to discuss, young man! You're marrying Vivienne before the week is out!" Lord Cardwell boomed, his round face mottled in outrage.

Susana Kavanaugh fainted on the spot, her body crumpling like a rag doll to the floor. Lord Cardwell rushed to assist her, momentarily forgetting his anger while he bent over the unconscious woman at his feet. At that moment Jackson Harlow appeared in the doorway behind Lord Cardwell. He stood silently, taking in the scene with hard eyes.

"Give me a hand, Harlow!" Lord Cardwell called in irritation.

Without a word, Jackson Harlow helped Lord Cardwell carry Lady Whitlock from the room.

"I'll be back in five minutes!" declared Lord Cardwell emphatically, with a final glance at the two shamed faces in the bed.

When the door closed, Aidan dared a glimpse at Vivienne, whose cheeks were a flaming scarlet. He flung back the blanket, leapt from the bed, and began donning his clothes as quickly as he could. He found Vivienne's pink nightgown on the floor at the foot of the bed and tossed it to her.

"Get dressed," he ordered coldly, "before your aunt and uncle return."

She still had not moved, the enormity of the situation weighing upon her. She shook her head woodenly. "I don't want to marry you, Aidan."

"Doesn't look like you have much of a choice in the matter now." His voice was clipped and harsh. "Neither do I."

He knew he should be kinder to her, for they had just been caught in a most shameless and compromising position, but he was too angry with himself. It was entirely his fault. He never should have come to her room in the first place. He lost all control when he was with Vivienne and he should have known better. Now he was going to have to marry her.

He watched as she quietly dressed herself, and found himself still amazed at her beauty. Her dark hair tousled, her cheeks flushed, her lips full and red from kissing him, she climbed from the bed, donned a wrapper from her wardrobe, and stepped into a pair of slippers. But God, it had been heavenly between them a moment ago. It was an excruciatingly frustrating and unfulfilling end to what began as a pleasure he hadn't had since . . . since the last time he was with Vivienne. *Ah, hell.*

There was a forceful knock on the door. Aidan glanced at Vivienne and she nodded her head. He opened it and her aunt and uncle entered. Lord Cardwell seemed to have calmed down somewhat, but Lady Cardwell, her lace nightcap flapping, fairly flew to Vivienne's side.

"Vivienne, darling, are you all right?" She put her arms around her niece in comfort as they sat on the rose velvet divan in the corner. "I must say the two of you gave us quite a shock."

"I apologize for that," Aidan said gravely, standing like a stone statue near the mantel.

"Your mother is recovering from the upset, Lord Whitlock, and would like to see you as soon as we are through here," Lady Cardwell said to Aidan, her tone surprisingly sympathetic.

Vivienne spoke, her voice trembling. "Aunt Gwen, Uncle Gilbert, I am very sorry to have shamed you both this way."

"No," Aidan admitted forcefully. "This was not

Vivienne's doing. It is I who must take the blame for all this. It was entirely my fault. I came to her room uninvited."

"You know what must be done then," Lord Cardwell stated with an implied threat in his words. "I won't have my niece's name ruined, Whitlock. You got her into this mess. You'll have to see it through."

"Yes, of course," Aidan stated hollowly. "I will marry her."

"But I don't want to marry him!" Vivienne protested, her voice rising in panic.

"Well, missy, you should have thought of that before you invited him to share your bed," Lord Cardwell muttered crossly.

Aidan cast a glance in Vivienne's direction. She sat huddled with a pink robe clutched tightly at her throat, her long black hair spilling around her shoulders. Her aunt sat beside her, patting her back soothingly. He felt terrible. Like a cad. A villain. A rake. Guilt, sorrow, and shame flooded him. But not regret. He only regretted that it had ended so abruptly and terribly. God, that thought provoked him. How had this happened? Where was his well-renowned self-control when it truly mattered?

"I gather this was not the first time?" Lady Cardwell questioned them in a gentle tone, glancing between them.

Neither Vivienne nor Aidan could honestly deny it, so both maintained a guilty silence, avoiding each other's eyes.

"I thought as much." Lady Cardwell shook her head with a resigned little sigh. "I suspected something was between you after you sang together at the musicale. Jane even questioned me about it."

"That settles it!" Lord Cardwell declared, looking pointedly in Aidan's direction. "Since she may already be carrying your child, Whitlock, you will marry her as soon as we return to London. I shall obtain a special license on Monday."

"Yes, of course," Aidan responded in a vacant tone. He had not thought of those consequences, and he very well should have. There was no way out of this one, he was the first to admit.

Lord Cardwell continued in a voice much lower than his usual volume. "We will do this discreetly. I want no breath of scandal to taint either family's name. We shall just have to say Whitlock asked for Vivienne's hand in marriage after the ball and I agreed, although that will be difficult for some to believe since earlier tonight I gave permission to more than a few gentlemen to court her. Perhaps it will look like I'm just indulging my love-struck niece. Luckily, Harlow gave his word to keep the matter quiet. I must say he was most disappointed, Vivienne, since earlier this evening he had asked my permission to court you when we returned to London. Unlike a certain gentleman in this room."

Once again Lord Cardwell gave a pointed look toward Aidan and Aidan took his meaning. Obviously her uncle was unaware of the history between him and Vivienne. Which perhaps was just as well. For what difference did it make now?

Lord Cardwell's voice echoed in the silent room. "So consider yourselves engaged to be married as of this moment."

Aidan finally looked directly at Vivienne. The anguish in her eyes caused his heart to sink. Once, in a different time and place, Vivienne had wanted to marry him.

Chapter 14

The First Engagement

Galway, Ireland
Ten years earlier . . .

"You will marry me, won't you, Vivienne?" Aidan asked lazily as he stroked her hair gently while she lay naked in his arms.

She smiled at him, full of love and adoration, "You know I'll marry you, you daft boy."

He had asked her to marry him at least a dozen times. Overwhelmed with their love, practically consumed by it, Vivienne would have gladly followed Aidan across the burning sands of an Arabian desert if he asked her to.

Aidan had talked of nothing else but marriage since the beginning of the summer when their long-time friendship had blossomed into a full-blown love affair. He wanted Vivienne to be his wife and live with

him at Cashelwood. He wanted to be with her forever.
And Vivienne felt the same way about him. Completely in love, they spent every free moment they had
with each other.

Best friends since childhood, their relationship grew
naturally from playmates to lovers because of the special bond between them. That connection linked them
together and made them irresistible to each other.
Over the years Aidan had matured from the attractive,
dark-haired little boy who befriended her on the beach
into a broad-shouldered, tall, muscular, and classically
handsome man. And Vivienne loved everything about
him: his English-Irish blended accent, his gentle hands
that caressed her so tenderly and aroused her so easily,
his full lips that kissed her with heated passion and
whispered words of love, and his intelligent, dark green
eyes, with long, dark lashes that seemed wasted on a
boy. She loved his cleverness, his genuinely good heart,
his strong sense of responsibility, his smile . . .

"Your mother hates me though," she added gravely.
Vivienne had always tried her best to be nice to Lady
Kavanaugh, but no matter what she did, she could not
make Aidan's mother like her.

"My father already gave his blessing so there is
nothing she can do to stop our marriage now. But
she'll come around eventually, once she gets to know
you better."

"I'm not so sure about that," she muttered, snuggling closer to Aidan's naked body as they lay wrapped
in blankets upon a makeshift pallet.

"She'll be fine. Trust me. My mother is not as bad
as she appears."

Vivienne rolled her eyes heavenward, but he did not
see it. She knew the only reason they had been

granted permission to marry was because Aidan's father happened to like her, whereas his mother patently disapproved. Lady Kavanaugh could not stop the marriage, but she certainly made her feelings against it clear enough.

Aidan kissed her cheek. "We'll get married in the little chapel at Cashelwood just as soon as your father gets here."

Vivienne's father had been informed of the match and was expected in port within a month or two. John Montgomery had met Aidan many times and welcomed him as a son-in-law.

"I hope he gets here soon. Aggie's almost finished with my dress." She could not hide her excitement. "It's so lovely, Aidan, wait until you see me in it."

"I think you look perfectly lovely just like this . . ." Aidan kissed her again, as he rolled over and covered her naked body with his. His lips pressed along her throat and neck, moving lower between her breasts. She felt herself consumed by her desire for him, her breath becoming rapid and shallow.

"Aidan," she murmured weakly. "It's time to get back home." Aggie would have her hide if she missed supper again.

Reluctantly he rolled off her, laying on his back. "I know, I should be getting home, too. But I hate to leave you, my beautiful little witch. I don't want to leave our house."

For weeks they had been meeting clandestinely in an abandoned cottage on the Kavanaugh's estate whenever they could arrange to get away. Their trysts at the cottage quickly became the focal point of their time together. They referred to it as their house, and indeed they had made it so.

Aidan kissed her one last time and they unwillingly left each other's arms and began to dress. Vivienne was just lacing up her black boots, when Aidan handed a small package to her. She glanced up at him questioningly.

He merely offered her a cryptic smile, his green eyes twinkling. "It's for you."

Vivienne unwrapped the brown paper and a shiny silver chain fell into her palm. Attached to the chain was a very delicate, heart-shaped silver locket. "Oh, Aidan," she whispered, "It's lovely."

"I want to show you how much I love you. Until I can give you the wedding ring," he stated, with his handsome face so serious and full of earnestness that Vivienne felt tears in her eyes.

She stood and put her arms around him, holding tightly to the beautiful locket. "You don't have to give me anything to show how much you love me. I know that you do. I feel it every time you kiss me. Every time you look at me. I love you with all my heart, Aidan Kavanaugh, and I will be yours forever."

He kissed her and then whispered in her ear, "Open it."

She popped the spring on the little heart-shaped locket and found a miniature painting of Aidan on the inside. It was a remarkable likeness, for the artist captured his handsomeness, his eyes, the thoughtful expression on his face. Vivienne smiled with delight. Engraved on the opposite inside panel were the words, *To Vivienne with all my love. Aidan.* She had never seen anything so beautiful. "Oh, thank you!"

She stood on tiptoe to place her lips on his, and once again they lost themselves in a passionate kiss. He finally said, "Let me put it on you."

She turned and lifted her long hair so he could place the chain around her and fasten the clasp at the back of her neck. She spun back around to show him, wishing there were a mirror in the cottage.

"It looks beautiful on you, *muirnin*," he said.

A sudden tapping on the cottage door startled them both. They looked at each other in perplexed astonishment for no one knew about their meetings in the cottage. Who could possibly be knocking on the door? Vivienne silently thanked the good Lord that they were both fully dressed and hurriedly attempted to pin up her hair in an effort to look respectable.

Aidan stepped toward the door and asked, "Who is it?"

"It's me. Finley," an urgent voice declared. "There's been a terrible accident, my lord."

Aidan opened the door and there stood a servant dressed in the Cashelwood Manor livery of dark blue, a young man of about Aidan's age with sandy blonde hair. Vivienne had met him at the manor once before.

"What is it?" Aidan asked.

"I'm sorry to interrupt, my lord, but I knew you were here. Your mother has everyone out looking for you and I thought it best if I came to get you." Finley gave a pointed glance toward Vivienne, his meaning quite clear. He knew exactly what was going on in the cottage.

Vivienne felt her cheeks turn scarlet and wished her hair looked more presentable and not like she had been rolling around the pillows with Aidan. Which she had been. She stepped closer to Aidan. He took her hand reassuringly in his.

Aidan looked worried, his dark brows furrowed. "What's happened?"

Finley hesitated for a moment then said, "It's your

father, my lord. He fell from his horse. They think his neck is broken."

Following Vivienne's gasp of shock, Aidan asked, "Is he dead?"

"I'm sorry to be the one to tell you, my lord, but the answer is yes. You're needed at home right away."

"Oh, Aidan," Vivienne murmured, squeezing his hand with hers. Aidan had no great love for his father, for he had been a harsh man, but still it must hurt to learn that he died. Aidan's expression became hard and drawn, and he suddenly seemed a thousand miles away from her.

"Finley, will you please escort Miss Montgomery back home? I'll return to Cashelwood immediately." Aidan turned to Vivienne and kissed her cheek, whispering, "I'll come see you just as soon as I can."

Vivienne's heart dropped to her stomach and a sense of foreboding crept over her as the three of them left the cottage. Finley, very loyal and discreet, walked her home, although she was perfectly capable of going alone. However, she didn't wish to upset Aidan at such a time, and she let his servant escort her back to town.

"So you and Aidan are marrying soon?" Finley asked in an attempt at conversation.

"Yes," Vivienne responded distractedly, thinking only of Aidan. "As soon as my father arrives."

"That's nice," he commented.

They said little more to each other on the walk home. She thanked him politely and he returned to Cashelwood.

As soon as she walked in the front door, Aggie said, "I heard about Lord Kavanaugh's terrible accident. It's all anyone is talking about this afternoon. How is our Aidan doing?"

"He's handling it well, I suppose. I didn't really have much of a chance to discuss it with him after we heard the news. Then he rushed home."

Aggie shook her head, her black hair pulled into a neat bun, "The poor lad. It's difficult to lose a parent. As you well know, Vivvy."

Vivienne nodded in agreement, although she could only imagine how Aidan was feeling. She never even knew the mother who had died giving birth to her, yet still felt her mother's absence keenly after seventeen years. But Aggie had been a wonderful substitute for her and Vivienne could not wish for more than that. Her grandmother had been everything to her since her father was away most of the time. Her upbringing with Aggie had been unusual, for Vivienne had more freedoms than most girls her age. She had been raised to read, write, and, most importantly, think for herself.

Aggie placed a cup of hot tea in front of her as they sat at the kitchen table. "I assume that lovely bit of silver is from Aidan?"

Vivienne could not help the smile that lit her face and her hand fluttered to the locket resting against her chest. "Yes. He gave it to me this afternoon. His picture is in inside." She opened the locket to show her grandmother.

Aggie stood and inspected the locket closely. "That's a fine likeness of him."

"He was so sweet to give it to me."

"You know," Aggie stated softly, closing the locket and adjusting it on Vivienne's neck, "she'll cause a bit of trouble now."

"Yes, I've thought of that," Vivienne said soberly. In fact, she'd thought of nothing else during her silent walk home with Finley. With Aidan's father dead, Susana Kavanaugh was bound to forbid the marriage. "What do you think will happen, Aggie?"

Aggie sat back down and rested her elbows on the table, clasping her hands together, in her usual thoughtful position. "Oh, I think she'll fuss and make Aidan's life a living hell, but in the end, what can she do? He's a grown man. He had his father's permission and blessing before he died. Everyone knows he's marrying you. And now he's the new Lord of Cashelwood and he can do as he likes. If I know nothing else in my life, Vivienne, I know that boy loves you. I've no doubt of that. I think he fell in love with you the first time he stepped into this house."

Aggie reached out and squeezed Vivienne's hand, her voice warm and soothing as she continued, "I won't lie to you either. It will be very difficult, marrying a man whose mother despises you. Susana Kavanaugh is a bitter and unhappy woman who believes you are not good enough for her son. But you and Aidan are young and strong and love each other. You are destined to be together, so it will happen. One way or another . . ." Aggie's voice drifted off and a strange look came over her face.

"What is it?" Vivienne asked, worried by her grandmother's pained expression.

She answered softly, "I don't know exactly. I just had a feeling about you and Aidan, but I must be mistaken."

"Tell me."

"I don't believe you will marry here in Ireland after all."

What could Aggie be thinking of? Where else would they get married but here in Galway? Her father was coming home. Aggie had made her a beautiful wedding dress. Of course things would have to be postponed for a while to mourn Aidan's father, but they would get married. It was what they both wanted. "But we will marry, won't we? I don't care where I marry Aidan as long as we get married. I love him," Vivienne said anxiously.

"You will marry him, of that I'm certain."

At her grandmother's words, Vivienne breathed a sigh of relief. Yet, she could not shake the feeling that something dreadful was going to happen.

A persistent drizzle sprinkled from the low, gray clouds during the funeral for Lord Joseph Kavanaugh. Vivienne sat beside Aggie in the Cashelwood chapel to pay their respects. Aidan was seated with his mother near the altar. Dressed in black, but unable to conceal the joy in her eyes behind her dark veil, Susana Kavanaugh attempted to give the appearance of a grieving widow. She may have fooled the chaplain but she did not fool Vivienne in the least.

The large turnout of mourners did not surprise her, for although he had been a harsh father to Aidan, Joseph Kavanaugh possessed a personality that inspired great devotion among his tenants. He was very popular with the locals as opposed to Susana, who was generally disliked, if not despised, by all who knew her.

In his own gruff way, Joseph Kavanaugh had grown on Vivienne and she had liked him, regardless of his crustiness and overindulgence in drink. She had to give the man a wide margin of error, for being married to a woman like Susana would turn any man into a miserable beast. At first Vivienne suspected that Lord Kavanaugh only approved of her betrothal to

Aidan merely to spite his bitter wife, but she came to believe that he genuinely liked her for herself before he died. If there had been any doubt, it lifted one of the last times she had seen him.

"Vivienne, darling, you're so pretty, if I were twenty years younger, I'd marry you myself," Joseph said during an interminably tense and formal dinner at Cashelwood one night after Aidan asked her to marry him.

Ostensibly, Susana had invited her, but Vivienne knew that Aidan had pressured his parents to spend more time with her. He had also wanted Vivienne to become more comfortable being at Cashelwood, for one day soon it would be her new home. That night she sat in the elegant dining hall at the highly polished table set with fine china, sterling silver utensils, and crystal wine goblets and thought of Aggie's cheery kitchen with mismatched chairs and chipped tea cups. Her life would change in more ways than she first realized once she became Aidan's wife.

"Thank you. That's the nicest compliment I've had in a long time, Lord Kavanaugh," Vivienne responded to her future father-in-law with a genuine smile.

"It's too late, Father." Aidan winked at her. "She has already promised to marry me."

"She's a good woman, Aidan," Joseph said approvingly. "She'll make a good wife to you."

"I know she will," Aidan agreed. "That's why I asked her."

"Have a big family, Aidan," Joseph advised. "I want lots of grandchildren running about the place. It will be good to hear laughter in the house again."

Vivienne blushed and could not meet Aidan's gaze.

Susana grimaced. "Could we please discuss something else besides marriage?"

"Marriage is not your mother's favorite topic, Aidan," Joseph Kavanaugh laughed gruffly then took a long sip of wine. "Choose something else for us to talk about, Vivienne."

Vivienne glanced uncomfortably between Aidan's parents. Amazed that two such disparate people as these two could have created a man as wonderfully loving and caring as Aidan bewildered her. There was a faint resemblance in Joseph Kavanaugh's green eyes that matched Aidan's, but Susana's face seemed prematurely aged and gray. Vivienne could see not a shred of similarity to her cold, sour features on Aidan.

But she could feel Susana Kavanaugh's blatant disapproval of her. She supposed that Susana would not have liked anyone whom Aidan loved more than his mother, but Vivienne sensed an intense and unfounded dislike from the woman that unnerved her. Even when she was a little girl, she instinctively knew where she stood with Susana Kavanaugh. Vivienne almost felt sorry for the woman, for it seemed her husband and her beloved son cared more for Vivienne than for Susana. And Susana was extremely aware of it. No one liked her. Her husband certainly didn't. Still, she was going to be her mother-in-law, so Vivienne made an effort.

"Please tell me what it's like in London, Lady Kavanaugh," Vivienne suggested brightly. "I've never been, but I hope to visit there one day."

For one brief instant the glimmer of a smile hovered near Susana Kavanaugh's tightly drawn mouth. "You cannot imagine a city as wonderful as London," she began.

Joseph guffawed loudly, his once handsome features bloated by drink. "Well now, little lady, you've hit on a topic that my wife is bound to like. But I for one am sick to death of hearing about how inferior we in Galway are to the high and mighty who live in London."

Susana stood up, and slammed her napkin down on the table angrily. "I'll not be made fun of at my own table, Joseph. I've had enough. If you'll excuse me." She turned and left the room in a huff, while Joseph laughed heartily and Aidan ran after his mother.

It had been a disastrous evening, although Aidan promised her that the situation would improve. She thought back to when she first met him, when Aidan referred to Cashelwood as a prison and how desperately he wanted to escape. She understood perfectly why he wanted to stow away on a ship.

Now, at Lord Kavanaugh's funeral, she felt the tremendous loss of her staunch ally at Cashelwood. As they filed out of the church that rainy day, she caught Aidan's eyes, and he nodded to her discreetly. She loved him so much. He looked responsible and dutiful escorting his mother, appearing incredibly tall and handsome in his black suit. She was proud of him and proud to become his wife. Meeting his family only reinforced how much Aidan needed her to bring warmth and love into his life. He was giving her so much materially, but she knew what she was bringing to their marriage was equal to, if not worth more than, the wealth Aidan possessed.

Then she felt Lady Kavanaugh's cold glare upon her. The utter malice in her brittle gray eyes stunned her. If she were not mistaken, there was a gleam of triumph in them as well.

A week passed after Joseph Kavanaugh's funeral before Vivienne and Aidan were able to meet once again at their little cottage. As usual Aidan sent a note telling her when to meet him there. When she arrived Aidan wrapped his arms around her and lifted her off the floor, swinging her in a wide circle. Placing her back down, he kissed her as though he had not seen her in months. "Lord, I've missed you."

"I've missed you, too." She leaned her head against his chest, feeling safe and protected in his arms. He had a way of holding her that made her feel cherished and utterly loved. She could not think of a lovelier place to be than in Aidan's arms. "How have things been at home?"

Aidan sighed heavily. "Complicated." They moved to their makeshift pallet on the floor that was their only means of furniture in the place, aside from the small table and two chairs in the corner. Aidan lay propped up on pillows and Vivienne cuddled into the crook of his arm.

"Tell me what's happening, Aidan. It's been torture to see you at the funeral and afterwards and not be able to really talk to you. Has your mother been trying to stop our wedding?"

"I thought she might, but she hasn't said a single word about it. Oh, she hasn't changed her mind, she still disapproves, but she hasn't put up any resistance in the usual way. Now that my father is dead, she wants to move back to England."

Vivienne's heart leapt at the prospect of Susana Kavanaugh leaving Ireland for good, and she could not help but smile. She had not been relishing the idea of sharing a house with Aidan's mother once they married. Even a house as large as Cashelwood. With Lady Kavanaugh out of the picture, her future as Aidan's wife just became that much sweeter. "So let her go."

"I would, but we received some news yesterday." He paused, hesitant to tell her.

Sensing his unwillingness, her brows furrowed in concern. What could be so terrible that he did not want to tell her? "What is it?"

"My father's uncle is the Earl of Whitlock. Sadly he, his wife, and their only son died in a fire last month. We just received the news today."

"That's tragic," Vivienne whispered in sympathy, yet confused by the topic. "But what does that have to do us?"

He took a deep breath and stated, "It seems I am the new Earl of Whitlock."

"Aidan!" Vivienne cried in surprise, her mind spinning. "You're jesting?"

"No, I'm not. The title should have passed to my father, but with him gone, I'm next in line. Much to my mother's delight, I must return to England to claim my title and estates, and apparently my quite considerable fortune."

Silent at first, a thousand thoughts spun through her head. "What will that mean for us? Will we still get married?"

"Yes, I'm still going to marry you, *muirnin*." He gave her a comforting squeeze and kissed the top of her head. "It also means that we shall have to marry a little sooner, perhaps before your father arrives, because I need to get to England as soon as I can."

"So we would have to leave Ireland? Forever?" She could not control the unease in her voice.

"Would you mind terribly?" he asked softly but also in a persuasive tone.

She instinctively knew he wanted her to agree with him. Although she would miss Aggie and Ireland, she answered him honestly, for Vivienne always spoke her mind. "As long as I'm with you, I don't care where we live."

Aidan kissed her thankfully. "You don't know how happy that makes me, Vivienne. I was so afraid you wouldn't want to come with me. That you would never want to live anywhere but here."

"I don't want to be anywhere that you're not. I don't like the idea of leaving Aggie, but she would be the first one to tell us to go. And we can always come back to visit. Can't we?"

He gave her a grin of pure delight that reached up to his eyes and said, "Any time you want, my love."

Vivienne loved when he looked at her that way. "Then there is no problem."

He sighed in relief as if a heavy weight just lifted from his shoulders. "My mother said you would fight me on this, that you were stubborn and would never agree to marry me if we had to live in England and—"

Vivienne interrupted him, pulling away from his embrace and sitting up straight. "Your mother does not know me well enough to predict my reactions to anything, Aidan. In fact, she hates me. Please don't ever listen to her where I am concerned."

He began to sit up as well, "Yes, but she was just—"

"She was just meddling and trying to turn you away from me is what she was doing," Vivienne contested vehemently.

"That's not true." He placed his hand on her shoulder. "And she doesn't hate you."

"Aidan, don't be daft! You're mother has hated me from the minute she met me!"

"Don't say that!" he protested.

"I'm not from a wealthy and titled family. She looks

down upon Aggie and me. She thinks my father is in the worst sort of profession. Although I'm half English, I might as well be all Irish in her eyes. I'm not good enough for you by her standards. Although I doubt anyone would be."

He just couldn't see his mother for the bitter woman she was. Susana Kavanaugh was trying to cause trouble, just as Aggie said she would. Vivienne supposed she couldn't fault Aidan for loving his mother, but it stung a little that he would have believed his mother over her.

"She's just upset at losing her husband," Aidan explained.

Vivienne laughed aloud. "Aidan, you cannot honestly believe that! Your parents despised each other and your mother has hated me long before your father died. And will for a long time after to be sure."

Aidan stood up and walked to the small window, looking out pensively. "I don't want her to hate you, Vivienne."

All the anger went out of her. "I know . . ." she said sympathetically.

She did not want to let Susana Kavanaugh come between them this way. She would not allow her to have that victory. Vivienne would simply have to get used to dealing with his mother, because she was certainly going to be a part of their lives, like it or not. Besides, she couldn't bear to be angry with Aidan.

Feeling contrite, she went to him and apologized. "I'm sorry for overreacting. I know it's not your fault that your mother is the way she is."

"I'm sorry too." He kissed her cheek tenderly, looking at her with an earnest expression. "Things are going to be all right, Vivienne. Trust me, please. I love you too much to let anything come between us."

"I love you too, Aidan. And I will come to England with you." She couldn't help but add with a mischievous grin, "I love you so much I'm willing to put up with your mother."

Aidan laughed ruefully at her remark and gave her a playful swat on the bottom.

She kissed him, pulling her to him. They began to kiss intensely, their passions rising, as they always did when they were together. He slowly began to unbutton the front of her dress, tracing a path with his fingers between her breasts. Once again they made love in their little cottage.

Less than a week later Vivienne received a note from Aidan asking her to meet him at their cottage. She told Aggie she was going for a picnic with Aidan, and she raced across the green fields of grazing sheep to the cottage. She arrived before he did, bringing a little picnic lunch for them, and she laid it out on the small round table that stood next to a pair of chairs in the corner. Then she filled the vase on the mantel with fresh pink roses she had brought from her garden.

She loved their little afternoon trysts. It was the only time they were ever completely alone together and she cherished these moments.

Impatient for Aidan to arrive, she plumped the pillows on their makeshift pallet and straightened up their little one-room cottage. Recalling how thrilled they were when they discovered it, she smiled dreamily. A typical white-washed dwelling with a thatched roof and a green door, the secluded cottage had been abandoned on the Kavanaugh property, and Aidan had claimed it as their private retreat. Secretly they made it more habitable and Vivienne had swept and scrubbed the floors and brought in little touches to make it more comfortable and romantic.

Daydreaming about being Aidan's wife, she longed for the time when she could sleep in his arms all night long and wake up to his sweet kisses at dawn. One day she would hold their baby in her arms. She loved Aidan completely and without reservation and he filled her with joy and happiness. Soon, very soon, he would be her husband and they could spend every day and night together and wouldn't have to meet in secret at the little cottage.

Or maybe they would, just for the fun of it . . . This long summer in their cottage had been incredibly magical and beautiful, and in many ways she would miss it.

She anxiously wondered what was keeping Aidan and grew bored. In anticipation of his arrival, she undid the top two buttons on the front of her dress and giggled thinking of his delight when he saw her. Getting into the spirit of her little game, she unpinned her hair, shaking the long dark locks loose, knowing that Aidan loved it when she wore it down. She removed her shoes and rolled down her stockings, setting them neatly in the corner. Bravely she unfastened a few more buttons down the front of her dress.

For a fleeting instant she toyed with the idea of removing her clothes completely and greeting him naked. Modesty won out. Instead Vivienne quickly removed her dress, recklessly slipped off all her underclothes, and put the dress back on. The deep blue dress had a demure neckline and she knew the color emphasized her eyes dramatically. Keeping the dress unbuttoned and open to the waist created an impressive view, exposing her ample breasts just to tempt him. She reclined on the pallet, in what she believed to be an inviting pose. She smiled thinking of Aidan's reaction when he saw her.

Suddenly the door opened, and she was momentarily blinded by the sunlight streaming through the entrance. The door closed, but it was not Aidan standing there.

Horrified, she clutched the front of her dress together and jumped to her feet.

"Nicky Foster! What in the world are you doing here?" she exclaimed breathlessly.

He smiled lazily at her. "Coming to see you, darling."

Vivienne burst out laughing at his remark. "Get on home, Nicky."

She had known Nicky Foster her whole life. In fact when they were children he used to tease her and called her a witch, but she had been aware for some time that he was sweet on her. Being a few years older than her, he had never paid much attention to Vivienne until last year. Tall and handsome with fair skin, auburn hair, and clear blue eyes, he was a decent, hard-working, and straightforward man. All the girls she knew from town were mad for him and competing with each other to be his wife. Nicky had escorted her to a few local dances and socials and they had a nice enough time together. She even allowed him to kiss her on the lips once or twice.

Of course, that was before Aidan came home from school, and her whole life changed that day on the beach when out of nowhere Aidan kissed her. Now that was a kiss . . . a kiss that left her senses reeling and left her without a doubt that she loved Aidan. Since then her heart had belonged exclusively to Aidan and she had not given Nicky Foster another thought. But now, here was Nicky in their secret little cottage. With her half-dressed.

"Did you follow me here?" she asked him somewhat irritably, wondering how he knew she was there. She had always been very discreet, and so had Aidan.

He grinned at her, his lazy smile wide and full. "I'd follow you anywhere, Vivienne. You know that, don't you?"

She shook her head ruefully. "Oh, Nicky, I haven't been very fair to you, have I?"

"I can make you happier than Kavanaugh can," he said, taking a step toward her. He possessed a beefy build with powerful muscles beneath his dusty work shirt. "We're the same kind of people, you and me."

"I love Aidan," she stated simply for that explained it all.

"You just love his money and fancy title. But he's not one of us. He's a gentleman. You don't belong with him and his kind. Besides, I know how it was when I kissed you. You're the girl for me, Vivienne."

She laughed at him again. "Oh, and I suppose you've said the same things to Bridget McDermott and Eileen Judge, for I saw you out walking with them just last week."

He reached out a hand to her, his voice serious and intent. "They don't mean anything to me. I've had to save face since you've been with Kavanaugh all summer, but it's you I love."

She took his hand and squeezed it gently, feeling a little guilty for how she had brushed him off. "Oh, Nicky. I'm sorry. But I love Aidan, and he loves me. You must know we're getting married."

Before she realized what he was doing, he pulled her to him so that she was pressed against his solid chest, his thick arms locked around her. "So I've heard. But you're not married. Not yet, anyway."

His mouth lowered over hers and he kissed her hard, in spite of her pushing against him. Vivienne could not believe this was happening, and if not for the insistent bruising force of his mouth on hers she would have laughed at the absurdity of Nicky thinking he could take her away from Aidan. Aidan, who would be there any minute and would set Nicky straight once and for all.

Nicky continued kissing her, his tongue forcefully entering her mouth. She kept trying to push him away, but he was a big fellow and Vivienne was no match for him in physical strength. She did not realize that, as she struggled against him, she had lost the grip on the front of her dress. Nicky, however, noticing her bare breasts, became even more aroused, and lowered her roughly to the pallet in one swift movement.

Apprehension engulfed her, for she had been waiting to seduce Aidan and ended up with Nicky Foster on top of her with his tongue in her mouth and his big hands on her breasts. That would teach her to play the temptress. Torn between screaming and laughing, for she couldn't for one minute think that Nicky actually meant to hurt her, she pushed at him with her hands.

"Nicky, please," she implored, out of breath.

"Vivienne!" Aidan's outraged voice echoed through the cottage.

Nicky turned his head slowly in the direction of the doorway, but did not let go of her. Vivienne twisted beneath him to see Aidan's shocked expression as he stared at her. Until the day she died she would never forget the look on his face as he saw her half-naked with Nicky Foster on top of her. His green eyes were wounded, hurt, angry. He stared at her accusingly, disbelievingly. His face was a portrait in absolute devastation.

With a sickening sense of dread, she realized what Aidan perceived was happening. Before she could blink, he whispered her name, turned, and left the cottage.

She called to him frantically while Nicky finally had the good sense to let her go. With trembling hands she pulled her dress together. The look on Aidan's face scared her more than she had ever been scared of anything in her life. She needed to talk to Aidan and explain, make him see that it wasn't what it looked like. Maybe he just needed some time to cool down, and then he would see how silly the whole thing had been.

"I'm sorry, Vivienne," Nicky said haltingly. "I had no idea . . ."

She looked at him blankly, her mind reeling with the implications of what just happened. Surely Aidan didn't believe she was really with Nicky Foster. "Go home, Nicky."

He turned toward the door but looked back at Vivienne and apologized again.

"Just go," she whispered.

"If you need anything, I'm here for you." He looked at her regretfully, then went out the door.

For a split second, she thought that was an odd statement to make, but it barely registered. As she dressed with shaking hands and a knot in her stomach, she reproached herself for trying to act the temptress for

Aidan. If she had been properly attired and had been more forceful against Nicky's overtures instead of laughing at him, Aidan would not have jumped to the conclusions he obviously had. After she had fixed her hair and was dressed completely once more, she slowly and carefully gathered up the remnants of their forgotten picnic lunch. She followed the meandering path to Cashelwood Manor deep in thought.

The way Aidan reacted had frightened her.

The liveried servant who answered the door when she knocked confirmed her worst suspicions when he informed her that Lord Kavanaugh did not wish to see her. On the verge of tears, she pleaded with the man to please tell Aidan that she needed to see him desperately. He shook his head imperiously and closed the door.

For the first time in her life, Vivienne did not know what to do. She needed to explain to him, but it seemed Aidan did not want to listen to her. Hiding behind his servants to turn her away, he wouldn't even face her. He had dismissed her and that angered her. How could he believe such an awful thing of her? That she would cast aside his love for another so easily? Her sadness then turned to anger as she marched home. Let him be stubborn then! If he was so quick to doubt her love for him, well, then . . . Maybe he didn't deserve her love!

By the time she arrived at her doorstep she had worked herself into a fine state of rage. Slamming the door shut, she startled poor Aggie, who jumped up from the sofa where she'd been sewing.

"Good Lord, child, you gave me a fright!" the older woman asked edgily, her sharp eyes taking in the stormy look on her granddaughter's face. "What's gotten into you?"

"Aidan Kavanaugh's gotten into me, that's what! He's impossible! That high and mighty—" Vivienne suddenly stopped, burst into tears, and ran to her grandmother. She cried as she had never cried before in her life. All the fear, hurt, and confusion of the last hour poured from her without restraint.

Aggie wrapped her arms around Vivienne and the two of them sank to the flower-print sofa. Vivienne sobbed into her grandmother's chest, taking comfort in her loving and reassuring arms, arms that had held her since she was a baby. Her gentle, care-worn hands stroked Vivienne's back in long, soothing motions.

"There, there," Aggie crooned softly. "I'm sure it's not as bad as all that."

"He won't talk to me," Vivienne cried, barely getting the words out between wrenching sobs. "How can I explain anything to him if he won't even see me?"

"Explain what?"

At that Vivienne sobbed louder. How could she possibly describe to Aggie what took place in the cottage when she wasn't even sure herself? It all happened too quickly. Waiting for Aidan. Nicky Foster appearing out of nowhere and relentlessly making advances on her. The sheer ridiculousness of the thought of her and Nicky together. Her protests against him. And Aidan standing before her, a mixed expression of complete revulsion and utter devastation. Her own panic and horror. That afternoon would haunt her forever.

Aidan hadn't come to her rescue. He'd believed her to be with Nicky Foster willingly.

The fact that Aidan wouldn't see her terrified her.

His action seemed final. The signal of the end of everything between them. Cold fear clenched her stomach with the dreadful certainty that she had lost Aidan forever. Aidan whom she loved more than life. Aidan who was supposed to marry her.

Aggie rocked her back and forth, but Vivienne continued to sob, incapable of speaking and unable to explain to her what had gone so terribly wrong.

Vivienne attempted to see Aidan the following day and was once again coldly turned away from Cashelwood Manor. She raced to their cottage, hoping against hope that he might come to look for her there. When she saw that the windows had been boarded up and the door padlocked, her heart broke. Their little cottage was not theirs any longer. He had completely shut her out, without even giving her a chance to explain.

By the third day she went to Cashelwood determined to see him even if she had to break down the front door. Instead, she received devastating news from the skeleton staff left to tend the manor.

Aidan and his mother were gone. They had left for England that morning. The house was packed up and they were gone for good. After everything that happened between the two of them, Aidan left without so much as a word of goodbye to her.

For days Vivienne cried inconsolably, torn between fits of outrageous anger and heartbreaking grief that he could so easily walk away from her, from what they had, from their plans for their life together without a backward glance. Without even letting her explain. She took to her bed, not leaving her room, and cried.

She could not eat a thing for the heartbreak left her physically incapacitated, and she slept fitfully, waking in the middle of the night to cry, and aching with longing for Aidan to hold her in his strong arms again.

After a week Aggie finally could take no more and dragged Vivienne out of bed, made her bathe, and forced her to sit at the kitchen table.

"That's enough now," Aggie declared firmly. "I'll not abide any more of this self-pity. You must get up and face the world again. It's not doing anyone any good to behave this way."

"I just want to die," Vivienne whimpered, wiping her red and swollen eyes with a handkerchief.

"Be careful what you wish for. You might just get it." Aggie quipped as she set a bowl of hot stew in front of her.

"Then I wish Aidan dies."

Aggie laughed heartily at that. "There's a bit of your spirit back!"

"I just miss him," Vivienne began plaintively. "I just don't understand—"

"Enough." Aggie interrupted in an authoritative tone that brooked no argument. "You're not hurting him with these histrionics. He's not here to care if you cry your eyes out or if you starve yourself to death. You're only hurting yourself. We've been over and around and under all of this a thousand times this week and we may never know what prompted our Aidan to take the steps he did. He was definitely wounded by seeing you with Nicky Foster. But he's gone now and he may never be back. So get used to it. Get on with your life."

"But you said he loved me, Aggie. You said we would get married."

A shadow crossed Aggie's fine features and a pained expression appeared in her knowing eyes. Slowly she nodded her head. "That I did, my dear, but I must have been mistaken."

Vivienne began to weep into her handkerchief again, overcome with emotions and distress.

"That's enough, I said," Aggie repeated, but more kindly than she had before, taking Vivienne's hand in hers. "You must regain your strength, Vivienne. I raised you to be a strong woman. And you're going to need your strength now. You have some other troubles to face."

Looking at her grandmother through her streaming tears, Vivienne asked, "What could possibly be worse than losing Aidan?"

Aggie gave her a pointed look. "Facing the scandal that Aidan left in the wake of his disappearance."

Puzzled, she questioned with a sniffle, "What scandal?"

"Oh, it's all over town that Aidan caught you half-dressed in Nicky Foster's arms, called off the wedding, and fled to England. The talk has been terrible about you and how it's my fault because I've let you run wild all your life. And Nicky's strutting about town like a proud peacock. He's been by a few times to see you while you were sulking in your room, but I sent him away. Although he had the decency to ask me for your hand in marriage."

Stunned enough to stop crying, Vivienne breathed deeply. "Oh, this is too much. What should I do?"

"You have some decisions to make. You can accept Nicky Foster's proposal of marriage—"

"I will never marry Nicky Foster!" she exclaimed vehemently.

"You can accept his proposal," Aggie continued as if Vivienne had not spoken, "and get on with your life, or know that no man in this town will ever marry you believing you have been with Aidan and Nicky both."

Vivienne's chin went up. "I don't care. I don't want to marry any of them anyway. I don't want to marry anyone but Aidan," her voice caught in her throat, "and if I can't have him, then I won't ever get married."

"I figured you'd say as much," Aggie said with a deep sigh. "I know you too well. If you marry Nicky, you would have a chance of respectability and a family of your own. By choosing not to accept his proposal, you are ruined. You must understand that you are re-signing yourself to a very lonely life, forever regarded as a tarnished woman."

Nothing Vivienne had ever done with Aidan had ever felt wrong or immoral. They were friends, they loved each other deeply, and were getting married, so that made their visits to the cottage justifiable to her. Aggie had raised her unconventionally, to be sure. She was brought up to think for herself and to be strong and independent. And even though Vivienne never outright told her grandmother what she and Aidan had been up to at the cottage, she was aware that Aggie knew. Aggie never said a word for or against Vivienne's discreet trysts with Aidan. That's just how she was, leaving it up to Vivienne and her own conscience to decide what was right, and Vivienne had never believed for an instant that she and Aidan were doing anything wrong. But now, seeing how it appeared to others with a less tolerant perspective, Vivienne felt ashamed for the first time, but she shook her head defiantly. "I haven't done anything wrong. I love Aidan. We were going to be married in a few weeks."

Again Aggie patted her hand in comfort. "I know, Vivienne, I know. But you must see how it looks to everyone in town."

Sadly she nodded her head. "It's not fair."

"Life is not fair, my dear," Aggie said pithily, but not without some compassion. "It won't be easy, to be sure, but we'll get by just fine. You come from strong and hearty stock, Vivienne. You'll survive this."

Vivienne nodded her assent halfheartedly, unsure if she had any strength at all.

Aggie continued pragmatically, "But let's just hope your reckless ways with the new Earl of Whitlock didn't leave you with a baby to remember him by."

Fully humiliated now, Vivienne cringed, placing her hand on her abdomen. In spite of the shame, a little part of her hoped that she did carry Aidan's child, for then she would be able to keep a part of him with her to love forever.

In time, however, she learned that she would not have a child of Aidan's. In time, she refused Nicky Foster's entreaties to marry him. And in time she became accustomed to the cool glances and disapproving frowns from the righteous folk in town. She was no longer invited to socials or asked to dances by the young men, because they expected other favors from her instead.

So she spent her days living an isolated life in Galway with her grandmother and keeping to herself. The lonely days spun into weeks. Then months. Then years.

Chapter 15

Consequences

England
Spring, 1870

"What were you thinking? Honestly, Aidan, you were naked in that harlot's bed in front of my very eyes!"

Susana Kavanaugh railed at her son, placing her hand dramatically on her heart as if the very memory of what she had seen eclipsed the actual event. She paced back and forth in front of him, her movements sharp and frantic. Usually pulled tight from her face, her gray hair now splayed out crazily in all directions and her dark blue dressing gown swirled wide about her slippered feet as she made each turn to walk back the other way.

"I was humiliated and disgraced tonight in front of Lord and Lady Cardwell, as well as Mister Harlow. And now . . . Now you are expected to marry that horrid girl!"

Aidan sat stony faced in his mother's room after

answering her summons. She had recovered quickly from her fainting spell in Vivienne's room and was fully enraged by the time he arrived. She began her tirade the minute he stepped inside but, then again, he had not expected anything less from her.

She could not be any angrier with him than he was with himself. He now had to marry Vivienne Montgomery. Caught with his hand in the cookie jar, so to speak; there was no gentlemanly way out of it. He had agreed to marry her, sealing his fate with hers forever. He'd been recklessly foolish with Vivienne, not just once but twice this week, and he knew full well the risk he ran if they were caught together. Now Vivienne would be his wife. His gut clenched at the thought and his head throbbed.

"How am I supposed to face the Winstons after this? Why couldn't you have been caught with Helene instead?" his mother wailed in impotent rage. "You simply cannot marry Vivienne Montgomery!"

After dealing with Vivienne and Lord and Lady Cardwell, Aidan was exhausted from the events of the evening and had very little patience left for his mother. "If it's any consolation, Mother, she doesn't want to marry me any more than I want to marry her."

And that stung. Vivienne seemed genuinely appalled at the idea of marrying him and the distraught look in her eyes turned his blood cold. Years ago they would have married each other joyfully, eagerly. Now she would rather face scandal and ruin than be his wife. Although being forced to marry her did not sit well with him either. He had not been given time to consider the travesty of a marriage they would have, nor did he want to give it any thought now.

"That's a lie!" Susana ranted and raved, her hands gesturing wildly. "That's a lie! She wants to marry you and always has. She planned this! She trapped you and tricked you! She planned it this way! She knew her aunt and uncle would discover the two of you together tonight and you would have to marry her."

Wearily he rubbed his temples and found himself defending Vivienne. "No, Mother, she didn't. Vivienne did not invite me to her room this evening. In fact, I only went to her room on a spur of the moment decision just to talk to her about . . . something. So there is no way she could have or would have planned to be caught in such a shameful manner by Lord and Lady Cardwell when she had no idea that I would be there in the first place."

"You . . . you went to her room uninvited in the middle of the night?" Her voice was incredulous, her gray eyes wide in total disbelief. Slowly, she lowered herself to sit in the armchair behind her, as if she were not capable of bearing her own weight under such circumstances. She stared at her son wordlessly.

"Yes," he said reluctantly, as it was not an easy thing to admit to his mother. He knew she was genuinely upset and embarrassed by his behavior and had every right to feel that way. Hell, he felt ashamed and embarrassed by his own behavior.

"Aidan, why? Why?" Susana began to cry. "You told me you were going to stay away from her. I suspected you were falling under her spell again, but I never imagined that you would do such a thing. To go to her bed! I never expected to find *you* with her." Her sobs became more pronounced and tears spilled down her pale cheeks.

In all his life, Aidan had never seen his mother shed so much as a single tear, let alone seen her in such a state. She had always been impeccably controlled and reserved, barely showing any emotion at all. Except for anger. He did not know how to comfort her now. Nor did he want to comfort her.

Yes, he had been caught in a very embarrassing and highly compromising situation and he had to marry Vivienne. And no, she was not his first choice for a bride. He and Vivienne had many issues between them to complicate their marriage. It was a dreadful mess to be in and he felt sick to his stomach about it, but his mother carried on as if her world had come to an end.

"I'm sorry," he stated awkwardly to her. "This is entirely my fault."

"Don't say that," she wailed loudly, crying harder. Her face looked ten years older suddenly. With her arms wrapped around her chest, she rocked back and forth, back and forth, sobbing. "If you had just stayed away from her tonight, this wouldn't have happened. After all I did to get you away from her, she won anyway. She got you. Oh, Aidan, why didn't you stay away? Why did you go to her tonight? Tonight of all nights?"

She rambled on hysterically, beside herself with despair, and Aidan could barely understand her.

"I'm going to sleep now. I'll see you in the morning." While she continued to cry, he patted her shoulder and left her room, gratefully closing the door behind him. He motioned to Mary, his mother's lady's maid. "Bring her some hot tea, will you, please? And stay with her until she calms down."

The thin woman nodded her head in agreement. "Of course, my lord."

Weary and emotionally drained, Aidan slowly made his way back to his room. Finley had been waiting for him but had fallen asleep in an overstuffed armchair near the fireplace, which burned low, the coals glowing red. He sat up and rubbed his eyes slowly when the sound of the door awakened him.

"You look like you've been through hell," Finley stated with a wide yawn, taking in Aidan's disheveled appearance. "Rough evening at the ball?" he asked sardonically.

"You could say that."

"What happened?"

"It seems I'm getting married this week."

Finley's eyebrows raised at his startling comment. "Indeed. Who is the lucky lady?"

"Interesting that you didn't automatically assume it was Helene Winston." Aidan remarked, sitting on the edge of the bed and kicking off his shoes.

"Isn't it Helene?"

"No."

"Then it must be Vivienne."

"You're quick," Aidan quipped dryly.

"I gather it was not a romantic proposal."

"Hardly. Her aunt and uncle found us naked together in Vivienne's bed."

Shocked, Finley said in amazement, "You're lucky the uncle didn't shoot you on the spot!"

"I know." Aidan sighed wearily at the thought. "It was not my finest moment."

"How is Vivienne?"

"Embarrassed. Shamed. Sick at the thought of marrying me."

"Is your mother aware of the good news yet?"

"Oh, yes. She happened to get an eyeful of the scene herself firsthand."

"Jesus." Finley shook his head and whistled low. "She must be fit to be tied."

"That's an understatement." Aidan stretched out on his back on the bed, too tired to remove his clothes.

"Imagine you and Vivienne getting married after all that," Finley said quietly.

"I can't imagine it."

Finley pondered aloud, "It almost seems as if you should have married her as you wanted to in the first place. Think of all the problems that could have been avoided."

"That was the problem, Finley," Aidan said in exasperation, looking up at the ceiling. "She didn't want to marry me then. She was with another man. *She* left *me*."

"But you left the country without talking to her about it."

Aidan rose up on his elbows and glanced curiously at Finley. "Whose side are you on anyway?"

"Yours, of course," Finley muttered softly, his brows furrowed. "It's just strange, that you're marrying her in the end after all."

Strange was an understatement. Aidan could not think of a more confounding situation than the one in which he currently found himself with Vivienne.

Jackson Harlow slammed his fist ineffectually into the wall, which was covered in pink cabbage rose wallpaper. He had no decent outlet for his considerable anger and frustration and he felt he would explode.

What the hell happened tonight?

He had slipped away to Vivienne Montgomery's room, anticipating a lovely interlude with her, perhaps even being able to persuade her to marry him. He had arrived a little later than he'd intended, due to some delicious antics with the insatiable Annabelle Worthington, and he had feared Vivienne would not still be awake.

Jackson could not believe his eyes when he reached her door. A flustered Lady Cardwell was rushing down the hallway with her fat daughter in tow. Lord Cardwell was having an apoplectic fit and Lady Whitlock lay out cold on the floor. His first thought was that something terrible had happened to Vivienne and, surprisingly, he felt his heart race in fear at the thought.

Then he glanced into her room and what he saw instantly explained the pandemonium in the hallway. Jackson could not breathe for an instant at the sight of Vivienne, his beautiful bride-to-be, huddled under blankets up to her neck, her cheeks scarlet, her long black hair loose around her. Next to her, unbelievably, the Earl of Whitlock, bare-chested, looked mortified. Obviously, they had interrupted a very intimate moment between the two.

What the hell was Whitlock doing in Vivienne's bed when she had sent him a note inviting him to her room the same night? He did not believe that he had imagined her willingness earlier that evening. Was she simply playing him for a fool? But to what end?

But no, he did not believe it was in her character. Admittedly, he did not know Vivienne all that well, but he just had a sense that she was a moral and honorable woman. He'd never met a woman of such noble character that he was so physically attracted to before.

Why the note? What was it she urgently needed to talk to him about? Had she feared a visit from Whitlock? She could not have expected Jackson to come to her room the same night she was entertaining Whitlock. Hell, he wasn't aware that there was anything between Vivienne and Whitlock to begin with. From what he had sensed, the two disliked each other intensely. Nothing about the evening made any sense.

And how did it happen to be that Whitlock's mother was present to witness such a scene? It was almost as if it were planned. But certainly Vivienne could not have planned to have herself humiliated and disgraced to marry Whitlock, when he had all but offered himself to her earlier in the evening.

Something was not right. Vivienne was not the type to play harlot games. He would bet his life on that. During the masked ball, she had eagerly agreed to see him when they returned to London. Hell, he'd even acted the gentleman for the first time in his life and asked permission to court her from that windbag of an uncle of hers. Then she sent that note to him. He was positive she had been in need of his help and that soon she and her fortune would be his.

And now they would both belong to that smug Earl of Whitlock, of all people. As if he didn't have more than enough in his favor already.

He wondered if Aidan somehow discovered that Vivienne had the deeds to the diamond mines and schemed to have himself caught not only in her room, but in her bed. That would explain why his mother happened to be walking by at that time of night. Perhaps he had completely underestimated the goody-two-shoes Lord Whitlock all this time. Maybe he was a worthy competitor after all, for somehow he had managed to ensnare Vivienne and her priceless deeds right out from under him.

Well, Lord Whitlock, you haven't married her yet!

There was still time to get Vivienne away from him. Uncle Windbag was procuring a special license for them this week. That would give Jackson a few days to work up a plan to get her back.

And get her back he would. Because Jackson Harlow played to win.

ONE SINFUL NIGHT

would be a miserable marriage.

Chapter 16

The Aftermath

As much as she wanted to, Vivienne could not cry when her aunt and uncle finally left her that night. She lay in bed in her darkened room, unable to sleep, unable to cry, feeling hollow inside. The evening had been a humiliating experience. To further her degradation, her aunt and uncle had made Glenda her guard. Glenda, with her self-righteous, malicious smiles.

"You're not so special now, are you, Vivienne?" she taunted her elatedly. "Now my parents and brothers know what you are really like. And it's not so pretty, is it?"

Glenda's vicious words had a ring of truth to them and wounded Vivienne deeply. No, she had not reflected well on her father's family. She was ashamed of herself.

Being discovered with Aidan in her bed was traumatic enough, but now she had to marry him. It

would be a miserable marriage, for he would never
trust her or respect her as he should. And then there
was his mother. Lady Whitlock was bound to blame
the entire scandalous incident on Vivienne.

In order to avoid joining the others at breakfast
downstairs the next morning, for she could not face
Aidan, or Susana Kavanaugh, or Jackson Harlow, Vivienne remained in her room and helped Lizzie pack
their belongings. Lizzie brought her some tea and
toast, for that was all Vivienne could stomach at the
moment. The calming, mundane task of packing
helped to calm her frayed nerves somewhat, although her hands shook as she placed the wooden
box from her father lovingly in the massive trunk that
held all her possessions.

The box brought back memories of her father's disappearance and her quest to learn the truth. Assum-
ing that Jackson Harlow must be appalled by her
disgraceful behavior last night, she realized she lost
her chance to find out what really happened to her
father. What Mister Harlow must think of her now! He
would never help her find her father after the shocking way she had behaved, and she didn't blame him.

Eerily, the whole incident reminded her of the
afternoon in the cottage in Galway when Aidan found
her with Nicky Foster. The confusion. The shame.
The terrible consequences. Honestly, how did everyone happen to be walking by her room at such
an hour? It was almost as if they were trying to catch
her with Aidan. But she certainly could not accuse
her aunt and uncle or even Lady Whitlock of entrap-
ping her into marrying Aidan. There was not a
chance of that.

Vivienne could only hide in her room for so long

before good manners dictated she venture downstairs to say goodbye. Squaring her shoulders, she attempted to control the nervous trembling in her hands as she descended the main staircase. The front hallway bustled in a flurry of activity as guests prepared to depart Bingham Hall. She saw Aunt Gwen talking with Aunt Jane. Glenda stood beside them, a self-important expression on her round, double-chinned face at the sight of Vivienne, waving at her pointedly. Yes, Glenda, for one, was thoroughly enjoying Vivienne's disgrace.

Thankfully, she did not see Aidan or his mother. She wondered if they had departed already, but she did not want to draw attention to herself by asking after him. However, Jackson Harlow caught her eyes immediately. He looked as handsome as ever; his golden blond hair neatly combed, his intelligent eyes the color of coffee with cream. Her cheeks flamed at the memory of how he had seen her last night, but his expression offered only questioning concern. He wanted to know if she were all right.

She smiled faintly at him. "Good afternoon."

"Good afternoon, Miss Montgomery." He looked at her with something akin to sympathy. "I trust you are well today."

She nodded her head in response, cringing inwardly at the recollection of last night's disgrace.

"I look forward to seeing you upon our return to London."

At his comforting words, Vivienne struggled to hold back the tears that would not come in the privacy of her room last night but now seemed ready to spill forth with ease. He still wanted to help her after he had witnessed her disgrace last night. That he could

still treat her so respectfully warmed her heart. He was
a good man and he really did care for her.

"I did not intend to upset you," he said gently.

"No, you did not upset me, Mister Harlow. I am
simply touched by your overwhelming kindness."

He moved a few steps closer to her and whispered
hurriedly, "I'm sorry I was not able to come to you
sooner last night. If I had been there earlier all that
happened could have been prevented."

Vivienne looked at him in startled surprise. What
was he talking about? Been there on time? On time
for what? Did he think he could have prevented her
sleeping with Aidan or her getting caught by her aunt
and uncle?

He continued to whisper to her, "I can help you out
of this situation, Vivienne. We'll talk more in London.
Everything will be fine, so please don't worry. Come
to my office Wednesday at noon. I'll be waiting for
you."

Jackson Harlow stepped away from her casually as
Gregory and George came striding into the hall. Puzzled, but grateful that he was still willing to help her,
she nodded her head in agreement. Jackson Harlow
bid her farewell, and turned to say good-bye to the
duke and duchess before he left. Confused by his odd
comments, Vivienne faced her cousins.

She could tell by the expressions on their somewhat
somber faces that they had been made aware of her
disgrace. Whether they heard the story from their
parents or Aidan himself, she did not know.

"Are you all right, Vivvy?" Gregory asked softly, his
expression full of sympathy.

She shook her head wearily at him.

He put his arm around her and whispered in her

ear, "It will be fine. Aidan is a good man, and you'll get on well together."

Again tears welled in her eyes but she blinked them back resolutely. Tearfulness seemed to be the order of the day for her. Just then Uncle Gilbert came in and announced that their carriages were ready. They said good-bye to Aunt Jane and Uncle Richard, who made them promise to visit again soon.

Eager to leave, Vivienne hoped that she could ride with the twins as they did on the way there, but it seemed her aunt and uncle weren't about to let her out of their sight. They insisted she ride with them. So Vivienne endured Glenda's presence for the entire journey back to London. And Glenda took great joy in taking up as much of the seat as possible, leaving Vivienne pressed uncomfortably against the wall of the carriage, with Glenda's elbow jammed in her side. The only saving grace was that once they arrived at the Cardwell townhouse, she would not have to share a room with Glenda anymore.

As they bounced along the road to London, Vivienne felt relieved that she had not had to face Aidan before she left Bingham Hall. She simply did not have the strength to look in his eyes yet. She could not bear to see the coldness, that utter lack of feeling for her, that would certainly be in his expression. She supposed the next time she saw him, they would be getting married. Her heart sank and her stomach knotted.

Ten years ago she was overjoyed at the prospect of marrying Aidan Kavanaugh. Now it only brought her misery because he despised her. He thought her unfaithful, morally loose, and conniving.

Why had she let him kiss her last night? Why had

she let him in her room? Even more confounding was what he was doing there in the first place. Ostensibly, he was there to warn her away from Jackson Harlow. If he hated her so much, why was he trying to protect her? She supposed he simply didn't want her to ever be happy with anyone. But couldn't that have waited until a more appropriate time? Why did he feel a pressing need to visit her at such a late hour in her bedchambers? Unless he simply wanted to take advantage of her again as he had in the portrait gallery. In which case, she had given him exactly what he came for and more than likely confirmed his worst suspicions of her immoral character. She should have resisted his seductive kisses, his caresses. She should have slapped his face. She should have thrown him out. Instead, she returned his kisses and melted at his slightest touch. She had welcomed him eagerly into her bed.

And for the briefest instant it had been magically beautiful between them.

It was almost as if they were back in their little cottage again, just the two of them, with all their love and passion for each other as if nothing had happened to ruin it. They were simply Aidan and Vivienne who had loved each other forever.

Then without warning her aunt and uncle entered her bedroom and those fleeting feelings of tenderness and love between them instantly vanished. That cold, hard look returned to Aidan's green eyes and once again they were at odds. Being forced to marry her was obviously intolerable to him. The cold expression on his face made her sick inside. She did not want to be the wife of a man unwilling to have her, of a man unable to trust her, of a man who did not love her. What kind of marriage would result from that? Not one that she wanted to be a part of. Yet it seemed she had no choice in the matter now.

Although Jackson Harlow's strange words haunted her.

"The bleedin' crook didn't pay me all wot 'e owed me. 'E was supposed t' give me the other 'alf tha money after I set the fire. But 'e didn't pay up. Tha's not good business now, is it?"

"Neither is setting a fire," Aidan responded angrily to the shifty fellow seated before him in the shipping office of Kavanaugh Enterprises. Grayson had brought the man in the morning after Aidan had returned from Bingham Hall. Still stunned by his impending marriage to Vivienne Montgomery, Aidan forced himself to focus on his business and on finding proof that Jackson Harlow was responsible for setting the fire that destroyed his warehouse.

Jimmy Travers scratched his thick skull, wondering at the meaning of Aidan's words. His thin, wiry form looked malnourished and, from the stench of him, he had not bathed in quite some time. His clothes seemed to be held together by the thinnest of threads and the scruff of a ragged beard covered his thin face leaving only his beady eyes and beak nose prominent. "But I 'eld up on my end. Wot's fair's fair. 'E said, 'alf before, and the other 'alf after I do the job. And I did. I's the one wot burned yer warehouse."

The man's questionable intelligence and pitiable plight led Aidan to go easier on him than he intended. Yet he played along. "No, it wasn't fair of him to renege on his end of the deal. Did you try to reason with him?"

Jimmy Travers shifted uneasily from one foot to the other as he spoke. "Sure I did. I goes t' 'is fancy office, not like ye 'ave 'ere, but 'arlow was outta town. So I waits fer days cuz I need the money 'e promised me. My sister's sick in 'ospital. Then this fella"—he nodded his capped head to indicate Grayson—"says that 'e'll 'elp me if'n I tells 'im 'oo set the fire. But I went t' 'arlow's 'ouse. I waited there till 'e come 'ome. I says t' him give me the rest a my money. 'E jus' laughed and says 'e don' know wot I'm talkin' about. Says 'e paid me all wot I agreed ta. 'Ad me thrown outta 'is 'ouse, tha's wot."

"I can imagine you are quite angry with him. Angry enough to lie," Aidan stated, appalled by Harlow's deplorable ethics. Not only was Jackson Harlow dishonest in his legitimate business deals, but he could not be trusted to follow through in his own underhanded transactions. Obviously poor Travers had no idea of the type of person he was in league with.

"'Tain't a lie, I tell ye," the man protested earnestly.

Aidan and Grayson exchanged knowing glances across Aidan's cluttered desk. Aidan's office was just that, a place to do business. His steady work habits were reflected in the no-nonsense furnishings and lack of pretentious effects. Aidan had worked tirelessly over the years to make his shipping business a success. Perhaps he had thrown himself into his work to forget a certain Irish beauty, but he wasn't about to have it ruined by Jackson Harlow and the poor, desperate souls he hired to do his dirty work.

"Do you have anything to prove that he hired you to set the fire?" Aidan asked, anticipating what his answer would be.

The slow-witted man shook his head with wide eyes, confirming Aidan's hunch.

"Thank you, Mr. Travers. We'll be in touch with you very soon."

"But wot about my money?" he asked urgently. "I gotta 'elp my sister."

"If you think I'm going to pay you for burning down my warehouse, Mr. Travers, you are sadly mistaken," Aidan stated in a cold tone. "You're very fortunate I haven't handed you over to the authorities. However, at this point, I am more interested in punishing the man who hired you than in punishing you. If you can help us prove it, there may just be a modest reward in it for you. Stay where we can find you."

The man, thoroughly cowed, dipped his head in reluctant agreement and shuffled reluctantly out of the office.

In the ensuing silence, Daniel Grayson said grimly, "I have the distinct impression the Harlows are trying to drive us out of business."

"And they have almost succeeded in doing just that." To Aidan's thinking, that was an understatement. Ever since Aidan had taken over Harlow Shipping's profitable routes to North America, he had steadily become Harlow's biggest competitor. As more and more merchants preferred to do business with Kavanaugh Enterprises, the company's profits increased greatly while Aidan earned a spotless reputation for honest, reliable business practices. On the other hand, Harlow Shipping, from what he had heard from various sources, seemed to be sliding downhill. The twin disasters of losing the shipment and the warehouse fire had placed Kavanaugh Enterprises on shaky ground.

His company had suffered a considerable financial loss, but Aidan was determined to do everything in his power to overcome this setback. And punish those responsible for trying to destroy him.

Grayson said intently, "We need to have proof to link Harlow to the fire. You and I believe this story of Travers, but no one else will."

Aidan hated to admit it, but Grayson had a point. "Keep your eye on Travers. He's the key to nabbing the Harlow brothers. Make sure you have a man follow him."

Grayson nodded his head in accord with this and made his way to leave the office. "I'll assign Jones first thing in the morning. He's very good at this sort of work."

Aidan called after him. "And find out what hospital his sister is in and make sure she's taken care of."

Chapter 17

The Other Option

"Now, please wait for me right here, Lizzie," Vivienne instructed her maid as they stood outside the imposing limestone building that housed Harlow Shipping International.

Still in disgrace, she'd managed to successfully escape Aunt Gwen's watchful eyes for the afternoon by telling her that she and Lizzie were going to shop for some items for her trousseau. And she had actually visited a shop and bought a ribbon or two, although admittedly rather quickly. Then she made her way directly to Jackson Harlow's office. It would upset her aunt to no end to find out that Vivienne was visiting Mister Harlow to discuss her father's disappearance, so it was better if she simply didn't know about it.

"I simply need to speak with Mister Harlow about my father. It shouldn't take much time at all. I promise, I shall be back momentarily," Vivienne continued to explain.

"All right, miss," Lizzie stated reluctantly, her wide eyes filled with worry, but she was far too loyal to Vivienne to challenge her wishes. And at the moment, Vivienne was not above using that fact to her advantage.

She gave Lizzie a reassuring pat on the shoulder, made her way up the neatly swept front steps, and bravely entered the building. She wore a smart day gown of a dusty rose, with an adorable bonnet in matching rose silk. Walking down the corridor and up a flight of stairs, she reached an imposing frosted-glass door with Harlow Shipping International painted in bold black letters on the front. She took a deep breath for courage and opened the door with feigned confidence. A young man, neatly dressed in a brown suit, greeted her with a solicitous air.

"Welcome, Miss Montgomery. Mister Harlow has been expecting you and is waiting for you in his office. May I bring you some tea?" His efficacious manner did nothing to calm her nerves.

"No, thank you," she murmured softly, clutching her reticule tighter in her hand.

The young man, obviously an assistant, escorted her politely into Jackson Harlow's office. Harlow Shipping obviously did a tremendous amount of business to be able to afford such a grand and elegantly furnished office. A thick cocoa-brown carpet covered the floor and heavy mahogany furniture and comfortable leather chairs were placed strategically around the room. Two tall windows that looked out over the street below were covered with gold velvet drapes. Various potted plants placed around the room added a touch of warmth, while dark green wallpaper and gilt-framed paintings of the Harlow fleet of ships adorned the walls. Her eyes immediately scanned the pictures for a glimpse of the *Sea Star*. She did not see it.

More daunted than she realized, Vivienne smiled nervously when Jackson Harlow stood in greeting when he saw her enter. He moved around to the front of his gleaming mahogany desk, and gracefully took Vivienne's small hand in his.

"I'm so pleased that you were able to meet me as planned, Miss Montgomery." He bent over her gloved hand in a gallant gesture and kissed it. "You look lovely, as always."

"Thank you, Mister Harlow."

"Please sit down and make yourself comfortable." He turned to the young man, who had escorted Vivienne. "You may excuse yourself, Francis."

"Very good, sir." The secretary headed out the door, closing it as he left.

Jackson moved to sit behind his desk once more and turned his eyes upon her in a steady gaze during the awkward silence that followed. He said softly, "I was beginning to think that you wouldn't come."

A nervous little laugh escaped her, as she adjusted her rose bonnet. "I was beginning to think I would not be able to get away from my aunt and uncle to see you."

"Obviously you were quite successful." He looked at her pointedly. "First things first. Are you well, Miss Montgomery?"

"I'm fine, thank you."

"May I presume to call you Vivienne?" He smiled at her in all his golden glory.

She could not resist his charm. The night of the Binghams' masked ball she had accepted Jackson's offer of courtship, then the poor man witnessed her in bed with Aidan. He was quite aware of her disgrace and inescapable marriage, and now, in a brazen maneuver, she had secretly arrived at his office unchaperoned. Allowing him to call her by her given name at this point seemed mild in comparison to her other transgressions. She merely nodded her head in helpless agreement to his request.

"Wonderful. Now you must call me Jackson."

Again Vivienne nodded her head. "Jackson it is then."

"Now, let's discuss your father, shall we, Vivienne?" He adopted a businesslike air and began to shuffle through the sheaves of papers on his neatly ordered desk. "I've been looking over the records from your father's voyages with us. Captain Montgomery had slowly taken over the trade routes to South Africa during the last five years, when he began piloting the *Sea Star.* He was an excellent captain, never lost a single shipment or crew member. He profited handsomely from our business with him."

"He did?" Vivienne questioned incredulously. If her father had been making large sums of money on his voyages, he certainly never shared much of it with her or Aggie. Between his intermittent visits to Galway, he always sent money to them whenever he could. Never knowing how much they would be getting or when the next allotment would arrive, she and Aggie spent the money sparingly, saving as much as they were able. Aggie suspected that her father was involved in gambling and the amounts he sent decreased sharply in the last years since he was employed with Harlow Shipping, leaving Vivienne worried for her future. After her father's ship disappeared, she and Aggie survived solely on what little earnings Vivienne brought in from her sewing.

"Are you saying you did not know of this?" Jackson asked in disbelief.

"That's exactly what I'm saying. I barely had enough money to keep food on the table. If my father was making large profits, he did not share them with me."

"That's most odd," he mumbled, his eyes still on the papers in front of them. "But it fits with my theory."

"What theory?" Vivienne's pulse quickened.

"This is difficult for me to admit to you, Vivienne. And I am only telling you this because of my feeling of responsibility for you, for it could cause quite a bit of trouble for me. And for my family."

Intrigued by his words she whispered, "You must tell me."

He paused for a moment. "I think there might have been some wrongdoing against your father on the part of my brothers, Davis and Miles."

Vivienne blinked, unsure how to respond while her sharp mind raced with possibilities. What was he talking about? What had his brothers done to her father? Had they stolen from him? Had they hurt him somehow? Even murd—No, she could not even say that word. "What do you mean, Mister Harlow?"

"Jackson," he corrected her smoothly.

"Jackson."

"I'm not completely sure just yet. But, brothers or no, I intend to find out. And to do that I need you to tell me everything about the time you last saw your father, from before he sailed until the last letter you received. Did he make any reference to Harlow Shipping or to either of my brothers? Did he mention any investments he made, any provisions for your future? No detail may be too small or insignificant. You must tell me everything."

Speechless, she stared at Jackson.

"I don't think it's a secret how I feel about you, Vivienne," Jackson uttered softly. "I only wish to help you in any way I can. I feel doubly responsible for your father's disappearance for I fear it may have been caused by my brothers' selfishness. You can trust me."

"I trust you, Mister—" she corrected herself, "Jackson."

"I'm happy to hear that, because I need your help in order for me to solve this mystery. We need each other. And for your own safety, we must not mention who you are to my brother Miles. He would know immediately that we suspect him. Fortunately he is out of town this week, but he will be back shortly."

"I see your point," Vivienne agreed. If his brother and foul play were somehow involved in her father's disappearance, then the logic in staying out of sight of Miles Harlow made sense. "But I don't understand any of this. Why would either of your brothers want to hurt a man who was in their employ for years? What could my father have done to incur their wrath?"

"This is very difficult for me to admit, Vivienne, but my brothers are greedy men. I have a feeling your father had something that they wanted. Quite desperately. He was merely in their way."

"What was it?" asked Vivienne, her hands clenched tightly in her lap.

"Diamond mines in Africa."

"Diamond mines? What would my father be doing with diamond mines?" Vivienne was in shock. Nothing made sense. How could he possibly be dead over something like that?

"Well, it seems he may have acquired some very profitable diamond mines in South Africa."

"My father?" she cried in disbelief. "Why, he knows nothing of diamond mines!"

"You don't need to know about them to become rich," Jackson explained. "You just need to own one. And Captain Montgomery apparently won deeds to some land in South Africa with my brother Davis. At first they believed the land to be worthless, and Davis sold his all shares to your father. However, it turns out that very same land holds some rich mines. They are worth a fortune and belonged completely to your father. Of course, my brother Davis bitterly regrets selling them to him."

Vivienne could not comprehend why her father would not have simply told her he owned lucrative diamond mines. "I don't believe any of this. Surely, my father would have written to me about something so important."

"That is why you must show me all of your father's letters to you," Jackson insisted. "There may be information in them that you may not comprehend, but will cast light on what happened. Can you bring them to me, Vivienne?"

"Of course," she responded woodenly, too stunned to refuse him. "He sent me a wood and ivory box from Africa just before he disappeared. With it was the last letter he wrote to me. He said that the box was very valuable and that he would explain everything when he saw me again."

Jackson's eyes lit up in excitement. "You must show

this box to me, but you must not tell anyone about what I have told you. It could place you in danger."

She nodded her head in agreement, falling silent. Overwhelmed by this information, she tried to make sense of it all. If her father had simply written to her about the diamond mines, she would not be in this perplexing situation. *Oh Papa, why didn't you just tell me the truth?*

After a few moments, Jackson stood and walked around his desk, moving to stand before Vivienne. He looked at her intently, his golden brown eyes searching hers. "In spite of what happened with you and Lord Whitlock, I still want you, Vivienne."

Startled by his abrupt change of topic, her cheeks flamed at the memory of the night at Bingham Hall when she was found with Aidan. It was a humiliation she wanted to obliterate from her memory permanently. "Please don't speak of that night."

"I ask that you allow me to speak my piece first. I can't help feeling this is all my fault. If I had only answered your summons sooner, perhaps I could have prevented Lord Whitlock from being in your bedchamber."

"My summons?" His words confused her again. She recalled he said something similar to her that last day at Bingham Hall.

"The urgent note you sent to me asking me to come to your room to help you."

Vivienne felt her heart overturn and she suddenly knew something deliberate had been planned that night. Something that had nothing to do with her, for she never invited anyone, least of all Jackson Harlow, to her room. Who would have written a note to Jackson asking him to come to her room in the middle of the night? What if her aunt and uncle had returned while Jackson was visiting her room? Who wanted to see her disgraced? And Jackson Harlow blamed for it? "What note—"

Jackson interrupted her, "Lord Whitlock was making inappropriate advances toward you before and you wanted me to stop him. You were afraid of him, weren't you?"

Oh, she was afraid of Aidan all right, but not in the way Jackson thought. Aidan would never physically hurt her or force her to do anything against her will. Of that she had no fear. Yet Jackson's concerned manner pulled at her heartstrings. He desperately wanted to help her, but she did not know how to respond to this information.

"I hope you consider me more than just a friend and I hope I'm not mistaken in believing that you may have feelings for me. I know of no other way to say this delicately, so I will be direct."

Vivienne waited expectantly, wondering what he would say to astonish her next, for it seemed this afternoon was to be full of nothing but surprising news.

"I am aware that your uncle is forcing Whitlock to marry you and that you are not happy about the situation. You do not have to marry him. I would like to suggest another alternative."

Vivienne's heart thumped loudly in her chest as Jackson elegantly knelt on one knee before her. He took her gloved hand in his with a tenderness that surprised her, yet she could not help the little shiver that raced down her spine.

"I would like to offer you my hand in marriage."

The ticking of the clock on the shelf echoed deafeningly through the silent office.

"You want to marry me? Even after—" Vivienne

could not help the incredulous tone from creeping into her voice. He still held her hand with a firm clasp.

"Yes. In due time and through the proper channels, I was hoping I would be able to ask you to be my wife, but it seems I was unexpectedly preempted by Lord Whitlock. I know you are a respectable and principled lady and that Whitlock took terrible advantage of you that night. He alone put you in this unbearable and shameful position where you were compromised. Now your family is forcing him to marry you." Jackson paused, his eyes holding her gaze. "I can offer you another option. You could marry me instead of Whitlock."

Vivienne could not believe it. This man—this man she had known for only a week—had more faith in her character and morals, than Aidan ever did. Jackson wanted to marry her. Whereas Aidan, who had been her friend since she was nine years old, had no faith in her at all. "Why would you want to marry *me*?" she asked incredulously.

"Because I think you are the most exquisite woman I have ever had the pleasure to know. I respect you and I appreciate your intelligence. I enjoy your company and think we get along well. I would be proud to have you as my wife."

Again an awkward silence ensued.

"You don't have to answer me right away," he continued soothingly, patting her hand. "Please take some time to consider my offer."

Vivienne could not help but say, "I only have until Saturday. Aidan and I are to be married on Saturday."

"Well, then, you'll have to answer me before then." A smile played faintly at the corners of his sensuous mouth.

"Thank you. I am honored by your very kind offer, Jackson, but really—"

"I'm not being kind. I'm being completely selfish." He squeezed her hand tightly. "I know it has only been a short amount of time that we have been acquainted with each other, but I believe I've fallen in love with you."

Fallen in love? She blinked at the handsome blond man who held her and asked her to marry him. Did she want to marry Jackson Harlow? Would that save her from the hopeless fate of an artificial marriage to a man who did not love or trust her? Attractive, charming, and prosperous, Jackson had much to recommend him as a husband. He offered her a respectable escape from her impossible situation with Aidan. Dare she take it?

At that moment raised voices, followed by angered shouts, could be heard outside and suddenly the door to Jackson's office burst wide open. An unkempt and obviously upset man stalked toward Jackson, while Francis, the assistant, yelled frantic apologies. "I'm sorry, sir! I tried to stop him!"

Startled, Vivienne watched in confusion as Francis scurried back out of the room and Jackson released her hand and abruptly stood, clearly outraged by the intrusion. He turned to face the boisterous ruffian who had stormed uninvited into his office. "How dare you interrupt me?" he cried indignantly.

"Ye 'ave to pay wot ye owe me!" the man in the tattered cap demanded, becoming more irate, if such a thing were possible. "I set tha' fire like ye said! I kep my end o' the bargain, but ye ain't kep yours! I need my money!"

"Travers, this is neither the time nor the place to discuss this—"

The man named Travers interrupted, "If not now, when?! I did my 'alf. I set the fire a fortnigh' ago. And ye owe me. I've already talked to Kavanaugh and if ye don' pay up right now, I'll go to tha police! I got nothin' to lose if ye don' pay me!"

Jackson's face darkened as he advanced on the man, causing Vivienne to intake her breath sharply at the sight. Confused by all that was happening, she instantly sensed the explosiveness of the situation and that Jackson was more than incensed by the man's interruption, although he attempted to remain cool and unruffled.

"I don't know what you are talking about. Now get out of my office," Jackson ordered through clenched teeth.

"Pay me first and I'll go!" the man persisted with mounting agitation, crossing his arms across his chest. "I ain't leavin' til ye pay me!"

Jackson's voice turned silky smooth as he told the man, "Why don't you come back tomorrow and we'll discuss your dilemma then."

Francis re-entered the room with two enormous guards following him. The beefy guards grabbed the irate man by his arms and proceeded to drag him kicking and screaming from the office.

"Yer a cheat, Harlow! Ye know ye owe me! Damn ye! Ye'll be sorry you didn' pay me. Ye'll be sorry!" His filthy curses and screams of dire retribution continued as he disappeared from view.

Jackson turned to face her with a regretful air and patted her arm soothingly. "I cannot apologize enough that you had to witness such a vulgar display,

Vivienne. The man is quite delusional. Apparently he is under the erroneous impression that I owe him money. Can you imagine such a tale? Please eradicate the entire scene from your mind."

Jackson's actions upset her. As well as the strange man's ominous words. A fire. The name Kavanaugh. Payment. Something underhanded had happened, of that she was certain. How much of the man's incoherent ramblings was true was anyone's guess. She wished she could erase it all from her head as Jackson suggested, but an odd memory niggled at the back of her brain. Something she ought to remember, but couldn't.

"I've erased it already." Vivienne forced a quick smile at him. "I should be going home now." She rose abruptly from her seat and grabbed her reticule. "My aunt will be wondering where I've been all afternoon."

Jackson stepped toward her, placing his hand upon her upper arm, his brown eyes glittering. "Vivienne, please consider my offer of marriage. I meant all that I said. I would be a good husband and I would take excellent care of you, of that you should have no doubt."

Avoiding the fervent look in his eyes, she merely nodded her head.

He flashed her a heart melting grin that set off his golden handsomeness to perfection. "Send me a message tomorrow. In the meantime, look through your father's letters."

Before she knew what he was about, Jackson leaned close to her. For a split second she thought he meant to place a light kiss on her cheek, but he moved slightly, cupping his hand behind her head, forcing her face next to his, and his lips covered hers possessively. Astonished at his boldness, she held her breath as he pressed his mouth against hers in a hungry kiss.

He felt warm and soft and he smelled nice enough, yet for some reason she shuddered. He released her just as abruptly as he had kissed her, leaving her off balance.

"And let me know your answer as soon as you can," he said urgently. "I'll be waiting."

Surprised, she took a step back, blinking at him. "I really must be going," she murmured as she hurried from the elegant office, knowing she appeared ridiculous.

She fled down the stairs, flustered by all that had happened during her visit. The incredible information about her father and the diamond mines. The unsavory characters of the Harlow brothers. The strange encounter between that angry man and Jackson. Jackson's declaration of love for her and his proposal of marriage. His mention of a note she supposedly sent to him. And then his kiss! She had not had enough time to absorb it all or make sense of any of it. She just knew she had been in his office too long and that Lizzie must be frantic with worry by now. She didn't dare risk upsetting Aunt Gwen and Uncle Gilbert again, after everything she had already put them through.

Hurriedly, Vivienne exited the front door. As she felt the fresh air touch her face, she stopped short and her heart sank to the tips of her stylish leather walking boots. Lizzie had vanished and Gregory Cardwell stood in her place at the bottom of the front steps, a stern look on his freckled face and his arms crossed over his chest. Obviously her cousin was quite displeased with her.

"What are you doing here?" she asked, flustered at

the change of events and still breathless from her mad dash from Jackson's office on the second floor.

"That's the question I need to ask you," he said stonily, eyeing her quizzically as she stood above him on the top of the steps.

Vivienne attempted to act nonchalant, casually adjusting her rose-colored gloves. "Where is Lizzie?"

"I sent her home. The poor, innocent thing. How could you make her an accomplice in your misadventures?" he scolded.

"I assure you that I'm not having any misadventures, Greg. Just taking care of some family business." She continued down the steps toward the sidewalk, brushing past him. "There's no need for you to get protective of me now."

Gregory grabbed hold of her arm, stopping her. "Maybe you could use a little protection, Vivvy. We need to talk, you and I. It's high time you cleared some things up for me. You have to tell me everything that happened between you and Aidan from the beginning. And what you were doing in Jackson Harlow's office just now."

Chapter 18

The Kiss

"Thank you for joining us," Lord Gilbert Cardwell said warmly as he welcomed the guests seated around the magnificent dinner table of his London town-house. "I thought it would be nice for our two families to spend time together in a more relaxed manner before the wedding on Saturday."

The families assembled consisted of the Earl of Whitlock, his mother, and the entire Cardwell clan. Aidan glanced around the table and could not help but notice that his mother, who sat rigidly to the right of Lord Cardwell, appeared as ill at ease as she certainly felt. She was barely feigning politeness and the strain of doing that much was apparent in the pinched frown marring her face.

His gaze then rested on Vivienne. He had not seen her since that infamous night in her bedroom. She sat calmly across the table from him. But of course she would be calm. Aidan wouldn't have expected anything less of her. He had to admit that she looked extraordinarily lovely. Wearing a gown of a deep lavender, the simple but tasteful cut of the dress showed off her figure to perfection and the color brought out the startling blue of her eyes. An involuntary rush of desire had flooded him at the sight of her and he steeled himself against it. He wondered what Vivienne was thinking as she sat with an unreadable expression on her face. More than likely she despised him for coming to her room uninvited that night. Lord knew, he despised himself for his unmitigated stupidity.

"Before we begin supper, I would like to say one thing," Lord Cardwell continued with a grand hand gesture, his auburn beard bobbing as he spoke. "I realize this is not a set of circumstances that any of us would have chosen, but the die has been cast, so to speak. We must make the best of a rather awkward situation. Our two families will be joined by marriage as of Saturday." Gilbert's broad round face smiled benevolently. "Two fine families united by fate."

"Here, here," Lady Cardwell chimed in sweetly.

Susana cleared her throat loudly, and began coughing as if choking on something she could not bear to swallow. Heads turned to stare at her as she then sipped water from the glass in front of her, ostensibly to calm her cough. Aidan watched Vivienne lower her eyes at the incident and he cringed in embarrassment. His mother's blatant disapproval of his marriage to Vivienne had been made quite clear to the Cardwells.

"I agree," Aidan made a point to say, nodding his assent to Lord Cardwell's statement. Aidan cast a stern glance in his mother's direction. Though she was biting her tongue, her hard eyes betrayed her seething anger and bitter disappointment at this sudden turn of events. At first she had refused to attend the dinner, but she feared offending the Duchess of Bingham too much to turn down an invitation from the duchess's brother. Aidan almost wanted to laugh at her impotent rage at his marrying Vivienne and not Helene Winston. The only saving grace in the entire sordid ordeal was that he had honestly broken things off with Helene and spoken to her parents about it *before* he was found with Vivienne later that night. For that bit of good foresight on his part he would be eternally thankful.

As supper was served, Aidan realized he had no reservations about marrying into the Cardwell family. They were warm, friendly, and infinitely likeable, and he had known them all for years. Gilbert and Gwen Cardwell were kind and decent people. George and Gregory were more like brothers than friends to him and, although he rarely saw them, their older brother Gerald and his wife, who had come to town for the wedding on Saturday, were wonderful as well. Aidan could even tolerate their petulant sister Glenda, where most people could not. No, the Cardwell family had much to recommend them. Coming from the perspective of an only child, Aidan welcomed being part of the large and boisterous Cardwell family.

On the other hand, marrying Vivienne was an entirely different matter. He did not thrill at the prospect of being her husband. Although they might enjoy each other in the bedroom, he could never trust her. There were too many years of resentment and hurt feelings to overcome. And he was still reeling from the shocking news that he received from Grayson regarding Vivienne's whereabouts that afternoon.

Aidan managed to sit through supper without having to speak to Vivienne directly. Luckily the Cardwells were an animated group and the conversation never lagged. They even managed to snare his dour mother into cracking a smile at one point. Even so, Aidan was grateful when supper had concluded and the men were invited into the library for cigars.

As Gilbert, George, and Gerald Cardwell sat drinking brandy and discussing the latest political news, Aidan and Gregory ventured outside to smoke on the patio. Between the twins, he had always been a little closer to Gregory than George. Perhaps because he met Gregory first.

"I know you don't see it this way, but I, for one, am very happy that you are marrying Vivienne," Gregory began in his usual blithe manner, leaning against the balustrade overlooking the Cardwell's rose garden.

"This is not something I wish to discuss," Aidan said wearily, exhaling on his cigar. "But since we're on the subject, I happen to be in need of a best man on Saturday."

Gregory laughed good-naturedly. "Happy to oblige, if that's what you were asking me."

Aidan nodded his head, with a rueful grin. "That's what I was asking."

"I'd be honored to be your best man." Gregory's voice lowered and his ruddy face turned thoughtful. "You know that Vivienne is a very special woman."

"You don't know the half of it," Aidan muttered bitterly.

"Oh, but you see, I do." Gregory smiled with a gleeful gleam in his eyes. "I had a lovely little chat with

Vivienne this afternoon. I finally know all about Galway and what happened between the two of you ten years ago." At Aidan's hard look, Gregory continued in a serious tone, quite unlike his usual self, "You're absolutely wrong about her."

Again that vivid image sprang unbidden into Aidan's head. Vivienne and Nicky Foster, arms entwined. It hadn't faded in the least over time. "I know what I saw, Greg. I saw her with him with my own eyes."

"Looks can be deceiving."

"Not that time."

"Give her a second chance. You loved her enough once to want to marry her," Gregory persisted. "And she still loves you."

"Did she tell you that?"

"She didn't have to," Gregory stated. "I can tell by looking at her face when you walk in the room."

"Then tell me, what was she doing at Jackson Harlow's office this afternoon?" Aidan countered with mounting skepticism. Then he added sarcastically, "Looking to book passage on a ship before Saturday?"

"How did you know she was there?" Gregory asked in surprise, his eyes narrowed.

"I just do," Aidan retorted. He was still surprised by Grayson's report that his man Jones followed Jimmy Travers to Harlow's office and saw Vivienne there. "And you can't tell me there's anything platonic in that relationship. Harlow is obviously after her. I'm marrying her on Saturday and today she's visiting another man, unchaperoned."

"She was not unchaperoned," Gregory defended her. "I was with her. And she only went there to find out what happened to her father. He was sailing on one of their ships when he disappeared. She thinks there might have been some other cause involved, perhaps even foul play. Harlow is just helping her investigate the matter."

Gregory's words gave him pause, but Aidan still snorted, "Oh, I bet he's helping her."

"If you think Vivienne is so faithless," Gregory challenged him, "then call off the wedding."

"Your father caught me in bed with her. He's obtained a special license. I can hardly back out now."

"You certainly could if you really thought she was two-timing you again. Only this time with Harlow," Gregory persisted.

Aidan was silent. Although he didn't like the idea of Vivienne visiting Harlow for any reason, if he were completely honest with himself, there was a part of him that deep down really did not believe she was two-timing him with Harlow. Gregory's reason was very believable. If Vivienne thought there was a chance her father was still alive or that his cause of death was suspicious and that there was actually something she could do to change the situation, it would be just like her to go charging off with a man like Harlow, believing he could help her. He felt a pang of regret that he could not help her find the truth about her father himself.

Still, he had seen the looks Harlow cast at Vivienne. And he had not imagined the looks Vivienne had returned to Harlow either. The man was consumed with lust for her and his interest was not merely to help Vivienne find out what happened to her father. Vivienne, just like that idiot Travers, had no idea what type of man she was really dealing with. Harlow's charm blinded her. Aidan supposed he was worried for her more than anything else. He knew better than to trust Harlow to be decent or chivalrous.

Aidan inhaled deeply on his cigar, blowing the smoke out slowly. "No, I can't back out now."

"Well, for what it's worth, I'm really happy you're marrying my cousin," Gregory stated with satisfaction. "In the end, I think it is going to work out well between the two of you."

"You're just relieved I'm not marrying Helene," Aidan quipped dryly.

"About that . . ." Gregory began hesitantly, with a sheepish look on his freckled face. "I . . . uh . . . I was wondering how you would feel if—"

"If you proposed to Helene?" Aidan finished his question. He had been expecting this from his friend and truly had no issue with Gregory and Helene being together.

"How did you know?" Gregory gaped in surprise.

"I'm not blind," Aidan said affably. "I think she preferred you to me all along, my friend."

"Thank you," Gregory said quietly, yet he could not contain his happiness. "I wasn't sure what you would think of me with Helene."

"I'm fine with it. I ended things amicably with her the night of the masked ball. You have my blessings if that's what you want."

"I do."

"Then you have them," Aidan said with a grin. He could not think of two more deserving souls than Gregory and Helene. "Be happy with her."

"Thank you, Aidan," Gregory uttered earnestly.

"Hello," a familiar feminine voice interrupted them. He and Gregory turned to see Vivienne before them, looking lovely in her lavender gown.

"Vivvy, we were just talking about you," Gregory

called to her as she stepped closer to them, and they both extinguished their cigars.

"Were you, now?" she questioned skeptically. "I can only imagine what that conversation entailed."

Aidan remained silent. Whenever Vivienne came near him, it seemed he lost the ability to think coherently. He nodded to her in greeting. She merely nodded back.

"Was I interrupting?" she asked them hesitantly after a moment. "Shall I leave you?"

"Please stay. We were just discussing the wedding," Gregory explained in his jovial manner. "Aidan asked me to be his best man on Saturday."

"That's wonderful," she replied, avoiding looking in Aidan's direction.

"Who have you asked to attend you?" Gregory inquired.

"Aunt Gwen," she paused and then explained, "I asked Glenda first but she said no, and I'm not yet close enough to any other girls here in London . . ." Her voice trailed off.

"I'm sure my mother is thrilled to do it," Gregory answered with a grin.

Vivienne nodded. "I think she is."

"I shall go and refresh my drink. I'm sure the two of you would like a moment of privacy. You must have some things to discuss before your wedding," Gregory began, knowing that to be the farthest thing from the truth. "If you will excuse me . . ." Then he fled the scene before either Aidan or Vivienne could utter a protest.

They stood uncomfortably together on the patio. In three days they would be man and wife, and now he could barely think of a civil word to say to her. An awkward silence ensued as Aidan stared at Vivienne. She looked enticing in the flickering light from the gas lamps illuminating the patio. Desire ran rampant through him, in spite of the anger that consumed him, and his body reacted physically to her presence. He wanted to touch her, to smell her hair, to kiss her, to pull her into his arms. He wanted to lift her skirts and have her.

"You don't have to marry me, Aidan." Her voice was low.

Startled by her remark, he responded instinctively, "Yes, I do."

"No, you don't. That night was my fault just as much as yours."

"I came to your room in the middle of the night, Vivienne. I take full responsibility and accept the consequences."

"I don't wish to marry someone who sees me only as the consequence of his actions. As a terrible sentence he must endure."

"You have no choice in the matter now. I'm marrying you on Saturday."

She looked up at him, her expression dark and accusing. "So you can punish me for the rest of my life?"

"What do you mean?" he asked incredulously. He was the one who would be tortured forever by that day in Galway, not her.

"You know exactly what I'm talking about. You will make me miserable, make us miserable. You will never trust me or believe in me again. You will hold Nicky Foster over my head and torment us both with what you think happened. You can never forget what you think you saw, and because of that, you will never give us a chance. We can never be at peace together. Are you ready for that?"

Aidan felt a twinge of remorse, but could not help but agree with her silently. Yet he managed to say through clenched teeth, "It will be fine."

She shook her head and said softly, "This marriage is a mistake. I know my family is making you do this, but you really don't have to marry me."

"I'm afraid that I do. I've given my word to your uncle."

"Correct me if I'm wrong, but you gave your word to me ten years ago yet that didn't stop you from breaking it then."

"That was different and you know it," Aidan retorted hotly. Again, she had struck a nerve with him. Ever since they were children she had always been able to do that to him. She always made him think and look at the other side of issues. But he didn't want to do that now. He was too angry with her. For the past. The present. For everything.

"No. I don't know," she demanded. "Explain the difference."

They did not speak for a moment. He had no response to that. The rational part of him acknowledged that she made a good point, but he was not going to admit that to her. Stunned and angered that she was attempting to get out of the marriage to him, he stood his ground. "I won't discuss that with you now."

"When will we discuss 'that,' Aidan, if not now?" she protested.

He stood firm. "There is nothing to discuss."

"You would think that," she said derisively. "We shouldn't marry each other. I can manage on my own."

"I doubt that," he scoffed at her. "Why were you visiting Jackson Harlow's office today?"

"That is none of your business," she snapped cuttingly.

By the startled expression on her face it was apparent she was surprised that he knew where she'd been. If he were not mistaken, there was some guilt in those sapphire eyes of hers. "It's absolutely my business when you are involved with a ruthless and dangerous man."

"Jackson Harlow is a fine gentleman," she defended him vehemently. "He's simply helping me with an important matter."

"Your father?" He raised an eyebrow at her.

"I see Gregory's been talking to you."

"Yes. But now you listen to me, Vivienne, and listen to me well." He stepped closer to her and put his hand beneath her chin, forcing her to look up at him like a child. If she were going to act like a careless, spoiled little girl, he was going to treat her like one. Her eyes widened and a defiant expression came over her exquisite features.

"Harlow is not interested in helping you, Vivienne. At least not in the way you think he is. He is set on ruining me and he'll ruin you to get to me. I told you once before. This is the last time I will say it again, and I expect you to obey me." He paused, then said very slowly and clearly, so she would not misunderstand nor misinterpret his meaning, "Stay . . . away . . . from . . . Jackson . . . Harlow."

She placed her hand over his hand in an effort to release her chin, and he reeled from the contact of her warm fingers on his.

"And I told you that you have no right to tell me what to do," she said between clenched teeth. She pulled away from his grasp triumphantly.

"I do as of Saturday when we marry."

"But we're not married yet, are we, Aidan?" she replied archly and gave him a withering glance before she turned to stalk away from him.

"Damn it, Vivienne!" he called after her, furious. Without thinking Aidan grabbed her with both hands and spun her around to face him. Her eyes glistened angrily and she struggled to break free once again. "You don't understand, do you?!" he cried.

"That you can tell me how to live my life? No, I don't understand, then. Nor will I ever! I can speak to anyone I want, whenever I want. You cannot tell me what to do!"

"When I'm your husband, you'll do as I say." He didn't know what he was saying. He had never been the kind of man who expected obedience in a wife.

She laughed at that, a mocking laugh, her eyes glittering fiercely as she struggled against his hold on her. "That's what you think!"

How dare she taunt him that way? She was going to be his wife and she still thought she could visit another man. A man who was obviously infatuated with her. *Not bloody likely!* And she hadn't a clue, a single clue, who she was dealing with. Aidan was not entirely sure what Harlow was up to with her, but he was positive it was nothing good. Harlow was not the altruistic type to do something for nothing. If he actually were helping Vivienne discover what happened to her father, he expected some payment in return. He wanted something from her desperately. Aidan wondered if Harlow were using Vivienne to provoke him. If Harlow harmed her in any way . . .

Aidan wanted to shake her, make her understand how dangerous Harlow was.

Instead he pulled her against his chest and his lips

crashed down upon hers. Instantly she stopped fighting him. Her rigid body softened and her soft, sweet mouth sought his. He wrapped his arms around her and her small hands clasped behind his neck. Their kiss deepened and he lost all sense of time and space, feeling only Vivienne in his arms once again. He breathed her in. Her softness. Her sweetness. The floral scent of her overwhelmed him. Their tongues intermingled and a little sigh escaped her.

His body tightened in response to the feel of her breasts pressed against him. God, how he wanted her. Wanted her writhing naked beneath him. Wanted to feel his body pressing into hers, over and over.

He wanted her to love him again. As she did once before. He wanted his Vivienne back. His friend. His lover. He wanted to forget everything that tore them apart.

He ran his hand down the length of her narrow waist, over the graceful curve of her hip, and around to the tempting flesh of her derriere. He squeezed. She pushed herself tighter against him, maneuvering herself between his thighs and he sucked in his breath. Their hot mouths moved over each other's. He walked her backwards until she was against the balustrade. She continued to kiss him fervently, their lips never losing contact. He lifted her so her bottom rested on the wide marble balustrade. She clung to him, her fingers in the hair at the back of his neck. He cupped her exquisite face in his hands, forgetting where he was, forgetting that she had angered him, forgetting the past. He was drowning in her. *Vivienne, Vivienne, Vivienne* . . .

"For the love of God, Aidan, can you at least keep your hands off her until after the wedding?" Lord

Cardwell muttered in exasperation as he joined them on the patio.

Instantly releasing her, Aidan looked abashedly toward Vivienne's uncle. How was it possible that he'd lost control again? In front of her uncle, no less! "I'm sorry," he said as he struggled to regain control of his senses. Good God! He had almost taken her there on the patio!

He assisted Vivienne off the balustrade and she stood trembling in front of him. He shielded her momentarily from view, to allow her to compose herself. And she looked incredibly appealing; her soft lips kissed to a ripe fullness, her satiny cheeks still flushed with unsatisfied desire. Yet he knew she felt as embarrassed and as mortified as he did. He wished he could protect her somehow. Instead he took her small hand in his, gave her a comforting squeeze, and let it go quickly. Before they turned to face her uncle, she glanced at him, her eyes full of emotions he dared not delve into.

"It's a good thing you're getting married on Saturday," Cardwell continued in his gruff voice. "I don't think you could hold out much longer than that. But please show my niece some respect in the meantime."

His mother had followed Lord Cardwell outside and, judging from the infuriated look on her face, she had also seen him kissing Vivienne.

"It's very late and time we were headed home, Aidan," she stated in a clipped tone.

"I think that's an excellent decision," Lord Cardwell echoed his mother's sentiment. "We'll see you at the church on Saturday morning. Ten o'clock sharp."

Aidan dared not look back at Vivienne as he left. He did not know if he had the strength.

Chapter 19

Another Plan

"I am offering you money to marry Vivienne Montgomery."

Jackson Harlow could not believe his ears. Yesterday he had received an unexpected and unusual invitation from the Earl of Whitlock's mother, and now he found himself seated before her in the expensively decorated drawing room of her London townhouse at an ungodly early hour. The invitation had intrigued him and he could not refuse to see her.

"Could you repeat that please, Lady Whitlock?" he asked with brows raised in surprise, not quite sure that he heard her correctly.

She regarded him astutely. She wore an austere navy blue gown, the darkness accentuating the silver-gray of her tightly coiled hair. She sat perfectly straight on the edge of her chair, her hands clasped firmly in her lap. "I had assumed you were a shrewd man, Mister Harlow.

Have I misjudged you?" she asked, one steely eyebrow raised above her icy gray eyes.

"I doubt you could do such a thing. Please continue," he encouraged her smoothly, intrigued by the possibilities she had presented to him.

"It's quite obvious to me that you desire Miss Montgomery. I observed you with her at Bingham Hall and I, for reasons of my own, want her out of my son's life permanently. Now I thought we could serve both our purposes. Are you interested in helping me?"

Hell, yes, he was interested! Lady Whitlock's plan would only further his own cause. She was practically handing him Vivienne Montgomery and her diamond mines on a silver platter. But he could not deny he was floored to discover that Aidan Kavanaugh's mother was such a cold-hearted bitch. He only saw her briefly at Bingham Hall, but he could not help but notice that she was a tough old dragon. Now he knew he had vastly underestimated her. Hell, he'd be doing Vivienne a favor by taking her away from Aidan. With this miserable woman as her mother-in-law, her life would be a living hell. Obviously Lady Whitlock did not deem Vivienne good enough to marry her precious Aidan. She preferred the elegant, blond Helene Winston for a daughter-in-law, which was not a bad choice either in his book. The woman must really hate Vivienne to manipulate her so callously, but far be it for him to judge another's ethics.

"What are you prepared to offer me in return for my assistance?" he questioned her coldly. He might as well make it worth his while. At this point he'd take Vivienne for free, but the old bitch didn't need to know that.

Jackson had been worried that he would not be able

to persuade Vivienne to marry him before Saturday and he would have to resort to more drastic measures. He had a soft spot for the Irish beauty and wanted her to come to him willingly, for he sensed she would be more uninhibited that way. He felt he almost had her convinced that afternoon in his office, then that idiot Travers burst in and scared her off with his unintelligible tirade. But he'd made Travers pay heavily for that interruption, and the pathetic man certainly wouldn't be around to bother Jackson ever again.

"The price is completely negotiable, Mister Harlow," Lady Whitlock continued briskly in a calm and business-like manner. One would think that she sold off her son's fiancées to the highest bidder every day. "Any amount that you require is possible. What I don't have to give you is time. We must move quickly. I want her out of London before Saturday. Then you must marry her as soon as possible. After that I don't care what you do with her. But it must look like she went with you willingly."

"What makes you think she wouldn't?" Jackson countered with a sly grin.

"Don't flatter yourself, Mister Harlow." She shook her head. "I've seen Aidan and Vivienne together. It might not be as easy as you think. She has her greedy claws planted firmly in my son."

Jackson admitted to himself that that statement surprised and somewhat wounded his vanity. He had been under the distinct impression that Vivienne cared for him, not Whitlock. "She has more feelings for me than it would seem."

"I don't care about her feelings," she retorted sharply. "I simply want her out of Aidan's life for good."

Curious to know the old dragon's motivation, he questioned her. "May I ask why?"

Lady Whitlock grimaced sourly. "Personal reasons, which go back many years and I need not go into with you. Suffice it to say, my son was well acquainted with Vivienne in Ireland."

"Ah, I see now." Jackson nodded his head in understanding. So Aidan Kavanaugh and Vivienne had a love affair years ago. It clearly explained why they were in bed together so quickly that night at the Binghams'. "Old love dies hard?"

"Something like that," she said in a dismissively clipped tone, brushing imaginary dust from her silky skirt. Then she folded her hands neatly in her lap once again. "I had arranged for you to be caught in her room that night at Bingham Hall. I sent you that note."

"You sent the note?" And suddenly it was all very clear to him. It explained perfectly why the Cardwells, as well as Lady Whitlock, had been at Vivienne's door that night. Only Jackson was the one who was supposed to be caught in Vivienne's bedroom, not Aidan. The Machiavellian woman had not only manipulated her son's miserable life, but she had played fast and loose with Jackson's own fate. Luckily for Lady Whitlock, it coincided with his personal plans, or he would have to vent his wrath upon her for attempting to ruin him. As it was, he would make her pay a heavy monetary price for her deviousness, which impressed him, oddly enough. "You are a cold-blooded woman."

"That is beside the point. Now, Mister Harlow, do we have an agreement?"

Jackson needed to marry Vivienne Montgomery as soon as possible. There would be plenty of time later to sort through her father's letters and find the deeds. Which would then legally belong to him. He had connections who could procure a special license for him as well. In fact, he could be married to Vivienne himself on Saturday instead of Lord Whitlock. Then it would be all settled. He could leave his failing family's shipping business and his miserable brothers and start a new life with a fortune in diamond mines and a beautiful wife by his side. He would take her to Paris. Italy. Maybe even New York. He was actually looking forward to being with her.

"Yes, Lady Whitlock, I believe we do. I'll have her out of town this afternoon."

Lady Whitlock looked at him quizzically, her sharp features alert. "What do you intend to do? Her uncle won't allow her out of the house until after the wedding, because he doesn't trust her to comport herself like a lady. And you can't very well go knocking on her front door and ask her to run away with you."

Jackson smiled his trademark, heart-melting smile and watched as Lady Whitlock flinched from the impact. "That's where you come in, Lady Whitlock," he said smoothly. "Vivienne could hardly refuse a summons from her future mother-in-law to make peace before the wedding, now could she?"

"I like the way you think, Mister Harlow." She smiled triumphantly, her gray eyes glittering.

"I thought you might, Lady Whitlock," Jackson said, and began taking steps to put this plan of theirs into effect.

That morning Vivienne sat at the dainty escritoire in her tastefully decorated bedroom at Cardwell House and idly wondered if she shouldn't take Jackson Harlow up on his offer and flee Aidan and his hateful mother once and for all. Marrying Harlow seemed like a simple way out of her disastrous situation with Aidan, but something held her back. Something changed that day in Jackson's office. Perhaps it was when Jackson kissed her. She could not envision being his wife when his kiss left her feeling cold inside. And distinctly disloyal to Aidan.

Not that Aidan deserved her loyalty.

Or perhaps it was Aidan's mind-melting kiss on the patio last night. Or when he squeezed her hand in a show of support when they had been caught together by her uncle yet again. If only she could make Aidan believe in her once more, there might be a chance for them to be happy together. That kiss last night sparked some hope in her that their marriage had a possibility of working. The feelings they had for each other were still there, just as when they sang together at the musicale and the night they were caught in her bedroom, even if Aidan attempted to ignore them. Were their feelings strong enough to overcome the obstacles they faced? They had to be. He simply could not kiss her that way and not care for her.

Could he?

Aidan evoked such powerful feelings in her. And she still loved him, still desired him. In spite of everything. In spite of all the years apart. They could be happy together if only Aidan would see the truth. But she was not certain if he ever would.

Vivienne focused her attention back on the matter at hand. That morning she had gathered all the letters her father had sent to her over the years and reread them methodically, one by one, searching for clues, anything unusual or hints at trouble with the shipping company he worked for. Yet nothing stood out. Each and every letter was perfectly, frustratingly normal.

Jackson told her that her father owned lucrative diamond mines. She could find no proof of that. Not a shred of evidence.

Vivienne could not imagine that her father would have priceless diamond mines and not tell her about it. If what Jackson told her were true, they had to be a fairly recent acquisition, for certainly he would have shared that information with her when she saw him last. That was two years before his ship supposedly went down sailing back from South Africa. His letters to her during that voyage seemed typical, displaying nothing out of the ordinary. He asked how she was, how Aggie felt, asked how things were in Galway. He mentioned the beauty of Africa and how he would love for her to see it one day. He did not refer to Davis or Miles Harlow at all. That left only the note that was attached with the wooden box he sent her just before he disappeared. The last words her father wrote to her.

> *My Dearest Vivienne,*
> *I'm sending this wooden box to you because it is a beautiful work of art from South Africa, and indeed, whatever is mine, daughter, is yours. I know you will care for it well and keep it safe until I return, for it is worth more than you know. Keep it close to you. I will explain its importance to you as soon as I return home. I love you very much.*
>
> *~Papa*

Rereading it now, she realized something peculiar and her heart quickened. Not only did he warn her not to let anyone take the box from her, claiming it to be worth more than she knew, but the phrase "whatever is *mine*, daughter, is yours" suddenly caught her attention. Was he alluding to the diamond mine when saying "mine"? She had no way of knowing for certain.

As she stared at the lovely wooden box again, she looked at the ivory diamond pattern with new insight. *A diamond pattern.* Was her father trying to tell her about the mines without actually telling her? Why the secrecy and mystery? Why not just tell her? For whatever reasons, he thought it best to keep his daughter in the dark. He obviously sensed some danger.

Lifting the lid of the box, she removed its precious cargo. Aggie's intricate Celtic cross. Now that she was in London, she wanted to buy a new gold chain for it. Her mother's wedding band. It made her wonder about her own wedding band, which certainly wouldn't be given with love. Then there was the silver locket from Aidan. Holding it in her hand, she popped the lock and gazed at his picture inside. He had not changed much since the picture was painted. He looked a little older perhaps, but the image still resembled him. In an unexplainable fit of sentimentality, she placed the locket around her neck. It felt strangely comforting to have it on again.

Now that the box was empty, she gave it a thorough inspection. There had to be something more to it. The box was the message, she was certain. Wondering why she never looked at it that way before, she ascribed it to the overwhelming grief she suffered at losing her father. She shook the box. And heard nothing. She turned it over and over, admiring the lovely ivory inlay, but seeing nothing out of the ordinary.

Until she examined the inside. And suddenly she knew. Why hadn't she thought of it before? Of course!

A false bottom. Delicately, she removed the dark blue velvet lining and set it on her desk. Underneath was a thin panel of smooth wood. She lifted it, and caught her breath in a little gasp of surprise. Folded papers nestled inside the bottom of the box. Trembling, she took the papers from the box and unfolded them carefully.

They were deeds, in John Montgomery's name, to diamond mines in South Africa. To think they were in the box the entire time! Her heart pounded at her discovery. Her father had owned diamond mines supposedly worth a fortune. Why on earth wouldn't he let her know such a thing?

Now the question was what should she do about it? What good was a deed, if it were even valid, to a place on the other side of the world? Oddly enough, her first impulse was to show Aidan. He would know exactly what to do and how to handle this situation. But he had no desire to talk to her. She supposed she should bring the deeds downstairs and let Uncle Gilbert take a look at them. Yes, that was probably the best course of action.

"Miss Vivienne, I have a message for you," Lizzie said cheerily as she entered Vivienne's bedroom.

"What is it?" she asked. Distracted, she gathered the papers and put them back inside the pretty inlaid ivory box.

"It's from the Countess of Whitlock." Lizzie handed her a sealed note in thick paper. "There's a servant waiting downstairs for a reply. It seems urgent."

Recognizing the intricate wax seal, Vivienne's interest piqued at receiving a note from Aidan's mother. She was the last person she expected to hear from and she read the elegantly scripted words in surprise.

Miss Montgomery,

   *Since you are marrying my son on Saturday, I wish
to spend some time with you and make peace before the
wedding. Please be at my house for tea this afternoon.*
                                                    Lady Whitlock

Vivienne laughed out loud. So the old harridan finally wanted to make peace, did she? Well, she had a
peculiar way of asking. More like demanding that Vivienne come to her. At least she kept up appearances
and said please! Vivienne supposed she should go see
her, although she certainly didn't relish spending any
time with Susana Kavanaugh alone. After the looks
that woman gave her at dinner the night before, there
was not a doubt in her mind that Lady Whitlock hated
her and would rather have any other woman on the
planet than Vivienne marry her son.

Certain her aunt and uncle would approve of her
visiting her future mother-in-law at her request and
not one to back down from a challenge, Vivienne
penned a brief note to accept Susana Kavanaugh's invitation. It would not be the most enjoyable afternoon
she ever spent, but making peace with her might be
worth it in the long run. She was actually a little interested in what Susana Kavanaugh had to say to her
after all these years. "Would you please take this to
Lady Whitlock's footman, Lizzie? It seems I'm to have
tea with Aidan's mother this afternoon."

"Why, Miss Vivienne!" Lizzie cried in amazement,
taking the note from her with round eyes. "I thought
she disliked you!"

"Oh, she does, I've no doubt of that. Perhaps she
just finally accepted that I'm marrying Aidan. I can't
imagine what she'll say to me," Vivienne said with a

little laugh as Lizzie left the room. Probably a long lecture on how not to disgrace Aidan's good name nor her standing in society. She tried to brace herself to be civil to the woman.

"He's dead."

Aidan glanced up from his desk at Grayson's surprising announcement. He knew instantly to whom Grayson was referring.

"What happened?" he asked. He'd been occupied at his office all morning, burying himself in work so he did not have to think about his impending marriage to Vivienne. It hadn't worked. His mind kept returning to her taunting words to him last night.

And that mad kiss on the patio.

He had been up all night reflecting on how she believed he would spend their marriage punishing her. There was some truth to her assertion. He was not proud of himself, but perhaps Vivienne was right about him. Could they be happy together if he gave it a chance? He did not want to be in a miserable marriage with her. Could their marriage be an agreeable one? They had so much in common, so much bonded history together, they could certainly make a decent go of it. Their love had been a rare and wondrous occurrence ten years ago. Could they reclaim that? Could it grow between them anew? If only he could forgive her . . .

She had adamantly declared her innocence in the incident with Nicky Foster. Had he seen something different from what really happened that day at the cottage? Had it truly been the way Vivienne depicted it? Could Foster have been taking advantage of her against her will? What if he had been wrong about her all these years? That question left him sleepless last night. But the answers haunted him as well.

And he had handled her badly last night. At this point in time he should know better than to think he could force Vivienne to do anything she didn't want to do. She was an independent soul and he had always loved her because of it. By forbidding her to stay away from Harlow, he just pushed her further under that man's influence. His frustration with her and fear for her had eclipsed his better judgment and he came across sounding tyrannical and irrational. He needed to go about it in a softer way with her, to get her to see his point of view. Harlow was dangerous, and maybe Aidan needed to explain to Vivienne just how dangerous he was.

Which brought him back to the conversation in front of him.

Grayson sat himself in a chair across from Aidan's desk and began the sordid story of Jimmy Travers' sudden demise. "Last night two men jumped him in the alley and knifed him. They sliced him up badly and it happened so quickly Jones couldn't stop them. He stayed to help, but the two men disappeared into the night. Travers bled to death before Jones could get him to a doctor."

"The poor fool," Aidan muttered in disgust, thinking of the thick-witted man and all the trouble he brought about. Aidan was positive that setting the warehouse fire had been the least of the man's sins, but it still seemed a waste of a life. Disappointment ran rampant through him. "It was all for nothing."

"There's a harsh price to pay for being foolish and greedy."

"Yes, and Harlow will be paying the price for this soon enough," Aidan predicted threateningly. He could hardly wait to see justice served up to that one. If he only had some proof.

"That's going to be harder to prove since he just killed off the only witness to his crime," Grayson said with a frown.

"That we know of," Aidan added, raising one eyebrow. "Keep investigating. There has to be something that we're missing. I am sure of it. He's not that smart and he could not have possibly covered all of his tracks. Let's put a trail on Harlow and his brothers first thing in the morning. We should have done that from the beginning."

"I agree." Grayson nodded, making ready to leave. "I think we have sadly underestimated Harlow's capabilities."

Which made Aidan all the more worried about Vivienne's involvement with him. Maybe he would stop by the Cardwells' this evening and make another attempt at reasoning with her. She was a reasonable woman, in spite of his protests to the contrary. If they could talk as friends again, as they once used to, they might be able to come to an agreement. Maybe they just needed more time together.

"Oh, did we follow up on Travers' sister?" Aidan called after him.

"Yes," Grayson turned to say with a grimace. "She's dying of consumption in the hospital. Doctor said there was no hope."

Aidan shook his head in regret as Grayson left the office, leaving him alone with his thoughts. There was so much misery in the world. Why would he insist on focusing on the sorrow in his own life? Could he concentrate instead on the good things he was fortunate enough to possess? He had once loved her with all his heart. She had once been his best friend. Was this a second chance at that happiness? Could he choose to be happy with Vivienne?

As Vivienne alighted from the carriage in front of Lady Whitlock's house, her pretty blue-striped tea gown swirling about her, she steeled herself for a tiresome and strained visit with Aidan's mother. She waved to the Cardwells' driver as he drove away with instructions to come back for her in an hour. Vivienne gave herself a moment before she had to knock on the door. She adjusted her skirts and took a fortifying breath. This afternoon was going to challenge her patience, of that she had no doubt.

"Hullo there, Vivienne!" a familiar voice suddenly called to her.

Startled, she glanced around to see Jackson Harlow waving from the window of a large, black-lacquered carriage pulled by four fine ebony horses. His gloved hand moved elegantly and he smiled brightly at her, his blond hair visible beneath a black top hat. As usual, everything about Jackson Harlow was elegant and stylish.

"Good afternoon!" she called back to him, grinning in spite of herself.

He ordered his driver to stop and he sprang from the carriage, landing like a tiger on the sidewalk beside her, his black cape swinging around him. His golden smile beamed at her. "Vivienne, what great luck! I was on my way to see you just now."

"Were you?" she asked in confusion. "I'm about to meet Lord Whitlock's mother for tea."

His expression clouded with disappointment. "Oh, then I suppose it will have to wait. I had some news for you."

"About my father?" she asked breathlessly.

"Yes, about your father." A smile tugged at the corner of his mouth. "Could you spare some time now? Otherwise it will have to wait a few weeks. I'm leaving town tonight on an urgent matter. I'm not sure when I'll be able to return to London. If you come with me now, I can show you the documents at my office before I leave."

Vivienne could barely contain her excitement. He had news about her father! Consumed with curiosity, she knew she could not wait weeks or perhaps months to learn what it was. She glanced toward Lady Whitlock's townhouse. Aidan's mother would be expecting her any moment now and would be exceedingly put out if Vivienne arrived late. Then she reckoned that Susana Kavanaugh would be put out with her for the rest of her life, and that being late for tea would hardly make a difference in her feelings toward her at this point.

Still, she harbored misgivings. "Would we be terribly long?" she asked him anxiously.

Jackson pulled a gold pocket watch from his vest and looked at it thoughtfully. He turned his golden brown eyes back to her, tilting his head to one side. "Well, that depends. I can't say for sure how long it will take, although you will more than likely miss tea."

"You couldn't wait an hour? Until after I've had tea with her?"

He shook his head in regret. "Honestly, I cannot. I

have an important engagement outside London that I must attend to immediately. I'm on my way now and thought I could quickly take you to my office before I leave."

Vivienne shifted nervously on her feet. She desperately wanted to know what Jackson had discovered. She would never get another opportunity to meet with him either. Once she married Aidan, that would be the end of that. Although faint warning bells sounded in the back of her mind because of the way he kissed her the other day, the prospect of learning more about her father outweighed her reservations.

She agreed to go with him.

Again he flashed his charming smile and extended his hand to her. "Come along, Miss Montgomery. What I have to tell you is something you certainly will need to hear."

Giving a fleeting glance back at Lady Whitlock's house, Vivienne accepted his hand and allowed him to escort her into his stylish and grand carriage.

have an important engagement outside London that

Chapter 20

The Truth

Aidan's mother was waiting for him in his drawing room when he arrived home later that evening. It was quite unusual for his mother to come to his house without an invitation and he was puzzled by her presence. She had her own elegant townhouse about six blocks away and preferred to have Aidan visit her on her territory. Their arrangement suited him perfectly and he wondered what had brought her there today. "What a surprise to see you, Mother," he greeted her.

She sat rigidly on a straight-backed chair, her hands folded primly in her lap. Her expression was grim, the age lines on her face seeming more pronounced than usual. Yet there was an undisguised gleam in her eyes. "I'm afraid I have some unpleasant news to tell you, Aidan."

A tightening in his gut told Aidan it had to do with Vivienne. He wondered what news his mother would have to impart about his future wife. "What is it?" he asked with a slight sense of dread.

"It seems Vivienne has run off."

"What do you mean?" he asked, his voice sounding as if it came from somewhere other than his own mouth.

"Vivienne and I have never had the best relationship, as you well know. For your sake, I thought it would be nice to invite her to tea this afternoon to try to smooth things over between us before the wedding. I was trying to make the best of this dreadful situation, Aidan. I was reaching out to her. I received a note from her accepting my invitation, but she never arrived."

"That doesn't mean she's run off," Aidan protested, feeling a little calmer. He was stunned that his mother made such an effort in the first place, and even more so that Vivienne had accepted an invitation from her.

There was a hard glint in his mother's gray eyes. "The Cardwells' driver left her at the steps to my door, but I never saw her. She never set foot in my house. He came to pick her up an hour later, but of course she wasn't there, and she has not returned home. No one knows where she is."

Aidan's mind was spinning. *Vivienne. Not again.*

Susana continued, "One would think a girl would keep an engagement with her future mother-in-law two days before her wedding. She would do well not to anger me and she knows that, Aidan."

No, it did not sound like Vivienne. If she were going to anger his mother, she would do it openly. And if Vivienne had accepted her invitation, she would have been there. Which gave him pause to worry. Vivienne was headstrong, to be sure, but not foolish. He would credit her that much. As a newcomer to London, she would never venture off alone in a city so large and unknown to her. Terrible things could happen to a young woman on her own in London. Aidan's heart began to race. "Something must have happened to her."

"Don't be a fool, Aidan," his mother snapped at him, her mouth twisted in a scowl. "The girl is just not the type to marry. It's quite obvious that she ran off with someone."

Last night, Vivienne had offered to release him from the engagement but he had stood his ground to honor his commitment to marry her. Had he been too forceful with her? Had she balked at his unyielding bitterness? She said she didn't want to marry someone who didn't want to marry her. He might have believed she was escaping their compulsory marriage, if not for that kiss. Their kiss last night meant more, and they both knew it. "I had agreed to marry her. Why would she run away?"

"I didn't say she ran away. I said she ran off with another man."

At first he rejected the idea. Then he thought of Jackson Harlow. Aidan felt sick inside. And livid. She had taunted him with that just last night—that he had no right to tell her who she could and could not talk to. *But we're not married yet, are we, Aidan?*

"She had to meet a lover," his mother insisted in a sharp tone. "A girl does not just wander about this city alone. She has done nothing but shame that family since they took her into their home. Those poor Cardwell twins are out searching the streets for her now, and her aunt and uncle are beside themselves with worry."

Feeling an icy sense of urgency settle over him, he asked impatiently, "Why didn't you send for me earlier? When you first learned she was missing?"

Susana stood up angrily, her voice rising in pitch as she spoke. "Why should I have bothered you? That girl has caused you trouble since the day you met her. It's obvious she has no true desire to be your wife. You deserve better than Vivienne Montgomery. Let her be another man's burden for a change. I, for one, am glad to be rid of her. As you should be."

"Go home, Mother," Aidan said with a distinct coldness, his disgust for her palpable. "I have to find Vivienne." He turned on his heel and left the room, ignoring his mother's repeated calls to him.

"Don't bother searching for her! She's not worth it! She doesn't want to marry you, or she would have been at my house this afternoon!"

Where could Vivienne be? In his heart he knew something was terribly wrong and she was in danger. And that somehow Jackson Harlow was involved in this up to his neck. He would go to the Cardwells' and join forces with Gregory and George. They would surely have more information on Vivienne's whereabouts than his mother did. He hurriedly made his way through the house and called to his butler, giving the man instructions. "Have Higgins bring my carriage around front as quick as he can. I'll be right down."

Taking two steps at a time, he raced up the long, elegantly curving staircase and down the corridor to his bedroom. A growing sense of alarm spurred him. Whatever had happened to prevent Vivienne from arriving at his mother's house was not good. He strode purposefully to the massive oak chest of drawers in the corner of his room.

Finley waited for him anxiously, but Aidan was barely aware of his valet's presence. "I need to talk to you about something important, Aidan," Finley said.

Aidan opened the top corner drawer and removed a heavy, black leather case. Inside was a pistol. Some sixth sense told him he might need it and, when he found Harlow, he wouldn't mind using it. He placed it in his coat pocket. "Not now, Finley. I'm on my way out." He continued to the door of the bedroom.

"It's about Vivienne."

Aidan stopped in his tracks and turned. He looked Finley directly in the eyes and demanded, "What about Vivienne?"

Finley hesitated, as if afraid to speak, his freckled face drawn in worry.

Aidan said impatiently, "Out with it, man. I haven't time to waste. I think Vivienne's in trouble."

That seemed to spur Finley into talking. "She never did anything wrong, Aidan. All those years ago, back in Galway. That day at the little cottage. When you found her with Foster. She was set up."

Aidan had the very breath taken from him. "Say that again."

"She was set up to look like she was with Foster, and to be caught that way by you. And for you to be angry enough to call off the wedding."

"How would you know something like this?" Aidan asked incredulously.

"Because I set it up. I was the one who arranged for Nicky Foster to be there before you arrived and for him to make it look like he was taking advantage of Vivienne. To compromise her."

"Are you telling me that Vivienne was completely innocent all this time?"

"Yes." Finley had the decency to look ashamed. "She was never untrue to you."

Aidan's head spun with this bit of news. Images and words raced through Aidan's brain. Making love to Vivienne in the portrait gallery. *"No one else, Aidan! There has . . . never been anyone else. Just you, Aidan. Only you."* Her anguish and tears in his arms afterward. *"My arms were not around Nicky. They were trying to push him off of me.*

And I was not kissing him. He was kissing me. Against my will." Her anger with him for not believing her. Then Gregory's words last night. *"You're wrong about her."*

Aidan had been completely blinded. So unyielding and callous. Full of wounded pride and righteousness. But another thought gripped him and he gave Finely a hard look. "Why would you do something like that?"

"I was told to."

"Who told you to do something like that?" he asked, although his head pounded with a sense of foreboding. He would not want to know the answer.

Finley waited a moment, his brown eyes meeting Aidan's directly. Then he confessed, "Your mother."

His mother. Her dislike for Vivienne was always blatant, but was she capable of that kind of hatred? To ruin Vivienne? To destroy the love of her only son? He thought of her waiting downstairs for him. An awkward silence followed before Aidan spoke again. "Do you know what you are saying?"

"Yes." Finley nodded with a definitive look.

It was too much. And yet it made sense. Finley had originally worked for his mother at Cashelwood Manor. He was the only servant who knew that Aidan met Vivienne secretly in the little cottage. He more than likely reported to her all Aidan's comings and goings. Finley would have been the logical choice to aid and abet his mother. Afterwards, Finley had been sympathetic and encouraged him to forget Vivienne and move on. That was when they had become friends. But Finley had never lied to him in all these years, and he certainly had nothing to gain by telling Aidan the truth now. Which posed another good question. "Why are you telling me this ten years after the fact?"

"Because I know better now," Finley asserted, the look on his face remorseful and contrite. "I knew it was wrong at the time and I have felt guilty about it all these years. I have wanted to tell you the truth many times, but I couldn't. I believed you would never see Vivienne again and it wouldn't matter anyway. But when she showed up at Bingham Hall, I couldn't believe it. I figured you must be fated to be together for some reason. Now that you're marrying her, you should know Vivienne never wronged you, and you both suffered for nothing. Your mother has been dead set against you marrying Vivienne from the start and, to be frank, I don't think she is innocent in Vivienne's disappearance today, either. I think she has her hand in stopping your marriage Saturday, just as she did the first time." Finley took a deep breath. "That's why I'm telling you now."

Again, Aidan was stunned speechless. His mother's scheming knew no bounds. It was unbelievable that she would go to such lengths to keep him from marrying Vivienne.

The implications of Finley's confession were devastating. His mother, *his mother*, had deliberately ruined his life.

"I'm sorry," Finley said with quiet resignation, his head hung low. "I'll pack my things and leave the house tonight."

Aidan shook his head. He knew Finley had only been following his mother's orders and at the time was not in a position to refuse her. "No, you don't have to leave. There has been enough unhappiness caused by this. I'm just thankful you told me the truth now. We'll talk more about this when I get back though. Right now, I have to find Vivienne."

"Thank you, Aidan."

Aidan left Finley and raced back down the stairs, calling to his mother. As he suspected, she had not left yet, for she was waiting to see what he was going do about Vivienne.

"Is it true, Mother?" he demanded angrily.

Regally, she turned her head toward him, her expression mildly curious. "Is what true, Aidan?"

"Is it true you ordered Finley to arrange for me to find Nicky Foster with Vivienne before we left Galway?"

Her gray eyes widened the slightest bit, but she rallied well. "I have not the faintest idea to what you are referring," she responded coolly.

"You deliberately made Vivienne look unfaithful to me all those years ago, didn't you? And you have conspired to keep her from me today. I knew you disliked her, but for the love of God, Mother . . . I never thought you capable of such malice. Where is she now?"

"I'm sure I don't know what you mean. How could I possibly know where that little harlot is or who she is with? It's good riddance as far as I'm concerned." She turned her back, dismissing the conversation and him.

For the first time in his life Aidan put his hands on his mother and spun her around to face him. Anger seethed through every vein in his body. Rage, betrayal, and fear for Vivienne. Especially fear for Vivienne. If anything happened to her due to his mother's hatred and his own blindness he would never forgive himself. "You arranged for someone to take her this afternoon, didn't you? Because you certainly didn't invite her to tea! Tell me who has her and where she is, Mother, or I swear to God you will never see me again."

Suddenly fearful, Susana Kavanaugh was aghast at her son's behavior. "Has Finley been talking—"

That sealed it. She was behind all of it, without a doubt. "Tell me who has her," he ground out between clenched teeth, giving her a little shake. "Is it Jackson Harlow?"

Maybe she finally felt remorse for once in her life. Maybe she feared losing contact with her only child. "Yes," she choked out on a bitter sob.

He released her in disgust, his worst fears confirmed. Before his eyes, his mother suddenly appeared weak and old, not the queenly, imposing figure she usually portrayed. She was his mother, but she had cruelly betrayed him. Not just once, but twice. "We'll discuss this later, and for your sake, you had better hope that I find Vivienne unharmed." He stalked away from her.

"Aidan," she called after him piteously, her sobs echoing in the high-ceilinged foyer. "I'm sorry . . . I just wanted what was best for you. I love you . . ."

He glanced back only to ask, "Do you have any idea where he was taking her?"

She shrugged with a sniffle, her thin shoulders sagging. "I . . . I didn't ask specifically, but one would assume he left London."

Now Aidan was positive that Harlow had left London with Vivienne. He just had to figure out where.

"You won't reach her in time," she cried to him as he opened the front door. "He's going to marry her."

His pulse quickened at her chilling words. Aidan would not let that happen, but now he knew time was of the essence. "No, I'm going to marry her." With that parting shot, he charged out of the house.

By the time he reached the Cardwell residence, the Earl of Whitlock was calculatingly calm, his mind having weighed various scenarios and possible outcomes between Harlow and Vivienne, but he needed more information. He followed the Cardwell butler into the comfortable parlor where Lord and Lady Cardwell paced frantically.

"How can this have happened?" Gilbert Cardwell blustered when he stopped pacing and noticed that Aidan had entered the room.

"Oh, Aidan, where can she be?" Lady Gwen Cardwell wailed, her pretty face drawn in concern.

"I don't know, but Vivienne did not go with Harlow willingly," Aidan answered without hesitation.

"I didn't believe so either. I've seen the two of you together and Vivienne is quite taken with you," Lady Cardwell continued. "But there was a note from Jackson Harlow stating they wanted to elope together."

Aidan shook his head. "It's a lie. A ploy to throw us off. Where are Gregory and George?"

"They went to Harlow's office first, hoping to find out more, and then went looking for you," Lord Cardwell said.

Lady Cardwell rambled on in nervousness. "I never would have suspected Mister Harlow of doing something so underhanded as to run off with Vivienne. He seemed such a nice gentleman. So charming. I knew he was quite smitten with her and disappointed that she was marrying you, but this . . . This is too much! I can't imagine the scandal this will cause. Do you think they are truly eloping?"

Aidan certainly hoped not yet anyway. "I think it's Jackson's plan, but definitely not Vivienne's. And not mine."

Gregory charged through the front door at that moment, with George close on his heels. Both of their ruddy faces were more flushed than usual and their expressions worried. Another man followed behind them.

"Aidan, thank goodness you're here!" George said in obvious relief. "We kept missing you. We stopped by your office and then your house, but you had just left ahead of us."

"Did you go to Harlow's office?" Aidan asked impatiently. "What did you find out?"

"His brother Miles was there, and just as anxious to find Harlow as we were," Gregory explained hurriedly, his usual easy-going manner now tense and troubled. "He's come here with us."

An older, slimmer looking version of Jackson Harlow stepped into the room. Miles Harlow stood shorter than his younger brother, seemed less vital, and wore thin wire spectacles. He removed his hat politely and nodded to the room in general. "Forgive my intrusion, but it seems this is an emergency. My brother has caused some serious trouble."

"That's an understatement," Aidan muttered in disgust. "What's going on? Do you know where he is?"

"I will try to be brief, since I know that Miss Montgomery's safety is at stake, and that is my main concern at this pront." Miles Harlow cleared his throat nervously and began to explain the complex story to them. "It has only recently come to my attention that my brother Jackson had been involved with some rather unsavory characters. He has plotted to destroy our competitors. He has spent wastefully, lavishly redecorating our offices and he has run up huge debts on his personal spending. His many creditors have begun hounding us. And he has just about bankrupted our family's business with his underhanded deals and has ruined our company's good reputation."

Aidan interrupted, "I was aware of that. I believe he arranged to steal a large cotton shipment of mine and had my storage warehouse burned to the ground."

Miles nodded his head wearily. "That does not surprise me. I'm sorry. It seems my brother has shown his true colors. I regret that I did not notice his wrong-doings sooner and put a stop to them. I've had my sus-picions of him for some time, but did not want to credit him with this sort of behavior. But just this af-ternoon Jackson made off with all the cash from our business safe. Every last cent."

"How does Miss Montgomery figure into all this?" Aidan questioned with an increased sense of urgency. It was obvious to him that Jackson Harlow was a desper-ate man, and desperate men commit desperate acts. The thought of Vivienne with him turned his stomach.

Miles continued in his quiet and earnest manner. "Apparently there was a falling out between our other brother, Davis, and Captain John Montgomery over some land they had claimed in South Africa. Captain Montgomery informed me of this situation and told me he was giving the land to his only child for her future. Unfortunately, I was very ill for many months, and not keeping up with the shipping business, and most of the duties fell to Jackson. During that time, Captain Mont-gomery's ship sank off the coast of Africa in a terrible storm. When I was finally recovered enough to resume my duties, I realized that Miss Montgomery probably had no idea of her father's wishes. Captain Mont-gomery was one of our best sailors and a fine man. I owed it to him to see that his daughter was taken care of properly. Because I was still too unwell to travel myself, I sent Jackson to Galway to find Vivienne Montgomery to inform her of the property her father owned in South Africa and allow her to claim it."

"You are referring to the diamond mines?" Lord Cardwell questioned.

Aidan's eyes narrowed at this bit of information. "What diamond mines?"

"Today Vivienne found deeds belonging to her

father that showed ownership of diamond mines in South Africa," Lord Cardwell explained in amazement. "She just gave them to me this afternoon, before she left to visit your mother. I sent them to my solicitor to have them verified."

Aidan turned to Miles, "And Jackson knew about these diamond mines, which now belong to Miss Montgomery?"

Miles concurred. "Of course he did."

"Then that's why he is so eager to marry her!" Gregory stated emphatically. "Vivienne told me that when she went to his office this week that Jackson offered to marry her even after—" His voice trailed off, but everyone knew the incident he referred to.

"What was her response?" Aidan's eyes pinned on Gregory.

"That she couldn't marry him, because she was marrying you."

At those simple words, Aidan felt relief wash through him. "I thought he was just trying to ruin my business and had a personal vendetta against me. But now I see that he has an even greater motive for taking Vivienne. He wants the diamond mines," Aidan stated with a deadly calm.

"So where do you think he went?" Gregory questioned urgently. "We have to move fast. He already has a good lead over us."

Miles spoke up first. "I'll bet he's headed to our family estate in Fair Haven. It's a little village north of here. But it's a two-day journey, and with getting such a late start, he'd have to stop for the night. Especially in this weather."

"Then let's get going," Aidan prompted them into action, for there was no time to lose.

Chapter 21

The Trip from London

It seemed their short trip to Jackson's office was taking longer than she expected. Vivienne was not familiar enough with London to know exactly what was wrong, but nothing outside the window looked familiar to her. She became concerned that not only had she missed tea with Lady Whitlock, but by now she would miss supper with the Cardwells.

"Where are we going, Jackson?" she had asked, perplexed by their northerly direction. She was positive his office was south of Aidan's mother's house. Perhaps she had simply become confused. "I thought we were going to your office."

"There's been a slight change in plans," he stated affably, grinning at her. "I must leave London and I need your help."

"Jackson, this is hardly the time for me to leave town!" she scolded in exasperation. "I was supposed to be meeting Aidan's mother and I'm getting married the day after tomorrow."

"So is that your answer to my proposal to you? You're getting married the day after tomorrow?" he asked quietly, pinning her with his steady golden gaze.

Confused by his tone, she responded uncertainly, feeling slightly guilty for she never did give him a definitive no when he asked her to consider his offer of marriage. "Well, yes . . . I truly appreciate your offer. It was very gallant of you to ask me given the circumstances and I'm honored by it. But I'm sorry, Jackson. I am going to be married to Aidan on Saturday."

"Do you love him?"

Now there was a loaded question. She definitely had feelings for Aidan and supposed she never did stop loving him after all that had happened. Especially during the past week. Seeing him again brought all her buried feelings back to the surface. "Aidan and I have a history together," she explained attempting to break the awkward silence. "We were engaged once before, but it didn't work out . . ." Her voice trailed off in hesitation. "Could you please turn the carriage around?"

"Aidan Kavanaugh doesn't love you."

Vivienne refused to be baited by that. "It's late and I really should be getting back home now. My family will be very worried about me. Please, Jackson, take me home."

"I'm afraid I can't do that." He grinned at her, shaking his head.

"This is not the time to jest with me. I insist you take me home this instant!" she cried in frustration and a growing sense of alarm. He could not truly mean he was not going to take her home.

"I'm not jesting, Vivienne. I'm actually quite serious."

He was not going to take her back to the Cardwells? Then where was he planning on taking her? Suddenly Vivienne was very afraid. She did not know the man sitting across from her in this fine carriage. Aidan's warnings sprang to mind too late. Ruthless and dangerous were words he had used to describe Jackson last night. *Harlow is not interested in helping you. At least not in the way you think he is. He is set on ruining me and he'll ruin you to get to me.* She had dismissed Aidan's warnings as the ravings of a jealous man. Now she wished she had heeded his prophetic words. He had been trying to protect her.

"You deceived me, didn't you?" she said, willing her voice to remain neutral. "You have no news about my father."

"One of the things I admired most about you, Vivienne, aside from your exquisite looks, is your quick wit. In answer to your question, yes, I deceived you."

She nodded her head in response to his grinning face. She shivered to think she had once thought his features handsome. Now she found them blatantly menacing. "May I ask why?"

"You're a wise girl, too. No hysterics on your part. I knew I was right about you."

Silence reigned in the carriage as she regarded him warily. An elegantly dressed gentleman in a fine carriage. He looked as if he were out making casual calls upon friends, not abducting a woman against her will. He carefully removed his top hat and gloves and set them on the seat beside him, next to his long, silver-handled black walking stick, and settled back in his seat across from her.

"Because you have behaved well so far, I shall answer

your question. I told you once, Vivienne, that I play to win, didn't I? That day at the picnic?"

The day she had innocently flirted with him beneath the shade of an elm tree and they talked about finding her father. She had felt pretty and engaging in her pink and white-striped dress and he had been dashing and charming. Such a contrast to how she felt now. "Yes, I remember that."

"I made up my mind that day to win you. The night of the masked ball I even asked your uncle for permission to court you honorably. Which, I will have you know, is something I have never done before. It just goes to show the extent of my feelings for you. You're a very beautiful and desirable woman."

His penetrating gaze moved over her appreciatively, causing her heart to pound in fear. She could not speak.

"I must say," he continued in the light tone he had been using, "that I was quite disappointed when I discovered you in bed with Whitlock. I had thought you a chaste young lady." He shook his head in disapproval. "Tsk, tsk, Vivienne. Who knew you were such a naughty girl? I despise the idea of Whitlock having had his hands on you first, but . . . that can't be helped now, can it?"

She did not know if he expected her to answer that, but in either case, she could not. Her throat was too tight. She felt the palms of her hands sweating inside her white gloves.

"Whitlock, that self-righteous, pompous, straitlaced mama's boy, managed to ensnare you into marriage before I could ask for you myself. That was hardly fair, Vivienne. Still, I wanted you. In good faith I offered to marry you, in spite of seeing you in bed with another man." He gave her a lopsided smiled, which chilled her to the bone. "Although I have to admit, that only spurred my interest in you, knowing you are not the prudish sort and that you would be a willing partner in *my* bed eventually."

Panic began to rise in her and she fought the desire to scream at the top of her lungs. The predatory gleam in his eyes terrified her. She needed to get him on another topic immediately.

"What about helping me? What about my father?" she croaked.

"I'm sorry, Vivienne, that I haven't better news for you." The look on his face changed to one of concern. "Your father did drown when his ship sank off the coast of South Africa. Before that happened however, he had a falling-out with my brother Davis. They had been partners in a land deal. Your father had the deeds to the diamond mines. My brother wanted them. So he sent them to you for safekeeping until he got home. Unfortunately he died before he could tell you about them."

"I found them this morning!" she blurted out, instantly wishing she could withdraw her words. Her hand covered her mouth a moment too late.

"Excellent news, my darling!" he exclaimed in excitement. "I knew you had to have them somewhere. You wouldn't happen to have them in your possession now by any chance, would you?"

She shook her head.

"No? I didn't think so. But it's no matter. We'll just have to stop back in London and retrieve them at some point. The money from those little deeds of paper will come in quite handy to finance our future."

She slowly removed her hand from her mouth. "Our future?" she murmured while alarm bells clanged furiously in her head. But she remained very still, not moving a muscle, her expression one of calm neutrality.

"Of course, Vivienne. I'm still going to marry you. Everything is all arranged. By this time tomorrow you will be my wife."

Pure, unadulterated panic rushed through her as she sensed the danger she was in. Her head spun with wild possibilities, none of them pleasant, as her heart thudded loudly against the wall of her chest. *Oh, God. Oh, God. Oh, God.* She was trapped. Trapped in a moving carriage with a man who had some nefarious purpose in mind for her. Her first impulses were to scream, cry, rant and rave, or, quite possibly, vomit all over him. She glanced at the window of the carriage and then back at Jackson, who still eyed her intently. She was no match for him physically. He could easily subdue her if it came to that, and she shuddered to think just how he would subdue her.

Then she heard Aggie's voice telling her, *Keep your wits about you now, miss.* Just thinking of Aggie helped. Her grandmother's spirit was with her. She could not overcome Jackson physically, but she certainly could outwit him. A cold calm took over her. Believing he would remain calm as long as she did, she forced herself to breathe and reminded herself not to say anything that might anger him.

"If you take me home, I'll gladly give the deeds to you," she suggested.

"No. You're staying with me. I thought I made that abundantly clear. Once I marry you the deeds legally belong to me."

Unconsciously Vivienne glanced out the window again, seeing dilapidated buildings pass by. It was beginning to rain. Her eyes lingered on the door handle. They were moving at a good pace. What would happen if she jumped from the carriage now? Would she be able to summon help? Or should she bide her time and wait for a better opportunity to escape?

His long black walking stick smacked down on the empty space on the seat beside her, cracking the leather like a whip. Vivienne jumped, gasping in startled surprise, her heart thudding wildly.

"Don't even think about it."

His threatening voice sent chills down her spine. She glanced back at him, and found his feral eyes gleaming at her. He sat like a tiger ready to pounce, watching, waiting, for his moment to strike. "At the moment, we're in a section of London where you would be raped the instant you hit the ground, then sold to the highest bidder. You would more than likely go for a high price." He grinned at her wickedly, enjoying the fear he instilled when she shuddered helplessly.

"You're better off taking your chances with me. I don't want to hurt you at all. I can make things very nice for you, Vivienne, if you will let me. For I have come to care for you a great deal. Be sweet. Be accommodating. Be willing. And we shall get along quite well together."

He lifted the walking stick and pressed it menacingly against her chest bone. As she gasped in shock, he uttered in an ominous tone, "But cross me once, just once, and you shall not live long enough to regret it. Are we agreed?"

No, you demented, repulsive, pathetic excuse for a man! You'll rot in hell for this! Stifling the words she longed to scream at him, she managed to murmur aloud a faint, "Yes."

"Smart girl." He removed the stick and placed it on the seat beside him once more. "Whitlock doesn't want to marry you anyway. His mother told me."

She glanced sharply at him, unconsciously rubbing the sore spot on her chest where he had poked her with his cane.

"Ah, that got your attention. You see, Vivienne, I'm really rescuing you from a terrible fate. Lady Whitlock despises you. She's the one who sent me that note, signed with your name, asking me to come to your room that night at Bingham Hall. She wanted to ruin you by having me caught in your bedroom and forcing you to marry me. That whole night was a set up for the two of us. And, quite frankly, I wouldn't have minded that at all. But apparently I showed up a little too late." He gave her a knowing look. "I'm doing you a favor by taking you from Whitlock. His mother would torment you relentlessly. I, on the other hand, offer you a mother-in-law-free marriage." He grinned happily at her, his golden gaze intense.

Vivienne's head spun as she thought of that night. Jackson's words explained so many things. Especially Lady Whitlock's being outside her door at the crucial moment. She did not doubt for an instant that Aidan's mother was capable of such behavior. How infuriated Lady Whitlock must have been when her plan went awry and Aidan was obligated to marry her after all! No wonder she fainted.

It also explained her sudden friendly overture to make peace.

"Then she orchestrated this with you, didn't she? That's how you knew I would be going to her house this afternoon. Lady Whitlock told you."

"But of course," he answered matter-of-factly. "Now

just relax, as we have a long journey ahead of us. I've a basket packed with some food just for you. Are you hungry?"

"No, thank you." Did he really believe that she would enjoy this as a merry, little jaunt to the country? That she would picnic with him gladly and thank him for rescuing her? The mere thought of food nauseated her. "Where are we going?" she dared to ask.

"Now if I told you that, it would ruin the surprise, wouldn't it?" He gave her a gleefully intimidating look. "And don't worry. No one is coming after you. I sent a note telling your aunt and uncle that we were in love and eloping together."

She had no acceptable words she could say to him in response so she kept quiet, her eyes lingering helplessly on the window and the rain falling outside. They were passing into open countryside. The sky hung low with gray and ominous clouds. Thunder rumbled overhead. It would be dark before long. She tried not to dwell on what might happen once they reached wherever it was he was taking her . . .

Instead she hoped her family would be worried enough to look for her by now. Surely they would not believe that she had gone out for tea with Lady Whitlock and ran off with Jackson Harlow. She counted on Gregory creating an uproar over her disappearance. He knew she would not leave willingly, especially after everything she told him about Aidan and Jackson Harlow yesterday. Gregory would be able to deduce that Harlow had abducted her and make Aunt Gwen and Uncle Gilbert believe she had not run away. But how would they know where to begin looking for her? She wondered if Aidan knew she was missing yet.

And, more importantly, would he even care that she was gone?

A powerful, dreadful thought occurred to her.

Aidan would automatically assume the worst of her now. He would think she ran off with Jackson rather than face marrying him, of course. She was certain of it. Last night he had warned her to stay away from Jackson Harlow and she had obstinately ignored him, knowing it infuriated him to think of her with Jackson. And he had been so high and mighty with her that she had wanted to infuriate him. But now he would believe she left with Jackson willingly. He would never think anything else. Why would he? With the words she had flung at him last night? She had deliberately taunted him. *But we're not married yet, are we, Aidan?* She cringed at the memory. How could she have acted so foolishly and recklessly? Who knew her words would come back to haunt her so soon and so irrevocably?

When she managed to escape this maniacal idiot, which she was certain she would, for she had no intention of sitting back meekly and becoming Jackson's wife, Aidan would never forgive her this transgression. Once again, it seemed she was doing something to deceive Aidan or to hurt him. Once again, she looked the faithless harlot in Aidan's eyes. Once again . . . How could it be that fate conspired to ruin her twice? For she would surely be ruined now.

Her heart sank. She had lost Aidan forever. *Again.*

As the carriage continued on the bumpy, puddle-lined road moving farther away from London and all the people she loved, Vivienne could not help the tears that spilled from her eyes. The edgy silence within the dim interior lengthened. She reached for a handkerchief from her reticule to wipe her eyes.

"Don't cry, Vivienne."

His soft voice startled her. She continued wiping her tears, ignoring him.

She wondered if he had been insane all along or if he had suddenly lost his mind this very day. For he was surely stark, raving mad. Maybe it was when he injured his head in the boat accident. In either case there was no doubt that she was in the captivity of a mentally unbalanced person. That gave her pause. She could outsmart an insane man, couldn't she? She couldn't simply sit there and cry. As Aggie always told her, she needed to keep her wits about her. Now more than ever. She needed to be alert and ready at a moment's notice to take an opportunity to flee him the second one presented itself. Perhaps if she played along, she might lull him into a false sense of security, and he might let down his guard.

"I'm crying because I had no idea you cared so much for me, Jackson."

In the growing dimness, she felt rather than saw his gaze on her, assessing her.

"I do care for you, Vivienne. I'm sorry things turned out this way. I know this is not how you imagined your wedding to be. I wish it could be different for us."

"I do, too," she whispered. She positively wished things were different.

They continued on for a long time in silence after that. It was now fully dark out and the rain continued to pour. The carriage rumbled to a halt. Jackson suddenly sat up straight, donned his gloves and hat, and threatened, "We're here. If you say one word to anyone you will regret it."

He removed his black cape and flung the door
open. Leaping from the carriage, he turned to help
her down. Vivienne tried not to flinch when he
touched her, placing his cape around her shoulders.
Raindrops pelted her face.

They were at the entrance of The Pig and Whistle,
a typical country inn. A tall gentleman rushed out to
greet them with a large umbrella. "Good evening, my
lord. We have your room ready for you, just as you re-
quested. Follow me through the back entrance."

Before Vivienne had a chance to catch the man's
eyes, Jackson quickly ushered her into the inn, grip-
ping her arm rather tightly, up the small wooden staircase, down a dim corridor, and into the end room
before she could make eye contact with a single
person. Obviously he did not intend for her to speak
to anyone. Her spirits sank. She stood nervously, waiting to see what Jackson expected of her.

"I'll bring your supper shortly. In the meantime,
make yourself at home." He flashed that chilling
golden grin at her, and held up a long key. "There's
no way out, so don't even attempt it, Vivienne." He
closed the door behind him and she heard the key
turn in the lock.

Trapped inside a strange building with a demented
man who terrified her, Vivienne looked around nervously. Apparently, the plain room had been prepared
for her. The lamps had been lit and a fire burned on
the hearth. It was acceptable enough, and at least it
was clean. The large canopied bed in the center of
the room gave her chills. Yet, relief flooded her at
simply being removed from Jackson's presence and
her knees almost buckled now from the strain she had

been under. Flinging off Jackson's offensive black cape, she sank onto a small divan, trembling.

Vivienne took a deep breath and willed herself not to cry and fall apart now. *Think. There must be some way out of this room.* She went to the door and quietly tried the handle anyway, knowing it to be a futile gesture. It was most definitely locked. She walked to the small rain-streaked window that faced out toward the back of the inn and peered into the darkness. A brief flash of lightning allowed her to see nothing more than woods surrounding the inn. Attempting to open the window, she discovered that it had been bolted firmly shut.

She sighed in resignation, leaning her head against the cool pane of glass. She was agile but she didn't know if she could survive a two-story drop without injuring herself, even if she could squeeze her petite frame through the small opening. And where would she go in the middle of the night, without a farthing to her name and no idea where she was? In the pouring rain? Wearing nothing but a thin tea gown and dainty slippers? That was providing that Jackson didn't catch her. The thought of him extracting his wrath upon her, stopped her from imagining she could flee from this room. There was no telling what he was capable of. She knew when she made her move to escape it would be when he had no chance to reclaim her. But she'd be damned if she would marry him tomorrow.

Think, Vivienne, think!

He said that he would be marrying her tomorrow. That would also mean that there would have to be a chaplain and witnesses. Vivienne would just have to say something to *make* them help her.

In the meantime she had the night to survive.

Glancing around the room for some sort of weapon, she noted a heavy china pitcher and a bowl resting on the small dresser. She could hardly surprise him with that. Oh, what wouldn't she give for a sharp pair of scissors or a butcher knife. Or a pistol. Her father had taught her to shoot one summer. She had fired many a shot into Galway Bay when she was fifteen.

The key turned in the lock and Vivienne almost jumped out of her skin. She faced the door as Jackson entered the room carrying a tray filled with food for her. He closed the door behind him. The tray was adorned with a single red rose in a small bud vase. Glancing furtively, she noted there was a fork on the tray. And a sharp knife.

He placed the tray on the side table. "I've brought your supper."

She merely nodded at him, attempting a faint smile.

He advanced on her, crossing the room in long strides. She would have backed away, but she was already pressed against the wall. He placed a hand on either side of her, bracing himself against the wall behind her, and she froze in place.

"You're so beautiful, Vivienne."

His frighteningly handsome face inched closer to hers, and she could smell the heavy cologne he wore. He breathed hotly next to her cheek and a wave of revulsion swept through her. His lips brushed along the line of her jaw, up to her ear, and he whispered, "You are awfully quiet, Vivienne. That's not like you."

Spurred by disgust and revulsion, she suddenly pushed away from him. "Honestly, Jackson, are you daft? Would you expect me to be anything else but quiet?"

Startled by her sudden move, he glared at her, his eyebrows raised in surprise.

Vivienne's anger and fear had gotten the best of her and she had lashed out, her Irish brogue in full force, as tended to happen when she was irate. "You misled me into coming with you! You're holding me against my will, taking me from my family and the man I love, and expecting me to marry you. I'd hardly call that cause for my rejoicing!" She had meant to lull him into a false sense of security. To lead him to believe she wanted to be with him. Too late now. Fear of his retribution settled over her, but she did not regret a single word she'd said.

Jackson regarded her appreciatively and chuckled low in his throat. "There's my spirited Irish beauty. The one who dared to visit me in my office unchaperoned." He stepped toward her.

There was no way to back up unless she went toward the bed and she was definitely not heading in that direction willingly, so Vivienne did not move a muscle. Jackson moved closer to her, bringing his hands behind her head, threading his fingers through her hair, slowly loosening it from its upswept style, sending chills down her spine. With a cold sense of dread in the pit of her stomach, she flinched as he pulled her head towards his. In an instant Jackson placed his mouth roughly over hers.

Chapter 22

The Capture

Aidan rode as if the devil himself were after him. With Gregory and George riding close behind him, they followed the road north from London to find Jackson Harlow. And Vivienne.

Vivienne.

Aidan could think of nothing but Vivienne and how he regretted blaming her and treating her so terribly. Especially when none of it had been her fault. He had been a fool, and she had been manipulated and devastated. Vivienne, who had always been a friend to him. His smart, brave, beautiful girl. All the lost time, all the wasted years, that they could have spent together. Now he wanted nothing more than to hold her in his arms again and tell her how sorry he was. And that he loved her. He always had and he always would.

He was damned if he would lose her a second time to the likes of Jackson Harlow. He could not lose her now. If only he wasn't too late . . .

They rode through the darkness, taking the mud-covered road toward the little village of Fair Haven. The three of them did not speak, they just kept moving through the rainy darkness. The journey was slow and the puddles deep. The rain was finally lessening to a drizzle, and Aidan urged his horse to go faster.

The dim lanterns in front of an inn flickered in the distance. He prayed he was following the right path. The wooden sign that blew in the wind declared the inauspicious place as The Pig and Whistle. He wiped the rain from his face and reigned in his horse. If Harlow had Vivienne captive inside that inn, Aidan wanted to catch him unaware, to prevent him from harming her. Gregory and George quickly caught up to him.

"You think he's here?" Gregory called.

"It's the only place to stop that we've come across. He's either here, or he pressed on ahead. But with the way the rain was coming down, I doubt he could have continued on this road in a carriage. I'd lay odds that he's inside. With Vivienne."

George said, "Let me check to see if his carriage is here first. We don't want to tip him off." He rode down the lane around and disappeared behind the inn to the stables.

"I can't just wait here," Aidan said after a moment. "I'm going in."

Gregory followed in agreement as they made their way through the mud to the entrance. Aidan dismounted and handed his reins to Gregory.

"Go ahead. I'll be right behind you," Gregory said.

Aidan entered the inn, which was fairly crowded with road-weary travelers seeking refuge from the earlier downpour. He scanned the main room quickly, seeing many faces, but none that belonged to Harlow. Or Vivienne. He walked to the large wooden bar and motioned to the innkeeper.

The balding, red-cheeked man smiled broadly at him. "How can I help you, sir?"

"Did a gentleman rent rooms for the evening? A blond gentleman named Harlow with a beautiful dark-haired lady?" Aidan asked.

"Don't know about the lady. Or at least the dark-haired part. Didn't get a good look at her myself. But we got a fancy blond gentleman by the name of Harlow upstairs with his wife."

Aidan's heart flipped over at that description. *Wife.* They couldn't have had time to marry. It was impossible. "That's not his wife," he said pointedly.

"Really, now?" The innkeeper's chubby face lit up with a greedy gleam in his eyes. "Then just who would she be?"

"My fiancée." Aidan handed the man a pound note.

"Ah." He nodded his shiny bald head in understanding, taking the money eagerly in his fat fingers and pocketing it. "Upstairs. Last room at the end of the hallway. Good luck to you."

Aidan turned to find Gregory standing right beside him. "Harlow had an accomplice in the stables. George is posted outside just in case Harlow tries to escape."

"He's not going to escape," Aidan said determinedly.

Moving with haste, the two of them made their way up the narrow staircase and down the length of the dimly lit corridor. Listening intently outside, the sound of muffled voices in the room panicked him. His heart pounding, Aidan kicked open the door to the last room at the end of the hallway. The wooden door splintered from its hinges and swung forward drunkenly. Inside he saw Vivienne sprawled on the bed, half-dressed, her dark hair spilling around her. With Jackson on top of her.

The image spun his mind back to another time and place, but to an eerily similar situation. This time he did what he should have done ten years ago.

Vivienne screamed when the door burst open. She screamed for all she was worth. She didn't care who came in, she didn't care who heard her, as long as it was someone, *anyone*, who could help her. She wanted Jackson to release her, to stop kissing her, stop touching her.

She had been fighting him tooth and nail for what seemed like forever. And she was exhausted. When he first kissed her, she had kicked him as hard as she could. Surprised by that move, he had hauled off and slapped her face, almost taking the breath from her. Then he pushed her toward the bed. That was when she first tried to scream. He placed his large hand over her mouth to silence her shouts for help.

That caused her to fight like a banshee. She bit his hand, drawing blood while still kicking him every chance she got. She managed to land a solid and satisfying kick to his groin, rendering him momentarily stunned. She broke from his grip and made her way to the door, but he still had the key. She pounded on the door, yelling for help. The only response was someone across the hall demanding they be quiet. She raced to the food tray and grabbed the sharp knife she had seen earlier. By then Jackson had recovered, and he had grabbed her legs and tripped her.

Both of them sprawled on the ground, knocking over the table that held the china pitcher and bowl. As the dishes shattered on the floor, he slapped her again, pulling the knife from her hand and calling her filthy names she had never heard before. She managed to utter a few choice epithets back at him, thanks to her bawdy tutelage from Gregory and George.

While she lay on the floor, Jackson pinned her arms to her side with his legs as he straddled her. He laughed at her, a gleam of admiration in his eyes. "You're amazing, Vivienne. Truly an amazing woman. But you can't beat me. I play to win. Remember?" He uttered menacingly, placing the sharp blade of the knife against the soft flesh of her throat. "I didn't want to play this way. But you started it."

The fight immediately went out of her. Then he kissed her again, his wet lips moving over hers insistently. Fearing the finely honed knife at her throat, she did not move, did not so much as breathe as his tongue entered her mouth. Revulsion filled her and she desperately wanted to shove him away from her.

Then he lifted his head and ordered coldly, "Now, get up and lie down on that bed or, as much as I'd hate to, I will slice your pretty face to ribbons."

Trembling, she did as she was told, all the while she felt the point of the knife at her throat. She lay awkwardly on the bed, horror sweeping through her. Jackson straddled her once again, his eyes feral and wild.

"This would be so much better if you were willing," he whispered low and close to her ear. "I don't know why you had to fight me like that. Be nice now, Vivienne. Be nice . . ."

He slowly moved the knife along her throat and slipped it beneath the collar of her dress. With one swift stroke he split open the front of her blue and white striped tea gown clear through to her chemise. He grinned lasciviously at her naked breasts.

Everything happened at once. There was a splintering crash, loud voices and shouts, the sound of heavy boots on the floor. Suddenly men rushed into the room. That was when Vivienne began screaming. Jackson's hand came back down over her mouth, silencing her. He hauled her up off the bed instantly, wrapping one arm around her, the other hand holding the knife to her throat once more.

The knife kept her from screaming.

Her heart pounded crazily with fright, but she finally managed to take stock of her surroundings, her eyes searching the room. She almost collapsed with relief when she saw Gregory, her endearing and faithful cousin, standing in the doorway. He was frozen in place, ready to protect her, but not daring to move for fear of endangering Vivienne's precarious position. Her terrified gaze moved toward the other man who had burst into the room. Powerful and dark, a look of undisguised rage on his handsome features, he stood to Vivienne's right. Aidan's familiar green eyes locked on her.

She wanted to cry then. Aidan had come for her. Aidan knew she did not go willingly with Harlow. He would not have been there if he believed she left him. His eyes told her so.

"Let her go, Harlow," Aidan demanded.

"Make a move toward me, and I will slit her lovely throat," Jackson responded.

"You won't kill her. You haven't married her yet," Aidan countered. "And you want those diamond mines of hers too desperately."

Aidan knew the truth. He knew what had happened. Vivienne was stunned.

Jackson laughed ruefully. "Get out of here and go marry that haughty blonde your mother chose for you. Leave Vivienne with me."

"Let go of her now or I will kill you."

Jackson laughed in derision. "You think you have it all figured out, don't you, Whitlock?"

"Yes. I have it all figured out." Aidan's voice was deadly calm. "And it's over for you."

"Did you know your mother paid me to take your fiancée today?"

Vivienne actually sucked in her breath at that dramatic revelation. She noticed that Aidan did not look surprised at all, but Gregory's mouth hung open wide. Susana Kavanaugh had surpassed all Vivienne's worst imaginings. The woman truly loathed her to go to such lengths to get her out of her son's life. She had been sold to a madman by Aidan's mother. But, thankfully, Aidan knew the truth.

Jackson continued to taunt Aidan. "She actually gave me quite a large sum of money to marry Vivienne. Something I was planning to do all along."

Aidan did not react, but said icily, "I know you stole that load of cotton from my ship. I know you set fire to my warehouse. I know that you bribed Travers to set the fire, didn't pay him, and then killed him when he harassed you for what you owed him. I know you've destroyed your family's business reputation and that you stole all the money from your brother's office today. I know that you *think* you're going to marry Vivienne to get the deeds to her father's diamond mines, which now belong to her."

"Get out!" Jackson yelled, pulling Vivienne closer to him.

"You're the worst kind of coward to hide behind a woman."

"Don't push me, Whitlock!"

"Let her go now," Aidan repeated, and he deliberately reached into his pocket and removed a pistol. He pointed it directly at Jackson. "Or I'll kill you." His intense gaze never left Vivienne.

Vivienne pleaded with her eyes, praying that neither of them would do something impulsive. She now had a knife at her throat and a gun pointed in her general direction. They were at an impasse and it did nothing to calm her. But suddenly she knew what she had to do to save herself. In a split second, she jerked backward, away from Jackson and the knife. With that fleeting movement she gave Aidan a wider target. The sound of a deafening gunshot echoed in the room and Vivienne screamed as she was rushed by both Gregory and Aidan as Jackson Harlow crumpled to the floor at her feet.

Gregory grabbed Jackson and held him down, taking no chances with him in spite of his wound. He was shot in the leg, for Aidan had aimed low in order to not hurt Vivienne. Bright red blood pooled on the floor around Jackson as Gregory made sure he couldn't cause any more trouble and began to bind the wound with a bedsheet. George rushed in, followed by the fat innkeeper while a group of patrons gathered at the door to the room. George hurriedly called for someone to send for a doctor and the constable.

Meanwhile Aidan had gathered a visibly shaken Vivienne in his arms, wrapping her protectively in his cloak. He lifted her off her feet in one swift motion, holding her securely, and asked the innkeeper to take them to an empty room. He carried her through the growing crowd of onlookers, and followed the innkeeper down the narrow corridor and into another small guest room. The fat innkeeper, instinctively knowing more pound notes would be coming his way, promised them anything they wanted and shut the door discreetly as he left the pair alone.

In the ensuing silence Aidan placed Vivienne on the narrow bed along the wall, and propped her up with pillows. He sat alongside of her and kissed her forehead tenderly. "Are you all right?"

"You came for me," she whispered, looking at him in wonder, as if she could not believe he was really there.

He felt a pang of remorse at the look on her face. "Did he hurt you?" He gently touched his hand along her cheek where the darkening colors of purple bruises were swelling in the shape of fingers on her white skin. He wished he had killed Harlow and was half tempted to go back down the hall and finish the job, but he couldn't bear the thought of leaving Vivienne now.

She shook her head wearily at his question. "I'm fine. You got there just in time. I don't think I could have fought him off much longer."

Aidan's heart had almost stopped beating when he burst in that room and saw Jackson with a knife at Vivienne's throat. The front of her dress torn apart, her dark hair tangled around her, and a panicked expression filling her sapphire eyes. She'd looked terrified and he could only imagine what Jackson had done to her.

"I thought you would believe that I wanted to be

with him," Vivienne whispered low, her voice catching. "I never thought you would come for me, Aidan."

"I know," he said ruefully, shaking his head. "I'm sorry."

"I'm sorry I didn't believe you. You warned me to stay away from him and I didn't listen to you. I thought he was trying to help me find out about my father, but now I know he only wanted the deeds to the diamond mines. You were right about him all along."

"Oh God, Vivienne, you don't have to be sorry." He shook his head again in regret. "You have been wronged more than you realize . . . My mother—"

"I know," she interrupted. "Your mother has always hated me. Jackson said she wrote a note to Harlow asking him to come to my bedroom at Bingham Hall that night. It was a plot to ruin me. They were supposed to discover Jackson with me that night, not you. That's why they were all there to find the two of us . . . together."

Aidan knew with a terrible certainty that Vivienne's words were true and felt sick to his stomach at his mother's treacherous manipulations. He recalled the night less than a week ago when he was caught in Vivienne's bedroom, and the talk he had with his mother afterward. What he had dismissed at the time as her hysterical ravings now had a new meaning. *I never expected to find* you *with her,* she had cried. *Aidan, why didn't you stay away? Why did you go to her tonight? Tonight of all nights?* Apparently she had expected to find Jackson Harlow in Vivienne's room. He had vastly underestimated his mother's hatred for the woman he loved.

"I didn't know that," he admitted regretfully, "but

at this point I'm not surprised to hear it. I'm very sorry, Vivienne."

"Your mother is a bit deranged, Aidan."

"Yes, she is." He nodded in reluctant agreement. "Quite deranged. And unfortunately there's more." Aidan was not sure she could handle any more news of the deception that surrounded her after everything she'd been through that evening, but he had to tell her the truth.

"More than that?" she asked in disbelief, her delicate brow furrowed in apprehension. "What else could there possibly be?"

He took a deep breath. "My mother arranged to have Nicky Foster come to the little cottage that day. She ordered Finley to set up everything. She wanted me to find you with Foster, so I would call off our wedding and leave Ireland without you. And she succeeded."

Vivienne's eyes widened as the momentous implications sunk in. "Oh . . ."

"I just learned about that tonight myself." Aidan shook his head, feeling sick to his stomach. "I don't know what to say except I'm sorry, Vivienne. Sorry that my mother is unbelievably conniving and cruel. Sorry that I reacted so badly that day at the cottage. Sorry I never talked to you about it, when I know you tried to see me and explain. I'm sorry I believed the worst of you. I'm sorry for all the time we've lost—" he suddenly stopped speaking when he noticed what she was wearing around her neck.

"Oh, Vivienne," he whispered softly, overcome by emotions at the significance of her symbolic gesture. He reached his hand out to touch the silver locket that he had given her when they were to be married. He recalled that extraordinary afternoon in the cottage when he fastened it around her neck. After all these years, he had completely forgotten about it, but obviously Vivienne had not. There was only one reason she would be wearing that locket two days before their mandated wedding.

She had wanted to marry him.

He looked at Vivienne lying in the bed, her pretty dress torn, her beautiful face bruised, her sapphire blue eyes wide with disbelief at the extent of his mother's scheming to keep them apart, and he was overwhelmed by his love for this incredible woman. She had not deserved any of the misery she had been forced to endure.

"God, I've been a fool, Vivienne, a great fool to ever doubt you. I can only say in my weak defense that I was young and impulsive, and seeing you with Foster that day completely devastated me. It wounded my heart, my pride. You were the only person in my life that I could count on. You were mine, the best part of my life, my best friend. In my eyes, seeing you with Foster managed to negate everything we had, everything we meant to each other. I thought the world of you, and it suddenly seemed that you thought very little of me."

"But I didn't—" she began to protest.

He stopped her from speaking, placing his finger gently over her lips. "I know that now, and I'm sorry I never gave you the chance to explain it then. I ran from you. I couldn't bear to think that you wanted another man, or that you only wanted me for my title and money, as my mother suggested. It was easier for me to run away and not face you. Which makes me a fool."

She stared at him, her expression curious. "And now?" she asked.

He owed her at least an explanation of all that happened, especially considering none of it was her fault. "Seeing you again has turned my life upside down, Vivienne. I tried to stay away from you at Bingham Hall. I tried to hate you. I tried to distrust you. I tried to put you out of my mind. And I couldn't. The day on the lake, I was terrified that you were hurt in the accident and I raced to help you. When we were in the portrait gallery I said awful things to you to push you further away, after we had been so intimate with each other. And that night in your bedroom . . . I only came to apologize for what happened in the portrait gallery and to warn you to stay away from Harlow. I didn't intend to end up in your bed. When we were discovered together and your uncle demanded I marry you . . . There was a part of me that was angry, yes. Angry with myself for dishonoring you. I realize how unfeeling I acted in front of you at the time. But oddly enough, I was mostly relieved. By being duty-bound to marry you, I could have you back, but not have to face or admit the truth to you or myself."

"The truth being?" she prompted him when he paused, her face expectant.

"That I still love you, Vivienne. I have loved you my entire life. And I want to marry you. I was coming to see you tonight, to talk to you. I had been thinking about the words you said to me on the patio, about me punishing you if we married. And I realized that you were right. If we had any possibility of a happy life together, I needed to give us that chance, which is what I wanted more than anything. When I learned that Harlow had taken you, I promised myself I would get you back or die trying, because it wouldn't be worth living without you. Now I want to spend the rest of my life with you. Just as we always planned. That is . . . if you can forgive my stubborn pride and all the pain that I have caused you."

"There's a lot to forgive," she said quietly, nodding, her eyes downcast.

"Was it terrible for you after I left Ireland?" he asked his voice full of remorse. He brushed a lock of her silky hair from her face.

Her expression clouded with sadness at the memory of that time. "More than you can imagine. No one in town would speak to me for years. I was humiliated. Scorned. So was Aggie, because they blamed her for my wild ways. But as time went by, people began to forget and forgive somewhat, since I created no new scandal and no baby appeared. Then I lost my father. And Aggie died shortly after that. I had no one left."

"I'm so sorry, Vivienne."

"But your coming for me today means more to me than you will ever know. I was so scared, Aidan. I thought you would believe the worst of me, thinking that I was betraying you yet again. Especially after the way I had taunted you last night on the patio. I knew you would never believe me this time. All I kept thinking was that I had lost you for good when I'd been so close to getting you back again."

Aidan touched his fingers to her soft cheek. "It's strange, but even before Finley confessed that you had been set up with Foster, my gut instinct was that you were not a willing partner with Harlow tonight. I felt you were in danger from the start. My only thought was to get you back."

"There has never been anyone for me but you, Aidan. It's only ever been you."

"I tried to forget you for years, my little witch, and I couldn't," he confessed.

There was a moment of silence in which they just looked at each other, taking in all that had happened.

She grasped his hand that touched her cheek. He took it in his and squeezed it tightly. Tears welled in her eyes and she whispered, "Can we start over?"

"Can you love me again after all I've done wrong?" he asked.

"I never, ever stopped loving you, Aidan. Even when I tried."

She was so beautiful and wonderful, and he was thankful to have her love him. "Will you still marry me, Vivienne?"

"Yes, oh yes."

"I love you, *muirnin*. More than you will ever know."

"And I love you," she echoed, placing a kiss on his lips.

He pulled her close to him, thankful for the second chance he'd been given to have her back in his life. They kissed, this time sealing their promise to each other. Sealing their fate together. His hands slid up her back as their kiss slowly deepened, his lips moving over hers with a possessive yearning. She opened her mouth to him and his tongue delved into the velvety sweetness of her mouth. Their need for each other was tangible, and she clung to him, her arms tightly around his body, as if she would never let him go.

He kissed her face, her eyes, her cheeks, breathing in the scent of her. With the utmost care, he removed the torn dress from her body, silently thanking heaven for arriving before Harlow had his way with her. He placed gentle kisses on her satiny skin, caressing her with soft strokes of his hand, erasing any touches Harlow had upon her.

His clothes soon following hers into a reckless pile on the floor next to the narrow bed. Naked, he crushed her down into the pillows, covering her body with the warmth of his. He needed to feel her, touch every inch of her. Her breathing became more frantic as the heat between them ignited into a fiery blaze. Her hands clutched him tightly, pressing him against her, as if she feared losing him. But Aidan knew he would never let that happen again. He could hear her heart beating frantically and his own heart constricted in response as his lips sought hers once more.

This was about forgiveness and absolution. They were starting over, with their love, with their lives. His hands moved reverently over her silky skin, absorbing her into his very being. He entered her slowly, his weight bearing down into her soft, warm flesh. Her fingers intertwined with his and they stared into each other's eyes for what seemed like an eternity. As he began to move within her, she began to cry. Tears trickled down her cheeks.

"What? What is it, love?" he asked, his brow furrowed in concern. His face next to hers.

Too overcome to speak, she sobbed lightly, "Too much—of everything."

He knew exactly what she meant, because he felt it too. So much had happened. To be together this way, and to know it was forever, was a dream he did not think could ever come true. He kissed her sweet mouth. He kissed her tears. He kissed her eyelids. He kissed the satiny smooth skin of her neck, breathing her in. He gave her delicate kisses. Cherishing kisses. Soothing kisses.

"I'm sorry," he whispered, stroking her hair, "I'm sorry . . ." He would spend the rest of his life trying to make up for all that had happened . . .

She touched his face, her fingers brushing along his cheek as if touching to make sure he was real. "I love you."

He continued to move within her, claiming her body, her heart, her mind more insistently. She arched up to meet his thrusts, her body quivering with the need to be with him, a part of him. Their breathing became hurried and rasping, their touches more possessive. He buried himself within her, wanting to lose himself in her and never be found. The need was endless and all-consuming. When she gasped out in pleasure and he felt her shudder beneath him, her body tightening around him, he joined her.

Afterward, Aidan held her cradled in his arms as she slept exhausted by the day's events, her breathing peaceful and even. His beautiful Irish witch. His Vivienne. He needed her like he needed air. Placing a feathery light kiss on her cheek, he sighed. He could not sleep, for fear it was all a dream. There was still much to be dealt with. Jackson Harlow. His mother. But he was not going to let Vivienne out of his sight until she was legally his wife. She was his once more and he didn't intend to ever let her go again.

Chapter 23

The Confrontation

Susana Kavanaugh, the Countess of Whitlock, paced nervously in her drawing room the next afternoon. She had slept fitfully during the night, wondering and worrying what had happened when Aidan rushed off to find Vivienne. Hoping against hope that Aidan had not caught her in time, and that Jackson Harlow had been able to marry her first, Susana tossed and turned in her bed. She had been up since dawn, still waiting for some news. Her stomach had been too upset to eat anything since the morning before when she had conspired with Jackson Harlow.

It had been a brilliant plan and she had been positive it would work, until Aidan had become so disturbed by Vivienne's disappearance and run out in search of her. She had not anticipated that; she'd expected him to be relieved to have her gone. Yes, he might be attracted to the girl physically, but she never believed for one minute that Aidan truly wanted Vivienne as his wife. Until last night, when he declared that he would marry her before Jackson Harlow did.

If only Aidan weren't so much like his father! Foolishly stubborn and appallingly simple in his tastes. Susana had tried her best to raise him to value the proper aspects of life as a titled gentleman of the nobility and the importance of high social standing. But he did not seem to care about any of the same things that she did. He even took to going into business! How that infuriated her, even though he was quite successful at it. She had endured enough from him. How was she supposed to accept him being compelled to marry the likes of Vivienne Montgomery? That awful night she saw him in Vivienne's bed would haunt her forever! And it had been entirely her fault that he had been caught with her. Which had eaten away at her ever since.

"My lady, your son just arrived," her butler announced, standing in the doorway.

Startled by her servant's presence, she instructed, "Show him in."

So Aidan had returned! Susana squared her shoulders and brushed her hands along the front of her dark gray gown. Now was the moment of truth. Now she would learn the outcome of her clever plan. She reminded herself to try to act somewhat compassionate if he were upset at losing that Irish harlot.

"Good morning, Mother," Aidan stated coolly as he entered the room.

The welcoming smile vanished from Susana's face and in an instant an icy look replaced it. Vivienne Montgomery walked in beside her son, her hand firmly in his. Susana's heart sank to the floor. Well, well, well. It was all over. The little witch had come back.

Vivienne had the temerity to glare at her. "Good morning, Lady Whitlock."

"I see you managed to find her after all, Aidan," Susana said, not caring for the possessive manner in which her son held Vivienne.

"Yes, I found her," Aidan responded not without some rancor in his tone. "We've had a most enlightening evening, have we not, Vivienne?"

"Most enlightening," Vivienne added. Her expression was unreadable, although Susana eyed her carefully. She had to give the girl credit for managing to string Aidan along all these years. She captivated him somehow.

"You owe us both an apology, Mother, but you especially owe one to Vivienne. Since she will be my wife as of tomorrow, I think she deserves at least that much from you."

"You're going through with it then?" Susana could not stop the hurt that welled within her.

Vivienne spoke. "Yes, we're getting married tomorrow. Finally. As we should have done ten years ago. We know everything about you now. How you managed to have me compromised with Nicky Foster. How you arranged for me to be compromised yet again with Jackson Harlow at Bingham Hall. And how you paid him to abduct me yesterday. Yes, Lady Whitlock, Aidan and I are marrying each other in spite of all you have done to prevent us from doing just that."

A charged silence reigned in the room as the three of them faced each other.

"It was all for you, Aidan," Susana uttered softly.

"No, Mother, be honest," Aidan demanded stormily. "It was all for yourself. You kept Vivienne from me because you were under the misguided perception that she was not good enough for me to marry. But that is where you were terribly wrong. I love Vivienne, and you cheated me out of a life that was rightfully mine. You cheated Vivienne. And you almost destroyed us both because of your selfish ways."

She defended herself calmly, "As your mother, I had to protect you."

"Protect me from what?" he asked skeptically.

"From her!" Susana pointed accusingly at Vivienne. He was still blinded by that girl's charms. "And from yourself and your destructive ways. You're just like your father. Too blind to know what's best for you. What else would you have me do?"

"I would have you be a decent human being and at least apologize for all the harm you have caused," Aidan said, his expression hard.

Once again Susana turned her gaze toward Vivienne, standing there in her drawing room, with her had possessively on Aidan's. "Well, Vivienne, I see you got your way."

"Did I?" she asked, staring at her with those uncanny eyes.

Susana felt unnerved by that comment and by the look Vivienne cast upon her. She wished the girl would scream at her. Susana knew how to handle that sort of behavior whereas Vivienne's unnatural calm disconcerted her. "Didn't you, though?" she countered with a disgusted smirk. "You got my son!"

"And you have lost him," Vivienne said softly with a pitying look, her expression sad. "I'm sorry for you, Lady Whitlock. You have lost your only son, the son you claim to love, and to what purpose?"

Susana could abide anything but pity, and the meaning in Vivienne Montgomery's eyes was quite clear. How dare the harlot pity her! Susana had expected a battle, a battle she could win. The girl infuriated her. "Aidan?" Susana looked questioningly to her son, but there was a coldness in his expression that she had never seen before. Her heart pounded and her hands shook.

"Sit down, Mother, while I explain," Aidan instructed her.

Shocked into obeying him, Susana sat upon the damask sofa, her body tense and rigid. He motioned for Vivienne to sit as well, and she placed herself in a chair across from the sofa. Aidan continued to stand. Susana held her anger in check, curious to hear what her son would say to her, although she was positive she would not like it, for it undoubtedly included his marriage to Vivienne Montgomery.

"The way we see it, Mother, you have two options available to you at this point." He looked at her meaningfully. "If you can apologize, treat Vivienne with respect, attend our wedding graciously, and generally behave yourself, you may continue to enjoy living in London as you do now. Or if you choose not to do that, I will cut off the majority of your funds and require you to retire to my small estate in northern Scotland, where Vivienne and I will not be obligated to see you or deal with you again. The choice is yours."

Silence filled the room and Susana seethed with impotent rage at being given an ultimatum from Aidan, who was certainly pressured to do it by Vivienne. So it had come down to this. Vivienne Montgomery, that poor Irish harlot, who dared to sit there with her pitying looks. Her beloved only son was forcing her to accept that awful Irish peasant as his wife or be banished from London for the rest of her life.

It was not a difficult choice for her to make. In fact, it was ridiculously simple.

Chapter 24

The Wedding

Vivienne and Aidan were married that Saturday in London by special license as originally planned by Lord Cardwell. It was a small, intimate affair and everyone in attendance agreed that it was quite obvious the bride and groom were madly in love with each other. The entire Cardwell family was there, as well as the Duke and Duchess of Bingham, and the Earl and Countess of Hartshorne and their daughter Lady Helene Winston. However, it was duly noted that Lady Whitlock had unexpectedly taken ill and was not able to attend the ceremony.

At a lovely breakfast at the Cardwell's townhouse following the ceremony, the new Earl and Countess of Whitlock were showered with good wishes.

The Duchess of Bingham cooed with happiness, "Why, Vivienne, Lord Whitlock swept you off your feet so quickly, we never even had a chance to see how many marriage offers you would get this season!"

Vivienne, wearing a stunning rose pink silk gown, responded blissfully, "But I accepted the only offer I wanted!"

Gregory pulled Vivienne aside, his freckled face bearing a gleeful grin, and gave her a hug. "My best friend and my favorite cousin. I'm very happy for you, Vivvy. I told you things had a way of working out for the best in the end."

"Yes, you were right, Gregory." Vivienne smiled at him, and glanced knowingly toward Helene. "About both of us." Gregory was beaming with happiness at finally winning Lady Helene's heart and hand. They were planning a grand wedding for the fall.

Aidan came to her with a kiss and a crystal glass full of champagne for her. "Hello, my beautiful wife."

"Hello, my handsome husband." She glanced up at him with a luminous smile. It had been a long time coming, but they were finally husband and wife. Vivienne was still stunned by all that had happened in the past week.

Even after they turned Jackson Harlow over to the authorities for the crimes he committed, more of his wrongdoings were brought to light. Vivienne revealed what she learned the day Jimmy Travers burst into Jackson's office, which linked him to the fire, and his brother Miles had a mountain of evidence against him, including the murder of Jimmy Travers. Jackson Harlow would be in prison for many, many years.

Obviously Aidan's mother had made her choice to face exile from London rather than accept their marriage. As sad as that was, Vivienne had to admit it was a relief to have the woman gone from their lives.

Then Glenda Cardwell had stunned everyone by confessing her involvement in Lady Whitlock's plan to ruin Vivienne that night at Bingham Hall. Aunt Gwen and Uncle Gilbert were outraged at her scandalous behavior and blatant lies and wanted her punished. But Glenda's abject misery and pleas for forgiveness swayed Vivienne to ask them to be kind to her. She still felt sorry for her cousin, in spite of the callous treatment she'd received at Glenda's hands. It probably galled Glenda more to have Vivienne stick up for her than any punishment her parents could mete out. But Vivienne still had it in her heart to eventually make friends with her cousin at some point and was determined to win her over.

Vivienne's life had changed dramatically since the day she visited Bingham Hall.

"I was thinking," Aidan whispered to her, softly nuzzling her ear, "of where we should go for our honeymoon."

She looked up into his green eyes and still felt her heart flutter in excitement. "As long as we're together, it doesn't matter to me where we go."

He kissed her again. "Then I would like to take you back to Cashelwood and start over there, my love."

Her heart skipped a beat at his romantic notion and she smiled. "I think that is a perfectly lovely idea."

The very next day they sailed to Ireland for their honeymoon.

As she and Aidan walked hand in hand down the beach along Galway Bay where they first met as children, Vivienne felt a wondrous sense of peace envelope her. She had come home, in more ways than one. Looking out at the horizon and breathing in the sea-scented air, she thought of her father. She still missed him every day and always would. She had finally accepted the truth that he was dead, although she would never understand why he had not confided in her about the diamond mines.

Her thoughts turned to her grandmother and she knew Aggie would be smiling, looking down upon her now. Her grandmother would be happy for her now that she was married to Aidan at last. Aggie's prediction had come true after all. She and Aidan were fated to be together, in spite of all the obstacles they had had to overcome.

Filled with an overwhelming sense of love, Vivienne stopped walking and turned to her husband. She reached up to him, cupped his handsome face in her small hands, and kissed him on the lips. They kissed softly, gently at first and then more intensely.

Suddenly Aidan moved his mouth from hers and looked at her meaningfully, a sparkle in his eyes. "So, that's the way of it then?"

Vivienne smiled at his imitation of her brogue and the words she had said to him all those years ago that day on the beach when he had first kissed her. "Oh, that's the way of it," she responded and kissed him again.